# THE SHOGUN'S GOLD

# THE SHOGUN'S GOLD

## Solving a Historical Mystery

SECOND EDITION

## CURTIS PIPER

*The Shogun's Gold: Solving a Historical Mystery*
Second Edition

Copyright © 2025 by Curtis D. Piper
All rights reserved.

shogunsgold@gmail.com

ISBN: 979-8-218-58844-1

*The Shogun's Gold – Solving a Historical Mystery* is a work of fiction. In this novel, any resemblance to persons living or dead is entirely coincidental, except for specific historical Japanese and American figures interacting with fictional characters.

Cover Design: Carol Stephens
Book Formatting: Maureen Cutajar, *gopublished.com*.
Map Outline: Courtesy of *d-maps.com*.

"Shogun Trove" article: Copyright owned by the *Charlotte Observer*. Reprinted with permission from the *Charlotte Observer*.

Cover Photos: Grateful acknowledgment to Stack's Bowers Galleries for permission to use the photos of two $20 gold coins. *StacksBowers.com*.

Adventure font: Neale Davidson created the font on the front cover title. His other creations can be found on *dafont.com*.

Printed in the United States of America

*Dedicated to*
*Ayako, Gary, Victor & Mary Piper*
*&*
*Kiku & Kristen Piper*

# Author's Note

Unlike well-known Japanese words such as samurai, sake, and sushi, several terms in my novel may be unfamiliar to readers. When they appear the first time, I have italicized them and provided definitions, usually by context.

Furthermore, diacritical marks are often used in Anglicized Japanese to indicate the union of two vowels. Shōgun is an example. I have chosen not to employ them.

Japanese surnames come before one's given name. Readers may find the following list of the novel's Japanese characters helpful.

Hara Ichinoshin: Historical figure. One of the last shogun's most trusted advisors.

Matsudaira Tokunari: A high-ranking samurai.

Nariaki: Matsudaira's son.

Tomita Yuki: The protagonist in Part One. A close friend of Nariaki.

Tomita Yoshi: Tomita Yuki's younger brother.

Tomita Tomoyoshi: Tomita Yuki's elder brother.

Ichi: A ne'er-do-well befriended by Tomita Yuki.

Kato Yozo: Yuki's trusted friend and former classmate.

John Manjiro: Historical figure. A shipwrecked teen who was rescued by an American sea captain in 1841 and raised in America.

Kansuke: A commoner whose American nickname is Shorty.

Johei: Shorty's son. Yuki gave him an American nickname: Ben.

Kuroi Taketo: Yuki's sworn enemy who betrays the shogunate.

Oki Izo: An anti-Shogunate spy working in the capital city of Edo.

Onishi, Kanbei, and Chobei: Kuroi's bodyguards.

Vice Admiral Enomoto: Historical figure. A shogunate naval officer.

Oguri Kozukenosuke: Historical figure. The shogun's financial and naval magistrate. Japanese samurai often changed their names, and one of Oguri's other names was Tadamasa.

# PROLOGUE

THE ARTICLE BELOW APPEARED in North Carolina's *Charlotte News* on September 15, 1941.

## *Shogun Trove*

### *Vast Japanese Gold Hoard May Be Uncovered Soon*

Chanting Buddhist sutras to pacify the spirits of the men murdered by his grandfather, Hidemori Kawhara of Japan is calmly digging away at the bottom of a hole 220 feet deep. When he reaches 250 feet he expects to uncover six large cabinets of gold worth billions of yen—enough bullion, in fact to increase Japan's gold reserve to five times its present size.

For seven years Hidemori has been digging, following the instructions contained in the aforementioned grandfather's will. It seems that back in 1868 the grandfather, Oguri Kozukeno-suke, was Finance, War and Navy Minister of the tottering Shogunate. Anticipating the fall of the Shoguns and the restoration of the Mikado, Grandpa Oguri gathered together all of the gold in the realm and buried it—deep. In order to keep his secret, Oguri resorted to a favorite trick of the Spanish Main

pirates. He had slain all of the carpenters, boatmen, coolies, and other laborers who participated in the burial and deposited their bodies on top of the treasure trove.

Hidemori believes that he is nearing the bullion cabinets, because he has struck a stratum of human bones and has excavated a sword bearing his family's crest.

According to Grandpa Oguri's will, the treasure is to be turned over intact to the Japanese Government.

If the treasure is uncovered, and if it is as large as reported, it will weigh heavily in the money marts of the world. It will restore Japan's impoverished treasury and, perhaps, stabilize the yen.

But no matter how rich it is, it will not enable Japan to buy the essential war materials she needs—rubber, iron and petroleum—from nations that have turned their backs on her international brigandry. Gold is not enough to win wars, as the United States, with its own vast store of the precious metal at Fort Knox, is beginning to discover.

Almost three months after this newspaper article appeared, the Japanese attacked Pearl Harbor, and Kawahara's search for the gold was forgotten. Rumors, however, persist about the Japanese cache, and treasure hunters still search for it. Historians call the story a fanciful myth, but they are wrong.

*Very wrong.*

# PART ONE
## The Shogun's Gold

# CHAPTER 1

*Present Day Pasadena, California*

WITH SWEAT RUNNING DOWN the small of his back, Parker West finished his daily 10K neighborhood run and returned home. He grabbed his cell phone and climbed the steps to the attic for the second time that day. He inherited the Mediterranean-style house from his parents, who died in a head-on collision with a drunk driver the year before, and he was cleaning up and getting rid of things.

He mopped the sweat from his neck and hands before picking up the coin he had found earlier. He hit the search button on his smartphone, and a second later, a photo popped up.

"What the...?" Parker bolted upright and glanced into the attic shadows as if he feared being spied upon. The gold coin in his hand was the exact likeness of the photo glowing on his cell phone screen. He reread the headline: "American 1866 Double Eagle minted in New Orleans sells for $345,000."

He examined Lady Liberty, whose head was encircled by thirteen six-pointed stars. Below her likeness was the date: 1866. The mint mark on the reverse side of his flawless coin would determine its value, and Parker held his breath as he turned it over. A ring of tiny stars and a burst of sunrays crowned the American eagle and its breast shield. Underneath the eagle were the words "United

States of America Twenty D." Immediately below the eagle's tail feathers, he found a little O, the New Orleans mintmark.

Parker swallowed hard, but the lump in his throat persisted. The coin in the palm of his hand was in better condition than the one pictured on his phone. Benumbed by his discovery, he slid the coin into its velvet pouch and gently placed it back in the battered wooden box containing the other puzzling items.

One was a disassembled rifle. Parker could tell it was old and guessed it was from the Civil War era.

But what he remembered most vividly was the Japanese sword. He was seven years old when his mother caught him playing with it in the attic—finding the sword and its flawless blade again after twenty years triggered ambivalent memories. Most of them puzzling. One hurtful.

Why the sword had caused such a fuss had always baffled him, yet his parents refused to discuss the matter. "Your mom doesn't want weapons in the house. Just leave it at that," his father said.

Parker sensed there was something more to it, but his last chance to learn the answer was lost with the deadly auto accident. He took a deep breath of the musty attic air and attempted to consign his painful memories to a cardboard box in the attic of his mind.

The file folder lying atop the rifle barrel was something he did not recall seeing before, and he wondered what it contained. He was about to thumb through it when a faded blue ledger with ACCOUNTS imprinted on its front cover caught his attention. He wondered if he might find one or two entries inside that would provide a clue to the origin of the double eagle.

But instead of finding columns of dollars and cents, he found twenty pages of characters written horizontally in pencil. *The sword is Japanese, so the writing must be too.*

He found some proper names and places printed in English, but the remaining 130 pages were blank. Embedded in a line of characters on page five, the English word gold stood out, and on page six, the date, August 15, 1867, caught his eye: one year after his newly discovered coin was minted.

He recalled hearing about a double eagle damaged by a bullet found aboard the hulk of the Confederate submarine *Hunley*. And he remembered reading about the thousands of such coins retrieved from the SS *Central America* that sank in 1857. They were appraised for much more than their melt value, given their historical significance.

Parker hoped his coin could tell a story too, but first, he had to research the ledger's origin and have the paper and the graphite sampled and tested. If the accounts ledger and the writing were as old as he suspected, he had a good chance of establishing the coin's provenance. And if a noteworthy historical event backed it, it would sell at a premium. *And maybe I can find out why Mom was so adamant about throwing everything out.*

Parker searched for more clues in the ledger, and on the center of page twenty, he discovered a brownish fingerprint next to four vertical Japanese characters. There were a couple of brown spots near the bottom edge of the page, and he knew blood on paper when he saw it. The following page was blank, but it bore numerous pencil marks and smudges. He guessed that each time the pencil point had become dull or broken, the writer had roughly fashioned a new point with a knife and honed it on the edge of the paper.

金　金　金

PARKER TOOK EVERYTHING TO his downstairs office. He had long since learned not to wear gloves when examining old documents. He washed his hands with soap and water, dried them thoroughly, and took a paper sample from a blank page and one of the apparent graphite smudges. He sent them by messenger to SoCal Forensics, his lab of choice. He crossed his fingers and waited. SoCal determined the age of such samples by employing fiber and chemical analyses and molecular spectroscopy.

If the ledger, the paper, and the graphite proved as old as he suspected, he would have one of the brown spots analyzed. *No sense in wasting money if I'm wrong about the paper and the smudges.*

His next step was to contact a professional translator, and he already had an idea who that might be. He had seen Jason Tanaka's name in an old file at his office and had asked his partner about him.

"He did some translation work for me about ten years ago. Long before you came on board," Marvin Greene, his business partner, had told him. "Quite a character and rich as all get out. He must be older than the magazines in my doctor's office. He lives in the San Rafael district of Pasadena, the last I heard."

# CHAPTER 2

INSURANCE COMPANIES RETAINED Greene & West, LLC, to investigate fraudulent claims, and Parker specialized in verifying real estate documents. As a detective of sorts, he was highly respected by his clients.

Early the following day, Parker took the box and its contents to the single tenant building he jointly owned with Marvin Greene. Marvin was a savvy investigator, but he was inept at selling his services, so their tie-up proved providential. Parker had earned a BS degree in marketing at USC, and on a whim, he had minored in forensics at Dornsife College of Letters, Arts and Sciences. Greene taught him what he did not learn at Dornsife, and their client list burgeoned with Parker's marketing skills. Four years later, Greene made Parker his partner.

Parker's clients included two real estate title companies and several banks. They sought his help in authenticating property-related documents. Intuitive by nature, he sniffed out fraud, and as hard as defense attorneys tried, they rarely shook his expert testimony. But over the past year, Greene's drug problem had gotten out of hand, and their partnership started losing clients.

Upon entering, Parker was dismayed to find the door to Greene's office closed. It meant trouble. He put down the box, quietly retrieved

Jason Tanaka's folder from the dead file cabinet, and jotted down the telephone number and address for Middlefield, Inc. It was an unlikely name for a Japanese translator's company, and Parker wondered about it.

He turned on the copier and started to copy the ledger. The first two pages came out clear, but the next three were streaked with toner.

"No one will be able to read this crap," he muttered.

He changed the toner cartridge and fumbled with the controls, but nothing worked. Disgusted, Parker was about to leave when Greene burst out of his office. His rumpled clothes and his dilated pupils said it all. He had been snorting up in his office.

"Parker. I thought I heard someone. What are you doing here so early?" Greene started humming, his eyes darting about as he wandered around the office.

"I tried to copy some personal stuff, but the damned copier is busted."

"Broken, huh? I'll call Eddy Blackwell. You've met him. His buddy Fumio knows how to repair this kind of stuff."

Parker had met Blackwell and thoroughly despised the man he suspected of supplying Greene with drugs.

Greene grabbed the five pages Parker was about to toss and examined the writing. "What the hell are these?" he said, wiping off the white powder clinging to his nose hairs. "Are you doing business with some Asian firm you haven't told me about?"

"No. They're from this old accounting ledger I found yesterday in my attic. I'm going to have it translated. I suspect the writing is Japanese."

"I'll give these pages to Eddy. He's fluent in Japanese, and I'm sure he'll translate them for you. He's coming over later today."

"Forget it. I don't want his help."

"Well, I'm gonna give them to him anyway," Greene said, folding the papers and sliding them into his shirt pocket. "If you don't find anybody else, you may wanna reconsider."

"Do what you want, but I won't use Blackwell under any circumstance. Just call someone and get the copier fixed, will you? I'm going to take a couple of days off. I still have a ton of things to do around the house."

"Be seeing you soon then," Greene said.

Without acknowledging his partner, Parker grabbed the wooden box and left.

# CHAPTER 3

PARKER MADE IT A point to work out every evening at the Cortez, a private club in downtown Los Angeles. He ran five miles on the rooftop track before working out in the gym. He was twenty-seven, six feet tall, and confidently carried himself.

At almost six o'clock, he checked off the last household chore on his to-do list and threw in the towel. He had passed on lunch, and his stomach was grumbling, so he decided to have dinner at his club after working out. Intending to visit Tanaka after he finished, he took the box and its contents.

But when Parker arrived at the Cortez Club, a lawyer buddy snagged him in the parking lot and persuaded him to play a few games of squash on one of the sixth-floor courts. They did not work out afterward, something they usually did. Instead, they showered and changed. Parker left everything in his locker, and they had dinner and wine in the Baroque Room. It was 9 p.m. when Parker called for his car.

Halfway home, he realized he had left the wooden box in his gym locker. He shrugged. *It doesn't matter. It's too late to visit Tanaka anyway, and the box is safe at the club. I'll pick it up tomorrow.*

AROUND THE TIME PARKER left his home late that afternoon, Eddy Blackwell was in his office, killing time until it got dark. He pulled out a tattered folder from his desk. The folder was the only thing of value he had inherited from his father. Taped to the inside cover was a blurry copy of a North Carolina newspaper article dated September 15, 1941. It read: *Shogun Trove—Vast Japanese Gold Hoard May Be Uncovered Soon.*

His father had convinced him that they could find the gold, but he died before they could. Eddy promised himself over his father's grave that he would locate the treasure when he grew up, and that afternoon, he received an astonishing clue.

He studied the copies of the five pages from Parker's accounting ledger that Marvin Greene had given him. The florid Japanese calligraphy stumped him, but he understood enough to realize the pages contained an important clue. It would take him at least a week to translate them, and he did not have time. Besides, he needed the rest of the diary. He punched three holes in the pages and added them to the folder.

Blackwell was a computer geek who considered himself more of a cyber artist. He was a modern-day urban hermit whose brilliant programming and hacking skills were essential to his drug operation. Three years earlier, he had hacked into the DEA and US Customs, but the government had yet to discover the breaches.

As a teen, Blackwell earned a black belt in karate, an essential skill for someone peddling drugs in East LA. He picked up Spanish and was the only one from the barrio who managed to get a Cal Tech scholarship. He majored in computer science and minored in Japanese. After graduating, he moved to Japan, where he cultivated contacts with members of the underworld, including Fumio, a young man in serious trouble. His *Yakuza* gang leader intended to have him executed, but Blackwell interceded.

In an agreed-upon show of remorse to his boss, Fumio cut off the little finger of his right hand. The whole episode was a boon for Blackwell. Because he spoke Spanish, he became an intermediary between Fumio's boss and an Ecuadorian cocaine seller. Blackwell took

Fumio under his wing and treated him as if he were a younger brother. After making enough to start his own business, Blackwell moved back to the States with Fumio in tow.

A sudden noise caused Blackwell to look up from his desk. He saw Fumio standing shirtless in the doorway with a wrench in hand. He had been working on Blackwell's car. Most Yakuza gang members had tattoos, and Fumio was no different. Sweat trickled down the scaly dragon covering his chest.

"Put a shirt on," Blackwell said. "We'll pay Greene another visit as soon as it is dark."

He pressed the shutdown button on his computer and grabbed his Kimber Micro 9mm pistol. "We will be visiting someone else, too. Get ready. We've got a long night ahead of us."

# CHAPTER 4

PARKER'S HOME OVERLOOKED THE ten-mile ravine known as the Arroyo Seco or Dry Creek. It was close to ten o'clock when he pulled into the darkened driveway, a bit buzzed from the bottle of white Burgundy he had shared at the club.

He fumbled with his house key, and when he inserted and turned it, he realized the door was already unlocked. He stepped in and reached for the light switch next to the door just as someone emerged from the shadows of his living room. Before he could re-act, his assailant struck him above his right ear and slammed him face-first against the wall.

"Fumio, the lights," he heard the thug say. Parker's brain flick-ered like lights during a brownout. He was too dazed to say or do anything, but he recognized Eddy Blackwell's voice.

Blackwell tossed Fumio the keys Parker had dropped. "Check out his car," he said. He yanked Parker's left arm into a hammerlock and spun him around.

Parker felt as if his arm had been ripped from his shoulder.

"You're killing me. What do you want?"

"I'll ask the questions," Blackwell sneered.

"There's nothing in the car," Fumio called out.

"You're breaking my arm. What do you want?" Parker groaned.

"Shut up," Blackwell said. He pulled Parker away from the wall and sent him sprawling onto the living room floor. "Come inside and keep an eye out for trouble," he said to Fumio. "If he tries to get up, you know what to do."

Blackwell checked out the shelves on either side of the fireplace. Not finding what he was looking for, he started tearing apart the adjacent study. Parker opened his eyes to see what was going on. It was his first mistake.

"You no look," Fumio said, making his point with a vicious kick to Parker's chest.

"No more," he wheezed. "Just take what you want and leave."

"I told you to shut up." Fumio kicked Parker again, this time in his face.

"That's enough!" Blackwell yelled. "Get back to the door."

Parker's nose gushed blood, and his ears rang, but he could hear Blackwell yanking the drawers out of his desk and dumping the contents. Papers fluttered, and books tumbled off the shelves and thudded on the floor.

Parker's head felt like it was about to explode, and he hoped they would find what they came for and leave. But the grisly truth hit him through a thicket of outrage and agony. *They have gloves on, but they're not wearing masks. They don't care that I recognize them because they plan on killing me.*

Having not found what he was looking for in the office, Blackwell dashed upstairs. Parker heard dresser drawers crashing on the floors and coat hangers screeching across closet railings. He swore under his breath when he heard a bottle of his favorite cologne shatter on the tiled floor of his bathroom. Then nothing. He sensed the end was near but was too hurt to get up and run.

Blackwell charged downstairs, dragging him to his feet and slamming him against the wall.

"What do you want from me?" Parker groaned.

"You know damn well what I'm looking for," Blackwell said.

"Money? There are two hundred bucks under the blotter on my desk. It's yours. Take it and leave."

Blackwell pulled out his Kimber Micro 9mm and pressed its blunt end under Parker's chin. "I'm not looking for money. Tell me where the...."

Fumio suddenly closed the front door. "Eddy, *satsu!*"

Blackwell released his grip, and Parker collapsed.

"Fumio, out the backway!"

Hearing the fence gate squeak, Parker surmised they were taking the narrow path down the arroyo escarpment. The house fell quiet except for the ringing in his ears. Dead quiet until he got up and stumbled outside. There, he learned what the word *satsu* meant.

"Freeze! Down on the ground," a cop shouted.

"Wha...?"

"You heard, down on the ground. Now!" another cop barked.

Parker dropped to his knees. His head throbbed, and his mind was in a freefall. One officer cuffed, pulled him up, frisked him, and read his Miranda rights.

"Sir, why the handcuffs? Two men just beat the crap out of me. They ran out the back door two minutes ago. You can still catch them."

"Mr. West, focus."

"Yes, but—"

"Listen up. We're taking you into custody as a person of interest."

"Person of interest? For what? I'm the victim."

"Tell it to him," the cop said, pointing to a plainclothes officer approaching them.

"I'm Detective Thomas Smith, Pasadena PD," he said, flashing his badge in Parker's face. "You had a little tussle with your partner a few hours ago, didn't you?"

It was an accusation, not a question.

"A fight with Marvin? Hell no. A guy named Eddy Blackwell and a Japanese goon named Fumio just beat the crap out of me. They can't be far from here. They're on foot. They're on a path behind my house that will take them to the bottom of the arroyo."

"Cut the bullshit, West. You and Greene got into a fight, and you killed him," Smith said.

Parker was too hurt to respond. He watched as an ambulance pulled into his driveway, flooding the yard with more flashing strobes.

The attendants pulled out a gurney and pushed it over to him. His legs began to wobble, and one of the medics grabbed him.

"Take this scumbag to the hospital and see that he's tested for drugs," Smith said.

Parker blacked out, but he came to when the ambulance pulled up to the emergency entrance at Huntington Hospital. He tried sitting up, but he was handcuffed to the gurney. The attendants wheeled him down a hallway, passing a small sign on the wall: JAIL WARD—Unauthorized Entry Prohibited. In the x-ray room, he fell unconscious again.

# CHAPTER 5

PARKER WOKE UP WHEN he heard nurses chatting somewhere down the hallway. He opened his swollen eyes and watched a line zigzag on the screen of the bedside monitor. He dropped his head back onto his pillow and dozed. Around two o'clock the next day, a doctor paid a visit.

"Mr. West, how are we doing?"

"Not so good."

"I can understand why. What happened?"

"Two crooks broke into my house and attacked me."

"Sorry to hear it. Your chart shows you have a mild concussion but no cracked ribs. Your chest has a couple of contusions. Pretty painful, I imagine, but nothing serious. The good news is that your nose isn't broken. Just ecchymosis in both eyes."

"Huh?"

"A couple of shiners, Mr. West."

Parker pointed to his wrist. "When did they take the cuffs off?"

"About an hour ago, when they moved you out of the jail ward."

"When can I leave?"

"I'm not quite sure yet. The best thing to do is get some rest now." The doctor scribbled a note on the chart and left.

As he lay in bed with an IV in his arm, Parker wondered why Blackwell had killed Marvin Green but not him. With nothing making sense, he drifted off to sleep. Eight hours later, he was awakened by a sound in his room. Even with his swollen nose, he could smell tobacco smoke on someone's breath. He forced his eyes open and saw Detective Smith peering down at him. The blood pressure numbers on the monitor jumped.

"Hey, Mr. West, it's me, remember?"

"Yeah, and I have nothing to say to you. Get the hell out, Smith."

"Mr. West, look at me."

Parker glared at him. "You said I murdered my partner."

"I'm sorry, but you gotta admit it did not look good for you. But that's all water under the bridge. You're a free man."

"Nothing like jumping to conclusions, right, Detective? I'm not talking until I contact my attorney."

"Whoa, whoa! Let's not go there, Parker. Can I call you Parker?"

"Just cut the crap and tell me what happened."

"Yeah, well, your partner got beat up pretty bad. Blood all over his office, just like in your living room. Got his neck snapped like a matchstick."

Parker winced.

"They had to be the same perps who attacked you. Your home was ransacked."

"So, I'm not a suspect?"

"No, I'm here to find out who did this to you. Where did you go after you left your office yesterday? I need to cover all the bases. What did you take with you?"

"Why?"

"Parker, let me ask the questions, okay? This isn't a case of two separate robberies gone wrong. Whoever they were, they were looking for something. They must have gotten your address out of Greene before they killed him."

"Yeah, and I know who they are."

"You mentioned them at the scene. A guy named Fumio and his buddy named Eddy Blackwell. I'm having checks run on them, and I should know if their names pop up today. We checked for prints, but we've come up with zilch."

"They were wearing latex gloves, but maybe they left prints in Marvin's office."

"Nope. Just yours, Greene's, and Natalie Burnes's, your bookkeeper."

"Did you check the video cameras? Everything is recorded on an iPad hidden under a stack of magazines in Marvin's room."

"Well, it's gone, and the cameras don't have memory chips."

Parker bit his lower lip, trying to absorb the news. "Tell me, Smith, what do you think their motive was?"

"Good question. That is why I need to know what you took from your office. I think they weren't after money. I have a reason to believe they were after an old accounting ledger."

Parker grabbed the bed rail and sat up. "What's that?"

Smith's eyes lit up. "A ledger. It had a bunch of Japanese writing in it."

Parker was sure Smith was on to something and considered telling him what he knew. But a little voice told him not to. He decided to wait and find out more before spilling his guts.

"Detective, how do you know all this?"

"Ah, well, that's a good question." The detective rubbed the back of his neck and looked up at the ceiling, averting Parker's inquisitive stare. "I found five photocopied pages in the wastepaper basket at your office. They have a bunch of rows and columns, and Japanese writing is on them. The pages must've gotten caught in the copier, and you tossed them. They were yours, right?"

Parker studied Smith's expression, sensing something about him he did not like. *Too eager. He's lying. Marvin took those copies and stuffed them into his shirt pocket. He said he was going to give them to Blackwell.*

"To answer your question, those pages were Marvin's, but what do they have to do with anything?"

"Quit the bullshit," Smith said. "They're not Marvin Greene's. They're yours. And to answer *your* question, those perps were after that ledger, or whatever you call it. They weren't after money."

"Say again?"

"The ledger you were trying to copy was a diary. Those guys were after it."

"A diary? Really? How do you know that?"

"A Jap officer at work translated it."

"I doubt Pasadena has any Japanese police officers. Americans of Japanese descent, perhaps. But a Jap officer? Detective, that's not very PC."

"Now, you listen to me, West. Tell me…"

A nurse entered the room before Smith could finish. "Sorry, Detective, you'll have to leave," she said brusquely.

Smith grunted, stood up, and patted Parker's pillow. "Think about it, Parker. Let's solve this together. I'll be back this evening. Here's my card if you think of something in the meantime."

# CHAPTER 6

PARKER ALMOST PULLED OUT the IV needle in his arm while tossing in bed. Despite the pain pills, the thought of the ledger kept him awake. That it might contain a secret worth killing for was a chilling prospect, and Detective Smith's outright lie about finding the five pages in the wastepaper bin bothered him.

It finally struck him the second time he thought about what had happened. The ledger was only a means to an end. Smith was right: Blackwell was after something else—something he had found in the photocopies. Parker sat up and called the Cortez Club. He asked the manager to have everything in his locker delivered to him. The box and his gym clothes arrived early in the afternoon.

金 金 金

AT SEVEN O'CLOCK THAT evening, Smith walked into Parker's room without knocking. His taut jaw muscles betrayed his effort to appear relaxed. He grabbed a chair and sat close to the bed. Too close.

"You look a lot better than when we last talked," he said. "Glad to see it."

"Lieutenant, I may look better, but I'm still not."

"But you've had time to recall where you put the ledger, right?"

"I still can't remember. I've got a slight concussion."

"Parker cut the crap. The doctor told me your cognitive responses are normal." Smith paused to wipe a small bubble of saliva from the corner of his mouth. "Do not toy with me. Where the hell is that ledger? Need I remind you that withholding evidence is a felony?"

"Sorry, I'm not trying to be evasive. Blackwell is undoubtedly after more than the ledger, and I know what it is."

Smith's jaw slackened. "You do?"

"Yeah. The ledger was in a wooden box with a sword and an old rifle. But what's more interesting is the gold coin I found inside— a so-called double eagle. It's worth over three hundred."

"Three hundred bucks?"

"No, three hundred thousand. It was minted in 1866 at the New Orleans mint. Very rare."

"Are you shitting me? A gold coin worth three hundred thousand bucks? I didn't find any sword or coins in your house or car, nor did CSI. Dammit, why didn't you tell me about this before?"

Parker forced himself not to laugh. Stringing Smith along was like flashing a laser beam on the floor in front of a cat.

"Come on, out with it," Smith said. "You took the ledger to a professional translator, didn't you?"

"Hell no. I would never give up the original. I just can't remember."

"One more time, Parker. Withholding evidence is a serious crime. Where the hell did you go after you left your office?"

"I told you; I don't remember."

Smith got up and gave the chair an angry shove. "I'm going to do some more legwork, but I'll be back here tomorrow, and you'd better have answers for me. You got that?"

"Sounds like a plan to me."

Smith looked angry enough to rip the door off when he left.

Thinking about his encounter with Smith, Parker began talking to his reflection in the wall mirror across the room. He called it a conference—something he often did at home.

"Smith and Blackwell are connected somehow. It's time to contact the Pasadena Police internal investigation unit and report him."

But before picking up the phone, he reconsidered. He would have to turn over the box and ledger.

"No way," he said to his reflection. "Parker, get with it. You minored in forensics at Dornsife. Find what this is all about. The cops can wait."

# CHAPTER 7

SMITH HAD BEEN ASSIGNED to investigate drug-related crimes six months earlier, and he soon made a name for himself by cracking a newsworthy case. Blackwell's *modus operandi* was to find out as much as he could about anyone who posed a danger to him and his operations, and Smith promptly showed up on his radar.

"Everyone has a skeleton in their closet," he told Fumio. "Find it but be careful."

Fumio broke into Smith's apartment a few nights later and discovered a backup drive buried in a can of steel-cut oats—not just a skeleton, but a veritable cemetery. There was over a terabyte of child porn on it, and a day later, Blackwell and Fumio knocked on Smith's door and returned the backup drive to the startled detective. After a heated argument laced with threats, they struck a deal. Smith promised to keep an eye out for any of Blackwell's aliases should they pop up on the police radar. In return, Blackwell would "reimburse" him for his trouble. It was blackmail, pure and simple, but Smith could do nothing about it except take what Blackwell called "cash for kids" and do what he was told.

The relationship worked smoothly until Blackwell gave Smith the heads-up about his plans for Marvin Greene and Parker West.

It was too much for Smith. Drug busts were one thing, but murder was another. He balked.

Blackwell assured him there would be no complications. Greene's security cameras would be taken care of, and no prints would be left behind. But Smith refused to have any part of Blackwell's plan— until he got an offer he could not refuse. He jockeyed his schedule to take charge of what was to have been the investigation of Greene's and Parker's murder. But things had gone sideways.

"Get over to Parker West's home and arrest him!" Blackwell yelled into his phone the night he murdered Marvin Greene. He was clearly out of breath. "You gotta get there ASAP. He's got some old accounting book with Japanese writing inside. It's hidden somewhere in the house. Find it and arrest him for killing Greene!"

While Parker languished in his hospital bed the next day, Smith got more calls from Blackwell than robocalls at dinner. The last one was not an invitation to have a friendly beer together. It was an order. Blackwell and his sidekick Fumio were waiting for him at the Starfish Bar in Seal Beach.

"You got no ledger, right?" Fumio said with an unusual amount of scorn.

"No, I don't have it yet." Smith wanted to slug Fumio, but instead, he turned to Blackwell. "Call your snapping turtle off, will you, Eddy?"

Fumio took one look at his boss, and his smirk evaporated.

"Look," Smith said, "I'll make West talk. It will just take some time."

"I have no time."

"Eddy, you do. West adamantly denies giving that ledger to a translator, and I am sure he's telling the truth. So just breathe easy and let me work on him a bit more."

Blackwell ignored Smith's plea and ordered a round of Kirin Dry. "Cheers. Drink up," he said, clinking Smith's bottle with his own.

Smith gulped down a mouthful. "Eddy," he said, wiping his lips with the back of his hand, "don't worry. Trust me on this. West is on the brink of spilling his guts."

"You're wrong. He's driven to find out what is in that diary, and he's worried you would impound it as evidence if you got a hold of it. He knows he might never get it back. He's an insurance investigator, a detective of sorts. He wants to figure it out by himself, but he will need a translator. Not just some Japanese housewife or even a college professor—he'll need a real expert, and I'll bet he's found someone and is ready to leave the hospital with or without a doctor's permission."

"What do you plan on doing?" Smith asked guardedly.

"Once he leaves the hospital, we'll be waiting for him. That's all you need to know."

Blackwell snapped his fingers, and Fumio produced Parker's laptop and cell phone. Smith had taken them from Parker's home office before CSI arrived. "Give them back to West and be quick about it."

It was a red flag to Smith. "Eddy, tell me what you did to them. I really need to know."

Blackwell pursed his lips and shot Smith an impatient look. "All right. Why not? I installed bots that link them to my computer and phone. They run in the background, and I get a heads-up when either device is on. Everything is connected to a zombie server."

"What the hell is that?"

"Simply speaking, it's a program that will route all West's phone calls, emails, and web searches to me. Every click and keystroke. Every word, spoken or written. All in real time. If he contacts a translator, I'll let you know, and you better jump on it right then and there."

"So that zombie thing is a kind of Trojan horse?" It was the only geeky term Smith knew.

"A worm, actually," Blackwell said.

"You hacked his computer and his cell phone? The Justice Department throws a fit every time Apple refuses to unlock one of their phones for the FBI. You are one hell of a genius."

"A piece of cake," Blackwell said, casually inspecting his fingernails against the light.

"Hold on, Eddy. West surely has antivirus programs installed on his computer and phone. Did you wipe them off? He'll know, won't he? He'll figure it out and blame me."

"Don't worry about things you'll never understand. It makes you sound stupid."

"You're right. I don't understand. I'm just asking."

"Quite elementary. The commercial antivirus programs out there can detect only known malware. I implanted a one-of-a-kind so that no commercial antivirus program can detect it. The bots are zero-day threats."

"Okay, I give up. What the hell are they?"

"They're threats new from day zero, the day they are implanted. West's antivirus software is top of the line, but the bots I've crafted are superior to anything out there. They'll never be detected, so don't worry."

"I'll be damned. Very clever." Having stroked Blackwell's ego, Smith figured it was the right time to ask a question that had been bugging him. "By the way, Parker mentioned something about a gold eagle. What's that about?"

"I have no idea. It's the first time I've heard about that."

Smith knew Blackwell was lying through his teeth. "So why is the diary so important?"

"Something in which I have an academic interest, that's all. I read Japanese, remember? Anyway, you've got your marching orders." Blackwell pulled a key and an envelope from his shirt pocket and dropped both on the table in front of Smith. Blackwell and Fumio got up and left before Smith could say thanks.

Smith stayed to finish his beer, staring at the envelope. It was thicker than usual, but he was troubled. Blackwell was acting erratically, and he was holding something back. It scared him to think about what he was planning to do next. *Way too many loose strings.* After thinking about it a few seconds more, he loosened up. *But that's Eddy's problem, not mine.*

He shrugged when he opened the envelope in his car and riffled through the hundred-dollar bills. But a broad smile parted his lips when he found a key with an address tag. "Academic interest, my ass, but thank you anyway, Eddy," he said.

金　金　金

A GRIZZLED, MIDDLE-AGED man opened the apartment door and eyed Smith.

"Don' yuh, hurt the kid," the drunkard stammered.

"Just get the hell out of here," Smith said. He pulled him out of the doorway and gave him one Ben Franklin. The man kissed the bill, and Smith slammed the door in his face. Once inside, he found the boy huddling next to a bedside nightstand.

Smith gulped. "Come here, you little angel, you," he said, wiping a trickle of spittle from his mouth.

Two hours later, Smith was back on the freeway, worrying over what he had done. He knew he was a dead man if his secret ever got out. Given what prison inmates did to pedophiles, a life sentence could be measured in months.

"Maybe it is time to put some distance between Blackwell and me," he said, speaking into the windshield of his car. He patted his pancake holster and his Glock 42. "I have to figure out how to do that."

# CHAPTER 8

THE DOCTOR GLANCED AT the chart and patted Parker's blanket-covered ankle. "Mr. West, things look pretty good, but I am still concerned about your concussion. I want you to stay another day."

"Anything you say, doc," Parker said, but he did not mean what he said.

As soon as the doctor left, he called Natalie on the hospital phone. She was Greene & West's bookkeeper. *Lucky she's not our receptionist,* Parker thought. Her arms were veritable tattoo art galleries, and body piercings would make Saint Sebastian wince. However, she was a diligent worker, and he respected her efforts.

"Parker, what terrible news about Marvin. I was worried about you, but a nurse said you were doing okay. Tell me what is going on. A police officer named Smith dropped by my house today and questioned me for a second time. Something about a wooden box and a diary, but it was my day off when Marvin was killed. Remember? I told him I never saw the stuff."

"Oh, yeah, I forgot about your new schedule, but I need your help pretty soon."

"Anything. Just tell me."

"I will be discharged tomorrow, and I need to go somewhere.

Will you have time to take me? I'll pay you fifty bucks to drive."

"You don't have to pay me. What's the address?"

"100 Carlyle Lane. It's a home in the San Rafael neighborhood."

"I remember that address. I once delivered some stuff to the owner, a fellow named Tanaka. It was before you started working with Marvin. Are you doing business with him again?"

"No, but I need his help."

"Well, as I recall, I had to deliver some documents, and Marvin had to make an appointment before I was allowed in through the front gate."

"Don't worry about that. I'll find a way in. I can be persuasive when I need to be. See you tomorrow morning at eight."

金 金 金

AT ELEVEN THAT EVENING, long past visiting hours, Smith arrived without knocking. Parker was startled when he opened his eyes.

"Sorry to bother you, but I have a surprise," Smith said.

"Don't tell me. Let me guess…rubber handcuffs?"

Smith ignored Parker's sarcasm and snapped open his briefcase. "Here's your laptop and your smartphone."

The detective's sudden munificence did not pass Parker's stringent smell test, but he was relieved to get them back. "Thanks, Detective," he said.

"No need to thank me. I was a bit rough on you. I got a search warrant and found them when I combed your house for clues. Our tech guys checked them out and couldn't find any suspicious or incriminating emails or phone calls. Here are the charges and cables. I also ordered your car out of impound," he said. "It's back in your driveway. Now, let's get down to business. Do you remember now where you went after you left your office?"

"Sorry, I don't," Parker said. To his surprise, Smith merely shrugged.

"Well, you have my card. Give me a call if you think of something." Smith shut his briefcase and pushed his chair back. "I gotta go."

Blackwell was waiting in the hospital parking lot near the front entrance. "West has his cell phone and computer," Smith said as he walked past the open window of Blackwell's car.

金　金　金

WITHOUT SMITH AROUND TO badger him, Parker plugged the chargers into the socket on the headboard of his bed. When he turned on his cell phone and computer, his anti-hacking apps started the scanning process. Minutes later, a message popped up on both screens: NO MALWARE DETECTED. Relieved, Parker socked the devices away in his gym bag.

At eight o'clock the following day, he walked past the nurses' station dressed in street clothes. His gym bag was slung over his shoulder, and he carried the wooden box with both hands. The lone nurse sitting behind the counter did not bother looking up from her computer. Luckily, the other nurses were in a room down the hall working on a patient in cardiac arrest. *Lucky for me, that is.*

Natalie was waiting for him. "You look a bit weak. Why not go home for some rest first?"

"No, I'm fine. Let's get going."

金　金　金

BLURRY EYED FROM LACK of sleep, Blackwell saw the car icon on his cell phone begin moving. Fumio was hiding inside Parker's house, ready to grab him.

"Fumio, he may be on his way. Get ready," Blackwell barked into his smartphone.

No answer.

"Dammit, Fumio, listen up."

Still no answer. When he checked his phone screen, Blackwell paled.

"Son of a bitch, the network's down."

He started his car and raced to the hospital's front entrance, but all he saw was an attendant and someone in a wheelchair waiting to be picked up. He had only one option left. He sped to the McDonald's down the street, intending to join the restaurant's network. But as he walked through the door, the link to his cell phone's network suddenly came alive. Slack-jawed, he watched the car icon moving west on Colorado Boulevard. Three minutes later, it crossed over the Arroyo Seco Bridge and entered the upscale neighborhood of San Rafael. It came to a stop in front of 100 Carlyle Lane.

# CHAPTER 9

100 CARLYLE LANE WAS a six-acre property in the exclusive San Rafael enclave. A tall, wrought iron fence encircled it. Inside, a three-story English Tudor overlooked Arroyo Seco. Natalie was about to pull up to the intercom when the exit gate swung open, and a Crown City Grocery van slipped past them.

"Gun it," Parker said.

She made it inside just as the gate swung shut. She drove up the winding drive and stopped in front of the mansion, and Parker unlatched his seat belt.

"Leave me here. I'll call later," he said.

Pain ricocheted in his head when he got out of the car, and he stopped halfway up the stone stairway to steady himself. He noticed a slightly built man standing amid several rosebushes in the garden below when he did. He wore work clothes, including canvas gloves and a tattered straw hat shielding his eyes. Parker assumed he was a gardener and gave the man a nod.

Parker spied a video camera leering down at him when he reached the front door. He pressed the call button, and a female voice crackled over the intercom. "Sir, you are trespassing. You had no right to enter without permission. Leave immediately."

He looked at the camera and smiled despite his insistent headache. "My name is Parker West, and I'm not selling anything. I'm here on business. I must see Dr. Tanaka. It's urgent."

"Dr. Tanaka sees visitors by appointment only. Now, leave."

A sudden cranial spasm staggered him, and he gripped the stairway handrail so hard his knuckles smarted. "Please, I have something to show him. It is a matter of extreme importance."

"Security guards are coming, so you'd better leave this minute."

Parker's knees started to buckle, and the gardener bounded up the stairs to steady him.

The intercom crackled alive again. "Uncle, get away from him. He looks dangerous."

"Terry, call off Crown Security. This fellow is hurt. Please open the door."

"I just came from the hospital," Parker said. "I have a mild concussion, but I'm okay. If only for a minute, I need to speak with Dr. Tanaka."

"I am Jason Tanaka," the man Parker had supposed to be a gardener said. "Are you able to stand by yourself?"

"Huh? I mean, yes. Just a bad headache. You're Dr. Tanaka?"

"I am," Tanaka said, pulling off his straw hat. "Allow me to help you with that box and shoulder bag."

The massive oak door swung open, and Parker came face-to-face with an irritated young woman.

"Come this way," she said.

"This is my niece, Teruyo," Tanaka said. "But she goes by Terry. She manages my household."

She led them to a pair of wingback chairs in a spacious drawing room and stood behind Tanaka, staring icily at Parker.

"So, what is it you wish to see me about?" Tanaka inquired.

"This," Parker said. He opened the box and pulled out the ledger.

Tanaka took a pair of reading glasses and hooked them over his ears. He opened the ledger and scanned the first page. Despite being dazed, Parker did not miss the look on Tanaka's face.

"Terry," he said, "this will take some time. Call Dr. Gallant and ask him to come over. I saw him on his backyard putting green a few minutes ago."

"But Uncle Jason . . ."

"Please do it now, Terry."

While they waited, Tanaka pored over the first page, unaware of how pale Parker had become.

"Quite interesting, Mr. West," Tanaka said. "But a challenging read."

It was the last thing Parker heard before he blacked out.

# CHAPTER 10

BLACKWELL SPED BACK TO his office in the scruffy commercial area of Eagle Rock, a northern LA suburb. The front windows on the brick building were boarded up and covered with gang graffiti, the area's preferred art form. The door was barred and padlocked, as were all the others on the same block. Minutes later, Fumio arrived.

"Boss, the network went down, and...."

"Yeah, I know. Just hold on," Blackwell said. He started tapping on his laptop keyboard. Three minutes later, he leaned back in his chair. "I'll be a son of a . . . Jason Tanaka owns 100 Carlyle."

"You know him?"

"Yeah. I've read four of his books. One was on the judicial system in feudal Japan. He's got a Ph.D. from Waseda University. If anyone can translate that ledger, it will be Tanaka. He'll probably invite Parker to stick around while he does the translation, and my guess is it will take him a couple of days to finish it."

"That long?"

"Give me a break. You tried reading the first page and gave up in less than a minute. But that's beside the point. Parker won't be sitting on his ass in the meantime. He will start the authentication process if he hasn't done so already. That's what he's trained to do."

Fumio watched Blackwell scan Carlyle Lane with his street view app. "Look here. See the Pac Bell junction box at the corner? Hard-tap Tanaka's line and attach a wireless transmitter when it gets dark. There's one in the safe. It will take a while to figure out which wires lead to Tanaka's residence, so get going. When you finish, park outside the cul-de-sac, just in case West tries to leave. I'll be waiting on the next block over. I don't think he will run, but I'd rather be safe than sorry."

"So, what do we do if he doesn't run?"

"Easy. We just watch and wait."

# CHAPTER II

THE LUMINOUS NUMBERS ON the bedside clock read 8:00 a.m. Parker opened the drapes, and sunlight flooded the room. He was surprised by the size of the bedroom. He explored the modest library and eyed a beautiful antique clock on the marble mantle over the fireplace. The bathroom was the size of his living room, and next to it was a sunroom with a table for two. On the stand beside his bed was a *yukata*, a light cotton robe, with a gift note from Tanaka.

The bathroom included a Japanese-made heated bidet with temperature control and pulsating water. He took a hot bath, shaved, and splashed some Creed Aventus cologne on his neck. *Never heard of it, but it smells good.* He put the yukata on just as a nurse opened the door.

"Hello, Mr. West. I'm Judy, your nurse. You don't remember, do you? You've been sedated for the last twenty-four hours. Just checking one more time before I leave." She took his temperature and blood pressure and listened to his heartbeat. "Everything checks out fine. Dr. Tanaka will be joining you later this morning. Goodbye, and stay well."

Parker relaxed in one of the wingback chairs in the library just as the mantel clock chimed nine times. A moment later, he heard a gentle knock on the door, and when he opened it, he came face-to-face with Tanaka, who was holding the wooden box.

"May I?"

"Dr. Tanaka. Of course, come in."

Tanaka placed the box on the table in front of the two chairs and gently shook Parker's hand. Instead of his gardening clothes, he wore a tan suit, a crisp white shirt, and a red Hermès tie. Parker assumed Tanaka was in his 70s, but he looked about twenty years younger. He was trim and tanned.

"You look a bit different from when I last saw you," Parker said.

"So do you," Tanaka snickered, pointing to Parker's yukata. How are you feeling?"

"A bit groggy but much, much better. Thank you for your hospitality. I'm sorry for the way I barged in on you."

"No apologies are necessary, and please, call me Jason. Dr. Gallant wants you to rest for a few more days. Frankly, I am quite pleased you came. By the way, I'm not always in my office downstairs, and I needn't tell you that my home is rather large. I sometimes work in my upstairs study, and I don't have a house phone handy there. I often use Terry's cell phone. Here's her number if you can't reach me on my landline."

"Thanks. I'll try not to bother you."

"Don't worry. If you need to talk, I need to listen. If you do not mind, would you be kind enough to tell me about the contents of this box?" Tanaka opened it and took out the accounts book.

"Everything belonged to my dad. But all I care about is the ledger. Have you translated it yet?"

"Hardly. It's rather difficult, but I am astounded by what I have already learned. But tell me, what's been going on? You look as though you were beaten," Tanaka said.

"I was. I went to my office to dig up your name and address and took the ledger to make a copy for you. But after spitting out five pages, the copier broke down. My partner, Marvin Greene, grabbed the copies and said a friend named Eddy Blackwell could translate them. That night, Blackwell and his partner, a guy named Fumio, murdered Marvin. When they couldn't find the ledger in our office, they came after me," Parker said, pointing to the bruises on his face.

"You know Blackwell?"

"Hardly. I always kept my distance. He used to visit Marvin from time to time. I think he was supplying him with drugs."

Tanaka sighed. "I read about Marvin's murder in the *Los Angeles Times*. So, you were his partner. Unbelievable," he said as he walked over to the fireplace mantel and checked the clock against his watch. "I guess you know he called me in on a case once. But that's beside the point. What else can you tell me?"

"That's about it, except I think the detective assigned to the case, a guy named Thomas Smith, is somehow involved with Blackwell."

Tanaka put on his gold-rimmed glasses and glanced at the unopened ledger. "I see. This is serious, isn't it?"

"It sure is. That is why I plan to leave today. It may be dangerous to have me here."

Tanaka shook his head. "No, I very much want you to stay."

Parker blinked. "Why?"

"Because I need *your* help, and you will be safe here. A dozen cameras monitor the grounds twenty-four-seven, and an alarm goes off if the property is breached. Just like when you dodged the entrance gate."

"I'm sorry about that. I was rather desperate."

"Not to worry. But given what you said, I will have guards stationed on the grounds around the clock. Crown City Security is the best in the business."

"Don't go to the trouble. I plan to call the police and blow the whistle on Detective Smith."

Tanaka shifted in his chair and leaned forward. "Parker, you want me to translate the journal, so do me the courtesy and allow me to finish it first. Keep this between you and me for now. It will take me several more hours, and I ask you not to do anything rash in the meantime. You'll understand soon enough why I am asking you to be patient. Oh, and don't say anything to Terry about Smith. She's rather protective of me."

"I gathered that."

"She will be here in a few minutes with your breakfast," Tanaka said, as he pulled off the box lid. "It will be a good chance for you two to get to know each other. It might take her a day or two, but don't worry. Terry will come around."

Tanaka picked up the clothbound sword and unwrapped it. "This is called a *wakizashi*, or short sword," Tanaka said. "They are usually paired with long ones. Samurai wore them together. Do you have its mate?"

"No, only that one."

"Too bad," Tanaka said.

Parker pointed at the velvet sack in the box. "Jason, did you see the gold coin? It's worth a few bucks."

"That's an understatement. I did a bit of research on it. It is 96.75 percent pure gold. It's far more valuable than its precious metal content, but its value pales compared to what I suspect the ledger is about to reveal. It is a diary of sorts. I wish I could tell you more, but the handwriting style makes it difficult to read."

"How so?"

Tanaka opened the ledger to the first page. "These are Chinese characters called *kanji*," he said, pointing to a line of them.

"Chinese? I thought they were Japanese characters."

"They are. The Japanese borrowed the Chinese writing system around fifteen hundred years ago. These kanji are written in an elegant, cursive style, a variant of the *Karayo* school of calligraphy. Elegant even in pencil. It is a style developed by Zen monks."

"A monk wrote the diary?"

"No, but the author, Tomita Yuki, probably took calligraphy lessons from one. By the way, family names always come first in Japanese. Yuki was his first name. He was a samurai from an aristocratic family. I believe he was a *rangakusha*."

"A ranga-what?"

"A rangakusha. A samurai scholar who studied the West. He most likely was a geopolitical expert who could read and write English. Do you know how the things in this box came into your father's possession?"

"I have no idea. When I was a kid, I discovered the box in our attic, but Dad never told me where it came from. And when Mom caught me playing with the sword one day, she went ballistic. She ordered Dad to get rid of everything, and he promised to do so. She was always the boss in our family."

"I'm sure she didn't want dangerous weapons in the house," Tanaka said.

"I don't know what she thought. She could sometimes be cold to me, but that's another story. What else have you learned from the diary?"

"Yuki kept it from early 1867 to April 1868, during which he visited the United States. He did not write very much; most pages are blank."

"Yeah, I noticed that. Why do you suppose he didn't write more?"

"Perhaps because he wasn't into keeping a journal. By the way, someone appears to have cut a small bit of paper from the bottom of the page with the graphite smudges on it."

"I did, and I sent the sample to SoCal Forensics. They will determine the paper's age and the graphite's composition. I need to check my email to see if they sent the report yet."

"Let me know when you get it," Tanaka said.

"Sure will, Jason. Oh, and did you notice the fingerprint on the last written page? I'm sure it is blood. I wonder what that's all about."

"It was Yuki's way of signifying the end of his journal. He wrote his name in large kanji on the last page. He must have lost his personal stamp called a *hanko*. The Japanese use them to stamp their names on important documents with vermilion ink. He used a bloody fingerprint instead. I would like to take a sample of blood to check the DNA. If, of course, it is readable."

"Why?"

"We may be able to establish a link with Tomita's living descendants in Japan, assuming there are any. We could do it through one of the Japanese ancestry sites. Would you mind if I have it tested?"

"Go ahead."

"Thanks. I've already contacted a friend at UCLA's medical lab. He is willing to run the test. It would be a travesty to damage the fingerprint, and there are a couple of blood specks at the bottom of the page that I can sample. I'll FedEx it today."

"So, what do you think about the other things?"

"The rifle is a collector's item. It might sell for five thousand dollars at auction. Oh, and by the way, I should have mentioned this earlier, but a certain Major Benjamin Butler and his daughter Mary were in Japan at the time, and he appears to have been assisting Yuki."

"Really? Do you suppose the major was a military advisor?"

"Hard to say. Maybe we'll never know." Tanaka reached into the box and picked up the green file folder. "I'm more curious about this. Did you go through it yet?"

"No, I was more interested in the ledger. Why?"

"I'll get to that later."

"Why later?" Parker asked, but Terry entered the bedroom with a serving cart before Tanaka could reply.

"You two get to know each other," Tanaka said as he stood up to leave. "By the way, Terry, I have asked Parker to stay with us for a few days while he heals."

"That's nice," she said.

Parker was surprised. She sounded as though she meant it.

# CHAPTER 12

TERRY HANDED PARKER A linen napkin with a wan, apologetic smile. "I'm sorry, Mr. West. I've been somewhat—"

"Protective of your uncle? I certainly understand. No explanation is necessary. And please call me Parker."

She smiled again, this time with an engaging look in her eyes. "We usually have a light Japanese breakfast. If you would prefer pancakes, I can take this back."

"Whatever you've made will be great."

"Do you mind if I stay while you eat? I brought an extra teacup."

"Please do."

She sat down across from him and poured two cups of green tea.

"An interesting pattern," Parker said, admiring the hatched lines on his cup.

"The pattern on each dish and cup is different," Terry said.

"Why is that?" he asked, swallowing some cold seaweed salad without chewing.

"Western-style chinaware comes in sets with the same pattern, but Japanese seek to collect a variety of colors, patterns, and textures. It's an important part of the dining experience."

"I never knew," Parker said.

When he picked up his chopsticks and attempted to hold them correctly, he caught Terry trying to hide her impish smile.

"Looks like I will learn a lot about Japan while I'm here," he said. "Maybe I'll start by learning how to eat with these."

"You do fine with chopsticks. It's how you look."

"Huh?"

"Your black eyes," Terry said, unable to muffle her giggle. "You look like a raccoon."

Parker winced when he reflexively touched the purple-green bruises under his eyes.

Terry reached over and patted his shoulder. "I'm so sorry. I should not have trivialized your condition."

"Quite all right," Parker said, taking a tentative bite of salmon and a sip of *miso* soup. "Jason is a real scholar, isn't he?"

"He is. And he's more like a father to me than an uncle. He and my aunt took me in when my parents died. Aunt Lily, Jason's wife, died two years ago."

"I'm sorry to hear that. And let me put your mind at ease. Jason wants me to stay here for a while, but I had better not."

She put a finger to her lips and hushed him. "I know your story. Your partner was murdered."

"That is precisely why I plan to leave. I don't want to put you two in any danger."

Terry gently grasped Parker's hand. "You don't understand. A change has come over Uncle Jason since yesterday."

"In what way?"

"He's not been himself since Aunt Lily died. But since you came, he has been like a new man. It's all about that ledger."

Parker stole a glimpse of Terry's delicate features while she gathered the dishes. *Maybe I will stay a day or two longer.* His musings were interrupted when Dr. Gallant knocked on the door and entered.

"Later," Terry said with a fleeting smile.

Gallant sat down and reviewed the nurse's notes. "You're a strong man to have taken such punishment," he said. "Do you need any pain pills? I've got some if you do."

"No, I'm fine."

"You look like you are. But I better change the bandage on the small of your back before I leave."

Parker undid the yukata, and Gallant peeled off the adhesive bandage. "Ha, your bruise reminds me of dermal melanocytosis."

"A what?"

"Dermal melanocytosis. It's a fancy name for a purplish birthmark. Its more inelegant name is a Mongoloid spot."

"It sounds ugly, but I know what they are."

"I'm surprised you do. Not many Americans have heard of them. Almost all people of Asian descent are born with a discoloration on the small of their backs. Many are spots, but some can be big patches extending from kids' buttocks to their necks. Many Native Americans have them too. Such spots usually disappear early in childhood."

Gallant finished and dropped the old bandage into the wastepaper basket near the door as he left. "Have Jason call if you need some help," he said.

金　金　金

STANDING IN FRONT OF the bathroom mirror, Parker inspected the black and blue discoloration extending beyond the edges of the bandage. Looking at it brought back a hurtful memory. He suppressed it by getting back to work. He turned on his laptop and checked his emails. "Ha, I knew it," he said when he read SoCal Forensics' executive summary.

It was enough for the morning. Parker closed the drapes, switched off the lights, and climbed into bed. An hour later, he heard a rustling sound in the darkened room. He opened his eyes just enough to see Tanaka rummaging through the wastebasket. When he pulled the blood-stained bandage out, Parker noticed he was wearing latex gloves. Tanaka quietly closed the door and left.

"What the hell was that all about?" Parker mumbled before dozing off.

# CHAPTER 13

AFTER A SEVENTEEN-HOUR sleep, Parker woke up with a ravenous appetite. Tanaka took him downstairs, where Terry had set out an American-style breakfast on the table. When they finished, Parker asked the big question. "Jason, is the translation done yet?"

Tanaka took a sip of coffee and patted his mouth with his linen napkin. "Not quite, but I can tell you that Tomita Yuki may lead us to one of the most impressive historical finds in recent Japanese history."

Parker stared at the last strip of bacon on his plate. "An impressive historical find? Can you tell me what it is? Just a hint?"

"Let us refrain from rash speculation until I finish the translation. We must also make sure the journal is authentic. Have you heard from SoCal Forensics yet?"

"Yes. I got a summary, and it looks good. How about the blood sample from the page?"

"I expect to hear from UCLA later today."

"That was quick," Parker replied.

"Indeed," Tanaka said. "Now, if you'll excuse me, I have many promises to keep."

"And miles to go before he sleeps," Parker muttered as he retreated to his room. "Why the heck is he so evasive?"

Rather than dwelling on it, he called SoCal Forensics and discussed the results of the paper and graphite tests. An hour later, Terry knocked on the door and pushed in a tea cart stacked with several boxes. "These are for you, courtesy of Uncle Jason."

"Wow, thanks, Terry. I'll pay him when I get my wallet back from the police," he said. The golden fleece logo on the boxes caught his eye, and he knew he would have to dig up some serious cash for the clothes inside.

"Terry, something has been bothering me. Your uncle is holding back on something."

"Parker, here are three pairs of trousers, four shirts, socks, two belts, and a sports jacket. I had to guess that you are a boxer shorts kind of guy. And a couple of pairs of size ten shoes. If anything doesn't fit, let me know."

"You're just like Jason, you know."

"Why is that?"

"You have selective hearing."

"Well, don't worry about paying for these. They are a gift. You can't be running around in that yukata all the time. Get dressed, and we'll take a walk outside."

Parker chose not to pursue the matter any further. When Terry left, he showered, shaved, and put on his new clothes. He was starting to feel good again.

Tanaka practically ran him over when Parker opened the door and stepped into the hallway. "Sorry, Parker, see you at ten in my office?"

"You got it," Parker said.

He found Terry waiting for him on the back patio, soaking in the warm sunshine. "Jason is really in a rush this morning," he said, hoping to learn why.

"He's been up since four this morning. I have never seen him so animated. Since you arrived, he's been like a kid with a new toy. That diary has had an amazing effect on him. He's talking about going to Japan to research it."

"Japan? Really?"

"Yes."

"Well, I'm getting a bit frustrated. He isn't quite as forthcoming as I'd hoped."

"Don't worry. He's just being meticulous. I'll tell you more about him. Let's just take a walk in the garden. I love it this time of year."

It was a smog-free day in Southern California. The sky was an intense blue, and the brilliant red roses were noticeably sweet-smelling. The San Gabriel Mountains seemed close enough to touch. Parker wobbled a bit, and Terry steered him to a marble bench.

"Terry, how is it that Jason became so, so...?"

"Rich?"

"I was going to say financially secure."

Terry laughed. "He inherited his parents' six-hundred-acre farm near Bakersfield. Cotton fields, mostly. It was called Middlefield Farms."

"That sounds really Anglo."

"That was the idea. When Jason's great-grandfather came to America, he changed his name. His name was Hiro Tanaka, but he changed it to Hank Middlefield. He had quite a sense of humor."

"How so?"

Terry took a small notebook and pencil from her jacket and drew a Japanese character:

"Look at this. It means field. Kanji are pictographs that evolved over thousands of years. Suppose you were in an airplane looking down at a rice field. Don't you see the four paddies? The character is pronounced 'Ta' in Japanese." She drew another character resembling a rectangle bisected by a vertical line:

"It means middle. Characters usually have more than one reading, and in this case, it is pronounced 'Naka.'"

"So, when combined, 'Ta' and 'Naka' mean field middle?"

"Yes, and, by reversing the characters and translating them, they become the very English-sounding name Middlefield."

"Interesting. So, what became of the cotton fields?"

"Chevron discovered oil there. They have the mineral rights, but they pay a nice royalty to Uncle Jason for every barrel pumped. Frankly speaking, he hardly knows what to do with his money. Because he prefers to continue his research for his next book on modern Japanese history, I handle most of his investments. He's self-taught in authenticating historical documents and an expert at handwriting analysis. That's why your partner asked for help to verify a Japanese signature in kanji."

"So why does he go by the name Tanaka rather than Middlefield?"

"He changed it back years ago. I don't know why."

Terry stood up, stretched her arms, and arched her back to absorb the sun's gentle warmth. "You're rather inquisitive, aren't you?"

"I guess it's in my nature. I'm sorry for being so nosey."

"Oh, forget it. Look, it's a beautiful day. I love the view," Terry said.

"Me too," Parker replied, referring to Terry rather than the San Gabriel Mountains. He sensed her serenity and untroubled innocence. Yet innocence was not quite the word. He felt a hint of something akin to sensuousness. He stood up, embarrassed to think Terry might notice that he had been staring at her.

A sound drifted over the lawn, interrupting his thoughts. Tanaka was standing outside his study, waving a sheaf of papers over his head.

"Parker, Terry, I've finished," he shouted.

# CHAPTER 14

TANAKA POLISHED HIS GLASSES with a linen handkerchief, hooked them about his ears, and set them precisely halfway down on the bridge of his nose. Parker and Terry sat in front of the massive desk and waited.

"Here are copies of my translation for both of you. I hope you can read my handwriting," Tanaka said. "The journal has as much to do with you, Parker, as it does with the man who wrote it."

"How so?"

"It's a bit complicated. You'll recall that Tomita Yuki, the samurai, wrote it. He lived at the very end of the Tokugawa shogunate, from the early 1840s to late 1868. You have heard of the shogun, right?"

"Oh, Uncle Jason," Terry said, rolling her eyes, "let's leave that lesson for another time. We'll be here all day if you start talking about Japanese history. Parker, all you need to know is that the Tokugawa shoguns were hereditary dictators who ruled Japan for over two hundred and fifty years. Please, Uncle Jason, let's get on with it."

Tanaka sighed. "I get the hint. But let me say that Tomita Yuki led an extraordinary life in an exciting period of Japanese history. He was fluent in English, which is probably why the shogun's government sent him to the US. He kept this journal in which he described some of the events that took place. Some, but not all."

"Jason don't get me wrong, but please, just get to the point," Parker said.

"It's not that simple. The journal speaks of something that has remained hidden to this day. I have access to several historical archives in Japan but have found nothing about this matter. Just rumors. Nevertheless, there is much circumstantial evidence. Yuki's uncle, whom he mentioned several times, was most likely a high government official. Under his orders, Yuki was sent to Boston. A Union Army officer and his daughter accompanied him."

"So, what is the impressive historical find you mentioned?"

"Just read the translation," Tanaka said, sliding two folders over. "Yuki is ready to lead you to the answer to many things."

"You're smiling again. What's this all about?" Parker asked impatiently.

Tanaka stood up and pointed to the door. "Just take your time and read it."

金　金　金

PARKER AND TERRY RETREATED to her upstairs study, where a double set of French doors opened onto a sunny second-floor balcony. She brought out an ice bucket with a bottle of sangria, glasses, a bowl of salsa, and a bag of tortilla chips.

"Why did Jason write this by hand?" Parker said. "I can read it, but I still wonder."

"He's always done translations this way. He'll input it on his computer once he is satisfied, but he likes to monkey around with his wording by hand. Japanese can be heavily nuanced, and getting the translation right takes time. So, let's dig in," Terry said.

They traded observations, spellbound from the outset. Terry started first. "When they were in Japan, Yuki described his nightly meetings with that Union Army officer's daughter. Listen to this: 'Mary and I spend intimate hours together in the teahouse.' It's rather suggestive, don't you think?"

"Not really. They were just getting to know each other."

"Parker, you are just like a guy. Don't you see? They were falling in love."

Parker chomped down on a salsa-lathered tortilla chip. "So?"

Terry sighed. "Never mind."

"Now, here's something interesting," Parker said a few seconds later. "Yuki implies but doesn't say exactly that he is being sent to the US on a secret mission. He also says he has a lot of 'wherewithal.' I wonder."

"Wonder what?"

"Jason said something about the impressive historical find. Maybe it was gold. I saw the English word in Yuki's diary."

"That's a thought," Terry said in passing. "He also mentions a Japanese guy the major befriended. They moved to Major Butler's house in Rhode Island when they got to Boston. A place called River Oak. Pretty weird. He was definitely holding back on things."

Both paused to take a sip of sangria while they drank in the view. A few minutes later, Parker broke the silence. "Wow, that Japanese fellow gets killed in a robbery attempt, and Yuki buries him in a cemetery along with his long samurai sword and 'many cases.' That's got to be the big secret Jason has been talking about. He must think 'the cases' are still buried in the US."

"I think you're right about that, but it's strange—Tomita never finished his next entry," Terry said.

Parker turned to the same page. "Yeah, I see what you mean. All he wrote was 'the map.' He probably was going to sketch a cemetery map showing where Shorty's grave was, but he was too distraught to do it."

Parker poured himself another glass of sangria, but Terry tapped his wrist, and he put it down. "What's wrong?" he asked.

"Mary is pregnant, and Uncle Butler dies. "Nothing was going right for them." She dabbed her eyes with a napkin and sniffed back a few more tears. "It's so sad. Did you catch Yuki's last entry? 'Dearest, I will return soon. I love you.' Parker, can't you see now? They were in love. They even talked about naming the baby. I cannot imagine how distressed Mary must have been. They weren't married, and Yuki was about to return to Japan. Do you think he ever returned?"

Parker crunched a chip and drained his glass. "I wonder," he said, missing Terry's searing frown.

"You are so incredibly insensitive. Don't you see? It's the story of Madame Butterfly in reverse. Yuki was the Japanese version of Lieutenant Pinkerton. Mary probably spent the rest of her life yearning for him to return. Or maybe she committed suicide, like Cho-Cho-San."

Parker put down his glass and wiped his mouth. "I get it now. Yuki was torn between two worlds. Oh, and did you read about Sarah, their housekeeper? He mentions her just once."

"Don't try changing the subject. What about Mary? You can't see it from a woman's perspective, can you?"

Parker tried dousing the California wildfire he'd ignited. "You're right. It was a tragic love affair, but we need to get on with it. I want to reread this whole thing. There's got to be a clue where the shogun's gold is buried."

"Humph," Terry said, puffing a strand of hair away from her eyes. "Sure. Forget about Mary. The gold, if that is what is in the cases, is more important."

"I see your point," Parker said. "But let's talk about it later."

Terry shrugged and started to reread the journal again. Parker used his iPhone to search for River Oak on the Internet. He found everything from a college in Florida to a church in Virginia but nothing in Rhode Island. Not long after, a sense of foreboding seeped into his mind.

Tanaka had meticulously translated the diary but was wrong about something important: Tomita's story was not a real secret. *Blackwell somehow knows more than is in the five pages Marvin gave him. Terry and Jason are in harm's way, and I've caused this.*

Terry's phone beeped, interrupting his thoughts.

"Uncle Jason wants us to come down for an early dinner. He's bringing the journal and wants to hear your report from SoCal Forensics."

Parker and Terry joined Tanaka in the kitchen, where a large platter of sushi and sashimi awaited them.

"I made this myself," Tanaka said. "Let's dig in."

# CHAPTER 15

THEY STORMED THE PLATTER, and a half-hour later, Parker chased down his last slice of flounder with a glass of Alsatian Riesling.

"Jason, let me give you the details on the SoCal Forensics report. Before I do, though, let me tell you what I learned about the ledger. It was printed and bound in 1858. A fellow named William Hartshorne was in the business of producing them in Brooklyn. I suspect the ledger gathered dust on Butler's bookshelf until he took it to Japan."

"What about the paper and the graphite?"

"According to SoCal, the paper was manufactured in the US around the same time. The mineral components entrained in the smudges are consistent with those found in graphite mined near Sturbridge, Massachusetts. SoCal concluded that the Joseph Dixon Crucible Company manufactured the pencil."

"Well, that's enough to convince me," Tanaka said. "I doubt someone would spend so much trouble forging such a document.

Terry looked perplexed. "So, can you tell us anything about the gold other than what is in the journal?"

"It was rumored that when Shogun Tokugawa Yoshinobu abdicated, his finance minister took all the bullion out of his master's castle and buried it in northern Japan to keep it away from the advancing Imperial Army. They were intent on installing the emperor in what became modern-day Tokyo. Historians have long pooh-poohed the story, but it looks like there was gold, and Yuki took it to Boston and buried it in a place called River Oak in Rhode Island. I couldn't find any reference to it online. Did you find anything?"

"Nothing at all."

"Parker, Uncle Jason, maybe Yuki returned to America and retrieved it," Terry said.

Tanaka shook his head. "That is highly unlikely. My guess is that Yuki did not, or could not, make it back to Boston. When he presumably returned to Japan, the country was in turmoil, and the Imperial Army was getting ready to attack the Domain of Aizu, Yuki's home province. I suspect that he was killed fighting there."

"Jason, that's all very interesting," Parker said, "but my main concern is that Blackwell and Smith know about the gold."

"I know, and I share your concern. We need to find the map before they do. If it still exists."

Parker gritted his teeth, and his eyes narrowed. "Jason, don't take offense, but I feel like I'm being subjected to your version of Chinese water torture. Information drip by drip. We didn't find any map."

"Sorry, I neglected to tell you," Tanaka said. He washed his hands in the kitchen sink and thoroughly dried them before opening the ledger. "Page seventeen is where Yuki wrote about burying Shorty, the sword, and the cases. He mentioned a map, but that was all."

"Yeah, we know that. So?"

"So, look here," Tanaka said. "There is a skip in page numbers. Page seventeen is called verso, a page on the left. The next two pages should be numbered eighteen and nineteen, but they are missing. The numbering starts again on page twenty. Look closely, and you can see where Yuki used something very sharp to remove the page. Probably a straight razor. He cut close to the binding, leaving just about an eighth of an inch of the page intact."

Parker slapped his forehead. "Jeez, it's so obvious."

Terry nudged his shoulder. "Don't obsess. The question is what happened to the map."

"That *is* the question," Tanaka said. "I suspect Yuki took it back to Japan. Think about it. Mary didn't need a map. She was a witness to what happened. Worst case? Yuki tossed it or lost it in Japan. In any event, we need to get started."

*Tossed it or lost it?* Parker drummed the tabletop with his fingers while considering Tanaka's unintentional rhyme. He concluded that there was a lot more work to be done. "I'll start checking the public records in Rhode Island for a property owned by Benjamin or Mary Butler. We won't need the map if we can find River Oak, but we'll need a metal detector. Thank God, Rhode Island is the smallest state in the Union."

Tanaka nodded. "Have at it. You've got all the real estate contacts. I'll search Butler's military records and the online grave registries."

"Good idea, Jason. Let's do it."

Terry slammed her chopsticks down. "Wait a minute, Uncle Jason. I have a stake in this as well. Give me something to do."

"She's right," Parker said. "Three minds are better than two."

"Thank you," Terry said, her jaw jutting out like the prow of an America's Cup sailboat. "At least someone respects my intelligence."

Tanaka bristled. "Terry, you're not to involve yourself in this. There's an element of danger, and…."

"I am already involved."

"But you shouldn't be."

Terry brushed a stray hair from her eyes. "No buts, Uncle Jason."

Parker wanted to seek cover. Terry seemed ready to blow the house down with her huffing and puffing, and Tanaka seemed to wilt when he caught a glimpse of her fierce expression.

"Okay, my dear. You can help. According to Yuki's diary, he was to leave Boston on April 1, 1868, but he doesn't say on what vessel he booked passage. Try to find a likely ship. No vessels sailed straight to Japan from the US in those days. He may have landed in Singapore or Hong Kong and boarded another ship to Japan from either of those ports. Give us the name of a likely ship, and Parker and I will take it from there."

"Are you trying to send me off to do some meaningless make-work just to keep me out of your hair?"

"Absolutely not. Think about it. If Tomita took the map back to Japan, we must retrace his journey. The map may be tucked away in an attic or languishing in the national library. It's late in the day, figuratively speaking, and we need to cover every base."

"Jason is right. We don't have much time," Parker said. "Eddy Blackwell and his buddy Fumio knew about the gold before we did, and now they've got two American names: Benjamin and Mary Butler. They appeared in Yuki's diary on the first page. If Blackwell digs up Butler's property records before we do, he'll be on his way to Rhode Island in a New York minute."

"Parker, do you always mix two states in that idiom?" Terry sniggered.

# CHAPTER 16

THE EASIEST WAY TO find River Oak was to check with a title company, but it was already seven at night. Parker had a friend at West Coast Title who could help him after hours, but he did not want to bother him. Instead, he googled "Rhode Island 1860 census" and found hundreds of digitized pages of handwritten records. He started with Providence County, running down name after name, looking for Benjamin Butler's or Mary's. But after two hours, he rubbed his eyes and gave up. He estimated it would take at least a week to comb through the raw data from Rhode Island's cities, towns, and hamlets.

Parker checked several ancestry sites, but neither the major nor Mary appeared on a family tree. He was exhausted and went to bed, but an old memory kept him awake. *There must have been another reason why Mom wanted Dad to throw everything in the box away…not just the rifle and the sword. Jason knows the answer, but he's been hiding it.*

Parker called his buddy Dave Chapman at West Coast Title at nine the next morning. The company made its money insuring owners against fraudulent title claims. It stored information on every property in California, and every property has what is called a chain of title that starts with its first owner. Parker once used the company to trace a title back to the 1700s when California was still part of Spain's New World empire.

"Hey, I heard about Marvin Greene's murder," Chapman said when he answered his phone. "Are you okay?"

"Yeah, but that's not what I am calling about. Dave, I'm looking for a property owned by a fellow or his daughter in Rhode Island in the 1860s, but I don't have an account with your East Coast division."

"Not to worry. Give me their names."

"Benjamin or Mary Butler."

"What? You've got to be kidding," Chapman shouted.

Parker pulled the phone away from his ear for a second. "Did I say something wrong?"

"You better believe it. Someone hacked our supposedly secure system last night. I received a no-damage report, but they did rummage through our records for any property owned by Benjamin or Mary Butler in Rhode Island. What's going on, Parker? This is serious shit."

"Marvin gave his killer five pages of a document I was working on. It bore those two names."

"Well, you have a lot of explaining to do. I'm going to report this."

Parker heard Chapman hitting his computer keys. "Please, Dave, don't push the send button. We can help each other. Just tell me one thing."

"What?"

"Did the hackers find the location of Butler's property?"

"Yeah. Benjamin Butler owned a house in Boston. He sold it in 1864. A water treatment plant sits on the site now."

"That's it? Nothing in Rhode Island?"

"Nope. *Nada*. So, what's all this about?"

"I think I know who hacked your system, but I have to make sure. I could get sued for defamation if I am wrong. Just give me a few days. We've worked with each other for what, six years? You know I'm on the level. I promise that you'll be the first to know. You'll probably be promoted when you break the case. Okay?

Chapman grunted.

I'll take that as a yes," Parker said. He hung up and rushed downstairs to tell Tanaka.

# CHAPTER 17

THE DOOR TO TANAKA'S study was closed, but Parker burst in, and Terry followed. "Jason, we've got a problem. West Coast Title was hacked by someone looking for the Butler property. Benjamin Butler once owned a house in Boston, but nothing in Rhode Island. In any event, your computer better be secure," Parker said.

"I can guarantee it. CyberSecure protects my desktop, Terry's laptop, and her smartphone."

"That's a relief. My things are protected too. It's a great company."

"By the way," Tanaka said, "I combed through something called the *Compiled Military Service Record*. Benjamin Butler's name and rank appeared, and his home in Boston was noted, but nothing else. I did find his grave on *findagrave.com*. He's buried in a Boston public cemetery. Nothing about River Oak and nothing about Mary Butler. It's like she never existed."

"It looks like we're at a dead end," Parker said. "What do we do next?"

Tanaka paused for a moment and stared pensively out of his study window. "Parker, let me clear up something. It hasn't dawned on you, has it?"

"What? I mean, no. What's going on, Jason? This is getting a bit old."

"I'm sorry. I should have been more forthcoming from the outset. While you were sleeping, I took that blood-soaked bandage from the wastepaper basket in your room."

"I know. I was half awake and saw you."

"Well, I had a test run on the sample from Yuki's ledger. Just as we supposed, it is human blood. But I also requested DNA tests on both samples."

"DNA tests?"

"Yes, and the results confirm what I initially suspected."

"And what is that?"

"Hold on, Uncle Jason," Terry said. "Are you saying . . .?"

"Yes, I am. There is a match between the two DNA samples. Parker, you are related to Tomita Yuki."

"What?"

"It's true. You are the direct descendant of Yuki and Mary Butler's love child. The DNA proves it."

Parker threw his head back and stared at the ceiling. "So that's the answer," he said, too choked up to finish his thought.

Terry reached over and put her hand on his shoulder. "The answer to what?"

"Why my mother could be so cold to me at times. She was a member of the Daughters of the American Revolution, and she never got tired of reminding us that she was a descendant of someone who came over on the *Mayflower*. She suspected that one of Dad's ancestors was Japanese, and the sword and the ledger were proof. But they were just tips of an iceberg."

Parker realized Jason and Terry were not quite following him. "You see, I was born with what Dr. Gallant called dermal melanocytosis. I'm sure you know what that is. Anyway, I overheard my mother tell Dad she felt humiliated whenever she saw the splotch on my back. She didn't let me swim at the beach or any public pool until it faded away. It wasn't completely gone until I was eight years old. That, and the box's contents, gave my mother all the proof she needed."

Parker choked up again. He peered out the study window to compose himself. "She realized Dad and I were not a hundred percent Caucasian, and it bothered her."

"Parker, don't be too hard on your mother," Tanaka said. He opened the file folder and handed two pages to him. "You need to read this letter."

Parker was a bit puzzled. He picked up the pages and began to read them in a hushed voice:

*"Son, if you check Ancestry.com, you will find the West Family tree that your uncle Robert put together. Your grandfather shared a secret with Robert many years ago, but not with me. I suppose Dad intended to tell me when I was old enough to understand, but he died before he could do it, and Uncle Robert waited until he was terminally ill before sharing the secret. It so happens that you and I are descendants of an Asian male. It has been a family secret because of the racial prejudice many Asians have been subjected to. I don't know anything about our ancestor—even his name. But I believe he was Japanese. I should not have kept this from you for so long, but I love your mother and did not wish to cause her more pain."*

Parker choked up and glanced pleadingly at Terry.

"It's all right," she said, kissing the back of his hand. "Finish it."

Parker swallowed hard and finished the letter:

*"I always wanted to have the ledger translated, but I dared not because your mom demanded that I get rid of everything. I'm leaving you this letter, the ledger, and the other contents of this box that I have been hiding for years. I lied to your mom when I said I'd thrown everything away.*

*Please forgive me, and please forgive your mother. She's starting to see the light of day. Her attitude changed when you got a scholarship and moved into that SC dorm. She misses you and has started to blame herself for how she reacted when discovering the truth hidden in our genes. It has taken time, but she is coming around.*

*I hope things will have already been ironed out by the time you find this letter. Trust me when I say that your mother truly loves you, as do I. And please know that I am very proud of you and your accomplishments. Stay well, son.*

*PS: You'll find something a bit ironic when you check out our family tree!"*

# CHAPTER 18

P ARKER STARED AT HIS father's signature and swallowed hard. "The letter is dated two days before my parents were killed in an auto accident. I had no idea," he said in a raspy whisper.

"Parker, cheer up. You have some very cool bragging rights."

"What do you mean?"

"Do I have to spell it out? You are the descendant of a samurai."

Learning that he was related to Tomita Yuki was a shock, and Tanaka and Terry waited until he absorbed the implications.

"Jason, thank you. Without your help, I would never have known."

"I should thank you for bringing the ledger to my attention. I hesitated to tell you about it because I did not relish opening a wound."

"Come on, guys, let's carry on," Terry said with obvious impatience. "I've finished my report."

金 金 金

UNTIL TANAKA HAD PRIVATELY brought him up to speed, Parker had known little about Terry other than she appeared to be well-educated. She had a master's in psychology from Stanford and was about to start working on her doctorate when Tanaka's wife died. Terry loved her uncle and was determined to help him overcome his depression.

He begged her to stay with him because he needed more than emotional support. He wanted to get back to his research on Japanese society, and he asked Terry to take over the management of his business affairs. She agreed to stay on when he promised to help her improve her Japanese. She took charge of the house and property and handled the estate's finances. And she negotiated contracts, including the end of a long-running dispute over oil royalties. In the end, she did not pursue her doctorate.

A few hours after Parker arrived and Tanaka began translating the diary, Terry noted a positive change in her uncle's demeanor. She realized he had a new purpose that drew him out of the remaining dregs of his depression. Parker had earned her gratitude, and she realized she liked him. Moreover, she sensed that he was attracted to her, but Terry had more than a pretty face, and she hoped he would come to respect her for that.

She handed copies of her report to Parker and Tanaka. "Let me explain all this. A ship called the *Lightning* picked up cargo in Boston and sailed to Hong Kong on April 1, 1868. You have a copy of a scratchy photo of it. It was a so-called extreme clipper ship, a high-speed English merchant cargo carrier commissioned in 1854. A three-mast schooner, to be exact. It carried almost 1,500 tons of cargo and a crew of 100. It sank in 1869.

Tanaka stared wide-eyed at Terry over the rim of his glasses. "Where did you find all this?"

"I accessed the Boston Harbor customs historical records online and learned from another source that the ship made port in Hong Kong on June 13. It discharged its cargo into lighters owned by the Jardine Matheson Company. The firm's archives are located at the University of Cambridge, and I contacted the records depository. A Dr. Carruthers Umpleby was kind enough to retrieve the digitized records and email them. After the ship's cargo was discharged, it took on a load of tea and sailed back to Liverpool."

"But, dearest, how can we be sure Yuki was aboard the *Lightning*?"

"On page three, you'll see a copy of the captain's log in which he noted that the ship took on three passengers in Boston." Terry turned to the next page and read the entry. "'An oriental by the name of Tommy occupies cabin #2.'" She smiled smugly and tapped her folder. "It's all here. Take your time and read everything."

"Remarkable," Tanaka said. "What a great job."

"Excellent work, Terry," Parker chimed in. "So, Tomita got as far as Hong Kong, but did he make it from there back to Japan?"

"I have that answer as well," Terry said. "An American ship called the *Sacramento* was anchored in Hong Kong Harbor at the same time, and it sailed to Japan a day after the *Lightning* departed. No doubt Yuki would have been looking for a ship to take him back home, so I made the reasonable assumption that he booked passage on the *Sacramento*."

"That's a big leap of faith," Tanaka said.

"Hold on, Uncle Jason, just be patient. I also learned Jardins delivered some cargo to the *Sacramento,* and I have a copy of the manifest on page six. The French consul in Hong Kong booked space for several crates of goods consigned to Léon Roches, the French ambassador in Yokohama. Here is the proof."

Terry slid copies to Parker and Tanaka. "Take a look at the section in the manifest I highlighted. You'll see that the American consulate in Hong Kong entrusted the captain of the *Sacramento* to forward a packet of mail to the American legation in Yokohama. Now, check out the captain's log that I also discovered."

Parker read it out loud. "A Nipponese male paid six dollars for steerage to Yokohama."

Terry leaned back in her chair. "That had to be Yuki, wouldn't you think?" she said with a self-satisfied grin.

Tanaka took his glasses off and checked the lenses through the sunlight streaming through the leaded glass windows of his study. "What I really think, my dear, is that you are a first-class detective. I should never have doubted your ability."

"I'll buy that," Parker said, gently patting her shoulder.

Terry returned his compliment with a demure smile. His touch seemed to inspirit her.

Tanaka got up from his chair and pointed to the door. "Let's break for an early dinner around five. I'll be ready to tell you about plan B by then."

Parker cocked his head. "Plan B?"

"At dinner," Tanaka said summarily. "In the meantime, we must keep looking for Benjamin or Mary Butler."

At five o'clock, Parker went to Terry's study. The door was open, and he pulled up a chair in front of her desk. She sighed, and he noticed a tear.

"What's the matter, Terry? You have been crying."

"It's just so sad," she said, sniffling into her handkerchief.

"What? What's so sad?"

"I've been rereading the journal and came across Yuki's entry on January 29, 1868. Neither of us has paid much attention to it:

> *What would it be like to be free from the turmoil I have encountered? Perhaps I can find peace someday sitting on the veranda at Daiten-ji contemplating the Fourfold Truths of Buddha, away from all the cares of the world. I yearn someday to be at peace. But what would become of Mary?"*

"Daiten-ji? Is that a temple?"

"Yes," Terry replied, making a brave attempt to smile. "Tommy was so torn, and Mary must have been desperate beyond words. It's just so sad."

Parker knew that whatever he might say to her would sound stupid. Terry saved him the trouble.

"Come on, Parker. Let's go down and hear about plan B."

金　金　金

EDDY BLACKWELL YANKED OFF his earbuds. He had spent hours glued to his computer tracking Tanaka and West while they searched for a place called River Oak in Rhode Island. And Tanaka's niece had traced Tomita Yuki back to Japan.

"I'll be damned. They know I was the one who hacked West Coast Title, and they are on to something. Something big. I can feel it in my bones," Blackwell mumbled.

"Maybe West will report Smith to Pasadena Police Chief now," Fumio said. "I think it's time to take care of him."

"Parker is not going to call Smith out just yet. If so, he and Tanaka would have much explaining to do, like why they withheld evidence. Besides, finding the gold is their top priority."

"So, what do you want me to do?"

"Get two first-class tickets to Narita tonight if possible. I suspect they are planning to go to Japan too. We need to beat them to it. I think I can find some important clues there with what I know now."

Left alone, Blackwell leaned back in his chair. He was eight years old when his father told him the story about the shogun's gold and showed him the yellowed copy of a news article titled "Shogun Trove." He had been obsessed with finding the treasure ever since. Over the years, he combed every historical record he could think of, but he came up empty-handed. Now, however, he had names, places, and new ideas to go on.

As he listened in on Parker's phone conversations with West Coast Title and read the SoCal Forensics analyses, Blackwell realized Parker was no amateur, nor was Terry Ando. He knew he had to act fast, or they would beat him to the gold. The diary translation was not on Tanaka's computer, which was a real drawback. Blackwell desperately needed the translation, but he knew he would have to wait.

金 金 金

TERRY HAD DINNER READY, but Parker had no appetite. After a few minutes, he pushed away from the table and began thinking aloud. "Yuki made it back to Japan. But then, what happened? It boils down to whether he had the map and whether it even exists today, doesn't it?"

Tanaka put down his chopsticks and took a sip of beer. "True, but remember that Yuki mentioned his younger brother, uncle, and cousin in the diary. He probably had other relatives, too."

"And?"

"And one of them may have stowed the map somewhere like your father did with the ledger. We might learn a lot if we can find Yuki's family records. Ergo, plan B. We're going to Japan and find your descendants. I'll grant you that it's a stretch, but the Japanese are excellent at record keeping. Even if we find no living descendants, the map could be in a document repository or a local museum."

Tanaka folded his napkin and placed it next to his plate. "I have already made our reservations, so get ready. We leave the day after tomorrow."

"In that case, I need to return to my house and get my passport. The cops never returned my wallet, so I don't have my driver's license. But I have a legal ID card. It's in my wall safe with my passport."

"I'll have two guards accompany you. You'd better get going."

# CHAPTER 19

AFTER RETRIEVING HIS PASSPORT, Parker joined Terry in Tanaka's study. "Jason, I'm frustrated up to here," he said, holding his right index finger below his nose. I've found absolutely nothing."

"Let's take a walk in the garden and clear the air."

As they wandered about, Parker and Tanaka recounted their failed efforts. Terry stopped to pick a blossom from an orange tree and held it up to Parker's nose. He sniffed it and gave her a wink.

Before turning to Parker, Tanaka peered down at the concrete wash at the bottom of the arroyo. "Let's see—Yuki mentions Boston and Providence in his journal, but that's all. We can't find the gold unless we find the cemetery, and we can't find that unless we find the Butler home."

"Maybe it was held by a corporation," Terry suggested.

Parker shook his head. "Even if it were, we would need the company name. Besides, the corporations that went out of business in Massachusetts and Rhode Island before 1900 are not in any database, so we can't look up any corporate officer's name."

"Then it's back to plan B," Tanaka said. "The first thing on our list will be to visit an old classmate, Dr. Imanaga Issei. He is an expert on the *Bakumatsu*, the period roughly from the 1850s to 1868."

"When do we leave?" Terry asked.

"Parker and I fly out on the private jet I've chartered. It departs tomorrow morning at eleven o'clock."

Parker looked at Terry and wanted to crawl under the orange tree.

"Hey, wait just one minute. What about me?" she said. "I am not going to stay here alone. There's nothing for me to do here, and you don't want me going out because you're worried some ninja is waiting to stab me. Besides, I hate the guards following me wherever I go."

"Ninja? Really? Ninjas are lurking around in Pasadena waiting to stab you?" Parker bit his tongue as soon as he said it.

Terry shot him an icy glare, and he took a sudden interest in the grass growing under his feet.

"Terry, I think..." Tanaka said.

"Yes, Uncle Jason, after all the work I have done to help, what exactly do you think?"

Tanaka cleared his throat and snapped off a small twig crowded with orange blossoms. He held it out to Terry as if it were a peace offering. "I was merely going to say that I think you need to start packing."

"Oh, Uncle Jason, you're such a dear." She took the twig, sniffed the blossoms, and flashed Parker a smug look.

金　金　金

WITH SOME FREE TIME on his hands, Parker logged on to *Ancestry.com* and found the family tree his uncle had put together. It started in 1870 with a woman named Sarah Saylor.

He had seen her name in Yuki's diary. She was Yuki's and Mary's housekeeper, and he concluded that Sarah had fostered their child after Mary died, but she never formally adopted him.

*She married a man named Steven West. He was my step-great-great-grandfather. Is that what I should call him? He adopted Michael Yuki and registered him as Michael West.*

Parker took some time to trace back Steven West's lineage. He learned what his father meant about his family tree being a bit ironic: Steven's ancestor was Deputy Governor William West of Rhode Island, born in 1733. And one of West's ancestors was George Soule, who came to America aboard the *Mayflower*.

Parker's father's letter brought closure, and Parker went to bed feeling a deep sense of peace. But he realized his search was not just about the gold anymore. It was also about finding out what happened to his ancestor, Tomita Yuki, when he returned to Japan.

But the more he thought about the pending trip, the more troubled he became. *Everything hinges on a scrap of paper that Jason hopes to find in a museum or someone's attic. It is not just a stretch. It's a shot in the dark.*

# PART TWO
## The Shogun's Gold

# MAP OF JAPAN
# 1868

*Showing locations noted*

*in*

*THE SHOGUN'S GOLD*

Hokkaido Island

Hakodate
Capital of Ezo Republic
in 1868

Honshu Island

Location where the gold was
rumored to have been buried

Aizu Domain

Imperial Capital of Kyoto

Edo (Modern-day Tokyo)

Choshu Domain

Yokohama

Kyushu Island

Shikoku Island

Tosashimizu
Location of Manjiro Museum

# CHAPTER 1

*February 1867—Edo, the shogun's capital*

LORD HARA, SHOGUN TOKUGAWA YOSHINOBU'S chamberlain and chief advisor, summoned his friend Matsudaira Tokunari to his manor. They sat on the matted floor in his study, examining an antique vase that Hara had recently acquired.

"Matsudaira-dono," Hara said, using the honorific employed when conversing with a fellow samurai, "our government is in serious trouble. The rebels are gaining strength."

The sudden switch in subject matter unsettled Matsudaira, and he responded guardedly. "I agree. Thousands will die, and the economy will be left in shambles if we are plunged into civil war. The so-called Imperial Army must be crushed. But why are you bringing this up? Does it have something to do with this vase?"

"No. The reason is I need your help."

"But I am retired. You know I'm past my prime."

"That is precisely why I need you. Rebel spies would never suspect an old codger like you to direct the secret mission I am planning."

Matsudaira gave Hara a gentle ribcage nudge in response to his friendly taunt.

"Does the shogun know you are thinking of doing something?"

"No, you are the only one besides me."

"Our conversation is all about my nephew, isn't it?"

Hara grinned. "You have seen right through me, haven't you? Tomita Yuki is an accomplished English-speaking geopolitical scholar."

"So?"

"I want you to summon him immediately."

"What is this all about? What are you planning?"

Hara arose and motioned his friend to follow. "It's cold in this room. Let's go to my study, and I will explain everything over some warm sake."

金　金　金

TOMITA YUKI SAT SHIVERING with his writing brush poised above a sheet of paper. It was early morning, and the charcoal embers in the *horigotatsu*, a recess in the floor under his writing table, were spent, and he found it difficult to write. His report on American military and naval uniforms for the *daimyo*, the hereditary governor of Aizu, would have to wait. "A complete waste of time," he muttered while cleaning his brush.

Moments later, Yuki heard something outside. He cocked his head, listening as distant shouts and the unmistakable sound of drumming hooves grew louder. He stepped onto the veranda and watched open-jawed as a squad of samurai reined in their horses in his modest courtyard.

"Tomita-dono, we have orders to wait for you," the leader said, nodding at a riderless mount. He leaned forward, his breath billowing in the cold air, and handed Yuki a small package.

Yuki retreated to his study, tore it open, and broke the familiar seal on a letter with his thumb; it was from his uncle. *There's a warship waiting for me in Sendai harbor to take me to Edo? What's this all about?*

He had no clue, but the prospect of returning to the capital galvanized him. Awakened by the commotion, his younger brother wandered into the study and peered over his shoulder.

"Is it another demand from the daimyo?"

"No, it is from Uncle Matsudaira. I must leave immediately for Edo. Yoshi, send for father's *aozamurai* and have him manage the household in my absence."

The lowest-ranking members of the warrior class, "green samurai," often had trouble making ends meet, and more affluent peers hired them to handle their households' mundane tasks.

"But I'm old enough," Yoshi said. "Why must I defer to an old man? In another year, I'll be a White Tiger."

Yuki could not have been prouder. The White Tigers were teenage members of an elite reserve unit in Aizu called the *Byakkotai*.

"That is the very reason you must do what I say. You're not to waste your time managing the household. Your studies and martial arts practice are much more important."

"Brother, it is my duty to obey."

Sensing his brother's frustration, Yuki mellowed, feeling a twinge of guilt about leaving him. The trauma of becoming orphans thirteen years earlier had made him exceedingly protective of Yoshi. He put his hand on the boy's shoulder and smiled. "Brother, I know you will. You are a true samurai."

His brother's eyes lit up. "Will you bring me some camellia seed oil for my swords' blades?"

"That's a promise."

"Thank you, brother," Yoshi said, his eyes widening in anticipation. "I am almost out of it, and oil from Edo is the best."

Yoshi returned to his room, and Yuki started packing. He could hear the horses trampling about, their hooves crunching through the crusty snow in the courtyard. He hastily donned his riding clothes and girdled his long and short swords.

Having thought about it, Yuki concluded that the growing threat to the *Bakufu*, the shogun's government, had something to do with his uncle's summons. The Bakufu faced a rebellion by disaffected anti-foreign samurai. Only Aizu's fiercely loyal army and its northern allies stood between the fifteenth Tokugawa shogun and the overthrow of his 250-year-old dynasty. The ramifications chilled Yuki more than the bitter outside air. He bade goodbye to his brother and mounted his horse.

"My apologies, sir," the impatient officer said. "The warship is on a tight schedule, and we have a hard ride ahead of us."

"The sooner we start, the better," Yuki said, digging in his spurs and bolting to join the lead rider.

Four days later, he boarded the *Kanko* in Sendai Harbor. The warship was a steam-powered personal gift from the king of the Netherlands to Shogun Tokugawa Yoshinobu.

# CHAPTER 2

Yuki was a fourteen-year-old orphan when his maternal uncle and guardian, Matsudaira Tokunari, enrolled him in Edo's Institute for the Study of Barbarian Books. He studied English and eventually became a *rangakusha*, a scholar specializing in the study of the West. In his case, it was Western geopolitics. After graduating, he was assigned to his home in Aizu, where he reported directly to the daimyo. Aizu was a backwater domain isolated from Edo's intellectual firmament. His uncle's summons, Yuki hoped, portended a reprieve from his boredom.

Seven days after leaving Aizu, Yuki paced the deck, ready to disembark. He stood 135 *sun*, or five feet ten inches tall, and was in fine physical shape from years of sword practice. He quickly negotiated the rope ladder and settled into the waiting longboat. Eight grim-faced samurai horsemen waited for him at the landing site.

The leader announced some unexpected news. "Your cousin Matsudaira Nariaki sends his apologies. He could not be here, but he awaits you at your uncle's summer estate."

"His summer estate? This time of year?"

The officer responded with an uncertain nod.

"Captain, what is going on? Why all the security?"

"Rebel *hitokiri* have infiltrated the city. We have been on alert for months."

The so-called man-cutters were rebel samurai who aimed to overthrow the Tokugawa regime and install the emperor as the titular head of what was to be called the Imperial government. They regarded the semi-divine emperor as the legitimate head of state rather than the shogun, whom they considered a usurper.

For almost seven hundred years, Japanese emperors had been nothing more than figureheads who survived only at the pleasure of the shoguns, or "barbarian-subduing great generals." Kyoto was the imperial capital where the emperor held court, but the rebels planned to install him in the shogun's castle in Edo.

Yuki feared an all-out war between the rebels and the shogun's army would result in social and economic chaos and the loss of thousands of innocent lives. Rattled by the thought, he nodded down the road. "Lead the way," he said to the captain.

They galloped through the streets of Edo and into the countryside. An hour later, they arrived at the main gate of Matsudaira Tokunari's summer retreat. An officer of the guard led him to a warren of apartments overlooking a vast garden. Yuki had never visited his uncle's estate in the winter, and the bleak grounds were a depressing sight.

Yuki spotted his cousin conversing with another officer among the soldiers scattered throughout the compound. When their eyes met, Nariaki broke off his conversation and rushed to greet Yuki. They had been raised together as brothers, and their bond had grown stronger even as their careers had taken them in different directions. Nariaki was now a high-ranking army officer of the Aizu domain. After a few hasty words, he asked Yuki to sit on the veranda overlooking the garden and wait while he attended to another matter.

Yuki was puzzled to see a paper bullseye target pinned to a tree about twenty yards from where he sat. And he was shocked when he noticed a young foreign woman watching him from a nearby apartment. When their eyes met, she turned away and disappeared, leaving him utterly perplexed. Moments later, Nariaki returned, but before Yuki could ask about the woman, he saw one of his former schoolmates, Kato Yozo, leading her and a foreign soldier toward the veranda. When they drew nearer, Yuki realized both were carrying rifles.

"That's Benjamin Butler, a retired American army officer, and the woman is his daughter. Her name is Mary," Nariaki whispered. "It is better to ignore her. I find her to be a difficult person."

Butler wore a blue army uniform and a rakish hat. He proudly strode to the veranda with a black cigar clenched between his teeth. Yuki found it difficult to estimate the ages of Westerners, but he guessed the major to be in his fifties.

His daughter was young, but how young, Yuki was not sure. There was an indefinable naiveté about her. She was neatly coiffed, but several careless strands of hair played about her face and neck. They stopped in front of him, and the major took a puff on his cigar and made a showy, Western-style bow. Kato, Yuki's former schoolmate, stood at a respectful distance and interpreted for Nariaki.

"Sir, I am Major Benjamin Butler, retired. I have come to your estimable country which Mr. John Manjiro recommends."

Yuki had once met Manjiro, who, as a young commoner, had been shipwrecked on a deserted island, where he almost starved. An American sea captain rescued the young teenager, took him to America, and raised him until he was old enough to return to Japan.

Butler smiled when he saw Yuki's surprised look. "Yes, sir, John Manjiro himself. I came here at his behest to assist your government in putting down the rebellion threatening your storied nation's tranquility. You may have heard of our great conflict in which rebels vainly attempted to divide our nation. Because your country is similarly threatened, the shogun's government has had the foresight to retain my services." Butler paused, pointing to Mary. "And now, my daughter will assist me in a demonstration."

She exchanged rifles with Butler, curtseyed in front of Yuki, and smiled engagingly. He acknowledged her with a slight, uncertain nod.

Butler interrupted Yuki's thoughts by brandishing his rifle. "Gentlemen," he said, "this is a French Tabatière. Emperor Napoleon III has offered to sell your government thousands of them. You may judge for yourself if it is a worthy replacement for those outmoded matchlocks with which some of your soldiers are still armed."

He motioned Mary to hand the other rifle to Yuki. A fleeting smile crossed her lips. Yuki pretended not to notice.

Addressing Nariaki, Butler pointed at the rifle in Yuki's hands. "That, sir, is a Spencer repeating rifle, made in America, but I will demonstrate the Tabatière first." Butler opened the lid of his Waltham pocket watch and gave it to Kato. "When you hear the first shot, begin timing me, and after two minutes, call me to stop."

Then, looking Yuki in the eye, he said, "Forgive me, but I've forgotten your name."

"I am Tomita Yuki. I am pleased to make your acquaintance. How is it that you know Mr. Nakahama Manjiro? I met him when I was a youngster."

"Is that a fact? I watched Johnny-Boy grow up in America. Mary, you were right," the major said, turning to his daughter. "This fellow is the one. He speaks English and very well at that."

He pointed to Yuki, paused, and bit his lower lip. "Mister, um . . ." An awkward moment passed as Butler struggled with Yuki's last name. "Mister Tow-me . . . hmm . . . Tommy . . . That's it. Mister Tommy! Please be kind enough to count my shots."

"Yes, sir," Yuki replied, humored with his new Western name but puzzled by the major's comment about his "being the one." He watched Butler insert a cartridge into the breech and cock the hammer of the Tabatière.

"Gentlemen," Butler said, "steel yourselves." The crack of the rifle sent two crows screaming skyward from a stand of nearby trees. Yuki counted as more shots shattered the cold air. A cloud of gun smoke drifted into the garden and enveloped three guards who started to cough.

"Two minutes!" Kato shouted. He retrieved the target and hung a new one.

"Now, Tommy, me boy, how many?" Butler asked.

Yuki counted the holes. "Nine, sir."

Butler poked his index finger into one of the holes that crowded the bullseye. "Not bad, I'd say. Mary dear, hand me the Spencer. And Mr. Kato, get ready."

Butler opened the end of the stock, inserted a spring-fed tube of cartridges, and prepared to fire. "Gentlemen, are you ready?"

Yuki and Kato nodded. The major aimed and squeezed the trigger. Blasts erupted one after the other, sending a shower of spent shells raining onto the ground in front of the veranda.

The major aimed and fired seven times before removing the empty tube from the stock and inserting a new one. He began firing, repeating the process a second and third time. A puff of cold air carried the acrid cloud of gun smoke to the veranda.

Kato coughed and waved the smoke away from his face to see the tiny second hand of the major's watch. "Stop!" he cried out.

This time, Butler's daughter retrieved the target and gave it to Yuki. He took the target but said nothing to her.

Butler smiled. Tommy, how many shots?"

Yuki counted the holes. "Twenty, sir."

"So, young man, you have seen it with your own eyes. Twenty dead rebels." Butler ejected the last unspent cartridge and thrust the rifle into Yuki's hands.

Yuki held the rifle by the stock, careful not to touch the smoking barrel. The English and American muskets carried by Aizu soldiers were nothing compared to the Spencer. "I am amazed," he managed to say, still shaken by the ear-shattering blasts.

Butler grinned. "Amazed, indeed. I think we're going to get along quite well together."

Before Yuki could ask Butler what he meant by his remark, Nariaki signaled the end of the demonstration.

Kato interpreted: "Thank you, Major Butler. "I and, and...*Mr. Tommy* must leave now."

Butler attempted to protest, but Nariaki dismissed him with a wave of his hand. The major made an awkward bow in the manner of his Japanese host, and Yuki placed the Spencer in Mary's outstretched hands.

"Miss Butler, the rifle is very hot. Be careful."

"Thank you, Tommy. I hope to see you soon," she said, smiling coyly.

Yuki bowed, and Kato led Mary and the major back to the inner rooms of the manor. Yuki followed Nariaki to the main gate, where they mounted their horses for their journey back to Edo.

"Nariaki, I presume the demonstration was for your benefit, not mine, but the major appeared to know of me. Why did Uncle want me to witness the demonstration?"

"All I can say is there are plans to buy Spencers to replace the last of our antiquated rifles."

"Am I to help negotiate a purchase contract?"

"Cousin, it is a state secret. I hesitate to tell you, but…" Nariaki said. "Father will tell you tomorrow."

# CHAPTER 3

MATSUDAIRA TOKUNARI WARMLY GREETED his nephew, and Yuki immediately pressed him about the rifle demonstration. His uncle deflected the questions with a wave of his hand. "I'll tell you tomorrow after you give me your opinion about some incense I've recently purchased."

"Incense? Uncle, I know nothing about incense."

Matsudaira smiled patronizingly. "Do not fret. I plan to teach you, but you look a bit drawn. Go get some rest."

Exhausted from his arduous journey and confused by his uncle's evasiveness, Yuki drank a flask of warm sake and fell asleep.

Early the next afternoon, Matsudaira led Yuki to his *chaya*, a tea-house located behind his primary residence. They sat across from each other in the center of the room. Next to Matsudaira was a *hibachi*, a sand-filled brazier. A small ash-filled cup and an incense box lay on the table before him. Reaching into the hibachi with a pair of bronze chop-sticks, Matsudaira shook the ash off the surface of a tiny charcoal ember.

"I have purchased something quite unusual. Let us see if it was worth what I paid for it." He placed the ember atop the ashes in the cup and shook a few grains of incense onto it. He closed his eyes and wafted a wisp of smoke under his nose before passing the cup to Yuki. "What do you make of it, nephew?"

"A powerful scent, sir," Yuki replied after taking a whiff.

"Powerful indeed. The merchant who sold it to me claims it contains the powdered horn of a *kirin*."

It was an unusual scent, but Yuki did not believe the nonsense about the mythological beast. Artists depicted the kirin as having wings, a dragon-like head, and a deer-like body. Yuki nodded politely and passed the cup back.

Matsudaira fell silent, staring at the hibachi as though he were searching for something in the embers and ashes. "The incense speaks much to us," he said. "The kirin is the destroyer of evil things, the second most powerful of the celestial creatures. Nephew, like this incense, I believe smoke from the barrel of a Spencer repeating rifle has similar properties. Both portend the destruction of the wicked. You saw firsthand the remarkable power of that rifle. What did you think?"

"I was astonished," Yuki said, unsure where the conversation was taking him.

"Astonished indeed. You are quite the diplomat. That is good because I am about to tell you a state secret. You must not reveal it to anyone."

Yuki bowed his head in obeisance. "Sir, you have my word."

"Then I shall continue," Matsudaira said, lowering his voice. "You may not know this, but the Shogunate has made light of the defeat we suffered this past summer against those who would seek to overthrow it, but in truth, our losses were severe. The rebels from Choshu Domain were armed with seven thousand modern Enfield rifles supplied by a conniving Scotsman. They forced our army to turn and run. The British government pretends to know nothing of the illegal arms sale to make matters worse. The bitter truth is that Great Britain appears ready to side with the rebels openly. If that happens, the Bakufu may not survive."

"But sir, Napoleon III's support is unwavering," Yuki replied. "I understand he is even prepared to provide naval support for us."

Matsudaira shook his head. "Hmph. I wonder about that."

Yuki knew that if the Bakufu fell, the result would be social and economic chaos. Some rebel leaders even proposed abolishing *shinokosho*, the samurai-dominated class system. If that were to happen, thousands of samurai would be forced to earn a living in commerce, sullying themselves by handling money and dealing with commoners on an equal basis. It was a troubling thought.

"Listen," Matsudaira said, "not all is lost. We have retained Major Butler to assist us in acquiring Spencers. As you saw yesterday, they can fire bullets quickly. English Enfields are much slower. If we are to defeat the rebels, we need ten thousand Spencers to arm Aizu's soldiers and those of two other Bakufu allies."

Yuki shifted uneasily on his *futon*. He had not realized the situation was so critical. His uncle had plans for him, but he was clueless about what they were.

While adding several more charcoal chunks to the brazier, Matsudaira continued. "With the Spencers, we will utterly destroy the rebel armies. However, make no mistake: the rifles are not inexpensive. Butler estimates that it will cost $40, payable in gold, for each rifle, ample ammunition, spare parts, bullet tubes, and tools to manufacture our bullets. The strain on the treasury will be enormous, but Japan cannot afford a civil war. I am convinced those rifles will save thousands of lives. That is why we have chosen you to handle the necessities."

"Uncle, you have chosen me to assist Major Butler?"

"Yes. You will accompany him back to *Meriken*."

"America?"

"Of course. You will be in charge. Kato, that fellow who assisted Butler during the demonstration, will be your assistant. And thirty samurai will be under your command. Nariaki and I have already started making the arrangements."

Matsudaira turned to warm his hands over the hibachi, giving Yuki time to digest what he had just heard. Meanwhile, an attendant entered with a tray of warm sake and poured two cups. They took tentative sips before draining them, and Yuki refilled his uncle's cup again before Matsudaira reciprocated.

"In the meantime," Matsudaira said, "you are to escort Butler and his daughter to Aizu. We need to keep them safe from prying eyes. Besides, Westerners are a capricious lot, and you will have an important opportunity to learn how they think. Make good use of your time while I finalize the arrangements."

Yuki swallowed hard. He could never have imagined that his long-held dream of going to America might be realized.

Matsudaira interrupted Yuki's thoughts. "The mission will be difficult and dangerous. I raised you like a son and respect your courage and judgment. That is why Lord Hara and I have chosen you."

"Lord Hara, the shogun's chamberlain?"

"Yes. Only he knows. In fact, he is the one who asked me to take charge."

Practically speechless, Yuki bowed, his hands pressed upon the tabletop, his forehead atop his fingers. "America? Sir, I cannot express enough gratitude for your confidence in me."

"Good. Then it is done. Work closely with Butler. Lord Hara promised him a generous reward, which would be paid only upon the delivery of the rifles. We will also give him a general's commission."

"A general's commission?"

Matsudaira flashed Yuki a sly smile. "A mere sinecure, yet he appears to covet it as much as the money. He is a curious fellow, but make no mistake, Butler is essential. He and Christopher Spencer, the man who invented the rifle, are close friends."

Yuki's uncle drained his cup of sake and urged Yuki to do the same with a nod. With their cups brimming again, Matsudaira finished what he was about to say. "Lord Hara has kept the shogun in the dark. Tokugawa Yoshinobu's judgment is sometimes flawed, and it is better that he remains unaware. Our plans must remain an absolute secret."

Yuki was shocked by his uncle's candor. "Sir, the secret is safe with me. You have my word. I will see the mission through even if I must give my life doing so."

Elated by his new assignment, Yuki returned to his apartment with visions of the United States of America glowing in his mind's eye. Americans were amiable but sometimes crude, a bit naïve, and always in a hurry. He was eager to learn more about them and their country, and now he had the chance.

But his primary goal, his only goal, was to bring back ten thousand rifles to put down the rebellion. It was clear to Yuki that Benjamin Butler was the key to success, and he dared not get crosswise with him. That meant he had to treat his daughter with more respect, no matter how awkward it would make him feel.

# CHAPTER 4

KUROI TAKUTO'S ANGER SEETHED over the news while he trudged through a gritty section of Edo. Tomita Yuki and his friend Kato Yozo had been granted plum assignments, but he did not know what they entailed.

"I was never even given a chance to apply," Kuroi grumbled. An umbrella peddler ran to the other side of the street when he saw the expression on the samurai's face.

Kuroi ducked into a *nomiya* patronized by down-and-outs and ordered a flask of warm sake. After graduating from the Institute for the Study of Barbarian Books with Tomita Yuki, he was assigned a minor position in the shogun's bureaucracy. But Yuki received a prestigious job working for the daimyo of Aizu. Kuroi considered the appointment a personal insult.

Hearing him swear under his breath, three patrons cast anxious glances at each other and quietly left. Ignoring them, Kuroi poured a cup of sake, swallowed it, and then another. *Without his uncle's connections, Tomita would never have been promoted. And that goes for that hanger-on Kato Yozo.*

What appeared to be flagrant nepotism made Kuroi's association with an enemy spy even more justified in his eyes. "It's time for me to get even." He slammed the table, and the last two customers scattered.

金　金　金

WARMED WITH A BELLYFUL of sake, Kuroi sought out Nibei, a commoner go-between for a rebel agent operating in Edo. The slight lapses in the man's Edo accent caused Kuroi to suspect that he was a *burakumin*, an untouchable. In fact, Nibei was an *Eta*, "a filthy mass," the lowest of the low. An Eta posing as a commoner would be executed without the slightest delay if he were caught. Kuroi found Nibei outside Asakusa Temple, peddling pornographic woodblock prints.

Nibei bowed and debased himself as usual. "Sir, how may I be of service to you?"

"Deliver this," Kuroi said, handing him a note. "You know where."

"Yes, Sir. As you say. Is there anything else?"

Kuroi despised Nibei's fawning obeisance, suspecting it was a guise to hide the man's contempt for samurai. "Leave me now," he said.

"Yes, Master. Thank you, Master." Nibei hastily grabbed his sheaf of colorful prints and disappeared.

The next evening, Kuroi discovered a thumb-sized scrap of paper under a pebble on the front step of his apartment. Only one character was written on it: 柳, *yanagi*, or willow.

# CHAPTER 5

D ISGUISED AS A *RONIN*, a masterless samurai, Kuroi hurried
to the outskirts of Yoshiwara, the notorious entertainment precinct. With no leggings, his legs ached in the
freezing air. Nearby, a willow once grew known as the "looking
back tree." It was said that patrons who indulged in the carnal
pleasures of Yoshiwara often glanced back at it, regretting that they
could not stay longer. The Yanagi was a sleazy inn frequented by
commoners and impoverished ronin.

Oki Izo was from the province of Choshu, a notorious hotbed
of rebellious samurai. More of a shadow than the man who cast it,
Oki posed a threat to the Bakufu, whose faltering intelligence service was unaware of his existence. As the Japanese would say, he
was a flea between a dog's teeth, an irritant not easily seen or dis-
lodged.

Kuroi had chanced to meet agent Oki at a brothel the year before. Being a man susceptible to flattery, he fell in with the shrewd
agent, who wheedled bits of privileged information each time they
met. Plied with sake and intoxicated with compliments, Kuroi
grew comfortable as a budding traitor. He was sure that nepotism
was the cause of his inability to advance up the bureaucratic ladder,
and Oki was always ready to stoke his anger and stroke his ego.

Kuroi and Tomita Yuki were from Aizu Domain, the rebels' fiercest and most hated enemy. Should the nascent rebellion result in the overthrow of the shogun, Kuroi knew that Aizu samurai heads would fall like a shower of October acorns. He was determined to avoid being part of the bloody harvest.

"Come drink with me in my room," Oki said.

Kuroi sat on a worn-out cushion and placed his swords to his right, their cutting edges facing outward. Placing swords to the left with their sharp edges out was a sign of mistrust and a grave insult. The heat from the horigotatsu warmed his feet and ankles, and he began to relax. A maid brought a tray of sake and scuttled off. The two conspirators toasted each other and drank.

"I feel insignificant in your presence," Oki said. "I envy your vast knowledge of the West and ability to read and speak a barbarian language. All your insights into the corrupt workings of the Bakufu have been quite helpful."

"It's nothing, really," Kuroi replied in a feeble attempt at self-deprecation.

"No, quite the opposite. The leaders of our Imperial movement are certain to reward you for your assistance. I know that for a fact, but of course, I cannot mention names."

"Say no more," Kuroi said effusively. "I am honored to play a small part in ..." He was at a loss for words to describe his treachery.

"Honored to play a role in destroying the shogun's corrupt government?" Oki offered.

"Yes, that's it," Kuroi said. He admired the way Oki finessed his words. "By the way, I have some important news."

"News?" Oki inclined his head like a robin listening for a worm in the grass. He poured another cup of sake for Kuroi.

"I've learned that an American army officer is being sequestered at Matsudaira Tokunari's summer estate outside Edo. I don't have any other details, but something important is going on. I'll try to find out what it is."

Instead of pouncing on the news, Oki shrugged and downed more sake. "Sorry, but your news is a bit old. Tomita Yuki, whom

I believe you know, was summoned there three days ago. Aizu troops had the whole area cordoned off, and gunfire was heard."

The news was as disturbing as it was unexpected. Kuroi panicked. Oki could have someone tailing him as well as Tomita.

Oki took one look at Kuroi's expression and laughed. "Do not look so crestfallen. Your information is always appreciated, and hearing the news from you adds credence to what I have already come across."

Sweat trickled down the small of Kuroi's back. He shifted uneasily, wondering how to respond. "My deepest apologies. I fear my news is a bit old."

Oki smiled dismissively, slipping his arms out of his kimono sleeves. His garment fell about his waist, and he motioned Kuroi to do the same. They sat with cups in their hands, their bodies glistening with sweat.

"Kuroi-dono, drink up. Enough of your unnecessary apologies. I'm eager to hear what else you know."

"Well, my guess is that the American officer came to Japan to advise the Aizu provincial army on Western battle tactics. Give me some time, and I'll try to find out what took place at Matsudaira's estate."

"Yes, that would be helpful," Oki said.

Kuroi swallowed his drink and waited for Oki to continue. He knew the spy had something up his sleeve, and he decided it was better to wait.

"I agree with your assessment of the American," said Oki. "He's dangerous, and we must eliminate him. I will need your help in furthering our Imperial cause."

Oki spoke so casually that Kuroi was not sure he heard correctly.

"Don't look so distressed. It will be easy."

"Are you suggesting that you and I kill him in Edo?"

Oki chuckled. "Us? Don't be absurd. The work will be accomplished in Aizu. My plans are already in play. Two Choshu samurai will arrive in Aizu by early summer and get things done."

Kuroi swallowed hard. "Oki-dono, sending assassins to Aizu is impossible. Security is unbelievably strict. Guards watch every road, and the daimyo's spies are everywhere. No one gets in or out without papers."

"Do not be the least concerned. I have a contact in Aizu who will smooth their entry and keep them hidden. But you can help by learning where the foreigners will be staying. It is probably located somewhere in the country. Find the location and provide my contact with as much information about it as you can acquire."

Kuroi had a good idea where the American officer would be housed, but he shuddered at the thought of being implicated. "It's getting hot in here," he said in a nervous attempt to change the subject.

"More sake?"

Kuroi held out his cup, and Oki filled it.

"Do not look so worried. All you need to do is pass along what you will learn. You'll never be suspected of complicity, I assure you."

Despite Oki's assurances, Kuroi wanted no part of the plan. Besides, returning to Aizu was impossible without permission from the government, something not readily granted to a low-level bureaucrat. His dangerous game of betrayal had brought him to an unexpected crossroad, and the thought of being involved in the plot caused him to unconsciously grab the back of his neck to protect himself from a sword blade.

Oki smirked. "Of course, Tomita will be taken out too. With him dead, you will be Japan's eminent rangakusha, and your value to us will increase a hundredfold."

"What? You intend to have Tomita Yuki killed?"

"Yes," Oki said. "If it weren't for his family connections, you might be in his stead right now—and be my target despite my respect for you. But you have had the good sense to serve our cause, and you needn't be concerned for your safety. But it is up to you to decide, isn't it?"

It chilled Kuroi the way Oki could turn things around. He had just delivered a deadly threat, not so subtly wrapped in warm assurances.

"Go now and think about it," said Oki as he stood up and opened the sliding door. "My man Nibei knows how to find me. If only you could be in Aizu to see Tomita's guts slip from his belly like eels dumped from a basket."

Kuroi returned home and drank himself into a stupor as he considered the possibility of being caught. He would be tortured and then taken to one of Edo's three execution sites, where Yamada Asaemon VII, the shogun's hereditary executioner, would mumble a prayer before lopping off his head. His liver would be cut from his belly and sold, and his head would be impaled on a stake in a conspicuous location as a warning to those who might consider treason.

Kuroi shuddered at what Yamada would do with the rest of his body.

金 金 金

LATE THAT EVENING, he heard a rattle on the front door. Thinking he was about to be arrested, Kuroi panicked.

A bold voice called out before he could reach for his sword. "Sir, I have an urgent communication from the Minister of Foreign Affairs."

Kuroi hesitated. He slid the door partway open and saw a government messenger holding out an envelope. Lightheaded from drinking, Kuroi grabbed it. The messenger left, and he tore open the seal and read the letter. It was from Minister Narushima Ryuhoku.

> *Kuroi Taketo: Henceforth, you will serve as my interpreter and translator. You may return to Aizu this summer to organize your affairs. You are to succeed Kato Yozo, who has been reassigned.*

Kuroi reread the letter and laughed. Emboldened by his promotion, he was ready to be Oki's willing accomplice. Kuroi had a good idea where the American and Tomita Yuki would be hiding in Aizu, and he agreed to work with the Choshu spy.

# CHAPTER 6

YUKI, THE GUARDS, AND porters waited at the front gate of Matsudaira Tokunari's town estate, where Major Butler and Mary were sequestered. Their move to Aizu had been carefully planned except for one oversight.

Mary flew into a rage when Yuki asked her to climb into the *kago*, a kind of palanquin that the porters were to carry. It was customary for people of wealth to ride in them, and he was shocked by her unexpected reaction.

"Mr. Tommy, get me a horse. I will not allow myself to be degraded in such a manner."

"Oh, come now, Mary," the major said.

"No," she said, stamping her feet on the icy road to make her point.

It was as though a bolt of lightning had struck amidst the gathering. The samurai grabbed their sword hilts. Mary had insulted Yuki, and the two porters ducked.

Surrounded by the guards, Mary was oblivious of her potentially lethal blunder. "Mr. Tommy, did you hear me?"

"Mary, we must be more accommodating," the major pleaded.

"I said no. I will not sit in that…that mousetrap to be transported like so much luggage by those pitiable creatures," she said, nodding at the porters.

Yuki struggled to keep his temper under control, yet when their eyes met, Mary's expression softened. She tried to grasp his hand, but Yuki stepped back to avoid her touch.

"Mr. Tommy, please be a dear. I am wearing a riding outfit, don't you see? Please find a horse. I cannot possibly fit into that box."

Yuki was mystified. Please be a *deer*? What kind of order is that?

The samurai guards and porters waited, staring at the bare branches of the trees, then at the ground, everywhere but at Yuki. *Do they expect me to decapitate her?*

He took a deep breath and considered the situation before turning to the guard leader. "This foreign woman is obviously too tall to sit comfortably in the kago. Procure a woman's saddle and find a gentle horse for her."

Turning to Mary, he attempted to calm her. "Miss Butler, I cannot be a deer, but I have arranged a horse and a sidesaddle for you. We will be delayed here for another day."

"Oh, Mr. Tommy," Mary said, "but you are a dear and quite the gentleman."

Yuki watched speechlessly as she and the major retreated to their quarters. Maintaining an amicable relationship with them was critical, and he realized his work would be more complicated than he had imagined. With no other recourse, he drew in a deep, chest-swelling breath and vowed to be more patient.

金　金　金

A DAY LATER, ARMED guards whisked Yuki and his party through the darkened city streets. From a Sumida River launch site, longboats carried them to the *Shohei*, anchored in Edo Bay. The Butlers' considerable baggage included five boxes of cigars and a case of rye whiskey. Standing on the deck, Yuki detected liquor on the major's breath, but he gave no thought that the man's drinking might be a problem in the future. What bothered him more was their foul-smelling body odor. Japanese believed that Westerners' meat-eating habits and their practice of taking infrequent baths caused their offensive smell. Samurai and many commoners bathed every day, and because most were Buddhist, they refrained from eating meat except for fish.

"It's colder than a mother-in-law's kiss," Major Butler muttered as they stood on the deck.

Yuki was puzzled. It was preposterous that a Japanese mother-in-law would have physical contact with her son-in-law. Even children did not kiss their parents. He concluded that his uncle was right; he had much to learn from the Americans.

During their journey, Mary peppered Yuki with questions, often quite personal. She wanted to know how old he was and why he was not married. The fact was that Yuki was too absorbed in his work to be bothered by the complicated niceties of a courtship. Go-betweens often suggested matches, but he rejected them.

He eventually found a way to stop Mary's impertinent questions. "When I complete my mission, Uncle Matsudaira will find me a suitable wife," he said.

The major remained in a jovial alcoholic daze during the voyage and subsequent overland trip to Aizu. Because the Butlers would create a stir if they were lodged in or near Tsuruga Castle, they were quartered at Matsudaira Tokunari's *yashiki*, a country estate. It was situated at the base of the foothills, about six miles from Aizu's capital. Walls surrounded the grounds, and a wide gate in front accommodated visitors on horseback. One samurai stood guard by a small door next to the gate, and two other guards patrolled the perimeter of the five-acre property.

Two rooms facing the garden opened onto a veranda through sliding *shoji*, doors made of wood-framed lattices covered with white paper made with the fibers of mulberry trees. Major Butler and Mary were given those rooms, and maids placed bedding on the floor each night.

"Americans are a practical people," Benjamin Butler said to Yuki. "We are born and raised to live our lives come what may. Sleeping on the floor bothers us none at all."

Their fatigue, borne of the rigors of their voyage to Japan and their journey to Aizu, eventually wore off, and the major and Mary began to settle in.

Each day, Yuki left his home outside the massive stone walls of Tsuruga Castle and rode to the yashiki. He wanted to spend his days planning their mission with Butler, but the major spent most of his days sleeping off his nightly drinking bouts. When they did meet, Yuki had trouble understanding his slurred speech.

Yuki was initially suspicious of the major's willingness to assist the Bakufu, concerned that he may have had an ulterior motive. The money required to purchase the rifles was enough for Butler and his daughter to live as aristocrats should they somehow make off with it. But it soon became apparent that the cunning offer of a general's commission appealed to Butler's vanity more than the generous compensation he had been promised.

Yuki concluded that the major was an uncomplicated, naïve man who viewed the world in dualities. Things were either good or bad, big or small, right or wrong. Facts never interfered with his preconceived notions. He saw the growing rebellion in Japan in the same light as the American Civil War. To him, the Japanese rebels, like the Confederates, were wicked, and the Bakufu was akin to the glorious Union. "I am bound to stand shoulder to shoulder with the shogun," he told Yuki. "Together, we will defeat those damned secessionists."

To Yuki's relief, Mary's mood gradually mellowed. Her maid taught her the rudiments of Japanese flower arrangement and entertained her with *origami*, the art of paper folding. Mary also started memorizing simple Japanese words and phrases, but she was lonely and felt a strong need to communicate in English with someone besides her father. Yuki was her only choice.

It was a perfect fit because Yuki believed her insights would help him better understand American culture and language. Book learning had provided him with a wide-ranging English vocabulary and a strong foundation in grammar, but he had some trouble understanding the spoken language, especially the major's.

Mary came to his rescue, and in time, Yuki became accustomed to what he once considered her overfamiliarity. When she offered to tutor him in English conversation, he quickly agreed. With a regimen of daily baths, her unpleasant body odor became a relic of her meat-eating past, and Yuki found it quite pleasant to sit across from her while they studied.

They were opposites in many ways, but they both had immediate needs the other could fulfill. As a graduate of Elmira Female College, Mary was conversant with various matters no Japanese woman would ever be allowed to explore. Thus, her presence was a boon to Yuki. He learned much more from her than the major, who was rarely sober. Conversing with Yuki helped Mary maintain her sanity during their sequestration. In time, they grew close, not out of necessity but out of mutual respect and understanding.

# CHAPTER 7

IN MID-APRIL, YUKI received a discouraging message from his uncle:

> *Shinsoku, the warship that was to transport your party to Boston, has suffered serious mechanical problems and is not yet seaworthy. Have patience.*

Yuki learned even more discouraging news: Kuroi Taketo was now the chief interpreter and translator for the foreign affairs magistrate. Yuki believed it was a poor decision to appoint him.

Upon arriving at the yashiki one morning, Yuki was disconcerted to discover Kuroi talking with the gate guard. He turned around and greeted Yuki in a surprisingly friendly manner.

"Tomita-dono, I apologize for my unannounced visit. It's been a long time. Two years, I think."

"Yes, it has," Yuki said, returning Kuroi's remarks with a perfunctory nod. "I'm surprised to see you here. Are you not overloaded with work in your new position?"

"So, you heard the news? I've replaced your friend Kato Yozo. Have you any idea what he is doing now?"

Yuki shook his head, hoping his lingering silence would make

Kuroi feel unwelcome. "Congratulations on your appointment," he finally said with forced sincerity. "You deserve it."

"Tomita-dono, your praise is much appreciated. Certainly, though, it was you who should have been promoted. You were always the better student."

Yuki acknowledged the compliment with a faint smile and waited for his unwanted guest to reveal the purpose of his visit.

"May I have a word with you?" Kuroi asked.

"Of course."

"Perhaps we should take a walk," Kuroi said, nodding at the garden.

Yuki willingly led the way out of the gate guard's earshot. "What brings you back to Aizu?" he asked.

"I was given some time to return here and put my affairs in order, but I was not allowed to return until now. Oh, and I have something important to ask of you."

"What is it?" Yuki asked warily as they approached the garden.

"I know you have two Americans here. Kato let it slip when we were discussing my new duties."

Yuki stopped in his tracks. "I'm sure you know it's a state secret," he said irritably.

Kuroi ignored Yuki's glare and edged toward the mansion. "Forgive me for my indiscretion. Of course, you're right. I should not have mentioned it."

Keeping his anger in check, Yuki pointed to the garden. "There is a finer view by the teahouse. Let me take you there."

Kuroi seemed not to mind. "What lies beyond those?" he asked, pointing to a line of evergreens.

"Just a wall. You can't see it from here. We have two guards patrolling the perimeter day and night."

"How about that small path? It doesn't seem something a guest would use."

"You are right. It leads to a gardener's tool hut, if you must ask. Kuroi-dono, I am swamped, and I am not feeling well. Please tell me what is on your mind."

"Sorry, I should have come directly to the point. I recently learned that your uncle had a hand in my promotion, and I wish to give him this token of my appreciation." He handed Yuki a small, lacquered box. "It contains some incense that may be of interest to him."

Taken aback, Yuki felt a sudden twinge of guilt. "Kuroi-dono, forgive my impatience. I have a headache. I'll be pleased to give it to him with your warmest regards."

"Then I must be leaving. Before I return to Edo, I have many things to do, so I probably won't see you for a while."

A familiar sound in the distance distracted them. A maid slid open one of the interior shojis, and Kuroi craned his neck in a blatant attempt to peer inside. Yuki quickly blocked his view and pointed to his horse. "Have a safe trip back to Edo."

"Very strange, Yuki muttered as he watched Kuroi disappear down the road. "It's not like him to be so friendly. He's up to something."

Feeling unwell, Yuki returned home without saying goodbye to the major or Mary.

金　金　金

Asai Soteki, a turncoat samurai, waited for Kuroi in a dilapidated shack in the countryside north of Tsuruga Castle. During his extended assignment in the imperial capital of Kyoto, the unit to which Asai belonged, ostensibly guarded nineteen-year-old Emperor Meiji. Being closely associated with members of the Imperial Household slowly turned Soteki against his Aizu compatriots. And he came to believe the shogun was a usurper of the emperor's rightful place as Japan's supreme ruler. After defeating Aizu and its allies, they intended to install him in the shogun's castle in Edo.

Kuroi pulled out a folded piece of paper as soon as he introduced himself to Asai. He dared not be seen with the Aizu traitor and wanted to leave as quickly as possible.

"I've made a sketch of the grounds showing where the guards and the foreigners are staying. I couldn't go inside the manor, but I believe the foreign man and his daughter have rooms facing the garden. Notice the tea house and the small gardener's shack. Your men should hide in one of them tonight. I suggest dispatching the foreigners early tomorrow morning as soon as it is light enough. Then kill Tomita Yuki when he arrives on horseback."

"The assassins will make good use of this," Asai said. He studied the map and asked a few questions. "This is quite helpful. I've already assigned a non-samurai soldier with an outmoded rifle to guard the front gate. His shift starts this evening. And two older samurai have been assigned to guard the perimeter. I made sure they did not get enough sleep last night. However, allow me to be frank; I am disappointed that you do not have the forged identity papers and the money I was promised. Make sure you have everything when we meet tomorrow night. It won't take long for Inspector Shimazu to figure out I planned all this. The two assassins and I must leave Aizu tomorrow after dark."

"You have my word," Kuroi said.

# CHAPTER 8

YUKI AWOKE THE FOLLOWING day with a blaring headache. He stumbled outside and vomited in his small garden. He wanted to stay home, but Mary and the major would be waiting.

He set off on horseback, and by the time he reached the main gate of his uncle's estate, a wave of nausea threatened to overcome him. He dismounted, failing to notice that a new gate guard watched his every move.

"Halt," the soldier shouted.

Stunned at the guard's impudence, Yuki glowered at him. "I am Tomita, and I am in command of you."

The soldier bowed apologetically. "Please excuse me, sir. I am new. I should have expected you, but in my ignorance...."

"Enough! What is your name? Where is the regular guard?"

"Kansuke is my name, sir. I don't know why the...."

"This is scandalous. An armed guard with no last name? A commoner?"

The guard appeared to be in his late twenties and relatively short, even for a Japanese. He wore an ill-fitting, semi-Western-style uniform, and his rifle was an outmoded Springfield percussion lock, the kind Aizu's army had abandoned a decade earlier.

"Who assigned you here? Speak up," Yuki demanded.

"The sector chief ordered it."

"Why is the regular morning guard not here?"

"I was not told, Master Tomita. I am new. I have just completed training."

"What?"

"Rifle training, sir. I…"

"Never mind. I'll see that you are relieved this afternoon. Here, take the reins of my horse. I intend on leaving shortly," Yuki said. He brushed past the guard but stopped and cocked his head when he heard a scream inside the manor.

Butler burst from his room, smashing through a sliding door, sending wood splinters and paper flying onto the veranda. He ran into the courtyard and yelled something incomprehensible. Yuki's first thought was that the major had become delusional from his drinking and, mildly amused, watched him stumble in the gravel and fall on his hands and knees.

"Thief!" the major bellowed.

A split second later, Yuki heard Mary scream. She burst into the courtyard and ran to him. She fell at his feet and clutched his ankles.

"Tommy, save us!"

"Mary, get up," he said.

"No, get down! The guard is going to shoot you!" she screamed.

Yuki spun around and saw Kansuke crouching on his left knee with his rifle leveled in his direction. Before he could duck, the rifle blast sent a .58 caliber slug zipping hornet-like past Yuki's head, and he heard Butler cry. Thinking the guard had killed the major, he spun around, only to find the bullet had found another mark. An intruder hovered over Butler with his sword poised to strike. Butler raised his arm to fend off the blade, but the swordsman faltered and dropped his sword. He grasped his bloodied chest and collapsed.

"Tommy!" Mary cried out again.

A samurai, his sword poised to strike, was almost upon him. Yuki drew his sword, knelt, and assumed a risky forward-thrust position. The assassin swung his sword, and Yuki lunged. The powerful thrust impaled the man, and his sword blade struck Yuki's arm when it fell. They stood heaving together in an awkward, deadly embrace for a moment. Bloody foam bubbled from the man's twisted lips. He tried to push himself off the blade, but Yuki grasped his sword's hilt with both hands and turned slightly to his left for leverage. Summoning all his strength, he gave his sword a powerful upward jerk. The blade ripped through the assailant's chest, and he died, collapsing in a pool of his blood.

Mary threw her arms around Yuki, but he was too weak to push her away. Instead, he stood still, filled with rage. He watched the major clamber to his feet and kick the body of his assailant. Certain the man was dead, he limped over to Kansuke and slapped the young guard on his back.

"You saved my life, me boy. God Almighty must have sent you," Butler bellowed.

"Master Tomita, what should I do?" Kansuke pleaded as he twisted himself out of the major's embrace.

"They are foreigners. Just smile and act politely," Yuki said dazedly. "His name is Kansuke," he called out to the major. "He doesn't understand English."

"Oh, Tommy, you've been hurt," Mary said, pointing to blood dripping from his wrist.

"I'm all right. It's just a small cut on my forearm."

He stumbled to the veranda, sat down, and pulled up his sleeve. Mary and her maid dressed Yuki's flesh wound. Tea was brought, but he could not keep it down.

"Find the perimeter guards and have them come here," he told Kansuke.

"Master, I just checked, and they have been killed."

The news stunned Yuki. He tried to swallow, but his throat was dry. "Then send the groundskeeper to Tsuruga Castle for help. You stay with us. Reload your rifle and stand guard. We must protect the foreigners."

The major reappeared with a pistol shoved into his belt, triumphantly waving his last bottle of rye whiskey. "I wish I'd had soldiers like you at Fredericksburg," he said, pointing to Kansuke. "If we can find a hundred boys like you, the rebels won't stand a chance." He swallowed a slug of whiskey and motioned Kansuke to do the same. The guard took a tentative sip, squinting as he swallowed the fiery liquid.

"Yes sir, me boy," Butler said, "we're gonna be the best o' friends."

"What does he want of me?" Kansuke pleaded.

"The major says that he has just appointed you to be his retainer because of your bravery."

The guard gulped when he heard the unexpected news. He leaned his rifle against a post and fell to his knees. "Foreign mister, sir, my greatest thanks."

The major grabbed him by the collar and pulled him up. "I don't know what you're saying, but there's no need for that, me boy. No man grovels such to another in America."

金　金　金

SIX EXHAUSTED SAMURAI ARRIVED five hours later. Their faces were dirt-streaked, and their horses were lathered and spent. Yuki recognized two of the men. The first to dismount was Shimazu Masumune, the chief police inspector of Aizu. He immediately ordered his subordinates to scour the perimeter. The second was the personal physician of Aizu's daimyo. He frowned when he took hold of Yuki's wrist and felt his pulse.

"Your body is on fire. Come inside and rest."

A few minutes later, Inspector Shimazu entered, carrying two swords. "Tomita-dono, both guards are dead. Tell me all you know." He placed the swords on the floor and produced a small mallet and punch from his satchel.

"These swords belonged to the assassins," he said. "They are very high-quality. Perhaps they can tell us more." He detached the handle of the first sword by striking the wood peg that kept it in place. He squinted at the exposed tang and read the characters stamped in the steel.

"'Shakudo, Choshu.' Just as I have surmised. The assassin was a rebel from the Choshu Domain. Tomita-dono, summon the foreigner and interpret for me."

"Major," Yuki called out, "come and tell us what happened."

"I encountered the one who attacked me sneakin' t'other way down that hall," Butler said. "At first, I thought he was a common thief, and I yelled at him. Then I saw his sword and realized my mistake. I figured I'd kicked a bear, so I ran clear through the door with him right on my heels. My guess is that the other cutthroat was lurking somewhere in the rear of the house. He was the one who came after you and Mary." He patted Yuki on the back. "Thank God for Mr. Kansuke and you, Tommy. We would have been killed."

After hearing the major's story, the inspector revealed what he had learned from his four assistants. "It's obvious the two perimeter guards were killed hours ago because their bodies are cold. There is no evidence of a struggle, and my guess is they were both sleeping. It was pitch black last night, so after the killers climbed over the wall, they hid in the gardener's hut until it was light enough to attack. They knew the lay of the land but next to nothing about the mansion's interior. My men informed me that the front gate guard is a commoner who was just assigned here. I am frankly shocked to hear it. It might be a coincidence, but I think not."

He removed the handle of the second sword with his mallet and punch and examined the exposed tang. "I thought so. Look here," he said.

Yuki hesitated. "I'm sorry, my vision is a bit blurred."

"It reads 'Kawaji, City of Hagi.'"

"Hagi? The capital of Choshu?"

"Precisely. They were not poverty-stricken ronin here to rob. They were rebel man-cutters here to kill."

"How could they have entered Aizu without being detected?"

The inspector lowered his voice. "Perhaps the question is best asked of the recently assigned sector officer."

"I, I do not understand," Yuki said, sounding dull and unsteady.

"His name is Asai Soteki. Until recently, he was with a contingent of our army in Kyoto guarding the emperor. He served there for three years. I think he may have fallen in with the Choshu rebels there. His primary duty here is to make the rounds of some of our remote checkpoints. My men informed me that Asai assigned the commoner here last evening, saying it was light duty, not requiring a samurai. And the two dead guards did not expect trouble out here in the country."

"Asai Soteki? I've never heard the name," Yuki said, his voice little more than a raspy whisper.

"Tomita-dono, you do not look well."

"Tommy," Major Butler said, "are you not well? The inspector is talking to you."

Yuki blacked out before he could answer.

# CHAPTER 9

KUROI CROUCHED INSIDE THE shack, waiting. He had witnessed men being tortured until they admitted their crimes, and if Asai were captured, he would do the same. Kuroi had to act quickly. Otherwise, he would be hunted down and hacked to death by Inspector Shimazu's men.

Two hours after dark, Asai appeared. "Where are you?" he called out.

"I'm inside," came a husky whisper. "Over here."

"Do you have the money and the documents? I need to get out. Shimazu's men are already looking for me."

Before he could say more, Kuroi rushed out of the gloom and slit Asai's throat, killing him instantly. He removed his victim's swords, pulled his body into a formal sitting position, and released his hold, causing Asai's upper torso to slump forward. Kuroi then bloodied the traitor's short sword and placed it by his body.

Satisfied that Asai appeared to have committed suicide, Kuroi rummaged through his victim's satchel. Among the items was a cotton kimono, and inside one sleeve was a message from Oki Izo, the Choshu spy in Edo. He flew into a rage when he read the last sentence:

*Asai-dono, you need not worry about Kuroi. I will take care of him before the government has a chance to detain him.*

Kuroi held the incriminating letter over the candle and let it burn to his trembling fingertips before dropping the last bit of paper onto the blood-soaked dirt. *Damn! He probably planned to kill me from the day I agreed to help.* He had his own letter, the one he had forged that afternoon. He slipped it into Asai's satchel, desperately hoping that it would clear him of any involvement in the assassination attempt when it was discovered.

But Kuroi's biggest fear was being arrested for having reconnoitered the yashiki. And that Tomita Yuki would be his accuser.

That night, he snuck out of Aizu. He had to get to Edo and kill Oki before he was captured and tortured like Asai would have been.

# CHAPTER 10

Y

UKI WAS DIAGNOSED AS AS having scrub typhus. Wracked with fever and severely dehydrated, his condition deteriorated. His doctor prescribed several herbal remedies and *natto*, a sticky mass of fermented soybeans usually consumed as a condiment. In Yuki's case, it was used to suppress diarrhea.

Mary took charge of caring for him, determined to save the life of the man who had saved hers. Along with the natto and steamed rice, Mary spoon-fed him *miso* soup, a fermented soy broth containing small cubes of protein-laden tofu. On the sixth day, Yuki's fever began to subside, and he was out of danger by the second week. Mary often cradled him in her arms, and though samurai were not supposed to show weakness, he was too sick to feel shame. Her gentle voice and confident bearing comforted him, and he did not pretend otherwise.

"You stood at death's door," the major told him, "But you are a strong man, and you never chose to open it."

Yuki knew otherwise. *Mary saved me.* He thought about her almost every waking hour. Although she lacked the deference and practiced reticence of a Japanese woman, he had become accustomed to her familiarity.

"You're nothing but a spoiled boy," Mary often told him. "Now, if you want to get better, you must do as I say." No maid or servant would have dared to put it like that, but Yuki readily did as he was told. Mary could be exasperating, but it no longer mattered. Her bold manner beguiled rather than annoyed him. And despite her assuredness, he noted a certain fragile innocence about her.

Yuki planned on returning to his house after he recovered, but he received a letter from his uncle before he could do so:

> *Remain with the foreigners under the pretext of your continued weakness. It will allow you to judge the major's character and enhance your understanding of how Americans think. Your observations will prove invaluable.*

Five additional samurai were assigned to the yashiki, and Kansuke became the major's bodyguard and constant companion. Yuki expected him to share sleeping quarters and take his meals with the groundskeeper, but the major would have none of it. Rather than face Butler's ire, Yuki ordered Kansuke to sleep in the small anteroom off the major's bedroom. To the commoner's obvious distress, Yuki also called him to take his meals with the foreigners—strangers clearly above his station.

"Master, please allow me to sleep outside and take my meals with the groundskeeper," Kansuke pleaded.

Yuki understood his discomfort, but the major despised Japanese class distinctions, and he would have it no other way. Besides, Kansuke was becoming more than just a bodyguard. He and the major prattled on for hours at night, each in their own language, yet they seemed to understand each other. It was soon apparent that they were becoming friends.

Kansuke's name proved too difficult for the major, and he named him Shorty instead. He was quick to pick up scraps of English, and the major treated Shorty more like a son than a bodyguard.

In one of his weekly letters to his uncle, Yuki described Butler's behavior:

*The major insists on treating Kansuke like a close friend. Despite his heavy drinking and willful disregard for our class system, I have complete confidence in Butler. Thanks to your advice about remaining at your manor, I have become comfortable with many American customs, and I am learning to speak better and understand everyday English.*

# CHAPTER II

MARY WORE WESTERN CLOTHES during the winter, but the intense summer heat and humidity were too much to bear, so Yuki ordered several light cotton robes to be made for her. After putting on the first one, she strutted down the veranda. "Look, Tommy, I am a Japanese princess." She stretched out her arms and twirled on the polished wood floor.

Yuki was astonished. Japanese women usually walked almost mincingly, but Mary boldly strode about in her new yukata. But when Mary chanced to stand between him and the bright sunlight, he noticed the lithe contours of her body through her thin summer robe. Her delicate figure and the outline of her breasts made an unexpected impression on him.

金 金 金

YUKI FOUND LIVING WITH the Butlers comfortable, but he sometimes needed to be alone. He often stole out to the garden at night and sat on a bench near the teahouse. A maid was always ready with a flask of chilled sake and a cup. He had to be secretive; Mary did not look kindly on drinking. "See what a slave it has made of my father," she once told him.

One evening, Yuki lit the candle in a paper lantern, drank a cup of sake, and mulled over a disturbing report from his cousin. Rebel samurai from the province of Satsuma and the domain of Choshu had resolved their differences and had become allies in their fight against the shogun. Time was running out, and Yuki knew the Bakufu was doomed without Spencer rifles. Lost in thought, he did not notice Mary coming his way.

"There you are. What are you doing out here, Tommy? The mosquitoes will eat you alive. And what are you drinking?"

Yuki decided it was time to be authoritative. "Mary, sit with me and be still."

"But Tommy . . ."

"Just be still, Mary. The full moon is about to rise above the trees. Let us enjoy it without distraction."

To Yuki's surprise, she meekly obeyed, and her attention soon turned to the teahouse.

"What sort of shed is that?"

"Shed?"

"Yes, you know, a storage house."

"It is called a chaya, a teahouse. I thought you knew." Spying the maid hovering nearby, he signaled her, and she disappeared.

"That shed, as you call it," he continued, "is where my uncle entertains his guests."

"You must be joking. In there?"

"Mary, do not be so quick to dismiss it. We Japanese prize the unadorned."

"It's certainly simple; I'll grant you that."

"But it's not simple. It is, how you say, rustic or, better yet, austere. It is made to be so. I'm sorry, there's no English word for it. We use *wabi* and *sabi* to describe something Westerners associate with rusticity, but the words are infused with deeper meanings. For Japanese people, beauty is not something ornate. This teahouse is an expression of the way we view our imperfect existence."

The maid reappeared and placed another cup and two fresh flasks of sake between them.

"Mary, it is the custom in Japan for one person to pour for the other," Yuki said. "Please hold this cup."

Unexpectedly submissive, Mary did as she was told, and he poured her a thimbleful of sake.

"Now, is it my turn?" She asked as if she were a child playing a game.

"Yes," he said.

She held the flask in two hands and carefully filled his cup.

"We sip it slowly, Mary."

"But Tommy . . ."

"Drink, Mary."

She brought the cup to her nose, sniffed, and took a tentative sip. And then another. She wiped her lips and sheepishly held out her cup for more when she finished.

"Wait. Let me show you the inside of the chaya," Yuki said, pointing to the entrance. "That little door is called a crawling-through-space. It is to remind us to be humble."

"Humility is certainly a virtue, but must I?"

"Yes," Yuki whispered. He handed her the lantern and carried the sake tray inside. They sat together and poured more for each other. Mary glanced at the *tokonoma*, the alcove with a hanging scroll depicting a carp swimming lazily in a pond. Below it was a simple flower arrangement that one of the maids changed every few days.

"So, what do you think? Does the chaya still remind you of a shed?"

"No, Tommy, you are right. It is simple, but it is elegant in its own way."

"Good. You are learning."

They fell silent, and in the apricot glow of the lantern light, Yuki saw Mary's expression change. Noting the troubled look on her face, he asked softly, "Mary, what is wrong?"

"Tommy, I am so afraid," she whispered as she slid next to him. "I cannot forget those assassins who almost killed us. You are the only one I can trust."

Yuki thought she sounded like a frightened child; her lower lip quivered, and a tear appeared. "I should not have forced you to drink. I am very sorry," he said.

Mary pressed a finger to his lips. "Tommy, please. You needn't apologize." She took his right hand and caressed it with her cheek.

"Promise that you will never leave Father and me here alone."

"I promise," he said.

"Please . . . please hold me."

Mary nestled her head against Yuki's chest and settled into his arms. He kissed her forehead as she had done to him during his illness, and soon their lips met. He felt the warmth of her body next to his, and he inhaled her delicate feminine scent. He blotted her tears with his yukata sleeve, and his right hand lingered on her cheek. She kissed him and reclined more comfortably in his arms.

Mary's silken hair and soft lips kindled a latent eagerness, and Yuki tugged at her sash. Yielding to him, she loosened her yukata and pressed his palm against her breast. Their hearts seemed to beat as one. Mary flooded him with kisses, and fervor seized them as he explored the delicate curves of her lissome body.

"Please, Tommy, be gentle," Mary whispered.

Their lovemaking was as desperate as it was passionate, and from that evening on, they secretly met in the teahouse. As the weeks passed, their mutual affection intensified, borne by their pressing emotional needs.

Years of study had unknowingly prepared Yuki for love in the Western sense of the word, the kind of love that now blossomed. Yuki and Mary became secret soul mates, finding refuge and solace in each other's arms.

Shorty soon learned of their secret and readily understood the need to keep the major occupied during their nocturnal assignations. Butler was only too happy to drink away his evenings with Shorty, and Yuki and Mary often heard laughter emanating from the manor as they made love in the chaya.

To please Mary, Yuki sent word to his younger brother, Yoshi, to deliver a set of tortoiseshell combs. He gave them to Mary one evening, and the next night she reciprocated by presenting him with a leather-bound accounting ledger that the major had never bothered to use. She also gave him a pencil and a small cube of India rubber to make erasures.

"Keep a journal, Tommy. It will someday bring back pleasant memories," she said.

It was a dangerous suggestion. The result would be catastrophic if the journal fell into the wrong hands. He, therefore, kept his entries vague and to a minimum.

# CHAPTER 12

A FARMER DISCOVERED ASAI Soteki's body and promptly notified the authorities. Given that Asai had learned he was about to be arrested, it was evident to Inspector Shimazu that he had committed suicide. And he did not consider that the lead assassin's letter found on Asai's body was a forgery. In it, the killer wrote that with Asai's help, he was sure the planned assassination would succeed.

"I forwarded the information about the Choshu spy in Edo to the Chief of Police there. He now has a name to go on, and his men should be able to track him down," Shimazu said.

Yuki remained unconvinced. And though he was sure Kuroi was involved, he kept his suspicions to himself and did not dispute Shimazu's findings.

But late that afternoon, as Yuki and Mary sat near the chaya enjoying a flask of chilled sake, he mentioned Kuroi's visit. He described how intently he had surveyed the layout of the compound. "He conspired with the assassins. I'm sure of it," he said.

"Tommy, the evidence is circumstantial. Are you sure your dislike of the man is not at the root of your suspicions?"

She placed her index finger across his lips before he could protest. "If you accuse Kuroi at this juncture, our return to Boston may be delayed. Do you really want that?"

Yuki exhaled a bitter breath of humid air. "You're right, Mary. An investigation would delay us. But mark my words—Kuroi must answer for this when the time comes."

# CHAPTER 13

A DAY LATER, a rider reined in his horse at the gate. The messenger dismounted and presented Yuki with an urgent message. In his study, he decoded it and found the news he had been waiting for.

"We are going to America!" Yuki announced.

When they arrived in Edo, Yuki's cousin greeted them first. "You and I have an important appointment tomorrow in Edo Castle," Nariaki said.

"But what about Uncle? How is he?"

"Not well," Nariaki said dolefully. "I dare not tell him the news I received this morning. Come, he is anxious to see you."

"Do not keep me in the dark," Yuki said, "What news?"

"Lord Hara was assassinated in Kyoto four days ago."

"The shogun's chamberlain?"

Nariaki's nod was almost imperceptible. He leaned over and cupped his hand over Yuki's ear. "Do not mention this to Father. You will see why."

Yuki's anticipatory thrill over the pending mission evaporated when he saw his uncle. He was thin, ashen-faced, and noticeably unsteady on his feet.

"Welcome back," Matsudaira said, his voice curdled with phlegm.

"Sit. We have much to discuss. Nephew, I need not tell you that we must have those rifles as soon as possible, or all is lost. Fortunately, we now have the funds."

"So, the *Shinsoku* is ready to sail?"

Matsudaira shook his head. "A month ago, Vice-Admiral Enomoto informed me the vessel is still not seaworthy for such a lengthy voyage. Fortunately, the American resident minister Robert Van Valkenburgh has arranged for you to sail on the USS *Lackawanna*, an American warship. It has been serving in the Pacific, making port last week. It will return to Boston to be refitted, and you and your party will be on it."

"An American warship? Can the sailors be trusted with Miss Mary aboard?"

"Certainly. But there is one problem. We had planned to send thirty Aizu samurai along with you, but you'll have to do without them. Even with the ship's skeleton crew, the quarters are cramped, and the captain has refused to accommodate more than six passengers. Major Butler and his daughter will have separate sleeping quarters, but you, your assistant Kato, and the two attendants will lodge below."

Yuki sat staring at his lap, attempting to sort out the implications.

"Yuki, speak up," his cousin said. "What are you thinking?"

"I am concerned about the lack of security."

"Don't be. Minister Van Valkenburgh has assured us that you and your party will be safe aboard the *Lackawanna*."

"Does Valkenburgh know the purpose of my mission? I've heard he has been increasingly uncooperative with our government. Why has he done us this favor?"

"He was informed that you will visit Boston to study America's republican governmental system, and he reportedly liked the idea. But it is more involved than that," his uncle said. "Van Valkenburgh is acting in self-interest. He knows about the assassination attempt and wants the Butlers out of Japan immediately. Had they been killed, he would have been in serious trouble. He has been secretly kowtowing to the rebels, and if the truth were to be known, an angry outcry from President Grant's opponents would force

Secretary of State Seward to recall him. Valkenburgh has gone so far as to grant the Butlers diplomatic status. It means that the gold need not be declared."

"Gold? I assumed payment would be made through a paper transfer between the two governments."

"That is not possible. Leave it at that."

"Uncle, if the American crew discovers the gold . . ."

"Nephew," Matsudaira said impatiently, "you need not be concerned. The gold cases will bear State Department seals and be locked up in one or two rooms under guard. No one will dare open them."

"But without a Bakufu ship and a company of soldiers awaiting our arrival in Boston, how will I protect the gold?"

"Again, you needn't be concerned," Matsudaira said. "The Bakufu purchased an ironclad corvette from France a year ago, and an experienced Japanese crew trained in Toulon, a French naval port. The ship has been renamed the *Tora*. Lord Hara has ordered the ship's master, Captain Gamo, to sail to Boston and await your arrival. He should get the orders in a month or so. He knows nothing about what your mission entails."

"Well, having the *Tora* waiting in Boston is encouraging," Yuki said, attempting to sound convinced.

"Again, do not worry. Is that clear?" Matsudaira said impatiently. He slid a packet of papers across the table to Yuki. "Give these to Captain Gamo. They are his orders to cooperate fully. Our soldiers must transfer the gold from the *Lackawanna* to the *Tora* before you even begin negotiating the rifle purchase. And the weapons and other equipment must be loaded onto the *Tora* before the gold is released to Christopher Spencer. Have I made myself clear?"

"Yes, sir."

"Then be ready. The *Lackawanna* departs in two days."

Yuki could not shake his skepticism, but it was time to acquiesce. "I am ready, sir. Thanks to you, the mission will be a complete success."

"Go, then. You have many things to do."

金　金　金

THAT EVENING, NARIAKI AND Yuki took dinner together. After three flasks of sake, Nariaki brought up the matter of Hara Ichinoshin's assassination. "Only five of us know of this mission now. The secret is safe with us."

The assassination gave Yuki the opening he needed to reveal his suspicions. "Cousin, I believe Kuroi Takuto was part of the conspiracy to kill Major Butler. You're the only one who knows."

Nariaki cocked his head. "Go on," he said, putting down his cup.

As Yuki described the events leading up to the assassination attempt, Nariaki's expression soured.

"Enough," he said testily before Yuki could finish. "Do not let your personal feelings get in the way of the facts. I assure you that Kuroi is no traitor. You could not have known this, but last month he played an important role in discovering the whereabouts of a dangerous Choshu agent named Oki Izo. Kuroi and our agents ambushed and killed him. It is a state secret, so I cannot be more specific, but trust me when I say that Kuroi's loyalty to the Bakufu is unquestionable."

A stilted silence followed Nariaki's rebuke. Thoroughly chastened, Yuki changed the subject. "You mentioned only five of us know about the mission. You, me, and your father. Who are the others?"

"I'll discuss that with you tomorrow. In the meantime, you need to get some rest."

Yuki's curiosity was piqued, but he chose not to pursue the matter because he was sure Kuroi was one of the others.

Upon his return to his quarters, Shorty was waiting for him. He asked permission to visit a friend who lived outside of Edo. Yuki agreed but warned him to be back by the following evening.

# CHAPTER 14

EDO CASTLE WAS A vast, maze-like complex of buildings. By the 1800s, more than nine miles of seemingly impregnable walls and moats enclosed the castle grounds. An officer led Yuki and Nariaki to the innermost confines of the castle grounds, where an official in his early forties greeted them with a broad smile.

He was Oguri Kozukenosuke, the shogun's finance and naval commissioner. An ardent modernist, he had been sent on the first official Japanese diplomatic mission to Washington in 1860. Due to his outspoken admiration of America, he was in the crosshairs of the anti-foreign rebels.

"Welcome, Tomita-dono," Oguri said. "I understand that you are a most accomplished geopolitical scholar. I am deeply impressed."

Being in the presence of Oguri humbled Yuki. He bowed and mumbled a few self-deprecating words.

"None of that, young man," Oguri said. "Come with me. I wish to show you something." He led the way to a blockhouse and lighted a Western-style lantern. "Be careful. It is quite dark inside."

They followed him down a stone staircase to an imposing iron-clad door. Oguri unlocked it and shouldered it open. Inside, he lit several other oil lamps, and Yuki's attention was quickly drawn to the sturdy wooden cases stacked against one wall.

"All of them are sized to accommodate American twenty-dollar gold pieces called double eagles," Oguri said. "The weight is roughly 100 American pounds, or forty-five and a half *kan* per case." He opened one of them and handed a coin to Yuki. "It was with great difficulty that I acquired them, given the need for secrecy and the scarcity of Bakufu funds."

Yuki examined the curious-looking goddess of liberty on the coin's obverse side. Thirteen six-pointed stars encircled her, but the exquisite design of the American eagle on the reverse side was what he admired more. It was the first American coin he had ever held.

"That coin made a circuitous route to the castle," Oguri said. "There isn't much American gold to be had in Japan, so the French obliged me by exchanging government bullion for fifty-franc Napoleons. With those, I acquired English sovereigns from another source." Oguri paused for a moment and flashed a conspiratorial smile. "In the end, the Hong Kong and Shanghai Banking Corporation accepted the sovereigns and made the final conversion to double eagles. Right under the British government's nose. Twenty thousand gold coins."

"Sir, you call them double eagles, but there is only one on the back of the coin," Yuki said.

"That is because the twenty-dollar gold piece is twice the value of the ten-dollar coin, which Americans call an eagle."

Oguri held out his hand, and Yuki returned the coin. "Is this the only gold left in the treasury?" he asked.

"Some gold is held in Osaka Castle, but that's all. So, you see, Tomita-dono, the fate of the shogun's government now rests on your shoulders. I wish you good luck."

金　金　金

THAT EVENING, YUKI MET with his uncle and presented him with a box of incense—Kuroi's way of thanking Matsudaira for having had a hand in his promotion. His uncle eyed it indifferently before setting it aside. "I will send him my thanks," he said.

Yuki did not mention Kuroi again. Instead, he gave his heartfelt thanks to Matsudaira. "Uncle, for your many past kindnesses, I vow once again to succeed in my mission no matter what difficulties I may face. I do so because I owe as much to you as I do to Japan."

"If I were sending anyone other than you, I would fear for our country. However, you will succeed, and I promise a great future for you upon your return. Stay well, my nephew."

Yuki wondered what his uncle had in mind by "a great future," but asking him would have been improper. He summoned Mary, the major, and Shorty to his apartment for supper that evening. As they dined, Yuki outlined the details of their pending voyage. Their glee was infectious, and, for the moment, Yuki pushed aside his concerns over the complicated mission.

# *FOXES:* SHINTO DEMIGODS

FOXES ARE MESSENGERS and guardians for *Inari*, an androgynous deity. Inari is believed to protect agriculture, farmers, sword makers, merchants, and, in the past, samurai.

Also known as Inari, fox statues often wear red bibs, which are associated with protection from evil.

About one-third of Shinto shrines are dedicated to the foxes. The grounds surrounding many of them are populated with hundreds of stone and ceramic figures, ranging in size from pebbles to larger-than-life statues.

Buddhism is known for its inclusivity. In Japan, Shinto shrines are often found on the grounds of Buddhist temples. Myogon-ji is a well-known one in Tokyo.

*Copyright photo by author*

# CHAPTER 15

NIBEI CLIMBED THE GRAY granite steps to Myogon-ji, a Buddhist temple near Edo Castle. It was almost dark when he passed through the main gate, and he stopped to catch his breath.

Nibei feared for his life, but he was trapped. He had no choice but to obey Kuroi Taketo's summons. The samurai who betrayed Oki Izo and took part in his assassination lurked nearby.

Shinto shrines often share space with temples, and Nibei cast a nervous glance at two stone fox statues flanking the incense urn in front of Toyokawa Inari Shrine. Being an *Eta*, an untouchable or a "filthy mass," was something he kept carefully hidden, but the Goddess Inari would know. When he was nineteen, Nibei murdered a commoner, stole his identity, and escaped the confines of the Eta enclave. He survived on the outside as a peddler and a thief.

In 1864, he fell in with Oki Izo, the Choshu spy, and served him as an informant and messenger. Oki paid him well, but Nibei's good fortune ended when Kuroi and a police squad hacked Oki to pieces at the Yanagi inn. In the aftermath, Kuroi hunted Nibei down and threatened him with death unless he agreed to become his agent and messenger. Nibei could do nothing but accede.

Kuroi and his new bodyguard, Onishi, waited near the shrine. Nibei bowed three times while uttering his gratitude for having been summoned.

"Well, get on with it," Kuroi said. "What do you have?"

"The man you assigned me to follow entered Edo Castle with another samurai this morning."

"Tomita Yuki?"

"Yes, Master. I am sure it was him."

Kuroi clutched the handle of his long sword. "Go on," he said.

"When they left the castle, I followed them back to the estate of Matsudaira Tokunari, who is...."

I know who he is," Kuroi said. "Get on with your story."

"Well, sir, two heavily laden horse-drawn wagons arrived at the Matsudaira compound late this afternoon."

"What were they hauling?"

"I could not get close enough, but I thought you should know."

"Return to Matsudaira's estate immediately and follow Tomita wherever he goes. Report to me every evening. Do you understand?"

"Yes, Master," Nibei said.

"Then, take this." Kuroi tossed a small cloth bag on the stone walkway.

Nibei immediately recognized the clinking sounds of brass coins. "You are much too generous, sir," he said, disappointed that it weighed so little.

"Then go," Kuroi said.

# USS LACKAWANNA

THE UNION NAVY'S USS *Lackawanna* was a sloop-of-war built at the New York Navy Yard and launched in 1862. Advanced for its time, it was a coal-fueled, steam-powered warship with a screw propeller. The number of sailors is unknown, but crews in similar ships carried upwards of 100.

During the Civil War, the *Lackawanna* was part of the Union's blockade effort in the Gulf of Mexico. It captured and sank several Confederate vessels and rammed a large enemy warship. Twelve sailors were issued the Medal of Honor for their actions in the Battle of Mobile Bay.

In 1865, she was decommissioned and re-commissioned a year later to serve in the Pacific.

*Photo courtesy of navsource.org. It is in the public domain.*

# CHAPTER 16

### August 1867

YUKI AND HIS COUSIN stood on the Yokohama customs pier the morning after Yuki said goodbye to his uncle. He had a bedroll slung over his shoulders with the ends of his swords protruding on either side. His heavy duffle bag had already been taken aboard. The SS *Lackawanna's* multi-colored signal flags snapped smartly overhead while Benjamin Butler wandered near the gangway. Mary stood nearby.

"So, you see, things are working out perfectly," Nariaki said to Yuki. "Even the weather is cooperating. You will undoubtedly return within the year, and we will move against the Imperial Army."

"Thanks to you and Uncle, I have every confidence of succeeding," Yuki said, gulping in a lungful of the invigorating ocean air.

Nariaki stepped closer to him. "Father wants you to know that he will see that the shogun appoints you to be the next magistrate of foreign affairs," he whispered.

"What?"

"It is true, Cousin."

"So that is what Uncle meant about a great future?"

"Exactly. But keep it secret for obvious reasons."

Nariaki's enthusiasm and the startling revelation boosted Yuki's spirits to a new high. Oguri Kozukenosuke had secured the gold, and everything had fallen into place just as his uncle had said it would. Nariaki had promised to tell him the names of the fourth and fifth persons who knew about his mission, but it no longer mattered. Yuki knew one was Oguri and suspected the other was Kuroi Taketo.

Shorty and his counterpart, a taller and stronger man, leaned wide-eyed on the warship's iron railing. At the same time, Yuki's assistant, Kato Yozo, his second-in-command, stood nearby, watching the American sailors laboring with the wagons.

The crew hoisted the heavy chests into a cargo net and slung them into the ship's hold. Sailors below decks placed them inside the smaller of two brigs. The first mate locked the iron-barred door when they were done while Kato looked on.

A crowd of commoners gawked at the warship from the roadside, and a knot of American merchants from the foreign settlement stood nearby puffing on their cigars, proudly pointing to the sloop-of-war that helped win the Battle of Mobile Bay during the Civil War.

Mary made her way to Yuki's side and nodded toward a rice shop. "Tommy, that man has been spying on us by the store."

Yuki had no trouble spotting him, but the man disappeared into the crowd when he strode down the pier to get a better look. Yuki shrugged and returned to Mary. "It is time to board the ship. You needn't worry. He was merely a curious bystander."

The sloop's boilers had been fired up hours earlier, and a hissing, black column of smoke belched from the midship stack. The screw shaft nestled in the belly of the warship groaned to life, and a sudden shudder ran through the vessel's bowels.

Sailors cast the last line off, and the *Lackawanna*'s great brass propeller began turning. Heading due south, the vessel plowed into the vastness of the Pacific. The voyage to Boston was expected to take 130 days.

# CHAPTER 17

MAJOR BUTLER AND MARY were quartered in small cabins while Yuki and Kato Yozo shared a large storage compartment to hang two hammocks. Despite the cramped quarters, Yuki and Kato were jubilant. They were en route to America. Shorty and Kato's attendant slept in the crew's quarters. During the day, one would go topside for fresh air while the other kept a watchful eye on the brig and the sailors.

But Yuki's euphoria evaporated three days after the *Lackawanna* took on a load of coal in Singapore. As the warship sailed through the Bay of Bengal, Kato complained of stomach cramps and a fever. He became dehydrated, and the ship's doctor was at a loss to alleviate his symptoms. Yuki watched helplessly as his friend rapidly declined.

"Don't let them take my swords," Kato said. They were his last words.

Yuki and Shorty washed and dressed Kato's body in his silk kimono, lapping the left side of the robe over the right, the age-old method used to prepare the dead. Yuki placed the swords next to his friend in a canvas shroud weighted with iron shot, and a sailor sewed it up. Four other sailors placed the body on a plank, tipped it over the railing, and saluted while Yuki watched disconsolately as it slid into the dark green water. He wondered how he could manage without his friend's help.

Several days later, Kato's attendant, the laborer who was Shorty's counterpart, began showing similar signs of distress. Bombay was the next port of call; by then, the man had become dangerously delirious. He made his way topside in an unguarded moment and leaped off the ship's stern into the turgid waters just as the *Lackawanna* weighed anchor. Yuki and Shorty were too late to stop him, and the ship's propeller sucked him under the muddy waters. His body never surfaced.

"Fate is working against me," Yuki said to Mary.

She brushed wayward strands of hair from his eyes and grasped his hand. "Don't be such a silly billy. It has been benevolent if there is such a thing as fate."

"How can you say that?"

"Think about it. If you and Shorty had not been assigned to guard us, those assassins would surely have killed Benjamin and me. It was God's will, not something you call fate."

Yuki was perplexed by her comment about God and how she sometimes called her father by his first name. In Japan, one would never address one's parent in that manner.

"Call it your God's will if you wish," he said, staring into the dark waters of the Arabian Sea. "I fear this is not the end of Fate's interference."

At the behest of the major, Yuki reluctantly commanded Shorty to share the storage room with him and sleep in Kato's hammock.

"Master, I am not worthy of sharing the same quarters with you. Please persuade the major to change his mind," Shorty pleaded.

"You are right not to forget your social position, but we must obey the rules of the Americans until we return to Japan. It is an awkward thing for both of us but remember the old saying: 'When in another village, one must obey its rules.'"

Shorty complied with great hesitation, but their mutual trust grew into an unlikely but providential friendship in the ensuing weeks.

# CHAPTER 18

BEFORE THE VOYAGE BEGAN, Yuki made only four entries in his journal, but he wrote four more with little to do aboard the *Lackawanna*.

*September 12, 1867*

*The major has become an English teacher, and his pupil is a fast learner. I am amazed at how Shorty has changed. It is as though he were a bit of moss clinging to a rock in Japan. But the relaxed social atmosphere the major has imposed on us has transformed him into a flowering plant. I will need his help more than ever now that Kato Yozo is dead.*

*November 15, 1867*

*We reached Cape Town yesterday, and last night Shorty and I bathed on deck, dousing each other with fresh water. Feeling clean and refreshed, I spent the evening with Mary. I must be careful. One of the sailors might take note. Shorty keeps the major occupied.*

*December 26, 1867*

*The major celebrated Christmas with several of the ship's officers and drank too much. Shorty spent his time below decks celebrating with his new sailor friends. I spent four intimate hours with Mary.*

*January 15, 1868*

*We made port in Boston today, and the harbormaster visited the Lackawanna. He informed the major that he had no news concerning the Tora. I fear the ship sank somewhere. The Lackawanna will soon be towed to a dry dock, and the captain gave us a two-day notice to remove our cargo and disembark.*

The major blew a cloud of cigar smoke and gave Yuki a friendly pat on his shoulder. "Never you mind about the *Tora*, Tommy, me boy. A storm probably delayed the ship. It will arrive soon, so we'd better visit Christopher Spencer today. It is time to commence negotiations."

They set off for the Spencer Repeating Rifle factory late in the morning. Mary chose to stay on board, and Shorty remained below decks to watch the brig.

YUKI WAS AWESTRUCK BY his new environment. Boston was a city at work. In the waterfront district, brick buildings stood row upon row. He held a kerchief to his nose as they walked past several tanning vats. Workers shouted, and tools clattered. The whole city was enveloped in sounds and smells.

Men and women walked side by side, unlike in Japan, where women were expected to walk several paces behind. And ordinary folk did not step out of the way when well-dressed citizens passed them by.

When they reached Spencer's factory, Yuki sensed trouble when he spied a pigeon sitting on the rim of a lifeless brick smokestack. Butler turned the handle of the front door of the small wood-framed office building, and they entered. A young man was bent over a desk, reading a newspaper at the room's far end. His starched collar was unbuttoned, and his bow tie dangled from his neck.

"Christopher Spencer, how the hell are you?" Butler called out.

Spencer peered at them through the gloom. "Benjamin Butler!" he exclaimed when he recognized his friend. "You are a sight for sore eyes. The last we met, you were lying on a bloody army cot in Washington, ready to die."

"Indeed, I was, Christopher, you sly dog you!"

They greeted each other with warm handshakes and reminisced while Yuki waited uncomfortably to be introduced. Spencer finally cast a bored look at him, and Butler patted Yuki's shoulder. "This here is an associate of mine. Just call him Tommy. He is a Nipponese man of importance."

"I am pleased to meet you, sir," Yuki said. "I am deeply impressed by the rifle that bears your name."

Spencer eyed Yuki with tired curiosity and nodded. "Nice meeting you too, Tommy. Have a seat." He turned his back and commenced making small talk with the major.

While he waited, Yuki watched as a worker entered the room with a mop and bucket and began mopping the floor within earshot of the desk.

The major did not appear to notice the man. Instead, he pointed to Yuki. "Tommy's here to buy some rifles and plenty of them. Ten thousand, to be exact. Spare parts, ammunition, Blakeslee ammunition boxes, and loading equipment. The works, my friend."

Spencer sank back in his chair, looking strangely troubled. "Ten thousand? That is a tall order. Why so many?"

"Well, sir," said the major, "that is a question we prefer not to answer, leastways not yet. But mind you, we're dead serious."

"I'm sure you are, Benjamin. I have never known you to be otherwise."

Butler pulled two cheroots from his pocket and gave one to Spencer. They bit off the ends of their cigars and spat them into a pewter spittoon next to the desk. Spencer lit his own and then held the match to Butler's.

"Christopher, me boy," the major said, exhaling a cloud of smoke, "we can take title to the rifles here in Boston on a date not too far in the future. Maybe even in a day or two. There's no need to get a bank or the government involved, if you know what I mean. A Nipponese ship is expected anytime now. You haul the rifles down to the dock for us when it makes port, and cash money will be waiting for you. In fact, Tommy is willing to give you some honest money up front if that's what it takes. We'll pay you forty dollars for each rifle and those other things I mentioned."

Spencer drew in a lungful of smoke and slowly released it through his mouth and flaring nostrils. "I wish you had come two months ago. You might have saved me from insolvency. As it stands now, I have lost control of my company."

Yuki did not understand the meaning of insolvency, but Butler's reaction said it all.

"What? How can that be?"

"It's a long story, Benjamin," Spencer sighed. He spoke so rapidly that Yuki understood only scraps of the story. What he did understand, however, alarmed him. Spencer had no rifles to sell.

"Surely we can find a solution," Butler said, shifting uneasily in his chair.

Spencer shook his head. "About ten thousand of them are sitting in a warehouse outside Washington, but the government has first call. It is damnably frustrating because I know they don't intend to buy them. I've gone to the War Department and buttonholed anyone who would listen. But they won't sign a release. The court is prepared to order the sale of my business to the Fogerty Rifle Company, and according to my lawyer, the best I can hope to get is a two-cent commission per rifle when they are finally sold. But until things are sorted out and the court has had its say, I'm dead in the water."

"Good God," Butler said, "How could this have happened?"

"It's a long, sad story. The government ceased purchasing when the war ended but never released its claims to the rifles I'd shipped to the army warehouse. To make matters worse, there are a couple of serious imitators—Fogerty and a fellow named Winchester. Competition has about killed me, and I can't pay my creditors. It's too late for me. Leastways, that's what my attorney told me yesterday."

Butler pulled at his collar and nervously twisted his neck.

"Christopher, me boy, surely something can be done. If you tell the court you have a buyer, the judge will surely have to listen. The War Department would have to comply with a court release order. We are ready, willing, and able to pay for the rifles immediately. Cut the judge in if that's what it takes. Tommy here doesn't ask for credit. He's ready to pay with gold. No contingencies."

Spencer set his elbows on the desk and lowered his head into the palms of his hands. "I truly wish that somehow...." Suddenly, he glared at the workman kneeling near the desk with a wet rag in his hand. It is evident to Yuki that he'd been listening in on the conversation.

"Mosely, take your stuff and finish up," Spencer said.

"Yes, sir." The worker stood up and mopped past the desk to the front door.

"Where was I?" Spencer asked.

"The rifles. We need the rifles," Butler said.

"Benjamin, I wish I could take advantage of your offer and get out of this mess," Spencer said as his voice trailed off. "But my hands are tied."

"Well, give it a try, for God's sake. We're desperate."

"I will. My lawyer is preparing another demand letter to the War Department to release the rifles."

"What's this about the court selling your company to that fellow Fogerty?"

"Sadly, it is a strong possibility, but that's a long story. Winchester is interested too. Where are you staying? I'll contact you as soon as I learn something."

"We're just off the boat. I'll let you know once we settle in."

Butler grunted as he rose from his chair. It was as though a heavy, unseen force weighed him down. "Please try, Christopher," he said. "We need the rifles. Come on, Tommy, we'd best be getting back to the ship."

Instead of saying goodbye, Spencer yelled at his worker. "Mosely, get the damn door for the major!"

The man opened it and stood at attention with the mop handle in hand like a rifle. Butler paused on the threshold and looked squarely at him for the first time. "Don't I know you from somewhere?"

The man took off his crumpled hat and shook his head. "No, sir, I don't reckon we've met."

Butler took another look and shrugged. "Well, then, I guess I'm the one what's wrong."

Yuki held Butler's left elbow and helped him down the stairs.

"It's not over yet by a long shot, Tommy. We may have to check with that Fogerty company Spencer mentioned. Let's hope the *Tora* is just a few hours out of Boston."

"Benjamin, if it isn't, we'll need to find a safe place for the gold tomorrow."

Butler had other thoughts on his mind. He bought a hip flask of whiskey on the way back to the *Lackawanna*. For the first time since Yuki left Japan, he no longer felt in control of the mission.

金　金　金

THAT AFTERNOON, THEY CROWDED into the major's cabin. Butler seemed detached, his breath filling the air with the odor of cheap liquor.

Yuki again stated the obvious. "Major, we must do something with the gold until the *Tora* arrives."

"I'm thinking a bank," Butler replied, bleakly looking at his empty whiskey flask.

"What bank would you suggest?"

Mary broke in before the major could reply. "Benjamin, have you forgotten the Panic of 1857? Banks went under, and their depositors, including you, lost every cent."

"You got a point," Butler said, rubbing his chin whiskers, "but what other place is there?"

"Let's return to River Oak. We can take the train to Providence and transfer to the Woonsocket trunk line. Tommy can use some of his expense money to buy a heavy freight wagon and a team of mules. I have already done the calculations. The gold weighs about 1,500 pounds, and you told me years ago that army freight wagons can haul almost twice as much on good roads. Surely you can find one to rent or buy. Just think of it. River Oak is our home. It's our haven."

"What is River Oak?" Yuki asked.

"I thought I'd told you about our home before. Oh, you'd love it there. I can see it now," she said. "It's where I grew up. River Oak is named after a great tree that grows on the property. The house sits along a river, surrounded by forests and fields. It's a day and a half from here, and the gold would be very safe there. Our nearest neighbor, Elmer Eiler, lives five miles away. He's been looking after the property for us. We'd have to stop there to get the keys, and...."

"Now, Mary, it's much too far," Butler said. "We must stay in Boston and wait for the *Tora*."

"Nonsense, Benjamin. There's a telegraph in Woonsocket. We can arrange to get the news within hours of the *Tora* making port."

"It's just too complicated," the major shot back. "We would have to load and unload the gold on two different trains. It would draw attention. There's no telling what would happen."

Mary was adamant and spent the next several minutes trying to convince Yuki and Butler that her plan was workable. But the major was adamant, calling her idea foolhardy. They reached an unsettled standoff and sat in the small cabin staring at each other.

Shorty broke the sullen silence when he punched his open hand with his fist. "We can do it, Master. Miss Mary is right."

Yuki shook his head. "No, Shorty, you don't understand."

To Yuki's consternation, Shorty ignored him. "Let's do it. Major, I take the rifle, and you keep pistol. I can shoot, remember?"

"I sure do, son," Butler replied.

"Master Tomita," Shorty said, "you have swords, and Major finished whiskey. He will be fine tomorrow. We ride wagon and train and stay with big boxes all way to that river place. Nobody gonna dare steal gold."

"Listen to Shorty," Mary said. "He has the right idea."

Despite Yuki's initial concern, Shorty's proposal began to make sense. Butler was an imposing authority who could easily keep any curious freight handlers at bay, and they were well-armed. "If you think we can do it, I am willing, but we must never leave the gold unattended."

"I guess you can count me in if Lieutenant Shorty says so," Butler snorted.

"We can do it," Shorty said with fierce finality.

They planned their journey to River Oak step by step. The following day, Yuki and Mary visited the harbormaster. Mary asked him to send a telegraph to Woonsocket in care of the major as soon as the *Tora* dropped anchor in Boston Harbor. He agreed, and Yuki gave him a silver dollar.

In the meantime, Butler went to Spencer's office. "We're moving to our place outside Woonsocket. As soon as you get an answer from the lawyers about the rifles, telegraph me in the care of the town's stationmaster. I'll arrange for the message to be delivered to us by horseback. Go to the telegraph office yourself. There's something about that worker I don't trust, and I don't want him knowing more than he does already."

# CHAPTER 19

EARLY THE FOLLOWING DAY, Butler engaged the services of a drayman and his heavy freight wagon. Marines from the *Lackawanna* supervised the stevedores as they muscled the heavy cases onto it, and the drayman covered the cargo with canvas. Yuki, Mary, Shorty, and the major walked to the train station alongside the wagon. No one paid attention to the small parade.

Butler hired four black laborers to load everything from the wagon onto a railcar. Yuki was impressed by their strength and dogged determination to finish the job quickly. But he felt sorry for them as they labored in the cold with clothes no better than rags. He hardly understood a word they spoke, but their gratitude was apparent when he gave each one a silver dollar, much more than Butler had promised.

The train ride to Providence, Rhode Island, took two and a half hours. Yuki dreaded the transfer to another train, but unloading and reloading the heavy cases occurred without incident.

They arrived in Woonsocket in the afternoon, but it was too late to proceed to River Oak. Yuki provided Mary and the major with some of his expense money, and Mary bought provisions. Butler purchased a heavy freight wagon, canvas, and six draught horses. And he hired four porters to load everything onto the wagon. That night, Yuki, Shorty, and the major bundled up against the cold and remained with the wagon while Mary stayed at a nearby hotel.

The following day, Mary set the major's Spencer on her lap, and he took hold of the reins. They all agreed it would draw too much attention if Yuki and Shorty were armed, so Shorty took the major's pistol and hid it under his shirt, and Yuki placed his swords under the canvas within easy reach.

Early in the afternoon, they made a brief stop at Elmer Eiler's farmhouse, where Butler retrieved the keys to the house. A half-hour later, they pulled up in front of River Oak. Yuki and Shorty lowered the cases and lugged them up the stairs and into the house. Because of the excessive weight, Butler directed Yuki to place them throughout the downstairs rooms. It took them hours to finish.

Seven days later, Yuki made a journal entry:

*January 25, 1868*
  *Mary is right. River Oak is safe. I have never experienced such pastoral quietude. Shorty and I sleep on the floor in the downstairs library. I placed my swords against the fireplace mantel just in case—Mary and the major sleep upstairs.*
  *The front entry leads to a large living room, where Mary often sits reading her Bible. The back of the house overlooks a small river, and a community cemetery is nearby. It is disquieting to have one so close. Shorty is superstitious and does not like it either. Mary says some of her ancestors are buried there.*

The next evening, Yuki made another entry:

*January 26, 1868*
  *Mary and I explored the estate's grounds today. A huge tree grows in the center of the cemetery, which is why the estate is called River Oak. The tree must be old because its trunk is quite large.*
  *The major took Shorty and me to the fields where we practiced shooting his pistol and Spencer rifle. We are both quite good at it.*

*When the major went to bed this evening, Shorty took a long walk, allowing me to share intimacy with Mary.*

*There has been no word from the harbormaster about the Tora, and I fear the worst.*

YUKI AND SHORTY SPENT most of their time in the library, where four cases of gold were stored. It was Sunday, and another day of waiting passed without a word about the *Tora*. Yuki concluded that a disaster had befallen the ship and raised his concerns during the evening meal.

After a prolonged discussion over coffee, Yuki reluctantly agreed to return to Boston with Major Butler, while Mary and Shorty remained at River Oak. If Christopher Spencer could not get the rifles released, the major assured Yuki he could cut a deal with the Fogerty Repeating Rifle Company and charter a ship.

But Yuki needed more assurance. "How can we keep the gold when we bring it to Boston? Where do you propose hiding it, and who will guard our cargo once you've chartered a ship?"

"Don't worry," Butler said. "We'll let Fogerty think the "funds" are in a bank in Boston. We'll not mention gold, so nobody would ever think of coming to River Oak to look for it. And when we're ready to pay, I plan on hiring several veterans in Woonsocket who are from my old command. I know them to be honest and loyal. I saved five of them from getting killed in Fredricksburg, and they all swore a lifetime of allegiance to yours truly.

"You and Shorty will have to load the gold onto the freight wagon and cover everything before my men come here. They will guard the wagon all the way to Boston. You, me, and Shorty will have weapons too, remember? And four of the veterans are widowers. I'm sure I can persuade them to join us on the voyage back to Japan. Of course, you'll need to be generous with your remaining expense money. I'll go to Woonsocket tomorrow to hire them."

With no viable alternative to suggest, Yuki agreed to Butler's plan. After dinner, Mary went upstairs to her bedroom. The major put on his old army coat and retreated to the back porch with a blanket. It was his favorite place to sip whiskey and rock away in the bitter winter air.

"I should go out and feed the horses," Shorty said. It was his way of allowing Yuki and Mary to be alone.

"No, stay with me this evening," Yuki said. "We need to discuss our plans." He wiped graphite dust from his pencil and pointed it to the edge of a blank page in the ledger, preparing to make another journal entry. But something seemed wrong. *The house is too quiet.*

Without warning, Butler came stumbling down the hallway with a man prodding him with a knife. "This is an outrage," the major cried out. "Who are you?"

"I'm Jesse. Pleased to meet you." He jabbed the major's back, pushing him into the living room.

Yuki grabbed his long sword, but the front door flew open, and a familiar figure strode in. The intruder's .44 caliber pistol was cocked and ready. Yuki held his breath. It was Mosely, Christopher Spencer's workman.

Mosely pointed his pistol at Yuki. "Put that damned sword down," he snarled.

Caught off-guard, Yuki had no choice but to obey and wait for a chance to catch Mosely in an incautious moment. He leaned the sword next to the fireplace and raised his hands.

"Get back in this here room with Butler," Mosely said.

"Who the hell are you?" the major bellowed.

Mosely ignored him when he saw Shorty crouching next to the library fireplace. "Get in here, you swarthy little Chinaman, or I'll blow a hole in your head."

"I am Nipponese," Shorty said.

"I don't care what you are. Get in here and stay clear of that sword."

Shorty held his hands up and stepped out of the library.

"Major Benjamin Butler," Mosely said, "we meet again, but we come for me and Jesse's compensation this time. A reward, you might say."

"A reward for what?"

"You see these?" Mosely said, pointing to red scars on his cheeks. "You were right to recognize me in Spencer's office. You and me seen each other before. I got these the day you marched me and Jesse straight towards Mary's Hill in Fredericksburg. You don't remember, heh? You should. We was like sheep to the slaughter. Me and Jesse was cooks, but you ordered us to the front with the rest of your godforsaken men, and I got a bullet clean through my left cheek and out t'other. I'm alive by an inch."

The major blinked when he studied Mosely more closely. "I remember you! Lieutenant Dickens had to prod both of you ahead with his sword in your backs while I was wounded rescuing some of my men. Men who were brave enough to sacrifice their lives. We were in desperate straits that day, but there was no fight in you two cowards."

"Cowards, huh? That's not how I remember it, but it don't matter none. Your leg wound got you mustered out, but they said my wound wasn't serious. They put me in the infirmary for a day or so before I could, could . . ."

"Before you could skedaddle? That's what you're saying, isn't it? You deserted your comrades and hightailed it back to Baltimore into that nest of secessionist sympathizers."

"Say what you want. It don't matter. I'm here to collect. I reckon the gold you and Spencer talked about is stored hereabouts, and it sounds like it's just about enough to make things even."

"Gold? I have no gold here. What have you done to my friend Christopher Spencer?"

"Spencer?" Mosely sniggered. "Good riddance. He ain't paid me and Jesse in over a month, and the sheriff locked the doors to his office four days ago."

"How in the hell did you know where to find us?"

"I overheard you tellin' Spencer the second time you met. It was right kind of you. We come to Woonsocket yesterday and found out where you live. I wanna thank you ahead a' time for your horses and the wagon. Now, dammit," Mosely said with menacing finality, "where is the gold?"

"It's on a ship bound for Boston," Butler said. "Don't be such a fool. I have eight silver dollars in a jar in the kitchen. Take the money and be gone."

Mosely spit a wad of chewing tobacco on the living room rug and pointed at something in the library. "What are those? It looks like blankets folded up on boxes what don't belong there. I reckon your China boy's been sleepin' on them, lookin' after the gold."

"Hey, boy, quit lookin' at that dang sword," Jesse yelled.

Mosely crossed into the library and inspected the cases. "Looks like they's what we're here for."

"Mosely, I told you there isn't any gold in this house. Now, get out," Butler said.

"Damn you," Mosely said. "Jesse shut him up."

Jesse slammed the small of the major's back with his fist, sending him sprawling on the floor.

"You no hurt the major!" Shorty yelled. He grabbed Yuki's sword, rushed out of the library, and stabbed Jesse in the neck. With blood gushing from his left carotid, he fell dead on top of Butler.

"Damn you, China boy," Mosely shouted. The blast from his pistol shook the crystals on the overhead chandelier, and the force of the slug knocked Shorty off his feet. He grabbed his chest and rolled over on his back.

Butler yelled and pushed Jesse's body off. "Shorty, Shorty," he cried out.

"I guess it's your turn now," Mosely said, turning to Yuki. But something caught his eye. He looked up the staircase and saw Mary aiming the major's pistol. It was locked and loaded.

Before he could duck, she pulled the trigger. The round struck Mosely's left hand, turning it into a bony mass of dangling fingers. Howling in pain, he fired back, but he missed. Mary returned his fire, but her aim was off, too. It was too much for Mosely. He tucked his mangled hand under his right armpit and rushed outside.

"Shorty!" Mary cried out as she rushed down the stairs.

The major cradled Shorty in his arms, and Yuki knelt beside them.

"Master, my wife Kayo…my son Johei… They live in Takahama near Edo Bay. Please, sir…" He closed his eyes, and his breathing shallowed.

"Kansuke-San, I give you my solemn promise. They will be taken very well care of," Yuki whispered. He pulled his sword from Shorty's hand. "I'll be back soon."

"No," Mary said. "Take this pistol. Your sword's no match against Mosely."

"I am a samurai. I must use my sword."

Yelping and swearing, Mosely fired a wild shot at Yuki and dashed headlong into the cemetery. He crouched behind a marble headstone with the river at his back and waited.

It was Yuki's sword against a pistol in the hand of a desperate man. Both weapons had their limits, and though technology held the advantage, Yuki was certain one's determination would ultimately decide the outcome.

He circled closer and ducked behind the great oak tree. He could not let Mosely bleed to death in the bitter cold. *Bushido*, the way of the warrior, compelled him to avenge Shorty or die in the effort. Yuki could not allow Mosely to die any other way. Duty demanded that he take his own life should he fail. He crept closer to the river. A twig cracked under his foot, and Mosely fired again. This time, the round came close, striking the headstone next to Yuki's head.

Mosely had two shots left, but Yuki knew one well-aimed shot would end his life. He took a deep breath, gritted his teeth, and lunged. Mosely fired point-blank, and Yuki felt a flash of searing pain near his belt, but he struck, severing Mosely's head. It tumbled into the weeds. In a fit of utter rage, Yuki grabbed the hilt of his sword with two hands and plunged it into the body. Ignoring his wound, he ran to the house, where Butler cradled Shorty on his lap.

"Shorty, stay with us. My friend, my great, dear friend," Butler cried out in a drunken blather, "Don't die. Don't leave on me."

Shorty lay still, unable to respond. Pink foam bubbled from his lips. He opened his eyes and smiled weakly. He tried to speak, but his eyelids flickered, and he was gone.

Mary hugged the major and wiped his tears with her handkerchief. "Uncle Benjamin, Shorty is in a better place now." She stroked his hair and wiped his forehead with her kerchief.

What Mary had just said puzzled Yuki. *Uncle Benjamin? Why did she call him uncle?*

Butler groaned and fell unconscious. Despite the nagging pain in his side, Yuki carried him upstairs to his bed, and Mary covered him with blankets.

"Yuki, my love, stay with us," she whispered through her tears.

"No, I am not finished."

# CHAPTER 20

YUKI DRAGGED JESSE'S BODY to the cemetery and dropped it next to Mosely's headless corpse. He pulled his sword from Mosely's chest and severed Jesse's head with an angry swipe. Yuki ignored the pain in his side and rolled the bodies into the river. After watching them disappear into the cold gloom, he dropped their bloody heads into a burlap bag he found in the barn. He put a large stone inside and flung it into the water. His face and hands were smeared with dirt and blood, and his shirt and trousers were warm and wet. He threw Mosely's pistol into the river, returned to the house, and cleaned his sword.

By then, the major had regained consciousness. "Did you do it?"

"Yes, it is done."

"Tommy, you're bleeding," Mary cried.

Yuki pulled off his shirt and checked his wound. Mosely's bullet had barely grazed his waist's upper layer of muscle tissue. Mary boiled a kettle of water over the fireplace, and Yuki sat stoically on a kitchen chair while she cleaned and dressed his wound.

After she retreated to her bedroom, his thoughts turned to Shorty, his loyal companion and friend. Much was demanded of commoner soldiers, but little was expected of them. They were considered nothing more than cannon fodder.

But to Yuki, Shorty had been a paragon of samurai virtue: loyal, honorable, courageous, and compassionate. He had saved the major's life twice, sacrificing his own the second time. No more could be expected of any warrior. America had erased the ancient Japanese class divide, and Shorty had become something he could never be in Japan: an equal. Yuki vowed to keep his promise to him. He could do no less.

# CHAPTER 21

THE NEXT MORNING, YUKI washed Shorty's body, and Mary laundered his clothes and hung them near the fireplace. When they were dry, Yuki re-dressed the body. Lastly, he slathered the blade of his long sword with scented bear grease he found in a can on the major's dresser. "You are a true samurai, my friend," he said over Shorty's body. "My sword is now yours."

He muttered a short prayer and turned to Mary. "We cannot keep the gold in the house," he said. "Christopher Spencer probably told others about our offer. Someone from his lawyer's office or another worker may have listened in. The house is not safe, so I intend to bury the cases next to Shorty's body in the cemetery."

"I agree," Mary said. "I want the gold out of this house."

Yuki spent two hours dragging the cases to the front staircase. Using a rope, he eased each one down the stairs and onto a makeshift sled hitched to one of the draught horses. It took the rest of the day to haul the cases to the cemetery. Having placed them next to Shorty's remains, Yuki and Mary clasped their hands and whispered prayers over the body.

金　金　金

UTTERLY EXHAUSTED, YUKI SCRIBBLED a barely readable entry in his journal. He wanted to pour out, but showing one's emotion was a weakness that samurai were exhorted to avoid. As was his habit, he dated the entry in English but wrote the rest in Japanese.

*January 29, 1868*
*Shorty is dead. He rests in the cemetery along with the gold and my long sword. He was no mere commoner. He was very much a samurai. I pray his spirit will guard the gold. The map*

Yuki did not finish the sentence. Instead, he turned to the next page and sketched a crude property map. He wrote "RIVER OAK" in English and drew a simple house and a few wavy lines to depict the river. He added several headstones crowned with crosses and sketched an oversized oak tree picture. He drew an X above it and finished the drawing by printing two kanji:

# 下木

It was a cryptic note that no one would understand unless Yuki was alive to reveal its meaning. He grew sullen when he thought about what would happen if he returned to Japan without the rifles. He might be ordered to give the map to Kuroi Taketo, who would return to Boston in his stead. If that were to happen, Yuki would be honor-bound to commit *seppuku*.

Yuki never bothered to finish his January 29th entry.

# CHAPTER 22

SHORTY WAS DEAD, and the major looked like he was about to join him in the cemetery. There was no word about the *Tora*, and it was unlikely that Christopher Spencer could come up with the rifles. Feeling helpless, Yuki sat with Mary by the fireplace and expressed his concerns.

"Without the Spencers, the rebels will crush our army, execute the shogun, and kill every foreign merchant and diplomat they can find. Russia, England, and France will invade Japan, and America will likely join them."

Mary snuggled in his arms and kissed his forehead. "You worry too much, Tommy. Things will work out."

"No, you're wrong. I need Benjamin, but we must face reality. He may die soon. He just sits in his rocking chair on the back porch staring at the river. What can I do?"

Mary had no answer. After she dressed Yuki's wound, they kissed each other and watched the flames in the fireplace consume a dying log.

Yuki's thoughts turned to why Mary sometimes called the major by his first name rather than calling him her father. From the beginning, he had been puzzled and could not forget the night Shorty was killed. He distinctly heard her call the major "uncle." He decided it was time to find out why.

"Mary, you called Benjamin your uncle the other night," he said.

Caught off guard, she sighed. "I wondered if you had heard me."

"What have you been keeping from me?"

She hesitated.

"Mary, tell me the truth."

She gazed at Yuki pleadingly. "I'm so sorry. I should have told you a long time ago. Benjamin is not my father."

"What?"

"Yuki, dearest, we had no vile motive in hiding the truth. Uncle Benjamin took me in when my parents died. He is my mother's brother. It is a complicated story."

Yuki said nothing. Prolonged silence was his way of drawing out the truth.

Mary squeezed his hand and sighed. "You see, my father was a prosperous Boston businessman, but he loved living here. River Oak has been the family seat for three generations. He loved it so much that he retired here, allowing his partner to manage the business. But during Father's absence, his partner swindled him out of all his money, and he was left with little more than this property. And he almost lost that, too."

"So, what happened?"

"It's a long story. Father rented out the fields and tried to get into the China trade. We moved to a cottage in Fairhaven, Massachusetts. It is a little seaport town that is a center for that kind of commerce. But the worst was yet to happen."

Yuki wiped Mary's tear-streaked cheeks, and she attempted a brave smile. "Seven years ago, Father had to mortgage River Oak to survive, and soon after, he and Mother died of diphtheria within a week of each other. I was only fourteen years old. Uncle Benjamin took me in and has been like a father ever since. I would have lost River Oak had it not been for him. He spent all his savings to pay off the mortgage, and when war broke out, he enlisted as a Union Army officer. In America, educated men of good character are often given command of troops in time of war."

Yuki got up and stoked the fire. "What happened to him?"

"In December of 1862, he was badly wounded in the Battle of Fredericksburg, a Southern town located in Virginia. That's where Mosely was wounded, remember? Uncle Benjamin was barely alive when they brought him to a hospital in Washington. I left Fairhaven and went to care for him. He survived, of course, and had to find work when the war ended. But times were bad, and he was reduced to taking odd jobs. I wanted to find employment too, but he insisted I go to college."

The glow of the dying embers in the fireplace illuminated Mary's wan expression, but Yuki waited until she was ready to explain what happened next.

"Anyway, Uncle Benjamin eventually became friends with Captain William Whitfield, who lived in Fairhaven. John Manjiro, the Japanese boy William rescued from a deserted island, lived with Whitfield and his wife. Uncle Benjamin met John many times before he returned to Japan. I have often wondered about him."

"I've wondered, too. I recall Benjamin mentioning Manjiro during that rifle demonstration. Remember?" Yuki asked.

"Yes, I do. And it was Captain Whitfield who wrote a letter to John Manjiro recommending Uncle Benjamin. That is why the shogun's government hired him as a military advisor. Soon after we arrived in Japan, the shogun's chamberlain heard about Benjamin's Spencer rifle, and you know the rest."

"Mary," Yuki said impatiently, "that is all quite interesting, but you have not answered my question."

"Oh, Tommy dearest, when an American man takes a mistress, he often tells people she is his niece. I did not want people to suspect me of being Uncle Benjamin's mistress, nor did he. That is why he chose to call me his daughter. Can you not understand?"

Guilt-stricken for having pressed her, Yuki gave her hand a gentle squeeze. "Mary, I never had doubts about you and Benjamin. I was merely curious."

They kissed, and Mary returned to her bedroom. Before he slept, Yuki made another entry in his journal.

*January 30*

*What would it be like to be free from the turmoil I have encountered? Perhaps I can find peace someday sitting on the veranda at Daiten-ji, contemplating the Fourfold Truths of Buddha, away from all the cares of the world. I yearn someday to be at peace. But what would become of Mary?*

# CHAPTER 23

THEIR NIGHTLY RITUAL RECOMMENCED after the shock of Shorty's murder subsided. Mary joined Yuki in the fire-lit library, where they sought solace in lovemaking.

Yuki's wound healed quickly, and the major's health improved, something he attributed to Gilbert and Parsons Hygienic Whiskey. Two weeks later, he declared himself fit for travel.

"Here's what I've been thinking all this time," Butler said, "I'm certain Valentine Fogerty or that fellow Oliver Winchester will gladly sell us rifles. But Christopher deserves one more chance. Let's visit him and explain the situation."

"This will take a lot of time, especially if you start bargaining with the companies and negotiating terms," Mary said. "We'll need a place to stay in Boston. Perhaps Reverend McLeod might find us quarters away from prying eyes."

"Who is he?" Yuki asked.

"The minister of the church to which Benjamin once belonged. The good reverend often scolded you for drinking. Isn't that so, Uncle?"

Butler flashed a sheepish grin. "Yes, my dear, perhaps you are right. Would you mind soliciting the good reverend's help? I fear he has long since given up on me."

Yuki was agreeable and confident that the gold would be safe with Shorty.

金　金　金

THEY DEPARTED FOR BOSTON in early February, leaving the draught horses and wagon in Woonsocket for farmer Eiler to retrieve. On the train to Providence, the man sitting next to Butler was reading the *Republican Herald and Post*. The headline caught Yuki's eye:

### GRISLY FIND AT THE MOUTH OF BLACKSTONE RIVER
*Two Headless Corpses Discovered*

They visited Reverend McLeod at his parsonage, and Mary explained their need to rent a house. "Benjamin is financially back on his feet and has an oriental valet. His name is Tommy," she said, pointing to Yuki.

"I have just the place for you if you don't mind paying a little extra," the reverend replied. "One of my faithful recently passed away and willed her home to our parish. The rent is eight dollars a month, including the services of Sarah, the deceased's housekeeper. My family doctor, Juda Stein, took her in as an orphan and taught her to cook and clean house. When she was old enough, he trained her to be a midwife. She rarely gets called upon, so I hired her. If you accept my conditions, you must promise your valet will act like a complete gentleman," he said, eyeing Yuki suspiciously. "I will not countenance any depraved behavior on his part."

"Oh, no worry. Tommy, here is a man of honor," Butler said. "I guarantee it."

"And, Benjamin," McLeod said without acknowledging the major's promise, "you must not drink or smoke in the house."

"I promise," Butler said sourly, and they moved in the next day.

THE SMALL ROOM WHERE Sarah slept was part of the detached kitchen. Yuki assumed she was no more than twenty years old based on her youthful looks.

"I am Sarah Sailor," she announced when they first met. She pointed to Yuki and smiled. "You Mashpee?"

"Mash pea? What is mash pea?"

Sarah peered into his eyes. "Ahh," she said, "I think maybe you a Mashpee Wampanoag, but no. Maybe you are a Celestial?"

Celestial was the polite American term for the Chinese. It alluded to the Celestial Empire, a term Chinese often used to refer to their homeland.

"My ma was Mashpee Injun from Cape Cod," Sarah said, "I thought you were from the Mashpee Wampanoag tribe like me."

*Does she think I look like her?* However, Yuki realized they did share certain physical features. Her hair was a glossy black, and her eyelids were similarly shaped. But the hue of her complexion was different.

"I am not Chinese, Miss Sarah. I am Nipponese," he replied with a gentle smile and slight bow.

"Chinee, Nipponee are all the same to me. I like 'em. Me? I am half. Ma said my pa is a navy sailor boy. He went to Sanfrisco. He never came back, and Ma died. Pa's name is Jack, but Ma didn't know his family name, so she said it was Sailor. So, I am Sarah Sailor. Someday I will find my Pa in Sanfrisco. It is far away. Someplace they call Ow-west."

Sarah's broken English and accented lilt sounded strange to Yuki, but he could understand her better than many of the sailors aboard the *Lackawanna*.

"What's your name?" Sarah asked.

"Just call me Tommy," he replied. She was the only Native American Yuki had ever met, and her engaging smile and amiability quickly won him over.

# CHAPTER 24

YUKI AND THE MAJOR put on their best clothes to visit Christopher Spencer. They found him in a small shed next to his old office. Spencer greeted them with a hangdog look.

"What happened to that fellow who was working here for you?" Butler asked casually.

"Disappeared on me some days after you left. It doesn't matter. He was a malingerer. I'm glad he is gone. Why do you ask?"

"Just curious," said Butler, casting a knowing glance at Yuki. "More importantly, what have you to tell us? It's been over a month since we talked last."

"Nothing but bad news. My attorney demanded the release of the remaining inventory to me, the ones in the US Army warehouse. But unbeknownst to us, the War Department had already taken the title and resold them to a Dutch firm. They were shipped out a week ago. Who knows where? The money I am supposed to get is tied up in court, and the legal fees are killing me. Benjamin, I'm sorry, but I cannot help you."

Butler sighed. "Then please understand that we must buy rifles from one of your competitors. We'll have to consider Valentine Fogerty or Oliver Winchester."

"Be my guest, but you won't be able to do business with either of them."

"What are you talking about?"

"Hold on a second," Spencer said, shuffling through a stack of newspapers on his desk. "Here, let me read this to you:

> *Our Washington office reports that Secretary of State Seward, British Ambassador Sir Edward Thornton, and French Ambassador Jules Berthemy have concluded talks over the rebellion in Japan. They deemed it a civil war and agreed that their countries should not interfere. Two days ago, they promulgated a declaration of joint neutrality.*
>
> *Henceforth, the export of cannonry, naval vessels, firearms, and other military material is prohibited. The prohibition extends to agents, representatives, and other intermediaries of the Bakufu, the Tycoon's government, and the so-called Imperial Government. Two or three other parties are expected to sign the agreement, including the Netherlands and the North German Confederation."*

All the names were confusing, but Yuki understood the appalling essence of the story.

"Mr. Spencer, what if we buy the rifles under the major's name?"

"Don't you see? Benjamin would be acting as an agent. No manufacturer will take the chance of selling rifles to him for fear of going to jail. And even if they did, he would be hard-pressed to find an honest shipowner to take on the cargo. The risk would be too great. Their vessels could be seized."

Yuki and Butler glumly returned to the house, lost in their grim thoughts.

# CHAPTER 25

THEY SAT TOGETHER IN the parlor, Mary reading her Bible and Yuki staring blankly out the window. It occurred to him that he was like the trapped cluster fly buzzing about the room. It struck the window several times before stunning itself and falling onto the sill. Yuki crushed the insect with his thumb and flicked it into the nearby wastepaper basket. *If it is to be, I hope my end will come as quickly.*

"Mary," he said, "the Joint Neutrality Declaration is the final blow. If the major and I are caught attempting to circumvent it, we will be jailed and the gold confiscated. It would be a diplomatic disaster. I fear the Imperial Army will decimate Aizu and our allies with their English firearms."

Mary closed her Bible and took his hand. "Tommy, maybe not all is lost. I have been thinking about the rifle demonstration at your uncle's estate in Edo. Certainly, you recall that father mentioned his friend Captain Whitfield."

"Yes, I remember. Whitfield rescued John Manjiro, the shipwrecked boy."

"Exactly. Whitfield still lives in Fairhaven, which is not far from here. I am certain he will help us."

"I'm a bit unsure about this. Why would he be willing to take such a chance?"

"Because he has been a vocal advocate for strong ties between America and the Bakufu. The rebels hate Westerners, and Manjiro will be hunted down and killed if they win. Once Whitfield understands the situation, I'm sure he'll do everything he can to aid the shogun. He is a very clever man and a respected sea captain. He can find a way around the embargo. I'm sure of it."

Yuki gazed out the window again, thinking about what Mary had said. He recalled meeting Manjiro at the Institute for the Study of Barbarian Books when he came to speak about his life in America. He described how Captain Whitfield rescued him from starvation in 1841 and took him back to Fairhaven. He and his wife raised him and sent him to school. Manjiro returned to Japan in 1850 when he was twenty-three years old. He was imprisoned for some time for having left Japan without permission. Still, his knowledge of English and his experience of being raised in America soon caught the Bakufu's attention. Commodore Perry and his "Black Ships" appeared in Edo Bay in 1853 and threatened to bombard the capital unless the Bakufu agreed to the US-proposed economic treaty. Manjiro was quickly summoned to Edo and given the rank of samurai. He was given two swords and chose Nakahama as his surname, the name of the village where he was born. He despised the anti-foreign samurai and worked hard for the Bakufu. A Dutchman did most of the interpreting, but Manjiro did translation work and advised the officials who dealt with the Americans.

Yuki rose and paced the floor. "Mary, you may be right. It's worth a try. When can Benjamin and I visit Whitfield?"

The major had a ready answer. "You stay here with Mary. I will go to Fairhaven tomorrow and impress upon Whitfield that Mr. Manjiro will likely have his head chopped off if the damned rebels take over. I know we can trust him to buy the rifles. Brazil, Paraguay, and Uruguay are fightin' tooth and nail right now. Whitfield can avoid suspicion by claiming he plans to sell the rifles to one of those countries."

Butler's convincing assessment galvanized Yuki, and he readily agreed to the plan. The major took the train to Fairhaven the next day, but he returned with unwelcome news.

"Captain Whitfield is on a voyage to Shanghai. His wife doesn't expect him to return for at least another five months. I'm sorry, Tommy. We'll have to think of something else."

Yuki decided that returning to Japan for help was the only option left. Mary became noticeably depressed that day, and he suspected she feared he was planning to abandon her.

The following day, while sitting at the breakfast table sipping coffee, Yuki decided to reveal his plans. He was about to speak when the major groaned and grabbed his chest. Yuki tried to catch him, but Butler slipped and fell off his chair. Sarah heard Mary's screams, and when she saw Butler on the floor, she threw off her apron. "You no worry, Miss Mary. I go get Dr. Stein."

Yuki carried Butler to his bedroom, and an hour later, Juda Stein arrived. After examining the major, he drew Mary aside. "I fear his heart is giving out, and I believe his days are numbered. See that he remains comfortable, and I will visit him in another day or two," he whispered.

# CHAPTER 26

BUTLER STEADILY DECLINED. "I'm just an old, worn-out penny what's time to be spent for the last time. Our mission was snakebit from the beginning, and now it's my damned heart."

Mary stroked her uncle's hand, and Yuki sat next to her. "Tommy," she said tearfully, "I know what you have been planning, but please, I beg of you, do not return to Japan. Wait until Captain Whitfield returns. I could not live without your help."

"Mary, I must go," Yuki whispered.

"Uncle Benjamin, please tell him to stay," she said as tears breached her eyelids and flooded her cheeks.

"Mary, Yuki knows what he has to do," the major said. "Tommy, I don't ask for much, but leave enough spending money here for us until you return."

"I will leave you more than enough, and of course, the gold will remain at River Oak until I return with help."

Butler raised himself by his elbows and looked Yuki in the eye. "Tell me, Tommy, what are your plans?"

"I won't know until I meet my uncle. He will certainly help. But you can be sure you and Mary will be well taken care of."

"Thank you, Tommy. I believe in you. Good luck."

They were Major Benjamin Butler's last words. That evening he died and was buried next to his parents' graves in a Boston cemetery two days later.

金　金　金

AFTER THE MAJOR'S FUNERAL, Mary continued to grieve. She rarely left her bedroom or spoke to Yuki, leaving him to take his meals alone. One morning, while reading the *Boston Herald*, Sarah brought him a pot of tea and a slab of buttered toast.

"When is Mary coming down?" he asked.

"Miss Mary, very sad," Sarah said guardedly.

Yuki failed to notice her uneasiness. Instead, he turned his attention to a front-page story:

> FAMED FRENCH WARSHIP SOON TO ARRIVE
> *The Couronne, a French ironclad, is expected to make port in Boston tomorrow. The warship will make a two-day courtesy call before departing for the French naval base in Toulon, a Mediterranean seaport. The steam-powered vessel is one of the most modern ironclads afloat today and is manned by over 550 crew members. The mayor and the city council will entertain Captain Gallant and his officers at a dinner in their honor at the Tremont Hotel. The Couronne is scheduled to depart for France the day after.*

Being permitted to sail on a French warship was unlikely, but Yuki figured he could persuade Captain Gallant to do him a critical favor. He spent the day writing two letters, coding the first one that only his uncle could decipher. He described the disasters that had befallen him but insisted he could succeed. He concluded with a plea:

> *Uncle Matsudaira, I will return to Japan as soon as possible. Vice-Admiral Enomoto must return with me to Boston on a*

*warship with a platoon of soldiers. Please commence making plans with him. He must be prepared by the time I return. And please ask John Manjiro to draft a letter of introduction to his benefactor, Captain Whitfield, on my behalf.*

Yuki addressed the second letter to the French ambassador in Yokohama, requesting that he forward the first one to his uncle. After finishing, he leaned back in his chair and stared pensively at the envelopes. *Everything depends on the goodwill of the French. If Uncle Matsudaira does not receive my letter, all will probably be lost.*

Yuki visited the *Couronne* the next day without telling Mary his intentions. The captain, who spoke fluent English, was initially suspicious and not disposed to listen. Still, he gladly agreed to deliver the letters when he learned they were mutual friends of Captain Jules Brunet, the French military advisor in Japan. Yuki offered to pay him for his services, but the captain refused.

"You are indeed fortunate," he said. "My orders are to rendezvous in Toulon with the *Dupleix*, a French corvette. It will sail to Yokohama soon after. I will send word for Captain Brunet to deliver your correspondence personally."

Yuki could not believe his luck. He had befriended Brunet when he and his men were sent to Aizu as advisors. He often turned to Yuki for help, and they spent many pleasant hours discussing military tactics over glasses of red wine.

"Thank you, Captain Gallant," Yuki said upon leaving. "I have every confidence the letters will be delivered."

# CHAPTER 27

MARY STARTLED YUKI WHEN she flung her arms around him as soon as he opened the front door. "Oh, Tommy, I thought that you had abandoned me. Please promise never to do so. I could never bear the thought."

Yuki was baffled. *Why the sudden change? What is bothering her?* He hugged her and planted a kiss on her cheek.

"Mary darling, I know you still grieve for Benjamin, and rightly so. But like you say, he's in a better place now."

"Yuki, it's not that. Can't you see?" she sobbed, gently stroking her abdomen.

"See what?"

"I'm with child."

Yuki cast an anxious glance about the room before it struck him. "*Our* child?"

Mary wrung her hands and stared anxiously into Yuki's eyes. Though they had known each other for a little over a year, they had overcome their differences in temperament, language, customs, and culture. She had been his nurse, teacher, friend, and his lover.

The revelation came as an outright shock to Yuki, but one that instantly increased, rather than diminished, his deep affection for Mary. Her devotion mattered, and he wondered what he could say to comfort her. He had often said that the Japanese expressed love by their behavior, not what they said, but it was now time to bend.

"Mary, my sweetest, I love you dearly. If there were more meaningful words, I would say them. You are my greatest treasure, more than the gold at River Oak. You worry I may abandon you, but I intend to prove you wrong. I will marry you before I go back to Japan, and I promise to return to you."

They sat on the parlor's loveseat, held hands, and kissed. "Oh, Tommy," she said, "You are the love of my life, but …."

"But what, my dearest?"

"Tommy, miscegenation is a crime. We could be jailed, and the baby taken from us."

"Miscegenation?"

"When two people of different races, you know…."

Yuki did know, but he had a ready answer. "Mary, I have kept a secret from you, but it is time to share it. If I succeed in my mission, I will be appointed the next Magistrate of Foreign Affairs. The shogun's chamberlain promised this. Cousin Nariaki informed me the day we departed Japan. Think of it. Our child will be a tangible symbol of a new era in my country."

He described a lavish Japanese lifestyle in which Mary would raise their child without want, shame, or fear. His fragile vision was wrapped in the thinnest tissue of hope, and Mary remained unconvinced.

"Tommy, do you really think your compatriots would welcome me?"

"Yes, you will be warmly welcomed and accepted," he said with as much conviction as he could muster. "People will have to. Scores of Americans and Europeans will clamor for our friendship, if for nothing else than to seek political favors." He could not have known that such a marriage would occur in 1879 between the new Japanese chancellor and a German woman.

Mary gazed at the ceiling, tears gathering in her eyes. "Tommy, dearest, it is impossible."

"What are you saying? Do you not wish to marry me?"

"Of course I do, but you don't understand. No minister would perform a marriage service given you are Japanese, and I am with child. And if Reverend McLeod learns of my condition, he will turn me out. And it is too dangerous for me to travel with you to Japan while I am pregnant. I could lose our child."

"Then what do you propose?"

"I need to think things over. I'll have an answer, but you must be patient."

金　金　金

THE NEXT MORNING, Yuki was surprised when Mary asked Sarah to join them for breakfast. It was the first time she had been invited to do so, and she squirmed in her chair, her wary eyes darting between Yuki and Mary. Mary gently grasped her hand, and it suddenly dawned on Yuki that Sarah had known of Mary's pregnancy before he had. In a few short weeks, she had become Mary's trusted, albeit disingenuous, confidant.

"Sarah, you have been like a sister to me," Mary said. "Tommy and I need your help."

Sarah blinked, and her wary expression was dispelled by a gentle smile that grew to replace it. "Anything for you and Mister Tommy," she said. "What can I do to make you happy?"

"Sarah dear, Tommy is returning to Japan for a few months, and I will need your help. Before my condition can no longer be hidden, I will move to my home in River Oak. That way, I'll be safe from prying eyes. Will you please go with me? It is in the country. Dr. Stein trained you as a midwife, and I want you there to help deliver my child. I have the greatest of confidence in your ability to do so."

"Really? I can go to the countryside to live wi' you?"

"Yes, but I have yet another favor to ask you."

"Anything you want, Miss Mary."

"You must tell people that the baby is yours, not mine. I don't have to tell you why, my dear. The child's features will most surely resemble yours."

Sarah seemed delighted by the irony of Mary's request and readily agreed. As soon as she left to work in the kitchen, Mary turned to Yuki.

"Tommy, I spent all night thinking this over. Of course, Captain Whitfield is the key, and I am certain I can persuade him to help. But we must guarantee he will not get into trouble for his efforts. Go back to Japan as soon as possible and return on Vice-Admiral Enomoto's ship. We'll retrieve the gold from the cemetery, and Whitfield will buy the rifles under his name. Winchester rifles seem like the best choice. You must prepay him for his services."

"Of course, but what then?"

"You, me, and our child will board Enomoto's ship in Boston and rendezvous with Captain Whitfield in Havana Harbor. Uncle Benjamin suggested he sail to South America, but the Spanish colony of Cuba is better to my way of thinking. Whitfield will not have to sail so far. Enomoto's soldiers will transfer the rifles onto Enomoto's ship, and your job will be to bribe the Spanish customs officials enough so that they will provide Whitfield with a satisfactory bill of sale. They are notoriously corrupt, and I'm sure they will do it for a price. The good captain must be able to provide our government with unquestionable proof that he has not violated the neutrality pact."

"That should be no problem, but what next?"

"I will prevail upon Whitfield to marry us. Being a ship captain gives him the legal authority to do so. Or we could ask Enomoto to perform a Japanese wedding ceremony. Our blessed babe will be old enough to make the voyage by that time. But in any event, Sarah must accompany us and pretend to be our baby's mother."

"So that Whitfield will not suspect us of being the parents?"

"Exactly. And she will no longer be our housekeeper. She deserves a better life, and I intend to provide one."

Mary's move to River Oak and her self-imposed seclusion made sense to Yuki. Sarah would keep her company and be there to deliver their child. Her idea to make the rifle exchange in Cuba also made sense.

But Yuki knew Captain Whitfield's willingness to help was not the only key he needed to succeed. Assuming his uncle received his appeal for help and Vice-Admiral Enomoto was agreeable, a seaworthy Bakufu vessel had to be ready as soon as he landed in Japan. Yuki and Mary continued to discuss the plan, assuring each other that it all would work. It had to. Yuki saw no other way.

A few days later, the first piece of the complicated plan presented itself when Mary found an announcement in the shipping section of the *Boston Herald*:

> *The Lightning, the extreme clipper built here in Boston fourteen years ago, is scheduled to make port on or about March 30 to take on a cargo of manufactured goods destined for Australia. It will make an intermediate stop in Hong Kong. There is a limited amount of cargo space, as are three passenger cabins. Those requiring cargo space or are interested in booking passage are advised to contact Mr. James Worthy, the agent for the Black Ball Line. He reports that the Lightning still holds several speed records. A few years ago, she made the Liverpool to New York run in 13 days, 19½ hours.*

Yuki booked passage and quickly readied himself. He slathered bear grease on his short sword, wrapped it in oilcloth, and stored it in Major Butler's wooden rifle box. Wearing one sword in Japan without its mate would draw dangerous attention. He asked Mary to keep the box and a few other personal items until he returned. He packed his other belongings in the major's army rucksack and took the pistol with which Mary had killed Mosely. His only problem was how to keep the map safe. Sarah had the answer. She gave him a tin tea canister with a tight cap to keep moisture out.

Before he left, he counted his expense money and gave half to Mary. The half he kept included a double eagle, a handful of five-dollar gold coins, silver dollars, and scores of Japanese brass and silver coins. He planned to give most of the money to Shorty's wife.

Mary gave him a locket. One side contained her porcelain image, and the other had several strands of her hair under glass. He hung it on his neck with a bronze skeleton key. A key he dared not lose.

On the morning of his departure, he made his last journal entry:

*April 1, 1868*
   *Dearest, I will return soon. I love you. Yuki*

They said their last goodbyes when they reached the harbor, but they dared not to hug or kiss. They both knew why.

Mary tearfully blew a kiss to Yuki from the pier as the *Lightning* slipped its lines. Standing at the handrail, he stoically waved goodbye.

A tug towed the cargo ship to the outer harbor, and it set sail for Hong Kong.

# CHAPTER 28

## June 11, 1868—Hong Kong

EIGHTY DAYS LATER, the *Lightning* made port in Hong Kong, and from there, Yuki booked passage to Edo on the *Sacramento*, an American merchantman.

He lay sleeping in his hammock below decks when the ship dropped anchor a few hundred yards from the Yokohama customs office and the jetty that led to it. He shook himself awake and got up.

While in Hong Kong, Yuki purchased loose-fitting trousers, a drab blue shirt, and a brown jacket-like garment that reached his hips. He wanted to enter Yokohama unnoticed, and the clothes resembled those worn by commoners.

He tightened the belt-like rope about his trousers and slid the major's .44 Colt inside his jacket. With the rucksack slung over his shoulders, he climbed topside. He was anxious. Everything hinged on his uncle receiving his letter and whether Enomoto was prepared to sail back to Boston.

He scanned the harbor, but he saw no other ships. Strangely, the customs house was shuttered, and no one acknowledged the presence of the *Sacramento*. Rain started to splatter the deck, and a stiff breeze arose. The second mate, Billy Jones, grew hoarse shouting orders to the grumbling crew. "Hey, Tommy," he called out, "Ye'd better ready yerself."

Crew members lowered three longboats into the water, and Jones called Yuki to join him in the third one. They cast off, and the sailors pulled hard, their oars straining in their locks. The other longboats followed. One was loaded with crates to be delivered to the French embassy, and in the other, ten sailors sat shielding their rifles from the salty spray. As they drew close to the shore, Yuki saw no one standing or walking along the waterfront.

"Tommy, where are all the people?" Jones asked as he scanned the area.

Yuki had no answer. He could only stare and wonder. The oarsmen maneuvered the boat midway along the stone jetty, and Jones climbed up first. A canvas packet inside his coat contained the ship's landing documents and a small mail pouch he was to personally hand over to the American resident minister, Robert B. Van Valkenburgh.

"Come on, you funny little Nipponese, hurry up," Jones called to Yuki. "I gotta clear customs."

The two other longboats sidled up to the jetty, and the sailors off-loaded the large crates addressed to the French ambassador, Léon Roches. The wind grew stronger, and a banging sound caught Yuki's attention. Jones heard it too. It came from the customs house.

"The damn shutters on them winders are coming off their hinges," Jones yelled through a gust of wind.

"Is anyone here?" Yuki called out in Japanese, but only the wind answered. He opened the door and shouted, "Summon the chief officer immediately." Still, no one answered.

They found several overturned chairs, smashed cabinets, and broken drawers inside. Wind-driven papers skittered across the floor like frightened mice.

"Tommy, what's goin' on here?" Jones said

Yuki shook his head, pulled the Colt from inside his jacket, and cocked the hammer.

"If this don't beat the Dutch!" Jones shouted above the wind and pelting rain. "Tommy, the cap'n won't keen on makin' this trip, and now I know why. Let's not go any fuhther 'til my men come up with the crates. Yer welcome to follow me. No sane man would dare attack us."

The sailors readied themselves, and Jones gave the order to fix bayonets. "Keep a keen eye out for trouble, men."

The armed escort marched to the foreign settlement, where French soldiers manned a *Canon de l'Empereur* behind a makeshift barricade. "Halloo!" Jones yelled.

When a French army officer appeared from behind the cannon, Yuki could not believe his luck: The man was Jules Brunet.

"Monsieur Tomita, what a welcome surprise. It has been a long time, *non?*" Captain Brunet grabbed Yuki's hand and pulled him close to whisper in his ear. "I have good news for you. I received your letter from Captain Thouars of the *Dupleix* and hand-delivered it to your uncle three weeks ago."

Yuki's spirits swelled at the news. "Captain, how can I repay you?"

"It was my pleasure to help," Brunet replied, "But what are you wearing? I hardly recognize you."

"I wore these clothes aboard the ship, but I plan to change as soon as I buy a horse. Surely a foreigner will sell me one. I will be meeting someone at a village on my way to Edo."

"A horse? Impossible, my friend. But why? It is hazardous to travel these days—*très dangereux*. We've learned that a Bakufu official was assassinated this morning, and the customs house was ransacked. The rebels are everywhere. Come stay with us. If security improves, I will visit Edo in a week."

"Thank you, Jules, but I must leave for Edo today."

He said his goodbyes to Brunet and Jones. He was unlikely to find any horses in town, but he had to try. He headed down a road leading to the commercial district of Yokohama. Wind fussed his back and spattered his legs with muddied water. His straw sandals were soaked.

When he stopped to wipe the rain from his eyes, he was shocked by something he saw. He drew closer and found two bodies lying near a closed *ramen* restaurant. One was that of a customs officer whose vacant eyes stared unseeingly into the sky, the sockets filled with rainwater. His black-lacquered helmet was still tied to the chin of his dissevered head. Yuki gingerly touched the officer's hand. It was cold. Looking at the other man's clothes, Yuki guessed he was the restaurant's owner.

A human voice startled Yuki. "You'd better leave them alone, or you'll lose your head too."

Yuki quickly traced the voice to a beggar squatting under the eaves of the restaurant. "How could this have happened?" he demanded.

The man had wandering eyes, but he squarely focused his left one on Yuki. "A couple of masterless samurai did this," he cackled. He shifted his weight and farted. "They claimed to be part of the Imperial army and threatened to kill anyone who disturbs these bodies."

Yuki drew closer, but not too close. "Ronin did this?"

"Are you deaf? I saw them cut these poor fellows down with my own eyes. Where have you been all this time?"

"I have just come from up north, if you must know. News is hard to come by there."

The beggar snorted. "You're dressed like me, but your haughty language betrays you if I may say so. You're a samurai, and by the way, you stink. You have been consorting with the barbarians, haven't you?"

Yuki was taken aback. The beggar had seen right through his disguise. "I have not," he protested.

"Is that a fact?" the beggar said dismissively. "Admit it. You came aboard that foreign ship anchored in the harbor. That's why you look so gaunt. I hear the food they eat is not fit for dogs."

"You seem to know all the news."

"Ah-ha, so, it's true. That ship explains it all. You've missed everything."

Yuki stepped away from the bloody puddle next to the customs officer's corpse. "Just tell me what has been going on."

"Edo and Yokohama are in chaos. Ronin have taken to pillaging shops and homes. The so-called Imperial Army occupied Edo Castle in April, and the shogun has capitulated."

"What's that you say?"

The beggar ignored him and studied the bodies instead.

"Are you going to answer me or not?" Yuki said.

"Oh, yes, your question. Well, the Satsuma and Choshu armies took over the imperial capital of Kyoto and ejected the Aizu soldiers who were there to protect the emperor. The shogun, the former shogun that is, has sequestered himself in the village of Ueno, just outside of Edo."

"Impossible," Yuki said.

The beggar picked his nose. "It is a fact, and it won't be long until Edo is completely in the hands of the Imperial Army. He flicked a bit of dried mucus off his finger and gazed expectantly at Yuki. "I've given you the latest news. Will you now, sir, give me some money so I can eat today?"

Yuki stared bleakly at the beggar. "Surely these are merely rumors," he said.

"No, it's true. Remnants of the shogun's forces, mostly samurai from Aizu, still occupy parts of Edo, but it is rumored they plan to move north. Aizu and its allies are readying for a fight to the finish."

"Aizu? Our army is withdrawing from the capital?"

"So, you are from Aizu? Be careful, or your accent will get you killed. Townspeople fear for their lives, and rightly so. They've closed their stores and homes tighter than barnacles at low tide. No place is safe anymore."

The news could not have been any worse, and Yuki began to worry that he was too late.

"Are you listening to me?" the beggar said, interrupting Yuki's dismal thoughts. "Might you have something for this poor old man?" His chameleon-like eyes focused on Yuki from two angles. "Perhaps a few brass coins?"

"Huh?" Yuki muttered, still lost in thought.

"Money, sir. I need money to buy some food."

Yuki bit the inside of his lower lip as he considered the beggar's plea. "I will give you twenty mon if you tell me what I need to know."

"Certainly. Whatever you want, just ask."

"Where can I buy a horse?"

"Buy a horse? Here? Nobody would dare sell you a horse even if they had one. They'd lose their heads. Tell me, where do you want to go with such urgency?"

"Edo."

"Ha! You'd be killed before you get halfway down this road. Wait a day or two and see what happens next."

"I cannot wait."

The beggar struggled up and limped over to Yuki. "I have an idea," he said in a whisper. "I'll show you a safe and quick way to get there. I want out of Yokohama too. I'll lose my head if I stay because I've been talking to you."

"You cannot come with me, so stop your nonsense and tell me the quickest way to Edo. Here, take these." Yuki reached into his purse and dropped five four-mon coins into the beggar's open hands.

"Thank you, kind sir. It has occurred to me that we have much in common. I was once a samurai myself. Surely you wouldn't think of abandoning a soul mate. I was wounded at the great battle of Yoshiwara, and as you can see, I have never fully recovered," he said, pointing to his eyes.

"You a samurai? What's this about a battle in Yoshiwara?"

"Of course, you don't know of it. You're from Aizu."

"Yoshiwara is nothing but a collection of brothels. No battle has ever been fought there except between whores."

"You are mistaken, sir. There was a fight between several drunkards and me. It was a terrible fight indeed. Don't get me wrong; I'm not proud I sprang from samurai stock. I eschewed that lofty rank long ago and became a scholar. I can assure you that I am not a mere beggar."

"A scholar? I doubt that. I'm tired of your prattle. Tell me a safe way to Edo and leave me." He shook his purse to make his point.

"We must go together," the beggar said as they started down an alley. "I dare not stay here. Come, or I will leave you behind."

"Damn you," Yuki swore as he hurried to catch up. "Tell me where you're going."

"To Edo on a boat, of course. It's safe now that the storm has largely passed. We'll follow the shoreline road to the first village we come across. Then, you need to open your purse and pay a fisherman to take us both."

"You've got a deal. There is one thing, however. I must land near Takahama, a small village south of the Shina River."

"No problem. I know where it is. But why?"

"Never mind, *omae*. Let's go. You'll know soon enough."

"Yes, my lord."

"Finally, some respect!"

"Yes, I am pleased to address you with the appropriate honorific given your station in life, but don't insult me by calling me omae. I'm not a nobody. You should at least call me by my first name. I'm Ichisuke, the scholar, but just call me Ichi."

Shorty taught Yuki compassion for commoners, and he suddenly felt a twinge of guilt. "Very well, Ichi-the-scholar, lead the way," he said with a bemused smile.

# CHAPTER 29

BY EARLY AFTERNOON, they had reached the shoreline of Edo Bay. Six fishing boats lay beached, and Yuki saw a lone fisherman pushing his boat toward the shore in the ankle-deep water.

"How is the fishing today?" Ichi called out to him.

"Terrible. It is always bad after a storm. Look for yourself." He brought his boat closer to shore and pointed to a basket resting atop a tangle of nets. Yuki counted five mackerel.

Ichi asked how much the fisherman would charge to land them near Takahama, and while they haggled, Yuki scanned the shoreline. A man, half-hidden behind an overturned boat, caught his attention. When their eyes met, he slipped behind a web of nets hanging on a drying rack. Yuki waited for him to reappear, but Ichi called him.

"It will cost a hundred *mon* for both of us. Climb in and sit across from me."

Yuki glanced at the drying rack again, but the man was gone. He climbed aboard, and the fisherman raised the luffing sail. He brought the boat about with one arm on the tiller and his other holding two ropes attached to either side of the tail boom. The sail billowed, and the crowded craft cut its way along the coastline. Ichi settled in on the pile of netting and took a mouthful of sake from the small gourd he carried.

Yuki nudged him. "We were being watched."

Ichi took another sip and plugged the wood stopper back into the neck of the gourd. "I know. He's been following us since we left Yokohama."

"What? You knew all along? Who is he?"

Ichi shrugged, pulled the wood stopper out, and took another gulp. "An agent? An informer? They're everywhere. Who cares?"

Bewildered by Ichi's blasé attitude, Yuki closed his eyes. *I've got to be much more careful, or I'll be killed.*

The wind was fickle, and for two hours, progress was slow. By the time they landed three miles south of the Shina River, a smudge of dirty rouge was all that remained in the sky. Yuki paid the fisherman and bought two mackerel.

"Lead the way," he said to Ichi.

"No, I can't go any farther. It's too dark, and my head is hurting." Ichi staggered a few yards, vomited into a bush, and collapsed in the sand.

Knowing it was too dangerous to proceed without Ichi's knowledge of the area, Yuki gathered an armful of driftwood and built a fire. *The sooner I'm rid of him, the better.* "Get up, drunkard, and prepare the fish if you wish to fill your stomach with something other than sake."

Ichi grudgingly gutted the mackerel and skewered them upright close to the flames. He opened his gourd and held it out. "Have a drink," he said.

Yuki had failed to fill his canteen before disembarking in Yokohama, and Ichi persisted. He relented, took a tentative sip, then a gulp. He took several more sips during their meager meal, and when they finished, they settled down to sleep.

Yuki pointed to a small cluster of shacks a mile inland the following day. "It's time to earn your reward. I'm looking for a woman named Kayo and her son Johei. Find them for me. If it is safe, come back and lead me to them."

Yuki shook his purse to make his point. Ichi's eyes lit up, and he set off for the village. It was almost noon when he returned.

"I found the kid. He looks to be about fifteen, but he acts more like a child. Anyway, it's quiet, and a farmer told me there aren't any ronin near Takahama because the villagers are too poor."

"How about Johei's mother?"

"I have no idea. The boy was alone, squatting in front of a shack. He just stared at the ground and didn't answer me. I could tell he'd been crying. His mother probably just gave him a beating."

They found the boy still squatting in the doorway when they reached the shack. Yuki handed a few coins to Ichi. "Go to the village and buy some food for us. The boy looks hungry. Get going. I'll deal with him myself."

Yuki was careful not to seem overbearing. He kept his distance and spoke gently. "Johei, I have come to see your mother and you. My name is Tomita. Pay no attention to the way I am dressed. I am just back from a long journey. I have news about your father."

"You know my father?"

"Yes," Yuki said. "But tell me, where is your mother?"

Johei pointed to a nearby mound of fresh earth. "I couldn't pay for a plot in the temple cemetery, so I buried her there yesterday. She died of bleeding lungs."

Yuki stared at the grave, dulled by the news. *This is going to be hard. There is no easy way to tell him.* "Johei, I have bitter news to tell you. Your father spoke highly of your mother and you. And I…"

Johei interrupted Yuki. "I hardly knew my father. I remember seeing him only twice. What message do you have from him?"

"The news is not good. Shorty was a great friend of mine. It hurts to tell you this, but he died in America."

"Shorty?"

"Uh, yes. It was your father Kansuke-San's American name."

"Sir, how do you know all this?"

"Shorty, I mean Kansuke-San, served me on an important mission for the Bakufu. It was a difficult assignment, and we faced many great dangers."

Johei dried his eyes with his dirty sleeve. "What happened?"

"Thieves attacked us, and your father saved his American friend's life and mine. But in so doing, he was killed. He was as brave as any samurai. Before he died, he begged me to inform your mother and you of his fate."

"Father was from Aizu," Johei said, "but I hardly knew him. He came here many years ago and married my mother. He could not make a living, so he returned to Aizu and became a soldier. Before he did, he arranged for me to be apprenticed to a fisherman, and I learned how to sail a small fishing boat. Father stopped by last year and told Mother he was going to *Meriken* on a secret mission. You must be the samurai he mentioned."

"I am," Yuki said, shaken that the boy knew something about his assignment. "Did he tell you anything about our purpose in going there?"

"No, sir. Mother said we must tell no one what little we knew."

"Good. Revealing your father's story could put you in danger."

"Yes, Master," Johei said, "but does he know?"

"Who?"

"Him," Johei said, pointing to Ichi, who had snuck up behind them and was sitting cross-legged under a persimmon tree.

Yuki reeled around. "Damn you. You've been spying on me."

Ichi shrugged. "I was merely listening. I dared not interrupt you, so I just kept my distance."

"What insolence! You heard everything, didn't you?"

"Yes, and what a sad story it is."

"I'll deal with you later. Remain where you are sitting and do not utter another word," Yuki said, struggling to control his anger. He took off his rucksack and pulled out a heavy pasteboard box containing scores of American and Japanese coins. All together they amounted to more than three hundred dollars.

"Johei, this is your father's reward for saving my life. There's a lot of money here, so spend it wisely and guard it carefully. You can buy a fishing boat and still have enough to live comfortably for a long time. If asked where the American coins came from, say that

your father often traded with foreigners and received them as payment."

Johei made no move to take the box. Puzzled, Yuki set it on the
ground and waited.

"Take it, you little runt," Ichi said. "If you don't want it, let me
have it."

Yuki exploded. "Enough!" He marched over to the tree and
grabbed Ichi by his collar. "Fool!" he shouted.

Ichi resisted, but Yuki threw him down and was about to kick
him when Johei scrambled over and stood in the way. "Master,
please, he means no harm."

Unexpectedly shamed, Yuki glared at Ichi, wondering what he
should do.

"Sir, I beg you not to hurt him," Johei said. "He is a nice man."

Yuki backed off. *The boy must think I am a monster. He does not
know what a danger this beggar poses.*

Ichi pulled Johei's arm from his neck. "It's all right, you little
rascal. What I did was wrong, and I deserve to be punished. Master
Tomita, I will never divulge what I just heard. I promise. I will go
and buy the food now."

Yuki pulled Ichi to his feet. "Just keep your promise and go. Now!"

Ichi brushed the dirt off his bare knees and bowed. "Yes, sir, I
am on my way."

Alone with Johei, Yuki again urged him to accept the money
box, but the boy refused again. There was a look of anxious anticipation about him, and Yuki was at a loss to know why.

To his surprise, Johei fell to his knees and bowed. "Master Tomita, I apologize for my impertinence, but I have a great favor to
ask of you."

"Have you changed your mind about the money?"

"No. It is about my father. You said he had a Meriken name.
Will you give me one too?"

Bemused by the boy's innocent request, Yuki gave it serious
thought. "Johei, stand up. There's no need to grovel. How about the
name Ben? Ben was your father's American friend whose life he saved."

"Ben? Like our word for diligent?"

"Yes, it sounds quite appropriate."

"Oh, thank you, Master Tomita. I am Ben!"

When Ichi returned, Johei announced his new name. Together they kindled a small fire in the shack's cooking pit, prepared fresh seabream, rice, and vegetables…and poured more sake.

"Johei, I mean Ben," Ichi said, "Let me tell you about the big city of Edo."

Ichi prattled on for what seemed like hours before Ben turned to Yuki. "Master, I want to go to Edo with you and Ichi-San. I don't want to live here anymore."

Yuki shook his head. "No. Edo is no place for a boy like you. It is too dangerous. You must stay here."

"Master, let him come with us," Ichi blurted.

"Silence! Do not test my patience again."

"I will not remain silent. Sir, you have demonstrated your compassion by coming here, but instead of helping Ben, you are giving him a death sentence, if you thought about it. He'll probably be robbed and killed if you leave him here with that money. Would you treat a son of yours like that?"

"Edo is crawling with criminals," Yuki said. "They would likely kill him and steal his money."

"You needn't worry, sir. I know of a safe place for us in Edo, and I'm sure you can find a way to send us to Aizu from there. I've considered it and decided to raise Johei and be his protector."

"You want to raise him? I wonder about that. Besides, I'm not sure Aizu is safe."

"Well, it has to be safer than Edo," Ichi said. "You have connections. You could find work for me. I could tutor a wealthy family's kid. Ben and I can go to Aizu by ourselves. I have decided to become his surrogate father. But you? How can you think of leaving a kid here to become a victim as soon as we leave?"

"Master," Ben said, "please do not be angered by our impudence.".

A strange sensation of remorse and annoyance overcame Yuki as he stared at them. *Ichi and Ben have somehow bonded, while I appear to the boy as an arrogant overlord.* He poked the dying fire with a stick, trying to shake off his guilt.

Ichi and Ben watched but said nothing.

Yuki sighed and tossed the stick into the fire when he came to a decision. "All right, you both may come with me to Edo. I will try to find work for you both. Perhaps my uncle or cousin can help. But if Edo proves too dangerous, forget about Aizu. Both of you must promise to return here to Takahama."

"I have no words that could thank you enough," Ben said. "Please forgive me."

"That goes for me too," Ichi said.

"Then it is done. We will leave early in the morning. We must get to the city by nightfall, so let's get some sleep."

# CHAPTER 30

AS THE GROUND FOG slowly dissipated, Ichi led the way down a small road. "It's a roundabout way to Edo, much but safer," he said.

Three hours later, he guided Yuki and Ben onto a well-trodden footpath. It veered north into an area of undulating hills. Birds chattered in the towering cedars while a gentle breeze teased at the leaves.

Ichi tended to meander, so Yuki impatiently took the lead. Minutes later, he sensed something was not right. The birds had fallen silent, and he saw movement in the brush twenty feet ahead. He stopped in his tracks when two men jumped out. One defiantly blocked the path. He wore two swords—a masterless samurai.

"Goro, get with it," the ronin said to his commoner underling. "Bring them up so I can see them better."

Goro pulled out a knife and prodded Ichi closer to Yuki.

"This is my path," the ronin shouted. "No one may travel on it without my permission."

"Please leave us be, kind sir," Ichi said. "We are just poor workers looking for jobs."

Goro took a closer look at Ichi. "Hey, I've seen you before. Don't try to deny it."

Ichi stared at his feet. "I told you already. We're just poor journeymen going to find work in Edo."

"You're lying. We saw you in Yokohama. You were drunk."

"Shut up, Goro," the ronin growled. He pointed to Yuki's rucksack. "What's that?" he said, tapping it with his sword blade. "What have you got in there?"

"Just some clothes, sir."

"Clothes, huh? That pack doesn't look like anything I've ever seen before. Stole it from one of those foreign devils? Drop it and show me what's inside."

"Certainly," Yuki said. *I'll gladly show you a bullet too. Just be a bit more patient.* He twisted out of one strap, but the rucksack slipped off his shoulders when he grabbed for the other.

Upon hearing the unmistakable clink of coins hitting the ground, the ronin grinned. "Well, now, what was that? Perhaps there's more than just clothes inside."

Goro crept behind Yuki and reached for the rucksack. "Stand back," the ronin shouted. "Mind that scum of a beggar and that brat of his," he said, grabbing one of the rucksack's straps.

When he did, Yuki slid his right hand inside his jacket, grasped the handle of his pistol, and cocked the hammer with his thumb.

The loud click startled the ronin. He dropped the strap and carved an airy circle in front of Yuki's face. "Untie your sash and show me what you hide underneath your jacket."

Yuki had to play for time with the ronin, who was close enough to slash his neck. He pulled out his hand and shook it. "See? It's empty. I have nothing."

"Is that so? Then why did you have your hand inside your jacket? Untie your sash, or I'll do it with my sword."

"Sir, all my money is in the rucksack, including several *koban*. Take everything. Just let us be on our way."

"Koban? Gold, you say?"

"Yes, they are yours. Just let us go."

The ronin snorted. "If you are so willing to give up the money, you must be hiding something more. Get down on your knees."

Seeing the look in the ronin's eyes, Yuki knew he could not play for more time. The major once said he could taste fear, and for the first time, Yuki experienced its cold, raw flavor. He had little hope of surviving the swipe of the ronin's sword, but he had to try.

"Hey, asshole, eat shit and drop dead," Ichi suddenly yelled. He pulled down the side of his collar and exposed his neck. "Go ahead and try to cut me first. You're no better than a mouse turd."

"Forget your scrawny neck!" The ronin exploded. "I'm going to gut you!"

"Run for it," Ichi yelled, but Ben froze.

"On second thought, I'll skewer the kid first," the ronin said.

"Blah! Eat my shit!"

"Let me gut the boy," Goro said.

"No! All three of them are mine. Back off."

With the ronin distracted by Goro and Ichi, Yuki slipped his hand into his jacket and pulled out his pistol. "Hey!" he yelled.

The ronin spun around, and Yuki pulled the trigger. The .44 caliber ball shattered the man's skull. Blood, bone, and brain sprayed the air, and the ronin's lifeless body collapsed on the path. Goro turned on Ichi with his knife, but Yuki shot and killed him.

Ben and Ichi ducked and clapped their hands over their ears. "No more, no more!" Ichi cried out.

It is evident to Yuki that neither of them had heard gunfire before. "There's nothing to fear," he said, offering his right hand to Ichi and pulling him to his feet. *This wretched beggar was willing to die to save Ben and me. Why? Why did he do it?*

Finding no answer, Yuki did something he would never have conceived of doing a year earlier. He bowed deeply, addressing Ichi as if he were an equal. "Ichisuke-Sama, I am forever grateful. You saved our lives."

Ichi bowed in return. "It was nothing. Any man would have done the same."

"You're wrong. No other man would have had the courage. You've earned my deepest respect. Come. We must make up for lost time."

"It's like nothing happened," he heard Ichi whisper. "Look at him, Ben. He is a real samurai."

Late in the afternoon, Yuki called a halt near the outskirts of Edo.

"Imperial Army soldiers are everywhere," Ichi whispered. "The city is more dangerous than I thought."

"Finally, you've come to your senses," Yuki said. "Please do not argue with me. Take Ben back to Takahama and keep him safe."

"You're just going to walk into Edo alone?"

"I went to school here. I know the city."

"I'm sure you are familiar with the very areas the rebels control."

Confounded, Yuki wiped his mouth with his wrist. "I suppose you are right," he said, clearly exasperated. "Where would you propose I go?"

"Not just you, all of us. I know a safe place in Yoshiwara."

"Yoshiwara? That ward is walled in, and much of it is surrounded by a moat. How do you propose getting in without being spotted?"

"Ah-ha. So, you *do* know all about the pleasure quarter," Ichi said with a smirk.

Yuki scowled. "I've never been there."

"Whatever you say, Master. But please trust me. I know a safe way to get in."

Ichi seemed so determined and sure of himself that Yuki gave up. "All right. Let's not waste time. Lead the way."

金　金　金

AROUND MIDNIGHT, they crept into the outskirts of Yoshiwara Yukaku, Edo's so-called pleasure ward. Clapboard brothels lined the road, and raucous laughter filtered through shuttered second-story windows. A listless prostitute, her face bruised and bloodied, staggered past them.

Yuki blocked Ben's view of her. "You needn't see such things," he said, casting a knowing look at Ichi.

A moment later, a street vendor appeared from a darkened doorway. "Interested in sharkskin, sir? I have a splendid specimen."

Yuki hesitated. He stopped under the faint yellow glow of a brothel lantern, and the peddler pulled back his straw hat just enough to reveal his disarming smile.

"I have a beautiful piece of it. Look, sir." He opened a lacquered box and pointed to a sheet of sharkskin slathered with a compound of black mud and secret preservatives. "It would make a suitable covering for even the finest sword handle."

"What use would I have of that?" Yuki said.

"You are a samurai, are you not?"

"Hardly. Do you see me wearing swords?"

"Some samurai no longer wear them to avoid being stopped by Imperial soldiers. I assume you to be a fine warrior by the confident way you carry yourself. If you have no interest in swords, perhaps you would consider a dagger. I can sell you a fine one for an excellent price."

Ichi stepped between Yuki and the peddler. "My friend is not interested. He is a merchant from Nagoya, so be off."

Ignoring Ichi, the man persisted. "If you change your mind, sir, I can be found right here. Everyone knows me. My name is Nibei."

Ichi pushed him aside and beckoned Yuki and Ben to follow. "Peddlers around here will try to sell you anything," he grumbled.

The encounter rattled Yuki. *The man knew I was a samurai. Is the way I carry myself that obvious?* It suddenly struck him; he had seen the man somewhere before. He cast a glance over his shoulder, but the peddler was gone.

"I don't like this," Yuki whispered. He pointed to a dark alley. "We will stay here and sleep until it gets light."

# CHAPTER 31

HEY WERE AWAKENED BY the rattling sound of doors and shuttered windows being opened. Storekeepers busied themselves in their shops, and itinerant vendors began spreading their wares along the road.

"Get up, and let's go," Yuki said.

Ichi rubbed his eyes and pointed to a nearby shop. "We need to buy a gift, so keep your purse ready. See that confectionary shop across the road? It's called the Togetsu, and they make the best bean jam confections in Edo. Beautiful, they are. Pay and don't act like a samurai who is too proud to handle money."

"Why do I need to buy a gift?"

"It's for the proprietor of the Bird's Nest."

"Bird's Nest?"

"Yes. It's a wonderful inn, not too far from here. I know the proprietor."

"*Irasshai*," a woman called out, welcoming them to her shop. She fell to her knees and bowed, obviously pleased to greet the day's first customers. "We have some fresh *manju*. My husband made them in the form of small peaches. It won't be long until we can eat the real thing, but in the meantime, buy these. They are very sweet. How many would you like?"

"I'll take seven," Yuki said. Giving an even number of treats, especially four, was taboo. The words death and four are pronounced the same in Japanese. Yuki paid her, and they continued down the road.

Moments later, Ichi pointed to a bridge over the moat separating Yoshiwara from the rest of Edo. "I cannot believe it," he whispered. "The guards have abandoned their posts. No need to bribe anybody. Let's go."

They crossed the bridge, and Ichi led them to a two-story wooden building fronted by an ornamental bamboo gate. "This is the Bird's Nest, one of Yoshiwara's finest inns."

The Bird's Nest was a brothel, and Yuki turned to leave. But he was too late. A girl slid the door open and spotted them. Her face brightened when she saw who it was. "Ichisuke-Sama, where have you been?"

"Shin-chan, it's been much too long. When can we get married?"

Shin-chan giggled. "Master, you are such a rascal."

"Who's here so early?" someone called from inside.

"Two gentlemen here to pay you a visit, ma'am," Shin-chan said.

The proprietress slid open the inner door, and when she saw Ichi, she put her hand over her mouth to muffle a cry. "Brother, where have you been, you old reprobate? You look so thin."

Yuki forced an embarrassed cough. "You are related?"

"I'm Ichisuke's half-sister," the madam said. She appeared to be in her early fifties, her hair neatly coiffed, but she wore a plain cotton kimono. Yuki wondered why.

Ichi nudged Yuki with his elbow. "Oharu is a fine woman, and the Bird's Nest is the best happy house in all of Yoshiwara. Its private bath is quite something. No other establishment has one as sumptuous."

"Ichi, enough of that nonsense," Oharu said. "I have been worried sick about you. And who is this illustrious gentleman?"

Yuki, knowing he looked anything but illustrious, made a shallow bow. "I am, Tomi . . ." he said, stopping short of revealing his family name.

"Welcome, Master Tomi," the madam said without looking the least bit doubtful. "A rather rare name, but I am sure it is that of a distinguished family."

Ichi turned to Yuki. "Sir, I'll explain it all later. We will be treated with great courtesy here." He stepped ahead of Yuki and addressed Oharu.

"Sister, we are not here to indulge in carnality. We just require two rooms, a hot bath, and good food. You must not reveal Master Tomi's presence to anyone and keep Shin-chan quiet about this."

Noting Yuki's troubled expression, Oharu flashed a reassuring smile. "Do not be concerned, Master Tomi. Your secrets are safe with us. Sadly, there's not much going on here in Yoshiwara. Since the troubles started, the rich have kept their heads down for fear of losing them to the drunken ronin who've swarmed into Edo. Only the low-class houses are busy. The last two of my girls disappeared yesterday morning for who knows where. And I must help Shin-chan clean because the other maid left too. I am at my wit's end, and I apologize for what I'm wearing. But don't worry. If you change your mind, I know where I can find a fine courtesan."

"That will not be necessary. Just show us to our rooms. We're exhausted," Yuki said.

After they removed their dirty straw sandals and put on slippers, Oharu led them to adjoining rooms upstairs. One overlooked a small garden and *koi* pond, and the artwork in both rooms appeared to be first-class. But after encountering the sharkskin peddler, Yuki wanted to keep an eye out, so he chose the smaller front room with a window overlooking the road.

"Please rest, sir," Oharu said. "You look hungry. I'll have Shin-chan prepare a snack for the three of you."

Ichi nudged Ben and nodded at the box of manju.

"My master brought something for you," Ben said, presenting it to Oharu.

"Oh, Master Tomi, how generous," the madam cooed as she opened the box and admired the confections.

"Is it possible to prepare the bath this morning?" Yuki asked, dropping his rucksack.

"Of course, but it will take a while to heat the water. I'll provide cotton robes for you, and I'll have Shin-chan launder your clothes after she stokes the fire."

"Kindly have her buy new clothes for us instead. They should be high in quality but not fancy. Nothing to draw attention."

Ichi slapped Ben's shoulder. "Hear that? What a generous friend we have."

Yuki removed his pistol and put it in his rucksack when they were alone.

"Neither one of you shall touch my belongings."

"No, sir, never. And don't worry about Oharu or Shin-chan," Ichi said. "Such is her business that Oharu prizes honesty and secrecy. Surely you recognize that by now."

"That may have been true a year ago, but now I trust no one."

Minutes later, Oharu returned with a tray of green tea and *yokan*, small blocks of sweetened bean jam made with agar.

"Madam Oharu," Yuki said, "please join us. I have been away for a while, and I'm anxious to hear what's been going on in Edo." He took a sip of tea, and Oharu sighed as she filled his cup again.

"There is no good news. As part of a brokered deal, the shogun exiled himself to a temple outside the city, and his castle was turned over to Imperial Army soldiers. Scores of them wander the streets looking to pick a fight. Bakufu stragglers are leaderless, but they are ready and willing to accommodate them. Just as bad are the ronin who think nothing of breaking into homes and stores and stealing things."

Yuki could hardly bear to listen. His uncle and his cousin might have been killed. He dismissed Oharu and dolefully watched Ichi and Ben finish their snacks.

Two hours later, Shin-chan announced that the bath was ready. They disrobed in the bath's anteroom and left their clothes in baskets. Ben had never seen a spa before, and Ichi cheerfully taught him the finer points of bath etiquette. They squatted on wooden stools and scrubbed the dirt from their skin with small bags of pulverized rice hulls. They poured bucket after bucket of hot water over their heads, and Yuki vigorously scrubbed his skin until he felt truly clean for the first time in months.

He stepped into the bath and gingerly lowered himself into the piping hot water. Ichi and Ben followed, But Yuki could barely see them through the steam. He put a damp towel on his head, closed his eyes, and leaned against the side of the wooden tub while Ichi and Ben chattered.

"You must call me *sensei* if I am to be your teacher," Ichi said.

"Yes, sensei."

"Can you recite the alphabet?"

"Yes, sensei: a, i, u, e, o, ka, ki . . ."

"No, no. I mean the alphabet poem, which contains all the syllables in our language.

Ben recited it without hesitation:

> *"Even as the scent still lingers,*
> *The flower's petals have scattered.*
> *What in this world remains unchanged?*
> *Arriving today on the other side of the mountains of existence,*
> *We will not allow ourselves to drift away, drunk by shallow dreams."*

"Perfect! Now tell me how to write the word for the cherry tree."

"That's easy," Ben said. "The tree character is on the left, long and thin, with two small shells on the right, above the character for a woman."

"So, there is some hope for you after all," Ichi said. They laughed, and Ichi began regaling Ben with absurd stories he seemed to invent as he told them.

While they chattered, Yuki repeated the Buddhist alphabet poem to himself. Every Japanese knew it. The poem reaffirms one of Buddhism's central tenets: the transient nature of all things.

They climbed out of the bath, their reddened bodies steaming in the cool air of the anteroom. They dried themselves, put on robes Shin-chan had left, and hurried to their rooms.

# CHAPTER 32

NIBEI STOPPED TO CATCH his breath at the top of the stone staircase leading to Myogon-ji, the Buddhist temple that shared space with a Shinto shrine.

He had important information for his new master and hoped to be rewarded for what he had discovered this time. He found Kuroi Taketo lurking in the shadows near Goddess Inari's shrine. Onishi, a down-and-out ronin bodyguard, stood nearby.

Nibei lost his job serving Oki Izo, the Choshu spy, when the latter was ambushed and killed by a squad of policemen led by Kuroi, who claimed to be a Bakufu agent. Nibei had his doubts, but it did not matter. He needed protection; The Choshu rebels had put a price on his head when rumors circulated that he had played a role in Oki's assassination. As he approached his new overseer, he noticed Kuroi looked tired, even worried.

"Well, what is it?" Kuroi snapped. "Out with it."

"Master, I saw Tomita Yuki. He is back in Japan... the samurai I tailed to the Meriken warship last year."

"Tomita? Are you sure?"

"I'm positive. He's thinner than the last time I saw him, and he disguises himself as a commoner. Three days ago, he landed in Yokohama aboard a Meriken ship. I caught sight of him surrounded by armed guards and sailors. They marched to the foreign settlement, where a French military officer at the barricades greeted him. They appeared to be friends, and while they spoke, the guards and sailors proceeded to the French compound, where they turned over several large crates."

Stunned by the news, Kuroi grabbed the hilt of his sword. "Are you telling me the truth, or are you just trying to wheedle money from me?"

"Oh, no, sir. I would never do that."

"Then go on," Kuroi said.

"Well, Tomita headed into town afterward, and I had to run to catch up. I discovered him standing by the body of a customs officer and a shop owner the rebels had murdered. Nearby was a drunkard. His name is Ichi, and...."

"Nibei, stop right there. You mentioned something about sailors and the crates they were carrying. How many were there?"

"The crates?"

"Yes, damn it."

"Five, sir."

"Describe them."

"They were cumbersome, wide, and quite tall. It took four men to carry each crate into the embassy compound."

"Ha, I knew it," Kuroi said, turning to Onishi. "His cousin Nariaki was right. Tomita failed, and now he is back."

"Is there anything else, sir?" Nibei asked, nervously staring at Kuroi's hand clutching the hilt of his sword.

"How could you see the Americans carrying the crates to the French compound? Foreigners do not allow men like you into their settlement."

"I have a secret way in. Near the warehouses. I saw everything quite clearly."

"There were no Aizu soldiers with Tomita?"

"No sir, no Japanese at all."

"The French?" Kuroi mumbled as he paced back and forth in front of his men. "Of course, the French—They must be involved. He left it with them for safekeeping."

"Left what?" Onishi rashly inquired.

Ignoring his bodyguard's indiscretion, Kuroi turned to Nibei. "Where did Tomita go afterward?"

"He and that drunkard I mentioned hired a fishing boat at a small village and sailed away. When the fisherman returned hours later, I learned that Tomita and Ichi had landed just south of the Shina River. I knew I couldn't catch up with them, so I paid another fisherman to take me to Edo."

"You lost Tomita?"

"No, sir, I knew where that scum Ichi is known to hang out, and I got there before they did. They showed up in Yoshiwara, just as I expected."

Relieved to see Kuroi relaxing his grip on the hilt of his sword, Nibei continued with more confidence. "A boy joined them somewhere along the way," he said. "I gather he's Ichi's son. They have taken rooms at a first-class bordello called the Bird's Nest."

Kuroi wandered over to the shrine of Inari, the deity variously revered as the goddess of the harvest, the protectress of warriors, and the guarantor of success. Two large stone likenesses of wily fox demigods, also called *inari*, guarded the walkway leading to the shrine. One held a stone scroll in its mouth, symbolizing its additional role as a messenger to the gods. Both glared down at Kuroi, who stood among hundreds of ceramic foxes scattered on the ground, some as small as pebbles. He was certain Inari was watching his every move from behind the two small doors of her shrine.

Onishi and Nibei tried to follow, but Kuroi stopped them. "Get back to the Bird's Nest and keep an eye on things. I expect Tomita will visit his cousin soon," he said. "Make sure he doesn't run into a rebel checkpoint to his uncle's estate. Follow him and protect him at all costs."

Nibei wanted to leave with Onishi, but Kuroi stopped him. "Put your hand out," he said.

"My hand?"

"Yes. Do it now. You look guilty. Do you think I'm going to cut it off?"

"No, Master. I would never think such a thing. It is my pleasure to obey your every word."

Kuroi burst out laughing. He reached into his purse and dropped a rectangular silver coin into Nibei's open hand. "Now, go do your work."

Greatly relieved and pleased with the unexpected reward, Nibei dashed off to catch up with Onishi.

# CHAPTER 33

ICHI, BEN, AND YUKI lounged in their new clothes waiting for their evening meal. Oharu, dressed in a red and gold kimono, served *kaiseki*, a special dinner consisting of several courses. She filled Yuki's sake cup while Shin-chan filled Ichi's and Ben's.

Shin-chan cleared the table when they finished the last course, and Oharu bowed and left.

Ichi poured more for Ben and himself. "A toast to our great benefactor, Master Tomita."

They drained their cups and drank a second round. Within minutes, their eyes were bloodshot, and their faces were bright red.

"Let's have another," Ichi said.

Ben held his hand to his mouth. "No more, sensei. Please excuse me. I feel dizzy." He pushed himself up from the table and stumbled into the adjoining room.

Yuki glanced disapprovingly at Ichi's sake flask. "You've had too much to drink as well," he said.

"You're right, sir," Ichi said with surprising determination, "No more for me. I'm swearing the stuff off as of now."

Pleased with Ichi's oath, Yuki decided it was time to tell him his plans for the next day. "Ichi-San, tomorrow I will report to my uncle. His country estate is a very long walk from here. You cannot accompany me, and you must not leave the Bird's Nest. I need not tell you how dangerous it is. I will return late tomorrow afternoon or early evening and prepare a letter of introduction to my younger brother asking him to find employment for both of you. He lives in Aizu."

"You are indeed a high-minded gentleman," Ichi said. He paused for a moment and bit his lower lip. "But sir, how long do you intend to remain in Edo?"

"I have business in Ikuta, a small village in Kawasaki Province. It will take me a day or so to get there. When I return to Edo, I'll spend the rest of my time at my uncle's estate."

"Ikuta? I've been there twice. It's depressing. Just a bunch of impoverished bumpkins toiling in the ankle-deep mud of their rice paddies."

"That may be true, but my elder brother's remains are buried in a temple cemetery nearby. It's the third anniversary of his death, and I am obliged to have a sutra recited in his memory. Do not mention this again. It's personal."

"Yes, Master. I beg you to ignore my indiscretion."

"Enough of that. It is time we slept."

Ichi retreated to his room, leaving the sliding door open the width of a chopstick. Yuki noticed, but he did not bother to close it the rest of the way. Sitting alone, he reflected on the events since arriving in Japan, but his thoughts soon turned to his plans for the next day.

Yuki was familiar with the Edo accent, and in the few days he had been with Ichi and Ben, he had learned to mimic it. But if enemy soldiers were to catch him and discover his pistol, they would dispatch him on the spot. He concluded that he must leave his belongings behind and hope to be let go if the rebels were to stop him.

A whisper of doubt about Ichi's constancy insinuated itself in Yuki's mind, but he recoiled at the thought. *How can I think such a thing? He put his life on the line for me. But Shin-chan might be sorely tempted. She could easily make off with my belongings.*

Hiding the rucksack in the closet was too obvious, but his eyes fell upon the tatami mat next to the window. He stood it on end and placed the rucksack between the floor joists. Satisfied it would not be found, he lowered the mat and slept.

Before dawn, he left the Bird's Nest, avoiding the main roads and the crowds. He changed directions several times, glancing furtively at people lurking in the shadowed alleys.

# CHAPTER 34

YUKI MADE THREE CIRCUITOUS detours to avoid Imperial Army checkpoints, arriving at his uncle's estate in a heightened state of anxiety. Bakufu officials might demand that he commit seppuku if they were to learn of his failure. Worse still, Kuroi might be chosen as his replacement.

The gate officer recognized Yuki and sent word of his arrival. While he waited, he scanned the grounds, surprised by the scores of soldiers camping in the garden. Another officer appeared and ordered Yuki to follow. As they approached the main house, Nariaki appeared. "You're back!" he shouted. "I knew you would make it. Welcome home!"

Yuki's pent-up anxiety eased somewhat upon hearing his cousin's welcoming voice. They entered the apartment and sat across from each other at a table in the middle of the room. Yuki asked about his uncle, but Nariaki's expression said it all.

"When we received your letter three weeks ago, we were relieved to learn you were safe. But Father blamed himself for what you had to go through. He passed away last week."

Taken aback, Yuki muttered a brief prayer. "I'm sorry, Cousin. He was like a father to me."

"I know," Nariaki said with a bleak smile. "Thanks to him, you and I became more inseparable than brothers could ever be."

They looked into each other's saddened eyes, Yuki wondering what other news his cousin had for him. Nariaki poured two cups of barley tea and slid one across the table. His mood noticeably changed. His eyes brightened, and a broad smile dispelled the gloom.

"Yuki, not all is lost. I have some good news to share with you. I am sending you back to America."

"What? You have the authority to do so?"

"Yes. Months ago, when Father knew his end was near, he petitioned the shogun and the governor of Aizu for permission to transfer his titles and duties to me. It was largely a meaningless gesture because the shogun was about to abdicate. But in effect, I became commander of all Aizu units scattered outside our home province. And more importantly, Vice-Admiral Enomoto has agreed to put what remains of the Bakufu navy at my disposal."

"This *is* good news, Cousin. Congratulations."

"No need for that. Tell me what happened to you."

Yuki spent two hours recounting his journey from Yokohama aboard the *Lackawanna* until his return.

"What about Butler's daughter?" Nariaki asked. "She was a very difficult woman, as I recall."

Yuki did not reveal their relationship. Instead, he praised her for saving his life and helping to solve their dilemma. "Mary knows Captain Whitfield, John Manjiro's benefactor, and she is certain that he will help us upon his return from his latest voyage."

"That is excellent news."

"Speaking of help, in my letter to your father, I asked him to secure a letter of introduction from John Manjiro. I wish to prove to Whitfield that I am a legitimate Bakufu representative. Did Manjiro provide him with one?"

"Sadly, no. Father died before he could contact him. Anti-foreign elements of the Imperial Army want to kill Manjiro, and Father dared not disclose his whereabouts."

Yuki shrugged and took a sip of tea, summoning his courage to ask the question that had plagued him for months. "Am I not to be punished?"

"Of course not. We failed you. No one is even alive who could demand it. You may recall that Lord Hara chose not to tell the shogun about your mission. Have you forgotten that he was assassinated shortly before you left?"

"No, I haven't, but Minister Oguri knows about the mission because he amassed the gold and prepared it for shipment."

Nariaki pursed his lips. "Another tragedy. Oguri was executed."

"How could that have happened?"

"The leader of the Choshu rebels agreed to make Edo an open city after the shogun abdicated, and they took over the castle. They expected to find a treasury full of gold, and when they found it empty, they assumed Oguri had absconded with it. They tracked him down, but he refused to divulge the truth. He was beheaded, as were several of his family members. His death is a great loss to our cause, but the point is that the mission has remained secret, and you will have a warship at your disposal three months from now."

"Three months? Cousin, that's much too long to wait. The round-trip voyage, including the detour to Cuba, will take at least three hundred days. Aizu will be overrun by then."

"Yuki, you've been listening to too many rumors. The ill-disciplined Imperial Army outnumbers us, but it is fraught with dissension between the Choshu rebels and their allies. I need not tell you that Aizu's army and our northern allies are stronger, better led, and more determined. I am in the process of gathering our outlying forces. Those you saw in the garden are just a few of them. In September, Enomoto's troopships will arrive in Kawasaki. The troops you see outside will sail north to Sendai and march to Aizu. Enomoto's flagship, the *Banryu*, is heavily armed and manned by an experienced crew."

Yuki smirked upon hearing the warship's name. It meant *Coiled Dragon* in English. "The name alone will scare the rebels into retreat," Yuki snickered.

Nariaki laughed. "I expect it will. Anyway, we will rendezvous with Enomoto in Yokohama and sail to Sendai. There, the *Banryu* will be resupplied, and then off you go. When you return to Japan with the repeating rifles, we will kill every rebel in our path."

"But what if they learn about your plans?"

"They won't. Though I trust Enomoto implicitly, I will not give him his final orders until we reach Sendai. That way, our secret can't slip out. And make no mistake, we will succeed. Ambassador Roches has promised to provide a warship to keep rebel ships from interfering with us on our way to Sendai."

"But the French are a party to the neutrality agreement."

"It hasn't stopped Roches from helping us."

"Nariaki, please be more specific. What happens when I return with the rifles?"

"The Imperial Army has neither the resources nor the confidence to move against Aizu. At least not yet. But by next year, there will be a showdown, and we will whip them with those rifles you mentioned in your letter to Father. What else is there to say?"

Nariaki's enthusiasm was encouraging, but Yuki remained unconvinced. "How can Ambassador Roches ignore Napoleon's orders to remain neutral?"

"He's a bit devious, that's why. Besides, Captain Brunet and his men are committed to us, and French naval vessels continue to prowl our coastline. Mark my words; if Roches sticks with us, we will prevail."

An attendant interrupted them and entered with a tray of rice balls sprinkled with toasted sesame seeds. They paused to wolf down the food, and when Yuki finished, he wiped his fingers on his sleeve.

"You play the role of a mannerless commoner rather convincingly," Nariaki said. They both laughed.

"Yuki, I am concerned about one thing. Are you sure the gold is safe in that cemetery?"

"I am positive."

"That's a relief," Nariaki said. "By the way, Kuroi Taketo will assist you on your mission."

Yuki had expected the revelation, but he was still shocked. "Kuroi? You know full well my opinion of him. He might not have been involved in the assassination attempt against Butler, but he is a real troublemaker."

"Let me put this bluntly," Nariaki said. "Be realistic. You will need someone who speaks English. If something…"

"If something, what?" Yuki fumed.

"Let me remind you that your former schoolmate, Kato Yozo, was second-in-command when you left on your voyage to America, but he died on the *Lackawanna*. That could happen again; only you could die this time. Can you imagine Vice-Admiral Enomoto landing in Boston without knowing how to find or even deal with Captain Whitfield and Butler's niece? Imagine him wandering about with a squad of samurai in Boston. How could he not attract unwanted attention? So, calm yourself. I've made the decision, and it stands."

Resigned to the inevitable, Yuki stared at the dregs in his teacup. "You're right. I allowed my lingering animosity to color my opinion of him."

"I'm glad you see it that way. Kuroi is a changed man. You will see when he visits us."

"Nariaki, I don't mean to be difficult, but please do not order me to stay here. I am planning to visit Tomoyoshi."

"Your elder brother? How is he? It's been years since you told me about him. Did he not become a wandering monk begging for his next meal?"

"Yes, but he took over the duties at Daiten-ji two years later. It's a small temple a day's walk from here. Tomoyoshi got married and now has a daughter. Needless to say, it's a long story. Please keep this to yourself."

Nariaki stroked his chin. "I suppose you would be safe in Ikuta. After all, the area is still quite loyal to the Bakufu. Do you know the Grand River Inn?"

"The one overlooking the Tama River?"

"That is the one. Let's agree to meet there on September twenty-four. It is the ideal place to finalize our plans while we wait for the *Banryu* to make port in Yokohama. If anything changes, I'll contact you."

"I deeply appreciate this, Cousin. I will certainly pass on your regards to Tomoyoshi."

"Yuki, back to the subject at hand — Just know that things will be different this time." Nariaki clenched his fists and squinted as though he saw the vibrant rays of a new dawn.

"With the Aizu army and our northern compatriots armed with those repeating rifles, we will relieve Edo and sweep westward, taking the head of every traitor. Vice-Admiral Enomoto's fleet will handily destroy the enemy navy and level Choshu's coastal batteries. Fence-sitting provinces will fall over themselves to join us in our march to victory."

Nariaki swallowed the remaining tea in his cup before continuing. "Oh, and by the way, as you are well aware, the daimyo of Aizu is related to the Tokugawa family."

"Yes, but what of it?"

"When we win, Tokugawa Yoshinobu will be reinstalled to his rightful position, and our daimyo has promised that you will become our new foreign minister plenipotentiary, just as Father promised."

Nariaki struck the table with his fist to make his next point. "Together, our generation of Aizu samurai will lead Japan into the modern world. Onward!" he shouted.

Awed by Nariaki's optimism and surprising news, Yuki no longer felt the gnawing despair he had lived with for so long. He leaped to his feet, grabbed his cousin's hand, and shook it Western style. "Nariaki, I do not doubt we will succeed, all thanks to you."

After the meeting, they briefly toured the camp, where Yuki visited several old friends. He was more convinced than ever that Nariaki's assessment was correct: The spirit of Aizu's army would carry it to victory over the Imperial traitors.

"I'll send a couple of men to guard you on the way back," Nariaki said.

"That's not necessary," Yuki replied. "I'll be safe." Buoyed in spirit, he set out for Edo alone.

# CHAPTER 35

KUROI STOOD NEAR THE snarling fox statues at Goddess Inari's shrine entrance. Two guards he recently hired lingered nearby. Kanbei was a rifleman and a deserter from one of Aizu's allies. The other was a local bully named Chobei, a name made famous by a thug who lived in Edo two hundred years earlier. He often bragged that he had been a sumo wrestler, and by his girth, Kuroi had no doubt the story was true.

Despite a monthly stipend from Yuki's cousin, Kuroi had little money to spare. He cautiously approached the shrine and stared warily at the scores of small granite foxes. He dropped two coins in the donation box in front of Goddess Inari's shrine and whispered a prayer. He had learned that assassins were out to take revenge for his betrayal of Oki, the Choshu spy, and he felt his back was against a wall. He needed all the protection he could get.

"It's taking too long. Nibei and Onishi should be back by now. Where are they?" he asked Chobei.

Chobei replied with a disinterested shrug.

"Damn your insolence. Go to the Bird's Nest and watch for Tomita."

"As you wish."

Kuroi did not miss the troubling smirk on Chobei's face. "Just watch. Don't do anything stupid. No drinking."

"I'm on my way," Chobei said without acknowledging Kuroi's warning.

"I'd better go too," Kanbei said.

Events were moving quickly, and Kuroi sensed rebel agents were getting close to discovering his whereabouts. "Remain here with me," he said, trying his best not to sound panicky.

Escaping from Japan was his only hope, but he needed money to live abroad. The shogun's gold was his only answer, and if Yuki were to be killed before he could get his hands on it, Kuroi knew his chances of survival were nil.

An agonizing hour later, Onishi and Nibei appeared. "We followed Tomita back as far as Yoshiwara. He's safe now," Onishi said.

"Good work. Now, get back over there and join Chobei. Don't let Tomita out of your sight. You and Nibei follow him wherever he goes. If he's caught, he'll be killed"

"You sent Chobei?" Nibei blurted.

"Of course. Why do you ask?"

"That scum Ichi owes him money. Chobei could cause trouble."

"Why was I not informed of this before?"

"Sir, I did not know you intended to send him."

"Never mind. Get over there now. The three of you."

Left to himself, Kuroi dropped several more coins into the shrine's donation box. "Great Goddess Inari," he murmured, "protect Tomita Yuki and me from harm."

Kuroi knew Aizu spies would sooner or later learn about his complicity in the attempted assassination of Major Butler. When that happened, the rebels would vie against Nariaki's agents for the honor of taking his head. Playing the traitor's game had backfired, and time was not on his side. His only hope was to buy his way to safety.

# CHAPTER 36

YUKI REACHED THE BIRD'S Nest after dark. The front door was locked, but he heard a familiar voice when tapping it.

"The Bird's Nest is closed. There is no one here."

"Shin-chan, let me in. It's me, Tomi. Where is Ichi?"

Seconds passed before she slid the door open and pushed aside the shutter, peering cautiously outside. "I'm sorry, Tomi-Sama. Everyone is gone."

"Gone?" He craned his neck and looked up the staircase. "Ben, Ichi, come down here. I'm back."

No one answered.

Shin-chan cowered, too distraught to speak. Yuki pushed her out of the way and rushed up the stairs. He threw open the sliding door to his room and saw the tatami mat by the window had been pulled up and cast aside. His rucksack was gone.

"Ichi did this, Yuki yelled in English. "He spied on me from the other room. I should never have trusted him." He rushed downstairs and confronted Shin-chan. "Where are my belongings?"

Trembling uncontrollably, she could barely speak. "Ichi and Ben took them and ran away. My master too."

"Ran away? Why? Where?"

"I don't know," she blubbered. "After you left, Ichi and Ben went out for a walk. When they came back, Ichi went upstairs and took everything. My master gave me some money and told me to buy some onions. When I returned, I found a note telling me to close the Bird's Nest until she returned."

"I should have known. Ichi has betrayed me." Yuki shouted.

Shin-chan hunkered in the hallway while he stormed through the inn, searching for clues Ichi might have left. "I was a fool to trust that shit-for-brains!" he shouted. "When I catch him, I'll blow his head off!"

It was an empty threat. Ichi had the pistol, and looking for him in Edo would be too dangerous. Yuki reached into his purse and nervously fingered the few coins he had left. *I must get out of Edo now. That rat must have poisoned Ben's mind and turned him against me.*

He dashed to the kitchen and started packing some food and water for his journey. Seconds later, a commotion erupted at the front entrance. He peered down the hallway, not knowing what to expect.

"Chobei, you're hurting me," Shin-chan cried out as the huge man shoved her out of the way.

"So, you're the one," Chobei shouted when he spied Yuki. He pulled out a knife and strode toward the kitchen entrance.

Yuki grabbed a knife but dropped it when he noticed a pot of water boiling on a charcoal brazier. He grabbed its handles with a towel, and when Chobei charged into the kitchen, Yuki heaved the scalding water into his face. Chobei dropped his knife and screamed, pawing his face as if he were fighting off a swarm of wasps.

Yuki pushed him aside, threw open the back door, and dashed into the darkness. A few minutes later, when he stopped to catch his breath, Yuki heard a familiar voice. He ducked between two derelict buildings and peered out from behind a pile of trash. He saw two men, one of whom he recognized as the sharkskin seller. The other was a ronin.

"Split up," Onishi said. "We need to find Tomita. Meet back at the bridge and be careful of Chobei. He's probably drunk."

Yuki remained hunkered down after they left, and a few moments later, Chobei came clumping down the alley, moaning and swearing. "Where are you, Tomita? I'm going to flay you alive." His footsteps faded, but Yuki waited a few more minutes before leaving the confines of Yoshiwara and sneaking down to the water's edge of Edo Bay.

A fishing boat appeared out of the gloom, gliding silently toward the shore. It landed, and a boy jumped out.

"Father, a stranger," he said, pointing at Yuki. The fisherman pushed his son behind him and pulled out a knife.

"Have no fear," Yuki called out. "I need your help. My wife is heavy with child, and I must return home. Can you take me as far as the Tama River?"

"I'm busy," the fisherman said. "Find someone else."

Yuki held out his last silver coin, and the man reached over the prow and grabbed it.

"Don't just stand there gawking," he said to his son. "Help me push off."

Yuki waded into the water and climbed in. A favorable breeze arose, and three hours later, the boat entered the Tama River estuary. They passed the dim lights of Kawasaki, and the fisherman sailed farther up before maneuvering the boat onto a graveled shoal. Yuki jumped off and scrambled onto the riverbank. Exhausted, he curled up under a gnarled cedar tree.

A few hours later, he awoke in a daze. The attack at the Bird's Nest made no sense, and his thoughts turned to Ben. *Is he in on the plot, or was he forced to betray me?*

Yuki had no answer. He had a long walk ahead of him and had to reach his brother's temple before nightfall.

# CHAPTER 37

IT WAS A BUDDHIST custom then, as it is now, to buy fortunes at temples written on strips of white paper. Believers tied the lucky ones onto the branches of a persimmon tree near the Myogon Temple entrance, hoping to be blessed with good fortune. The morning after Yuki fled Edo, Kuroi pulled a lone slip of paper from the lowest twig. It was a message from Nariaki.

"We must leave immediately," Kuroi said to his men.

"Where to?" Onishi asked.

"Tomita is safe at his uncle's estate, and I must meet him. Nibei, you stay in front of us and watch out for any trouble."

"What about Chobei?"

"He's lucky I didn't carve his guts out. He can stay behind and nurse his burns."

Four hours later, Kuroi was greeted by a guard, and he saw Nariaki talking with Captain Jules Brunet near the pond. *What luck! This is no accident. They must be discussing the disposition of the gold at the French embassy.*

Kuroi tried to listen to the conversation, but a senior officer kept him at bay. When Brunet departed on horseback with a squad of French soldiers, Nariaki greeted Kuroi and led him to his apartment.

"I have important news," he said. "Yuki has just returned from America. Things are falling into place."

Kuroi feigned surprise. "This is good news," he said. "Where is he? I did not see him outside."

"He's not here. He's in Edo, but you will see him soon enough."

"Nariaki-dono, he needs to get out of Edo now. It is far too dangerous. Do you know where he is? Let me afford him some protection. Better yet, I'll bring him back here."

"There's no need for worry. I expect he's already left Edo."

"He's on his way?"

"Yes, but not here. Somewhere just as safe."

"Does this mean we will soon be leaving for America?"

"No. That is why I've summoned you. Vice-Admiral Enomoto is having problems assembling his flotilla. He will not be ready to sail anywhere until late September."

The news was grim. Kuroi feared Nariaki's agents were close to uncovering his duplicity; when they did, he would have no place to hide. Both the rebels and Nariaki's men would vie for the chance of hacking him to pieces.

"What must we do in the meantime?" he said.

"The three of us will rendezvous at the Grand River Inn overlooking the Tama River," Nariaki replied.

"That's a good place. I know it well. But what about the gold?"

"Enough of your questions. You will know soon enough. Remain here with your men until we depart."

"Please, sir, I must attend to many personal matters in Edo. I am well-protected thanks to your generous stipend."

Nariaki considered Kuroi's plea while he tightened the shoulder belt of his Western-style uniform. "Very well, but you must check for messages at Myogon Temple every day. The situation is in flux, and our plans may change again."

He led Kuroi to the front gate and gave him a final warning. "Keep your temper under control and your curiosity in check."

Nariaki's rejoinder angered him, but on his way back to Edo, one thought calmed Kuroi's fury. It made no sense that Captain

Brunet's visit was to coordinate the transfer of the gold to Nariaki at the encampment. Only a handful of French advisors were in the area, while the Imperial soldiers were numbered in the thousands. They could easily overwhelm the French, kill all of them, and make off with the crates. *Ambassador Roches undoubtedly agreed to safeguard Yokohama's gold until Vice-Admiral Enomoto's arrival.*

"We've got a lot to do before September," Kuroi told his men.

# CHAPTER 38

*Late June 1868*

YUKI CAUGHT SIGHT OF the Grand River Inn through the twilight murk, and moments later, he came across two ferrymen about to beach their craft. He shook his last few coins into their hands, and they poled him across the river.

An hour later, he stumbled upon a three-foot granite column beside the road. Unable to see the chiseled characters, he read them with his fingers. "Daiten-ji: Temple of the Great Heaven," he said. "I've made it."

Yuki felt his way up the hill's uneven stone steps. Close to the temple gate, something snagged his left ankle. Dried bamboo canes clattered overhead, and when he bent down to disentangle his leg, something hard and heavy struck him between his eyes. He crumpled onto a mossy bank, and for a moment, he lay in a semiconscious daze. He squeezed his eyes shut, attempting to wring the excruciating pain from his head.

A dim light passed back and forth in front of his face, and he heard agitated voices. He felt strong hands lifting him by his armpits, and someone grabbed his ankles. Then nothing.

Hours passed before the sun's rays spread across the floor. Yuki sensed he was not alone. He could hear someone breathing.

"Brother, are you awake?"

Yuki forced his eyes open upon recognizing his elder brother's voice. Buddha of the Western Pure Land gazed placidly down at him from the temple's altar.

"Tomoyoshi, what happened? Where am I?"

"Just rest. I made your bed in front of the altar."

Someone whimpered nearby, but Yuki was too weak to turn his head.

"Master, it's me," Ben said. "Please forgive me. I was the one who clubbed you. It was dark, and I thought you were a thief."

"Master, it's not Ben's fault. I made him stand guard on the path last night."

Yuki recognized the voice through his clouded mind. It was Ichi's. His head throbbed, and it took time for Yuki to absorb what Ichi had said. He did not speak until a door to the left of the altar slid open, and a young girl peered at him.

Yuki could not sit up, but he turned his head. "Saori-chan," he said groggily, "how you've grown. Come here. Let me see you more clearly."

Saori blushed when her father motioned her to sit by Ben, who was sitting next to Ichi.

Seeing Ichi and Ben again sent Yuki's mind into a spin. *What are they doing here?*

"Do not blame either of them," his brother said. "I planned everything. Last month, thieves stole all my rice and broke into the donation box. We did not expect you until today. Why did you come at night?"

"W-when I...I returned to the Bird's Nest, Ichi and Ben were gone, and so was my rucksack. Then a thug—Chobei was his name, tried to kill me. I wrongly suspected . . ."

"It is understandable you would have suspected me," Ichi cut in with surprising impertinence, "Yes, we took your belongings, but you forgot about our conversation over dinner at the Bird's Nest."

"What about it?"

"You told me of your plans to visit your brother's grave in Ikuta. Daiten-ji was easy to find. But imagine my surprise to learn your brother is quite alive."

"I shouldn't have lied to you, and it was wrong of me to suspect you of stealing my things. Please accept my apology."

Ichi turned to Ben. "Shall we accept an apology from a raccoon?"

Ben glanced at Yuki's two black eyes and burst out laughing.

Yuki laughed, too, though his heart hurt more than his head.

Sensing it was better to leave, Tomoyoshi motioned Saori and Ben to follow him outside.

Yuki struggled up with Ichi's help. "I'm glad you took the rucksack," Yuki said when they were alone. "Otherwise, it would have fallen into the wrong hands. But why didn't you wait until I returned?"

"Because we were in danger. Despite your warning not to leave the Bird's Nest, I visited a friend in his nearby cutlery shop. I'm alive for having disobeyed you. I was sitting in the back having tea when Chobei ambled in. I ducked just in time. He asked my friend's wife if she'd seen you, me, or Ben, but she said she hadn't. And on my way back to the Bird's Nest, I spotted that sharkskin peddler. That is when I knew we had to get out of Edo."

"Well, it was good that you disregarded my warning," Yuki said. Tired and still in pain, he slumped back down on the *futon*. Ichi left, and Yuki closed his eyes.

*That sharkskin seller shadowed me from the day I landed in Yokohama. My mission is not a secret. How stupid of me not to realize it before. Who gives him orders? The Imperial Army?*

The thought chilled him.

YUKI TOSSED ABOUT ON his bed, trying to understand how the secret of the mission and his return to Japan had gotten out.

He considered returning to Edo to warn his cousin, but he dared not go. Instead, he chose to wait things out.

That evening, he staggered outside to breathe the fresh air and watch the fireflies flash about the cemetery. "Mary, I love you and miss you so very much," he said to the new moon rising above the temple. "I will return to you. I promise."

# CHAPTER 39

To EXPLAIN THE PRESENCE of three strangers, Tomoyoshi asked Ichi to pose as a novice monk. He readily agreed, and Saori shaved his head. During the shogunate, Japanese children attended temple schools where the local priest taught them to read, write, and use the abacus. Ichi gladly assumed Tomoyoshi's teaching duties. His wandering eye and warm but eccentric behavior quickly captured the hearts of the village children. Tomoyoshi also informed the curious that Yuki was another novice monk who had come to the temple to recuperate from an apparent injury. Saori shaved his head as well.

Ben became Saori's cousin, and he joined her in class. He helped her draw fresh well water each morning, and he helped her in the kitchen each evening. Tomoyoshi, Yuki, and Ichi spent the warm evenings on the temple veranda while the two teenagers strolled about the grounds with fireflies flashing about their feet. They often heard Saori giggle at Ben's rustic accent.

Yuki told Ichi and his brother about his pending mission, confident that the secret was safe with them. But Ichi seemed more interested in another mystery. "*Osho-Sama*," he said when he addressed Tomoyoshi, "may I ask why you chose to eke out a living as a Buddhist priest? After all, you were a samurai from a proud Aizu family."

Tomoyoshi took a sip of tea and gave Yuki a knowing glance. "Ichisuke-San, it's a long story. One rainy day, a fishmonger splashed mud on the hem of my kimono as he dashed by. He did not stop to apologize, and I chased him down. I was sorely tempted to behead him."

"Did you?"

"No. I was suddenly struck with the contemptibility of my vanity. It was as though an unseen hand kept me from unsheathing my sword. I had never experienced such shame. I told the man to be more careful and sent him on his way."

Ichi finished his tea and stared at Tomoyoshi in disbelief. "What did you do next?"

"An instantaneous transformation overcame me. I cannot explain it save that Lord Buddha called upon me. I spent several weeks meditating and fasting, almost dying from the lack of food. In the end, I renounced my samurai status and announced my decision to become a monk. My father tried to dissuade me, but I refused. He disowned me in anger and had my name stricken from the Tomita family records."

"Then what happened?" Ichi asked.

"It is a story that happily changed my life. After two years of study and strict discipline at a monastery, I began wandering the countryside with a begging bowl, seeking enlightenment. However, I realized that Lord Buddha wanted me to minister to the sick and poor rather than selfishly meditate on my existence's meaning. One day, I happened upon Daiten-ji while looking for a safe place to stay the night. The priest was on his deathbed and pleaded with me to take over his duties. How could I not? He died. I married his daughter, but she died after our child was born. Only Yuki and his cousin Nariaki have known about me until now."

"Do not worry," Ichi said solemnly. "Your secrets are safe with me."

"I'll vouch for that," Yuki said.

# CHAPTER 40

*September 1868—Daiten-ji*

YUKI LEARNED FROM A villager that the Imperial Army had wiped out a contingent of Aizu soldiers in a battle not far from Edo. Ex-shogun Tokugawa Yoshinobu had been captured and sent to a distant province under house arrest. Yuki feared for his cousin Nariaki, but he could do nothing but wait and pray, something he did with his brother.

Another villager told him a "big Bakufu sea general" was starting something called a "republic" on Japan's northernmost island. Villagers spread rumors daily, but the last was the most outlandish one Yuki had ever heard. Hearing them made the days seem to drag by.

金　金　金

SEVERAL DAYS BEFORE HIS long-awaited rendezvous with Nariaki and Kuroi, Yuki wandered the temple grounds with his brother. Near the entrance to the small cemetery, Yuki told him more about his pending voyage to America.

"Have you thought about Ichi and Ben?" Tomoyoshi asked.

"Given the uncertain situation, please allow them to stay here until I return."

"That's what I was hoping you'd say. Ben is a bright boy and very helpful. And I cannot do without Ichi's help in the classroom."

Tomoyoshi began to finger the wooden beads of his rosary. His lips barely moved as he muttered a silent prayer.

"What is it, Brother?" Yuki asked.

"Can I not persuade you to forsake this mission? The cause of the Bakufu is hopeless, and there has already been too much bloodshed. Do you want to be part of that by bringing back those monstrous weapons?"

"Cousin Nariaki is counting on me. "Besides," he whispered, "a personal reason compels me to go."

"Oh? And what might that be?"

"There is an American woman who carries my child. Perhaps she has already borne it. I plan to wed her."

Tomoyoshi did not appear to be shocked. "Are you so attached to her?"

Yuki smiled and nodded.

"Ahh, now I understand. That explains how you've mellowed. Only a woman could accomplish such a miracle."

"America changed me, Brother. I can no longer call myself a samurai," Yuki said.

"On the contrary, you are an exemplary one. You are as driven as you have always been, but there is certain compassion about you now, something you lacked before. It's obvious by the way you treat Ichi and Ben."

"I suppose it is a defect we share," Yuki said.

"An agreeable defect, nonetheless," Tomoyoshi replied.

They wandered back to the temple, where Yuki gave his brother the heavy pasteboard box. "Take it. It is expense money that I never used. There is enough to keep you, Saori, Ichi, and Ben in comfortable circumstances for a long while. I was going to give it all to Ben, but his circumstances have changed for the better."

"We can manage, Brother. You needn't be so generous."

"Consider it a donation. Ichi and Ben want it this way too. Please pray for my success."

Moments later, Ichi barged in. "Tomita-Sama, Ben and I have decided to go with you."

Yuki shook his head. "It is not possible. Besides, you are needed here."

"No, no, we want to see Meriken."

"If it were in my power, I would allow you to come, but I have no say in the matter. I must follow the orders I have been given, and I expect you to follow mine."

Ichi attempted to argue his point, but Yuki's growing impatience was a warning he could not ignore. "Master, please forgive my indiscretion," he said as he bowed deeply, "I will do as you say."

Later that evening, Yuki sat cross-legged with his hands on his lap. He closed his eyes, and his brother chanted the Heart Sutra in front of the seated statue of Buddha:

> *Form is emptiness, and emptiness is form,*
> *Life was transient. Life was suffering—*

After the ceremony, Tomoyoshi went to his study and returned with a bundle in his arms. He sat down and unwrapped it. "You surely recognize these," he said, pointing to two swords and a dagger. "Why I have kept them, I do not know, but you may need them now."

Tomoyoshi's face was devoid of expression, but Yuki sensed his brother's deep, unfathomable sadness. Killing another human, even an enemy soldier, was an anathema.

Yuki picked up the long sword and ran his fingers across the lacquered surface of the scabbard. "I would be honored to have these, but I would have no use for them in America. You should sell them."

The swords were meant to kill, and Yuki knew that Tomoyoshi's love for his brother and fear for his safety overcame his pacifistic vows. To accept the blades meant that he might kill with them, and Yuki was not about to burden his brother with such guilt.

"However, allow me to take this," Yuki said, picking up the eight-inch *tanto*, or dagger. It could serve only one purpose as far as he was concerned, and he wondered if Tomoyoshi knew what it was.

Yuki got his answer when tears welled in his brother's eyes.

Later, while everyone slept, he sat down and wrote a letter to thank his brother for agreeing to take in Ben and Ichi.

# CHAPTER 41

KUROI SLIPPED INTO YOKOHAMA in early September and met with a Dutch shipping agent. For twenty guilders or approximately 225 US dollars, the shipping agent agreed to book Kuroi on the *Kosmopoliet II,* a Dutch clipper ship. It was expected to make port around the twenty-third of September. A week later, it was to set sail for Batavia, the capital of the Dutch East Indies.

Kuroi also agreed to pay an additional seven guilders in equivalent dollars to transport five heavy crates of personal items, all payable before boarding. With plenty of money he assumed was awaiting him at the French embassy, Kuroi gave the agent a gold *koban* as a down payment. Batavia would be the perfect place to start a comfortable new life, safe from an assassin's blade.

He wanted to introduce himself to the French ambassador, but he feared that Nariaki or Yuki might learn of his meeting, so he reluctantly returned to Edo. Doing away with Nariaki and Yuki would have to come next, something he thought would be easy. But Ambassador Roches' willingness to release the gold was the big question.

IN LATE SEPTEMBER, Kuroi received an urgent message from Nari-aki. He was to join him on the first leg of their trip to Komae, a small village not far from the Tama River. The Imperial Army avoided the area, and Komae was considered safe. Kuroi sent his men ahead to lie in wait near the village, and on September twenty-second, he and Nariaki set out with a retinue of more than two hundred soldiers.

"We will spend the night in the village with two of my body-guards while the rest of our troops continue to the port town of Kawasaki," Nariaki said. "A troopship will be waiting for them. Vice-Admiral Enomoto will land in Yokohama on his flagship to-day or tomorrow and be waiting for us."

"But what about Tomita-Sama?"

"We'll meet him at the Grand River Inn and stay overnight. It will give us time to rest and strategize before continuing to Yoko-hama. Captain Brunet and the French ambassador will be waiting to meet with me upon our arrival."

Nariaki's comment reaffirmed what Kuroi believed to be true: the French had the gold. "I can hardly wait to reconnect with your cousin and Captain Brunet. "But does Enomoto know of our plans to sail to America?"

"No. But after we set sail for Sendai on his flagship, the *Banryu*, I will inform him of his mission. You, Yuki, and I are the only ones who know about this. I will disembark in Sendai, and the ship will be provisioned for your long voyage to Boston. Thirty of my best men will accompany Yuki and you, and I will lead the rest of my troops to Aizu."

Everything was falling into place for Kuroi's plan to succeed, save for three problems. He was confident he could solve two of them, but the third one troubled him: Ambassador Léon Roches.

Kuroi knew he had to prove his right to take ownership of the gold, and he supposed Yuki or Nariaki possessed some sort of cer-tificate allowing a holder to take possession. He believed Roches would never release the gold unless he could present him with such a document.

Late that afternoon, Nariaki and Kuroi stopped in Komae to spend the night. They took separate rooms at a small inn, and the two guards were ordered to patrol the perimeter. The remaining two hundred Aizu soldiers continued their march to Kawasaki.

Just before dawn, Nariaki heard a rifle shot. He sat up and reached for his long sword, but Kuroi burst into his room and thrust the point of his sword within inches of his neck.

"Make one move, and you die," Kuroi said. "Tell me what I need to know, and I promise you won't suffer. What arrangements have you made to load the gold onto Enomoto's ship?"

Nariaki stared at the sword blade without flinching. "I should have listened to Yuki. You are a traitor."

"I'm warning you, where are the documents?"

"Documents?"

"Documents for the release of the gold. Do you have them, or does Tomita keep them?"

"You have no idea what you are talking about."

Kuroi quickly scanned the room and saw something. "Maybe I won't need your help," he said, reaching for a satchel on the floor next to Nariaki's sword.

Nariaki slid both hands under his bedcovers, and Kuroi heard him pulling a dagger blade from its sheath. Before Nariaki could pull it out, Kuroi plunged his sword into his heart.

Blood seeped through the cotton bedcover, forming a growing red blotch while Kuroi rummaged through the satchel. He grabbed a heavy purse full of coins but found no documents. He took a kerchief from his sleeve and squeegeed the blood off his sword as he pondered where they might be. A red drop fell from the blade's tip and landed on his right *tabi*, one of two split-toed socks worn with sandals. He ignored the stain and went outside.

He found his men standing by the two dead guards. Chobei was arguing with Onishi.

"The entrance guard was mine to take care of, but you killed him," he yelled at Onishi. "Master Kuroi, I should get a reward, not him."

"Stop arguing with one another. All of you have done well," Kuroi said. "There's no need to argue." He shook out a handful of silver coins from Nariaki's purse and dropped a few into each of his men's open hands.

"We've got to leave now. Nibei is waiting for us across the river, and so is Tomita. Do not forget that I want him taken alive."

# CHAPTER 42

RELOADING THE MAJOR'S PISTOL took time. Yuki carefully measured out gunpowder and packed it under a lead round in each of the six chambers. He then inserted six brass percussion caps on the nipples upon which the hammer would strike.

After he finished, Yuki said a last goodbye and set out for his rendezvous. When he reached the Tama River, he saw the same two ferrymen he had hired in June. They sat on their punt-like ferry having lunch and did not bother to look his way. One hundred paces downstream from them, an older man was busy caulking the hull of his beached fishing boat.

Gladdened at the prospect of seeing his cousin, Yuki started up the hill to the Grand River Inn. He saw Kuroi waiting for him on the veranda as he drew closer. *Where is Nariaki? Has he not arrived?* Yuki's heart began to race. Something seemed amiss.

"Welcome, Tomita-dono," Kuroi said. "It's been far too long since we last met. A meal has been prepared for us. Let's go in and eat."

Yuki stepped onto the veranda, where he and Kuroi perfunctorily bowed and uttered the usual flattering greetings. When he bent down to untie his sandals, Yuki puzzled over what appeared to be fresh blood on one of Kuroi's tabi. A maid ushered both guests inside before he could ask about it. A table in the center was set only for two.

Yuki's concern mounted as he unshouldered his rucksack. With Kuroi closely watching, he removed his brother's dagger and placed it on the floor, keeping his pistol concealed. When both were seated, the maid served them a tray of appetizers and drinks.

They poured sake for each other, but Yuki had no time for a toast. "Kuroi-dono, where is my cousin?"

"You have not been told?"

"Told what?"

"It happened in June when I was at your uncle's estate. Our mutual French friend, Captain Brunet, had just left. Your cousin set today for our rendezvous and started to tell me the details of our mission."

"So, where is he?"

"It is hard to tell you, but I must. I heard the crack of a rifle shot and your cousin collapsed in my arms. He had been struck by a bullet and died within the hour. Gate guards chased down a Choshu sniper and killed him. I would have told you earlier had I known where you were hiding."

Yuki was dumbstruck. He stared into his sake cup as he fought to keep control of his emotions. His cousin was dead.

Seemingly unaware of Yuki's despair, Kuroi gulped down his sake and poured more for himself. He called out to the maid, who was waiting outside the room. She brought another tray of sake and set two more flasks on the table.

After the maid left, Kuroi continued. "I regret that I must be so abrupt in your time of sorrow, but now we must discuss our mission."

"What is there to discuss?"

"Our plans have changed. Vice-Admiral Enomoto will not rendezvous with us in Yokohama."

Yuki's mind was muddled in grief upon hearing the news—so much so that he could not fully comprehend.

"Listen up, Tomita, the Bakufu is no more," Kuroi said, using language used when speaking to an inferior. "Enomoto and our remaining forces are gathering in Hokkaido. Believe it or not, he has established a republic."

"A republic? Where did you hear such a thing? Enomoto has probably already landed in Yokohama and is waiting for us."

"Not so. I've made other plans. You must understand that I'm now in charge of the mission. Enomoto appointed me to head it. He is *not* on his way to Yokohama. He has his hands full running the new government. Tomita, you must face the bitter facts."

A villager had told Yuki about a new government on Hokkaido Island the week before, but he had dismissed the story as another bizarre rumor. But he now realized it could be true.

"Kuroi-dono, if what you're telling me is true, all is lost," Yuki said. "We must return to Aizu and help defend it against the Imperial Army."

Kuroi shook his head with a scowl and banged the table with his cup, spilling his tea. "The enemy is not strong enough to attack Aizu for at least another year, and I have had the foresight to charter a Dutch ship. It will sail to the Netherlands and Boston with the gold you left at the French embassy. I will buy the rifles and deliver them to the Ezo Republic. The *Kosmopoliet* may have already made port in Yokohama. You are to return to Aizu, and I will take care of the rest. Ambassador Roches must release the gold to me. Surely, you were given a voucher as proof of ownership. I'll need it to claim the gold."

*The gold? So that's what this is all about?* Yuki ground his teeth so hard his jaw hurt when an image of Kuroi's blood-stained tabi flashed in his mind's eye. *He murdered Nariaki.*

Kuroi ignored Yuki's harsh glare. "Tomita, will you please give me the proper documents? And I want you to write a note to Roches explaining why I am to take custody of the gold."

"Listen, Kuroi-dono. I agree with you. The gold must be re-trieved," Yuki said, "but...."

"Good. You've come to your senses. The *Kosmopoliet* will leave as soon as the gold is taken aboard.

"Nariaki did not tell you, did he?" Yuki said, casting a furtive glance at Kuroi's sword.

"What do you mean?"

"The French do not have the gold. I don't know where you heard such a thing."

"What?"

"It's true. I left it in America."

"That's absurd. In June, you returned on an American ship, and armed American sailors transported the gold to the French embassy. Brunet was there. My agent saw it all happen."

"Oh, so that's it. The sharkskin seller is *your* spy. I wondered who he was. But never mind him, let me set you straight. I did meet Captain Brunet that morning. He was charged with guarding the entrance to the foreign settlement. He said the crates your agent saw contained Western clothing for the ambassador's mistress and furnishings for the French embassy."

Angered by what he believed was Yuki's attempt at deception, Kuroi gulped down the rest of his sake. "Do you expect me to believe you left the gold in America?"

Yuki's mocking grin ripened into a contemptuous laugh. "I'm telling you the truth. I was unable to conclude a deal for the rifles. I'm sure Nariaki told you that much, right?"

"Yes, but the gold, damn you, where is it?" Kuroi sputtered.

"It was too dangerous to bring it back to Japan. How could I? As you must know, our classmate Kato died aboard the ship on our way to Boston, and so did his attendant. The *Tora* never showed up, Kansuke, my attendant, was murdered, and Major Butler died of a heart attack. I had no choice but to leave the gold with my American mistress. She hides it."

"Nonsense," Kuroi said, grabbing the hilt of his sword. "The French ambassador has the gold." Yuki reached for his pistol, but a commotion erupted outside, and both men leaped to their feet.

Ichi charged into the room, almost out of breath. "Sir, I came to say one last goodbye, and you must take Ben with you. We are all in danger," he shouted, pointing at Kuroi. "His henchmen are hiding behind the inn, and I overheard them. They plan to torture you."

"Damn you!" Kuroi shouted. He started to unsheathe his sword, but when he saw Yuki pulling out his pistol, he overturned the table and slammed it against Yuki's arm. The collision caused the gun to discharge, and the bullet struck the ceiling. Kuroi bashed his way through the maid's door in the back of the room before Yuki could fire again.

"Master, leave him," Ichi said, waving the gun smoke from his eyes. "We must get out of here now. That sharkskin seller is here too. He is hiding near the ferry."

Yuki grabbed his belongings and jumped off the veranda. Ben was waiting with a bedroll slung over his shoulder. "Master, they're coming," he said, pointing uphill.

Yuki took off toward the boat he had seen on his way to the inn. "Ichi, Ben, follow me," he yelled.

"After them!" Kuroi shouted, and his men followed, dashing down the hill.

The startled elderly fisherman dropped his spool of caulking twine at the river's edge and shoved his boat into the water.

"Help us, or they will kill you too," Yuki said, shaking his coin-laden purse. "I will pay you well." He and Ben followed the fisherman into the water and climbed aboard.

"Master, they're after Ichi-sensei," Ben cried out.

Yuki was alarmed to see Ichi intentionally luring Kuroi's men away. Ichi tripped and fell on the ferry mooring line tied to a large rock, and the two ferrymen scattered when they saw what was about to take place. Onishi got to Ichi first, pulled him up, and he and Chobei dragged him back to Kuroi, who stood waiting near the shore. Chobei shoved Ichi down and pulled out his knife.

金　金　金

THE FISHERMAN'S FEVERISH PADDLING sent the boat onto a sandy shoal in his haste to maneuver the boat into deeper water. He jumped out and grappled with the prow.

"Good luck, Master. Keep Ben safe," Ichi shouted.

"Tomita, if you want to save his life, come back," Kuroi yelled.

Yuki pulled out his pistol and cocked the hammer. "Chobei, drop your knife and let him go, or you're a dead man."

"Tomita, this is what you get for throwing scalding water in my face at the Bird's Nest," Chobei shouted. He reached down and slit Ichi's throat.

"Sensei!" Ben cried out. He tried to jump overboard, but Yuki grabbed him.

"Don't do it. Ichi forfeited his life so that we could escape. Be still for me." Yuki wrapped his arm around Ben's chest and set the pistol barrel on his shoulder. "Plug your ears, and don't move."

He fired, but the round kicked up the sand in front of Chobei's feet.

"Ha!" Chobei shouted.

Yuki fired again. This time he did not miss. Chobei fell face-first into the river sand and did not get back up.

Alarmed, Kuroi and Onishi retreated, but Kanbei stood his ground and raised his rifle.

"Kill the fisherman," Kuroi yelled.

Yuki fired at Kanbei. The round came close but missed its mark, and Kuroi's rifleman scuttled away from the shoreline.

The jittery fisherman pushed the boat free and climbed back on board. Yuki started to paddle, and the fisherman maneuvered the ship into mid-river with his tiller.

When he saw the boat pulling away, Kuroi started running. "To the ferry!" he shouted to his men.

Nibei was waiting for them with the mooring line in hand. They jumped in and found two poles used to maneuver the ferry. Nibei and Onishi started to pole the boat toward the middle of the river, where the deepest water was.

The tidal waters of Edo Bay largely governed the Tama River's flow. The tide was in flood, slowing the river's current. Yuki paddled as hard as possible, but the ferry kept pace.

The Grand River Inn faded in the distance, and Ben, thoroughly dispirited, choked back his tears. He started reciting the alphabet poem he and Ichi had done so many times before:

*"Even as the scent still lingers,*
*the flower's petals have scattered—"*

# CHAPTER 43

KUROI PACED THE DECK of the flat-bottomed ferry, shouting orders to his men. Onishi and Nibei synchronized their poling, and the larger craft kept pace with the fishing boat. Kanbei steadied his rifle on the prow and waited.

Yuki helped the fisherman hoist the sail, but it drooped in the still air. The hull leaked badly, and the old man ordered Ben to bail. An hour later, they entered the Tama River estuary, and the sound of Kuroi's ranting grew louder as the ferry began to close the gap. Kanbei pulled the hammer back on his rifle and waited for Kuroi's command to fire.

"Tomita, surrender now," Kuroi yelled.

"Pay no mind to him. Steer us into the bay," Yuki said to the panicked fisherman.

"No, I dare not. My boat is leaky and too small to cross open water. We'd be swamped."

"I will pay you in silver."

"No, I must land the boat."

"Fisherman," Kuroi yelled, brandishing his sword, "pull your boat about, or I'll slice you up for bait!"

The panicked fisherman pushed hard on the tiller and forced the boat to veer toward the port-side shore.

"Get down!" Yuki yelled.

Kanbei fired, and the fisherman grasped his chest, groaned, and fell overboard. Yuki grabbed the tiller and tried maneuvering the boat away from the shore, but it started to wallow.

"Ben, jump! Swim ashore and run," he yelled.

"No, Master. Out of my way. I am a fisherman's apprentice, remember? I can sail this boat." He calmed the luffing sail and pointed to the tiller that Yuki was ineptly pulling and pushing. "Master, I beg you, remove yourself and leave it to me."

Yuki hesitated, but noting Ben's unexpectedly determined expression, he scrambled past him and knelt on a pile of netting. He steadied his pistol on the gunwale and bit his lower lip. Ben grabbed the tiller and fed out the rope attached to the starboard side of the sail boom.

Moments later, Yuki saw his chance, took a deep breath, and fired. Kanbei's rifle fell overboard, and he fell dead on the deck. Yuki cocked the pistol hammer again. Kuroi ducked, but his head and shoulders were visible. It was a difficult target, but Yuki aimed and fired.

The bullet missed, and to his amazement, Kuroi stood up, seemingly unafraid. Yuki cocked the hammer and squeezed the trigger again, but the hammer struck a spent primer. Kuroi had kept a count of the shots, but Yuki had not. With no time to reload the pistol and only a dagger to protect himself and Ben, Yuki knew the chances of survival were nil.

"Tomita is out of bullets," Kuroi shouted. "Pole harder. We're almost within reach."

"Stay down," Yuki said to Ben. "I'm going to swim ashore, and they'll go after me. When I jump, land the boat on the far shore, and run. Find your way back to Daiten-ji and tell my brother what has happened. Good luck!"

Yuki tore off his sandals and grabbed his rucksack. But when he took one last look at the ferryboat, he saw Onishi and Nibei staring at each other with their poles out of the water.

"Dammit! Start poling!" Kuroi yelled. "We're losing them!"

"The water is too deep," Onishi shouted. "The poles can't reach the bottom."

Kuroi could do nothing but watch while the current carried the ferry toward the opposite shore. Yuki dropped his rucksack and patted Ben on his shoulder.

"You did it. You saved us."

"Sit down, Master. You're in my way." Ben pulled on one rope and fed out the other, holding the tiller steady under his left arm. The sail billowed, and the fishing boat entered Edo Bay minutes later.

Yuki noticed an ominous bank of clouds to the southwest. "Ben, stay close to shore and set your course for Yokohama," he shouted.

Ben sniffed the air and looked at the clouds sweeping in. "Master, the wind will not favor us. We'll be swamped if I try. We must sail across the bay and wait until the storm passes."

Yuki gripped the gunwale and stared bleakly at the receding shoreline. Over 200 of Nariaki's men were stranded in Kawasaki and rescuing them would be Vice-Admiral Enomoto's top priority. If Yuki did not quickly show up in Yokohama, Enomoto would likely not wait, and returning to America would be impossible.

# CHAPTER 44

KUROI KICKED AT THE sand in a silent rage. Onishi avoided eye contact while Nibei squatted, poking a bleached oyster shell with a stick.

Kuroi pointed to several fishing boats beached nearby. "Nibei, how long will it take to get to Yokohama on one of those?"

Nibei glanced skyward while he calculated. "Three, maybe four hours, sir."

"Hire one of them and be quick."

They landed in Yokohama in the late afternoon and found the foreign settlement in a state of panic. With Edo Castle in the hands of the Imperial forces and the shogun under house arrest, Westerners feared the worst. They were well acquainted with the fearsome rebel slogan *Sonno joi*—Revere the emperor and expel the barbarian. The main entrance to the foreign settlement, Yoshida Bridge, was blockaded. Dutch and French artillerymen stood nervously behind barricades; their cannons gorged with grapeshot.

Japanese were prohibited from entering the settlement unless a Westerner accompanied them, but Nibei knew a way in. They crossed a wide, stinking ditch and squeezed between two warehouses.

"*Bonjour, mes amis,*" Kuroi called out to the first French soldiers they came upon. A corporal and two privates stopped in their tracks and raised their rifles. Kuroi held up his arms and forced a brave smile. "*Parlez-vous Anglais?*" he said in his tortured French accent. When the corporal nodded, Kuroi continued. "I must see *le Captaine* Brunet. He is *mon ami*. I am Kuroi Taketo from Aizu."

The uncertain soldiers motioned Kuroi and his men to squat in the dirt while the corporal ran to the French ambassador's compound. In the meantime, Kuroi watched dozens of civilians and soldiers scurrying about the embassy grounds with luggage. It was apparent they were preparing to decamp.

A few agonizing minutes later, Captain Brunet appeared, the man Napoleon III had personally chosen to advise the Army of Aizu. Brunet's face lit up. He dismissed the guards and gave Kuroi a hearty handshake. They kissed each other on both cheeks while Onishi and Nibei looked on in disbelief.

Brunet greeted Kuroi in English because his Japanese was limited. "My dear friend, how unfortunate we must meet under such circumstances. The rebellion has jeopardized the French diplomatic mission, and Napoleon has ordered the embassy to be temporarily closed."

"Has your emperor abandoned us?"

"Yes," Brunet said with fire in his eyes, "but my men and I will remain here without our government's blessing. Be assured that we will never betray you. We are brothers born of the sword and will fight at your side until victory is ours. His Excellency Ambassador Roches has reluctantly acceded to my demands. We sail tomorrow morning for Hokkaido Island aboard the French corvette *Dupleix*," he said, pointing to the warship at anchor.

"We will pick up stragglers along the way and join Vice-Admiral Enomoto's soldiers to defend the Republic of Ezo. But enough of that," Brunet said. "You and your men look exhausted. I'll see that you are given rations and a place to sleep. By the way, how is your colleague Monsieur Tomita? It has been three months since I last saw him."

Kuroi's spirits soared upon hearing Yuki's name. "You must have met him here in late June."

"Yes, I did, but all too briefly. He returned on an American merchant ship. He told me that he had been on a secret mission in Hong Kong."

Kuroi moved away from where his men stood and addressed Brunet in a hushed, confidential manner. "That is true, and Ambassador Roches agreed to take temporary custody of some heavy wooden crates for the Bakufu until Tomita-Sama or I came to retrieve them."

"I clearly recall them. They were quite heavy, but none of them were consigned to your government. They contained clothing, various furniture, and housewares for Ambassador Roches. Monsieur Tomita asked about buying a horse, but none were available for sale. I assume he made it safely to Edo."

"There is some misunderstanding," Kuroi said. "I was informed that Tomita delivered those crates to the ambassador for safekeeping. I'm sure of it."

"No, monsieur," Brunet said, holding his hand close to his mouth to whisper. "Excellency Roches showed me their contents. The finest furniture from Paris and beautiful lingerie for his Japanese mistress."

Kuroi scanned the bay, but the *Kosmopoliet II* was not at anchor. All he saw was the *Dupleix*, and he started to hyperventilate.

"Monsieur, are you feeling unwell?" Brunet said.

Kuroi caught his breath and pointed to the harbor. "I don't see Vice-Admiral Enomoto's warship anywhere."

"Ah, yes, the *Rancune du Dragon*, the *Banryu*, as you say in Japanese. When it approached the mouth of the bay this morning, three rebel warships closed in on it, and Enomoto barely escaped. It is said he will sail to the town of Hakodate, where we believe the defining battle of the rebellion will be fought. We can only hope for a favorable outcome," Brunet muttered.

Kuroi looked down and kicked a pebble. *And my only hope is that Tomita has survived the storm. Goddess Inari, I beg of you, save him!*

After Brunet left, Kuroi gathered his men and addressed them in a whisper. "I expect Tomita to show up in the next few hours, or at the latest, early tomorrow morning. We must get to him before he can contact the French. Hide outside the settlement along the road leading to Yoshida Bridge. If you spy him, he must be captured, and you must let me know immediately. I will stand guard by the warehouses. Kill the boy, but I want Tomita alive."

"What if Tomita fails to show?" Onishi asked.

"In that case, he's probably already making his way to Aizu."

金　金　金

YUKI AND BEN DID not show up, and Kuroi met with Brunet the following day.

"Captain, it is imperative that my men and I get to Aizu and join forces with my comrades. Will you allow us to accompany you to Sendai? Tomita Yuki is said to be in Aizu standing on the castle battlements, and I expect to fight alongside him."

"Of course, you may, but we will pick up stragglers from the Northern Alliance along the way. Why not join us to fight for the new republic?"

"Duty demands that I stand with Tomita Yuki to defend Aizu."

"Ah, *quel courage*. Such spirit will surely prevail over the rebels."

"Courage, yes. But all of us are in a race against time."

# CHAPTER 45

Late in the afternoon, the storm turned the gentle wave-
lets of Edo Bay into spitting whitecaps. Ben piloted the boat
close to the opposite shore and eased it atop a six-foot wave,
sending the craft crashing onto a stony beach. He and Yuki
watched benumbed as the surf smashed the hull, and the wind
ripped the sail.

"Look, a lean-to," Ben said, pointing to a dilapidated hut. "It's
a temporary shelter for fishermen."

They huddled together until the storm moved on and the sky
cleared. Yuki scanned the bay one last time, but the *Banryu* was
nowhere to be seen. He bitterly concluded that Kuroi had told the
truth; Vice-Admiral Enomoto was not waiting in Yokohama to
pick him up.

The oilcloth-wrapped contents of Yuki's rucksack and Ben's
bedroll were dry, but their clothes were soaked. Using Benjamin
Butler's tinderbox, Yuki started a small fire, and Ben nursed it into
a roaring blaze. They put on dry clothes and hung their wet ones
in the lean-to rafters.

While they sat, Yuki removed the cord from his neck. He wiped
Mary's locket dry and tested the key he had worn since the night
of Shorty's murder. It was still tightly attached to the cord. Finally,

he oiled his brother's dagger, disassembled the pistol, and oiled each part with a cotton cloth.

"To a samurai, such firearms are profane. I spent many years perfecting my skills with a sword, but I am no match for this. With a few minutes of practice, you could easily kill a samurai. But doing so with such a device would be shameful. It has no soul, unlike the cold purity of a blade." Yuki gave the pistol cylinder a spin as if to make a point.

Ben crept closer. "Sir, may I hold it?"

Yuki held out the pistol, but Ben shook his head. "No, not that, sir. The other one," he said, pointing to the locket.

Surprised, Yuki clicked it open and handed it to him. Ben delicately brushed Mary's porcelain likeness with his little finger.

"Are you keen for her?" he asked. It was an indirect way to ask if a person loved another.

"I am," Yuki said, "I'll tell you about her some other time, but it is time for us to sleep." As the stars gazed down upon them, he considered Ben's fate.

*If I survive all this, I shall adopt him and petition the Daimyo to give him samurai status. It is the least I can do for Shorty.*

# CHAPTER 46

Yuki counted on finding a Japanese coastal freighter bound for the north in the small port town of Kizaru. He guessed they were ten *ri* or about twenty-four miles from the town, but within the hour, he detected the unmistakable odor of coal smoke and heard the throbbing beat of a steam engine. A minute later, he spotted a column of black smoke.

Yuki and Ben ran to the top of a small ridge, where they spied a three-mast, paddle-wheeled gunboat. An unfamiliar pennant whipped wildly atop the mainmast. They crept closer and saw soldiers lining up to board. A pennant bearing the Tendo Domain crest, an Aizu ally, was affixed to one soldier's backpack.

"Let's go!" Yuki shouted. They ran down the slope to the pier just as the last soldiers were trudging up the gangplank. Through the din, Yuki heard someone call his name.

"Tomita-dono, it's me, Toshio."

Yuki quickly recognized Ishida Toshio, a samurai from Dewa Province, another Aizu ally. He and Ben scrambled aboard, and Ishida greeted them.

"What's happened to them?" Yuki said, nodding at the troops.

"Elements of the Imperial Army cornered my unit. We broke out, and this ship, the *Takao Maru*, miraculously came to our rescue.

Imperial forces now control everything to the south and west. Our province joined the Northern Alliance, and Vice-Admiral Enomoto has established something called a republic on Ezo Island. People are starting to call the island Hokkaido. Don't ask me why."

"Is this vessel bound for it?"

"Yes. The great fortress in Hakodate Harbor is now Enomoto's provisional capital. That's the Northern Alliance's pennant," Ishida said, pointing to the mast where a black flag emblazoned with a white star whipped in the wind.

"Aizu is part of the new alliance, right?"

"No. Aizu Domain has chosen to go it alone."

The time spent at his brother's temple had isolated Yuki from the catastrophic, fast-moving events, and the new information was appalling. Aizu was planning to go it alone against the Imperial Army.

"Where is the rest of Enomoto's flotilla?"

"Somewhere north of here if Choshu warships haven't destroyed it. The *Takao Maru* managed to evade them, but three other troop-carrying vessels were captured. Tomita-dono, the situation is bad. Very bad. The *Banryu* was seen steaming north yesterday with three rebel warships in hot pursuit."

"Yesterday?" Yuki said, unable to hide his growing desperation.

"All I know is what the captain told me," Ishida said, grasping Yuki's shoulder. "Are you coming? The sailors are getting ready to raise the gangplank and cast off."

"Will the *Takao Maru* make port at Sendai?"

"No. It's in the hands of the Imperial Army already. We expect to pick up stragglers in Yotsukura, a small port south of Sendai, and then proceed to Hakodate. That is if Choshu warships don't intercept us." Ishida paused a moment to let the news sink in. "Tomita-dono, you must decide quickly. Are you with us? You need to disembark now if you aren't."

With a battle brewing in Aizu, Yuki assumed his brother Yoshi and the White Tigers would be defending the daimyo's castle. He had no other choice. "Ishida-dono, we will sail with you, but because Sendai is out of the question, we'll disembark at Yotsukura. I am undecided whether the boy will come with me. If not, I will pay you to care for him."

Ishida agreed, and Yuki glumly watched the sailors raise the gangplank and drop the last line. The steam engine shuddered, and the paddle wheels began churning. All eyes scanned the horizon as the *Takao Maru* entered the open waters of the Pacific. A stiff wind arose, and the captain ordered the sails to be unfurled. The smokestack belched one last cloud of smoke, the engine pounded to a stop, and the wind-swelled sails carried the warship northward through the cobalt blue waters.

As dusk overcame the vessel, Yuki stared bleakly at the waves below. *Fate is preparing a final blow. Unless Aizu defeats the Imperial Army, I have no hope of being with Mary again.*

Yuki and Ben were each given a rice ball and some hot tea that evening. They sat eating with their backs against a bulkhead, and when they finished, Yuki announced his decision. "Ben, you must sail to Hakodate with my friend. The town is far from any fighting. When it is safe to return, I will call for you."

"But Master . . ."

Yuki flashed an impatient look, and Ben demurred. He knelt and pressed his forehead on the wet deck. "Master, I promise to obey you."

Yuki pulled him to his feet as tears welled up in Ben's eyes. "Crying is unbecoming of you. You are no longer a child. Find a place and sleep. We both need to rest."

Yuki followed him below to get out of the wind. With the pencil and one of several sheets of ledger paper he had squirreled away, he composed a letter:

*Dearest Mary,*

*No doubt you have learned that the Bakufu has collapsed. Thus, my plans to return to you are in doubt. I am on my way to Aizu, where a great battle looms, one in which I intend to participate. If we achieve victory, I will return to you and finish the business you are familiar with. However, should you not hear from me again, take comfort in knowing I will have honorably faced my end. But trust that, in any case, I will always love you. The gold . . .*

Yuki paused to consider what he had just written. He erased the last two words, and added more:

*Keep our secret. Use what I have left in your care to your advantage. If you have borne a son, raise him to be a man of letters, not a man of the sword. If you have given birth to a girl, raise her to be like you. Know that I will always love you.*
*Tommy*

He fashioned an envelope with another sheet of paper and glued it with a bit of paste he made with his saliva and the few remaining grains of cooked rice he'd saved. He inserted the letter into the envelope, sealed the flap, and addressed it to the Maple Street address in Boston.

The boilers were stoked at dawn, and Yuki climbed topside to watch a dozen sailors scrambling up the masts. They furled the sails and cinched them to their spreaders. Soon after, the paddle wheels began to churn. Ishida stood, clutching the handrail.

"What's going on?" Yuki yelled above the noise.

"We'll soon make port."

"Yotsukura? So soon?"

"Yes. If you are still going to Aizu, you had better get ready. We won't be there very long."

The ship hugged the coastline for another half-hour before Yotsukura came into view. Yuki slung his rucksack over his back just as Ishida pointed to something.

"Look to the east," he cried out.

Yuki saw black smudges of smoke, and as the minutes passed, two ironclads came into view, steaming toward the *Takao Maru*.

"Those must be Admiral Enomoto's ships," Ishida shouted.

As Yuki stared wide-eyed, trying to make out the lead ship, he was startled by the screech of the boatswain's whistle. The gun crew dashed to the bow, knocking Ben off his feet.

"Choshu raiders!" someone yelled.

When he saw a yellow pinpoint flash from one of the ships, Yuki grabbed onto the handrail. A second later, an ear-shattering explosion sent him and Ben diving to the deck. The shell hit the water three hundred yards from the stern, and a few seconds later, four more bullets whizzed overhead, landing a hundred yards aft.

"They're range-finding us!" Ishida shouted. Ben tried to get up, but Yuki grabbed his sleeve and yanked him down. The gun crew returned fire with its smooth-barreled cannons, but the shells exploded well short of the leading ironclad. Silence gripped the crew, and Yuki clenched his jaw, waiting for the next enemy shell to hit.

Instead, the gunners burst into a raucous cheer. The enemy ships had inexplicably broken off and were heading back out to sea.

"We're in luck. That must be Enomoto's flagship, the *Banryu*," Ishida shouted.

Yuki's spirits soared when he saw a vessel pursuing the enemy warships. It seemed to have appeared out of nowhere. The gunners cheered, and soldiers crowded along the handrail to watch. A half-hour later, only faint wisps of smoke were visible on the horizon.

"Very strange," Yuki said. "Enomoto's flagship never fired a shot."

"Who cares?" Ishida said. "We're still alive, aren't we?"

The attack caused Yuki to reconsider his plans for Ben. The *Takao Maru*'s wooden hull would not stand a chance if the ironclads struck again. Reasoning that the so-called Ezo Republic would not be any safer, Yuki gave him a choice.

"You may accompany me to Aizu if you wish. But you must promise to stay with the caretakers at my uncle's country estate. It's far from Tsuruga Castle, where the fighting will take place. If the situation becomes impossible, you must return to Daiten-ji by yourself. What do you say?"

"My father's duty was to serve you," Ben said with boyish solemnity. "It is now my time to do the same."

"Then, ready yourself. We are about to disembark."

The *Takao Maru* sidled against the pier, and a group of soldiers glumly pushed and shoved their way on board. Only a few carried rifles, all of them obsolete. A young Aizu officer followed close behind.

"Where are you from?" Yuki demanded.

"Who are you to ask?" the samurai answered, eyeing Yuki's ragged clothes and haggard look.

"I am Tomita Yuki."

Hearing Yuki's commanding voice and noting that he had a surname, the officer snapped to attention. "I'm Lieutenant Kawada Toshio. Please accept my apology. I should have known you were one of us."

Yuki flashed a disarming smile. "Never mind what I'm wearing. It's a long story," he said, making a show by brushing dirt off his cotton jacket. "Your men look beaten. Where are their rifles?"

"Two days ago, an enemy squad ambushed us. My men dropped their rifles and scattered like leaves. I started with one hundred of them. Now I have only forty-two. They are commoners, and their lot will be the same whichever side wins. They have no fight in them."

"Have you any news from Tsuruga Castle?"

"Our army is dug in around the town, but rumors have it that the enemy is hauling in new English cannons from Sendai. I'm not sure our troops can withstand a heavy bombardment."

"I'm on my way to join the fight," Yuki said. "What is the best way to get there?"

"It will take you at least eight days."

"Why so long?"

"You had better skirt the main road and stick to the rugged trails. That way, you'll avoid enemy patrols. They're everywhere."

Kawada handed a cloth-wrapped bundle to Yuki. "Sir, these swords belonged to a fallen comrade. You'll need them. And here's a map I drew. It shows the trails to take and those to avoid."

Yuki thanked Kawada, tucked the map away, and joined Ben on the pier. Together, they watched the *Takao Maru* chuff out of the harbor before heading out of town. It was late afternoon when they reached a lonely inn hugging the side of a hill. There was a plume of steam rising behind it.

"See that, Ben? The inn has a hot spring. We are going to have a bath tonight."

They scrubbed the briny grime off their bodies and soaked themselves in the pool until they could no longer bear the heat. The owner's wife served them a hearty meal back in their room. She apologized for her delay, explaining that her kitchen help had disappeared the day before. "There is no good news," she sighed.

The next morning, she packed two boxes with *inarizushi*, rice balls stuffed in fried tofu pouches. After filling their canteens with barley tea, Yuki and Ben set off and followed Kawada's map. They walked fifteen miles a day, sometimes fewer, sometimes more. The temperatures hovered just above freezing at night, but Yuki dared not light a fire. The child side of Ben reasserted itself, and he huddled close to Yuki at night. Yuki suspected he did it more out of fear of his surroundings than for warmth.

# CHAPTER 47

KUROI CLUTCHED THE STARBOARD railing and vomited over the *Dupleix's* handrail. The ship's impromptu defense of the *Takao Maru* had made him seasick. Nibei and Onishi hid their faces, smirking as he staggered about the rocking ship's deck.

The gutsy French captain of the *Dupleix* had chased the Choshu warships away, but he dared not violate the neutrality agreement by engaging them. It was apparent that the Choshu commander of the two Imperial Navy warships also had no stomach for a fight.

After giving up the chase, the *Dupleix* sailed to Yotsukura, and when it tied up, Kuroi led his men off the ship past a squad of bedraggled Aizu soldiers.

"Tomita is no fool," Onishi told Kuroi. "Even if he and the boy survived the waters of Edo Bay, there's no guarantee he's on the way to Aizu. This is a complete waste of time."

Kuroi needed Onishi and Nibei more than ever, but aboard the *Dupleix,* Nibei had acted disturbingly churlish, and Onishi had become increasingly truculent. His remark was another indication that he and Nibei were tired of Kuroi's secrecy and frequent tirades.

"It isn't a waste of time," Kuroi replied, keeping his temper in check. "I know for a fact Tomita will be coming here if he survived, and, knowing him, I am sure he has. He'll find his way aboard a large fishing boat or a coastal freighter, but we are days ahead of him, and I know exactly where he'll go when he gets to Aizu."

"So, what?"

"So, we'll remain here overnight, and I'll treat you both to dinner and bath at a decent inn. After all, you have been faithful companions," Kuroi said.

He made a show of opening the purse he'd taken from Nariaki's body and counting out coins. "Here is your reward for helping me so far."

He handed two gold *ryo* to Onishi and dropped ten silver coins into Nibei's open hands.

"You're paid up, and you're free to leave," he said, gazing at their startled looks. He watched the *Dupleix* cast off, allowing his men time to absorb his unexpected generosity. "By the way, if you help me catch Tomita, there will be much more for you. You both have wondered why I had you shadow him in Edo, right?"

Onishi and Nibei nodded warily.

"You will recall that I even demanded that you protect him."

"Yes, but you never told us why," Onishi said.

"Well, it's time I let you in on my secret. Perhaps you heard the news that the Imperial Army found the Bakufu's gold reserves missing when they took over Edo Castle. Rumors continue to circulate that the shogun's minister, Oguri, took the gold and buried it north of Tokyo."

"Yeah, and Choshu samurai caught up and beheaded him. They said there was no such treasure."

"The truth is that Oguri did not take the gold. Tomita's cousin had it removed and buried weeks earlier, somewhere near Yokohama. After Tomita returned from his diplomatic mission, Nibei tailed him. Remember? I rightly suspected that Tomita was in on Nariaki's plans."

"Why did Tomita's cousin take the gold in the first place?"

"I learned he was in negotiations to buy modern weapons from the Dutch, but it's too late if you ask me."

"And how do you know all this?" Onishi asked.

"The night we stayed at the inn near the Tama River, Nariaki told me about his negotiations. But he refused when I demanded to know where the gold was, and we got into a fight."

"And you killed him," said Onishi."

"I had to. It was either him or me."

"Then you don't know where the gold is buried?" Nibei said.

"No. That's why Tomita is important. He knows the exact location, and I intend to make him talk. I will make you rich if you men are in on this with me. Very, very rich."

Nibei stared at the silver coins in his hand. "Master, you are much too generous. Count me in," he said, dropping them into his purse.

Onishi seemed undecided, but as he rubbed the two gold coins together between his fingers, a faint smile grew into a wide grin.

"Count me in too. And don't worry about making Tomita talk," he said, patting the hilt of his short sword to make his point clear.

"I know how to do it."

As they wandered around Yotsukura, Kuroi muffled a guffaw in his coat sleeve. *They gulped down my story like warm sake in a snowstorm.*

金　金　金

THEY LEFT YOTSUKURA THE next day, and just before nightfall, they stopped at another inn. That evening, while Nibei stood guard, Kuroi and Onishi soaked themselves in the hot mineral waters of the outside pool. After they climbed out, Nibei was allowed in.

It was midmorning the next day when they got up. Fully rested, Kuroi and Onishi sat together having breakfast while Nibei ate in the kitchen, making small talk with the owner.

"Not much business these days, huh?" Nibei said, holding out his empty bowl for more rice.

"A man and a boy were here yesterday and your group today," the old man said while filling Nibei's bowl. "Nobody else in more than two weeks."

"What's that, you say? A man and a boy?"

"Yeah. A down-and-out ronin. My wife thought the boy was his catamite, but I don't think so."

"Really? What did they look like? I may know them."

"The ronin was fairly tall and well-spoken. The boy's name was Ben. Unusual, don't you think? They were in a rush to get to Aizu. Strange, they would want to."

Kuroi was dumbstruck when Nibei barged into his room and told him the news. Instead of being days or weeks ahead of Yuki, they were hours behind him. Kuroi grabbed his swords. "If you two want a share of the gold, we must cut Tomita off before he gets to Aizu."

"Let's go!" Onishi shouted.

# CHAPTER 48

*Aizu Domain—October 8, 1868*

AFTER A DEMANDING TWELVE-DAY passage through the mountains, Yuki gazed at the narrow footpath leading to Aizu. He calculated that it was October eight by the Western calendar. For a few moments, he listened to the incessant rumble echoing throughout the hills. It was an ominous sound, one he recognized for what it was: cannon fire.

Yuki shook Ben awake. "The battle for Aizu has begun. Let's eat and get on our way. You'll be safe where I'm taking you."

They sat together, each with a rice ball and a cup of barley tea. When they finished, Yuki pulled out his pistol. "I prefer the swords that Kawada-San gave me. I want you to take this."

He pulled the hammer back with his thumb, explaining why it was necessary. He then demonstrated how to aim the pistol. "If you must defend yourself, wait until your target is close enough so you cannot miss. Now, watch closely."

Ben clapped his hands over his ears, and Yuki fired at a nearby pine tree. The lead ball struck the trunk, sending bark fragments into the air.

"Now you try it," Yuki said, handing Ben the pistol.

Ben pulled the hammer back, aimed, and squeezed the trigger. The ball hit the tree close to where Yuki's bullet had struck.

"I did it, Master," he shouted, "I did it!"

"Yes, and I'm proud of you," Yuki said while reloading the pistol. "Do not use this unless you are in immediate danger. Do you understand?"

"Yes, Master."

"Good. Now, let's get going. A big dinner, a hot bath, and warm beds are waiting for us at my uncle's estate."

The sound of cannon fire grew louder as they followed the winding path, making Yuki even more determined to join his brother Yoshi on the castle's ramparts. His uncle's estate was far from the battle zone, and he assured himself that Ben would be safe and well-taken care of there.

The optimism that his cousin Nariaki had instilled in Yuki was a thing of the past. Nothing had turned out the way they had expected, and the only hope of restoring the shogunate rested upon the shoulders of Aizu's soldiers. They were fierce in spirit, but so were the imperial soldiers who were armed with modern English rifles. Yuki's mission had failed, and he was ridden with guilt.

The incessant cannon fire plagued him with thoughts of chaos and carnage. He feared for his brother Yoshi and prayed he would not be part of the human harvest.

金　金　金

A SCHOLAR OF RARE intelligence, Yuki knew more than the English language. His brief stay in the United States opened a world only a few Japanese knew. Samurai accounted for less than ten percent of the population, but farmers, artisans, merchants, and untouchables had little chance of bettering themselves under their rule.

Yuki was torn between two different worlds. Mary and the major had taught him to respect the individual, man or woman, regardless of social status. In so doing, he learned the virtue of showing benevolence to those less fortunate. Shorty, Ben, and Ichi were beneficiaries of Yuki's newfound compassion.

But he still clung to the past. Not out of a misguided desire to preserve Japan's class system but out of his belief that the anti-foreign sentiment had to be extinguished so that Japan could open itself up to the New World. And in his mind, only the Shogun's government could do it.

As he and Ben trudged along, Yuki could hardly have conceived what awaited them. But he did fear their story might become buried during the unfolding battle.

A DAY LATER, Kuroi made his way out of Aizu—alone. Nothing happened the way he had planned. The Imperial Army was close to victory, and remnants of Aizu's intelligence unit learned he had murdered Yuki's cousin. They were out to get him, and Imperial agents were closing in on him, determined to seek revenge for his part in killing Izo, the Choshu spy.

If Kuroi were caught, he would pay with his life, and he knew the payment process would be painfully slow. He barely escaped three Aizu samurai on a snowy mountain path, and days later, he avoided an Imperial Army ambush by sheer luck.

Nevertheless, he could not have been more pleased with how things had turned out.

It took him two months to reach Yokohama, dressed in the clothes of a peddler he had murdered along the way. He booked passage on an English merchantman with the remaining money he had stolen from Nariaki. Not to Batavia in the Dutch East Indies, but to Boston.

# CHAPTER 49

## February 1869—Boston

JUDA STEIN INSISTED THAT Mary remain in Boston and not go back to River Oak as planned. Confined to the Maple Street home and cared for by Sarah, the neighbors never knew of her pregnancy and the subsequent birth of her baby. For the first four months of life, the child thrived.

But not Mary. She began to feel unwell several days after visiting Benjamin Butler's grave despite Stein's admonishment not to leave the house. On a bleak, snowy morning, Sarah could hardly stay awake. The day before, Mary's coughing appeared to presage nothing more than the onset of a cold. But by midnight, Sarah began to fear the worst.

"I'm so tired. Please hold Michael Yuki for me," Mary said.

Sarah recognized the warning signs. She gently lifted the baby out of Mary's arms and kissed his forehead. "You're very sick, Miss Mary. I go get Dr. Stein."

"Sarah, if I should pass away, don't let anyone take baby Michael. The money I have is under this bed in a box. It is yours to live on until Tommy returns. Tell him what happened. You may return with him to Japan with baby Michael Yuki, where you will have a wonderful life."

It was too much for Sarah, and she burst into tears. "Mr. Tommy, take me to Japan? I won't go. Please, dear Miss Mary, don't die."

"Do not cry, my dear friend. Tommy will not force you, and he may even wish to remain here."

SARAH RUSHED TO SUMMON Dr. Stein, but Michael Yuki lay crying next to his lifeless mother when they returned. Mary had succumbed to pneumonia, but Sarah and the baby remained in good health.

"Sarah, if anyone asks about the baby, you tell them Michael is your child. He bears some of your features, don't you think? No one will suspect otherwise," Stein said.

Stein gave her a ceramic papboat, a small, long-necked vessel with a handle, and taught her how to feed cow's milk to the baby. He also arranged for Mary's burial in the same cemetery where Benjamin Butler's remains rested. But two days later, he visited Sarah and gave her some disturbing news.

"I failed to inform the authorities of Mary's death properly, and they've learned she was living in this house. If they come and find you here, they may conclude that Michael Yuki is not your child. If so, they will send him to an orphanage. Come to my house. I will pay you to be my housekeeper. If the health officials visit me, you must hide until they are gone."

Sarah retrieved the wooden box, and with Mary's baby strapped to her back, she followed him to his house.

But Master Michael, as Sarah called the baby, did not take well to the papboat. Stein tried hiring a wet nurse, but none would agree to nurse what they called a half-breed. Michael's condition began to decline.

A police officer interrogated Stein and demanded why he had failed to file a death certificate. Boston had suffered a cholera outbreak in 1866, and the city was still on edge. Stein assured the policeman that Mary had died of pneumonia and promised to file a certificate that day. Sarah cowered in the cellar with the baby until the officer left. That evening, she announced her plans.

"Baby Michael needs to drink a mother's milk. I will go to Mashpee reservation and find a wet nurse."

The Mashpee reservation was a two-day journey from Boston, located at the base of Cape Cod, just south of the glass-making town of Sandwich. A Mashpee mother, who had recently given birth to a baby girl agreed to nurse Master Michael for one silver dollar a month. Thriving on the mother's milk and Sarah's loving care, baby Michael Yuki regained his strength.

In early March, Sarah visited the village medicine woman who lived alone in a *wetu*, a domed hut with wattled walls. She was known throughout the reservation for her ability to communicate with unseen spirits, those who exerted significant influence over the lives of the Mashpee. Sarah pleaded with her for protection and watched as the elderly woman fell into a trance in the smoky hut.

She chanted for over an hour, calling on the benevolent spirits of the Mashpee Wampanoag to protect Sarah and the baby. But she suddenly stopped. "The Evil One is looking for you and the baby. He intends to kill you both. You must be careful."

Sarah was sure the policeman who had interrogated Dr. Stein was the Evil One. "Make me powerful medicine to keep us safe from him. I pay you a five-dollar gold piece."

Three days later, the medicine woman presented Sarah with two leather pouches containing magic ingredients. "You and the child must wear them. No harm will come to you if your heart is pure. This medicine will cause the Evil One to lose his way."

Confident that she and Master Michael were safe, Sarah returned to Dr. Stein's house and resumed her role as his housekeeper. Soon after, Stein found a wet nurse, a desperate, newly arrived Irish immigrant, and Michael continued to thrive.

# CHAPTER 50

Kuroi landed in Boston 187 days after embarking in Yokohama. He bought a suit of Western clothes and, late in the afternoon, found his way to 125 Maple Street. Now, almost penniless, he knocked on the door, prepared to tell Mary the story he had concocted, one he hoped would convince her to reveal the whereabouts of the gold. If guile did not persuade her, Kuroi was prepared to use force.

"No one lives there," a woman next door called out from her doorstep.

"Please excuse me," Kuroi said, doffing his stovepipe hat. "I'm here to visit Major Benjamin Butler and his daughter, Mary."

"Major Butler, you say?"

"Yes, a very close friend and hero of mine. And what little ability I have in speaking your language, I owe to Miss Mary's skill and patience as my teacher."

"Oh dear," the woman said. "You must be one of their oriental friends. I should have known." She set her broom down and blew her nose. "I have some unfortunate news for you. Major Butler died quite some time ago, and poor Mary died a few months later, or so I was told. Such a tragedy."

Kuroi clutched the handrail to steady himself. He was no closer to his goal than two years earlier. "Dead? How?"

"Their housekeeper, Sarah, can tell you more, but I warn you, she's a trollop."

"Where can I find her?"

"If you must know, ask Dr. Stein. He lives over on Elm Street. Number 201." She pointed to the corner. "That's Elm. His house is on the left, up three blocks. She is his housekeeper now."

Kuroi arrived at Stein's home out of breath, prepared to tell a new story. He calmed himself and knocked.

"*Ja?*" Stein said, opening the door partway. "Who are you?"

Hat in hand, Kuroi bowed. "I am Taketo Tomita, and I have come for my brother. He disappeared in Japan earlier this year, and I believe he returned to Boston."

"You are Tommy's brother?"

"Tommy?"

"That is what Mr. Tomita was called. I know for a fact that he has not returned."

"Oh, no. That cannot be true. He must be somewhere about. Where is Miss Mary? She should know."

"*Ach*, sweet Mary. Sadly, she has passed away, but please come in and tell me what you know of Tommy." He sat down at his rolltop desk and offered Kuroi a chair. "I must tell you that your brother and Miss Mary entered an inappropriate relationship. After he left for Japan, she bore a child named Michael Yuki. But tell me, why do you think Tommy came back to Boston?"

"During our civil war, we were separated, and I could not find him. Tommy believed he had fathered a child here, and he was desperate to return and marry his child's mother. If Tommy did not return, I must conclude he was killed in Japan. Thus, I am desperate to visit his child to see that he is in good hands. Who is caring for him now?"

"Mary's maid, Sarah Saylor. Sarah could not have been closer to Mary if she had been her sister."

"So, Michael Yuki is my nephew," Kuroi said, nervously fingering the rim of his hat. "Kindly tell me where I may find him and Miss Saylor. I was told she is your housekeeper."

Stein pushed his chair away from the desk. "No longer, I'm afraid. Mr. Tommy failed to return, and we believe he met a tragic end. That is why Sarah took Michael Yuki as her own. It was for the best. This society does not welcome mixed-race children, but Sarah loves the child."

"I am warmed to hear Miss Sarah cares so much for him," Kuroi said. "Can you tell me where she lives?"

"Well, sir, Sarah is very superstitious. She claimed that an evil spirit was scheming to kill her and the child. She left Boston and went to San Francisco."

Kuroi slumped in the chair. "San Francisco?"

"*Ja.* Sarah believed that her father lived there, and she left to seek him. She bought a second-class ticket on America's new transcontinental railroad with Mary's money. It cost her fifty-six dollars. I know because I took her to buy the ticket."

"San Francisco? My brother said he left some belongings here. Miss Sarah surely did not take them."

"Mr. Tomita, there was not much to take. Only his sword, a rifle, and a few other items. Oh, and your brother's journal. Mr. Tommy kept it while he was here."

"A journal?"

"A diary, sir," Stein said.

"Ah, yes. My brother's diary. He told me about it. I would like to have it as a keepsake."

"I saw it only once. It was full of those funny chicken scratches with which you people write. I saw a few words he'd printed in English, but nothing else made sense."

"Did Sarah take some hefty boxes with her?"

"Luggage? No, only the things I told you about. They were packed in a wooden box. She took that and a bag of clothes." Stein paused when he saw Kuroi fidgeting in his chair. "Mr. Tomita, you look pale. Are you feeling ill?"

Lost in his dismal thoughts, Kuroi failed to answer.

"Mr. Tomita, I ask you again. Are you not well? Why do you ask if Sarah had luggage?"

"Oh, the luggage—I fear she and my nephew are ill-clothed. May I ask why you seem certain that she went all the way to San Francisco? She could have gotten off somewhere in between."

"I have proof, sir. Let me show you." Stein pulled open one of the small drawers in the rolltop. "Here it is," he said. "I received this letter some time ago. Someone wrote it for her."

The room was almost dark, and Stein paused to light an oil lamp. "The letter is dated April the tenth. Let me read it to you:

> *Dear Dr. Stein, I arrived safely in San Francisco but have not found my father. People think that I am a Celestial. Master Michael is healthy and growing strong. I have met a kindly gentleman. Steven West is his name. He wrote this letter for me. Yours truly, Sarah Saylor.*"

"Did you reply to Miss Sarah?"

"Yes, but I have yet to hear from her," Stein said.

"Doctor, I must see my nephew. Can you give me Miss Saylor's address?"

"Mr. Tomita, are you being truthful with me, or is it your intention to take the baby? You cannot be so cruel."

"No, I merely wish to bring Sarah news about my brother and thank her. I agree that my nephew should remain with her."

Stein settled back in his chair. "Then you are a true gentleman, and I thank you. You may have the envelope and the letter."

Kuroi read the return address: Steven West, General Delivery, Market Street Post Office, San Francisco, California.

"Thank you, Dr. Stein. You have been most helpful, but I have one more question. Did Major Butler own the home on Maple Street?"

"No. His house is not far from Boston, but I don't know where."

"Think, Doctor. Please try to remember."

"You ask the impossible, Mr. Tomita. What is so important about the major's house?"

"I merely wondered," he said. "Thank you very much, but now I must take leave."

Stein led him to the front door, but Kuroi stabbed him in the back before he could open it.

"*Mein herz,*" Stein gasped. He staggered two steps and collapsed.

Kuroi rummaged through Stein's desk and found a cashbox. He pried it open and counted out eighty-three dollars in greenbacks. "Sayonara, Dr. Stein," he said.

He picked up the glass oil lamp and threw it against the wall, sending a spray of flaming whale oil onto the drapes and carpet. He pulled the dagger from Stein's body and walked out into the night. The fire engulfed the house, and the fire department could not save it.

金　金　金

THREE WEEKS LATER, Kuroi stepped off the train in San Francisco and found his way to the Market Street post office. The postmaster acknowledged having met a man named Steven West.

"He came here with a half-breed kid and his redskin woman. Somebody from Boston sent them a letter three or four weeks ago, but they haven't been back to get it. There's no way of knowing where they live. Could be the next block over or in Timbuktu."

Kuroi was desperate. He combed the neighborhoods around the post office, asking shopkeepers and passersby if they knew of Steven West. But his efforts came to no avail.

He dared not return to Japan even if he had the money. To survive, he hired himself out as a common laborer and eventually settled down to live with a former prostitute in China Town. In 1902, he fathered a son, and when the boy was old enough to understand, Kuroi told him about the missing gold.

# PART THREE
## The Shogun's Gold

# CHAPTER ONE

*June 7—Present-Day Tokyo*

EDDY BLACKWELL LISTENED TO Parker and Tanaka discussing the missing map. Why they sometimes called each other in the house on cell phones rather than conversing face-to-face puzzled Kuroi. But he did not care. He had something to go on. He knew Japan and had a list of places where he might find the map or at least a clue to where it was if it existed. He pulled off his earbuds as the Narita Airport express train rolled to a stop at Shinjuku Station. He shut down his laptop and grabbed his backpack.

"Listen up," he said to Fumio. "Tanaka has plans, and he and West are coming here. But I have a good idea where to look. I'll be on the road, so don't let him out of your sight."

"What about Tanaka's niece?"

"Her too."

*39,000 feet above the Pacific*

FLYING ON A PRIVATE jet was a first for Parker. He had plenty of room to stretch out, and the flight attendant quickly brought him the drink he had ordered. He opened his briefcase and reread

Jason's translation of the Tomita diary. Nothing stood out. No clues. Not even a hint. He closed the file and allowed his mind to wander. Terry occupied the seat on the other side of the aisle, and the scent of her delicate perfume sent his mind wandering. Slightly buzzed, he gazed out the window, imagining they were romantically involved. *Paris? No. Some palm-studded beach in Tahiti? Yeah, holding hands and gazing at each other...* He closed his eyes and did not wake up until the plane landed at Narita International Airport.

A white-gloved chauffeur with a Toyota Century limo was waiting for them. An hour later, they arrived in the Shinjuku Ward.

"This is one of Tokyo's biggest entertainment districts. Just about anything goes here," Tanaka said as they rode down Shinjuku Dori. "We're staying in a section called Kabukicho. It's a bit seedy but a lot of fun. When I was a student, my buddies and I came here to drink and play mahjong."

The driver turned off the main avenue and inched down a narrow street flooded with pedestrians. Parker saw a samurai, a zombie, and Minnie Mouse walking past the car.

"What's going on? Some sort of festival this evening?"

"No, they are just cosplayers. The streets are choked with them during weekend nights," Terry said.

"Cos-what?"

"Parker, where have you been? It's all the rage in Japan. Cosplayer is the shortened form for costume player. It's the way the Japanese let it all hang out. They dress up, usually like *manga* or comic book characters, and party here. I've even seen cosplayers gallivanting about in Pasadena's Old Town."

"We're here," Tanaka said moments later.

Parker's room was on the tenth floor, and he watched a crowd of cosplayers milling in front of a nearby high-rise hotel.

"What the heck?" Parker had to look twice. The giant head of what appeared to be a Tyrannosaurus rex, bathed in purple light, its claws clutching the edge of the hotel roof, glared down at the crowd with angry yellow eyes. Suddenly, the monster's gaping mouth turned red, and his steamy breath shot from his throat. His roar was so loud that Parker could hear it inside his room. "Shinjuku," he said, flopping down on the bed. "This looks like one hell of a fun place."

The following day, Terry took him for a walk. Parker was wide awake despite the time difference, and Shinjuku had him in its grip. They wandered past the Robot Restaurant and dropped in a few shops. They ended up at an owl café, where they fawned over barn owls and sipped ten-dollar cups of coffee.

On their way back to the hotel, Terry took Parker to a shrine squeezed between two high-rises. They passed under a *torii*, a gateway consisting of two upright granite pillars with two stone crossbeams.

"Buddhists have temples, and Shintoists have shrines. Sometimes they share the same ground, but not here," Terry said, showing him how to rinse his hands in a stone water trough. She tossed a few coins into the donation box and rang a bell to summon the god whose spirit resided behind the closed doors of the small, box-like shrine. She clapped twice, closed her eyes, and prayed.

"You looked like you were serious about praying. Do you actually believe in these gods?" Parker said.

"I believe in preserving ancient traditions. What do you believe in?"

"I guess I never thought about it. What did you ask for? Or is that a secret?"

"I asked the spirit residing inside to guide you to the answer you seek," she said, handing him a five-hundred-yen coin. "You try it."

Parker tossed the coin. Feeling a bit self-conscious, he clapped and prayed.

"So, what did you ask for?" Terry asked.

"It's a secret," Parker said, flashing a sheepish grin.

He noticed a man wearing aviator sunglasses and a baseball hat as they wandered out. He was standing near the torii, inspecting one of the columns. His interest in the dull gray pillar seemed contrived, and Parker became suspicious. As they passed him, the man turned away and entered the compound.

That evening, Tanaka shared a bit of bad news. "I spent five hours at the Diet Library and found nothing."

Parker shook his head and cast an I-told-you-so look at Tanaka.

"Don't be so pessimistic, Parker. Let's see what Uncle Jason's friend can tell us tomorrow," Terry said.

# CHAPTER 2

D R. IMANAGA GREETED THEM in Waseda University's faculty dining room. His Queen's English was impeccable, and with a head of feral hair, Parker thought the professor could pass as an Asian Einstein.

A waitress brought a tray of beer, and they toasted each other. Imanaga wiped a bit of foam from his mustache and turned to Tanaka. "I am always honored when you visit me, Jason. What is the purpose this time? The last time we met, you were researching public safety in nineteenth-century Edo. Is there another book in the pipeline?"

"Perhaps I should let my friend Parker explain," said Tanaka.

Parker launched into the story he and Tanaka had rehearsed earlier. "Dr. Imanaga, Jason told me that you are an expert on the end of the Tokugawa shogunate, the Bakumatsu, as you call it."

"Oh, so you are a doctoral candidate?"

"No, far from it. I'm embarrassed that I know very little about Japanese history."

"So why are you so interested in the end of the samurai era?"

"I have a purely personal reason. An ancestor of mine was Japanese. Jason has agreed to help me trace my family tree."

"Indeed," Imanaga said. He put down his glass of beer and took a closer look at Parker's features.

Parker smiled. "No, Dr. Imanaga, you will not see any visible signs. My Japanese genes are rather diluted."

"Hmm. I do see some features, however. Your black hair, mainly." Imanaga gulped down a half glass of beer, pausing to wipe the foam off his mustache again. "The Bakumatsu—that would place your ancestor right around the late 1860s."

"Close enough."

"Then I must assume he was a sailor or a merchant who fathered a child by a Japanese lady of the night. Probably in a seaport like Yokohama." Imanaga paused for a moment to gauge Parker's reaction. "Am I correct?"

"Actually, no. The evidence suggests that my ancestor, Tomita Yuki, traveled to America in 1867. It was there that he fathered a child."

"Really? He had a family name, so he must have been a samurai. Do you have evidence proving he visited America?"

Parker was ready with an innocent lie. "Not much. Just some written reminiscences from his grandson."

"Incredible. Japanese were not allowed to travel to America without government permission in those days. What could have taken him to America? Do you have any idea?"

"No idea, sir."

Imanaga turned to Tanaka. "Jason, can all this be true?"

Tanaka nodded. "Just one of those interesting little footnotes in history."

Imanaga stared pensively at his glass. "So, you're helping Parker with his genealogy? Do you expect me to believe that the illustrious Dr. Tanaka came here to help Mr. West research his family tree? I think there's more to his story than you are willing to divulge."

Imanaga's sudden directness caught Tanaka off guard. "Yes, well, ah, what he said is true."

"Oh, come on, Jason. There's another angle, isn't there? Share it with me."

Terry spoke up before Tanaka could reply. "Uncle Jason, admit that you've fibbed to Professor Imanaga."

Parker took a sip of beer and fought hard to keep from choking on it. *What the hell is she doing?* He put the glass down and nudged Terry's knee under the table, but she acted as though she had not felt anything.

"Imanaga-sensei, it is supposed to be a secret, but I am sure it will be safe with you. Allow me to explain," Terry said.

Parker nudged her under the table again. "Terry, let me handle this."

"Shush," she said. She smiled fetchingly at Imanaga. "You see, Parker and I are engaged."

"*Ah, so.* Now, it all makes sense. Congratulations, Mr. West," Imanaga said. "You are marrying into an illustrious family. It's a Japanese thing, you know, making sure there are no skeletons or black sheep in the family closet. We Japanese often hire detectives to check out a prospective bride's or groom's roots."

Imanaga paused to study Parker's features again. "So, Mr. West, admit it. It's Jason who wants to trace your lineage."

Parker forced an apologetic smile. "Yes, it's true—Yuki being a samurai and all."

"You would certainly have bragging rights, but so would Jason."

Tanaka changed the subject as he poured beer into Imanaga's empty glass. "Issei-San, how can we find a registry containing Tomita family names?"

"Centuries-old family genealogies may sometimes be found in temples along with something called a *kakocho*. It's basically a record of deaths. Unfortunately, a wave of anti-Buddhist sentiment followed the fall of the Bakufu, and the temple in Aizu, where I suspect the Tomita records were stored, was destroyed. The government took what was left for safekeeping. And during World War II, everything was stored in a cave. They moldered there for over a decade before a prefectural office in Fukushima City took them over. I do not think any historian has ever bothered examining them. Go to Fukushima. You might find a clue to the whereabouts of living relatives if there are any."

For the rest of their lunch, Imanaga and Jason reminisced about their university days. Afterward, Tanaka, Terry, and Parker took a taxi back to Shinjuku.

"Terry, that was a clever ploy. It threw Dr. Imanaga off track. I had no idea that you could be so deceptive."

"Yes, very clever," Parker said.

"I didn't mean to embarrass either of you, but Dr. Imanaga wasn't swallowing the story," Terry said.

Parker fell quiet and barely listened as Tanaka spoke about his plans for the next day.

"We'll check out the Tomita family records in Fukushima, assuming there are any. Then, we'll go to Aizu Wakamatsu, where Yuki was born and raised. If any relatives are living there, we'll visit them. If not, there is a reasonable chance of picking up a clue somewhere like the John Manjiro Museum on Shikoku. It is the smallest of Japan's four main islands. It's where Manjiro was born and raised."

"The castaway kid Yuki mentioned in his diary? Jason, forgive me for saying this, but it sounds like a stretch. A big one."

"I'll grant you that, but he may be our last, best hope. We leave on the bullet train tomorrow morning at six. Better get some sleep."

金　金　金

THEY ARRIVED AT THE prefectural office in Fukushima City the next day at noon. Tanaka pressed the elevator button, and they descended one floor to the Abandoned Family Records Office. A gnome-like clerk greeted them with a friendly smile. Tanaka introduced himself and presented him with his business card the Japanese way, with two hands.

"Ah, Americans. From California, no less. What a good chance to practice my English," he said. "Nakamura Kenjiro at your service. How may I help you?"

Pleased that Nakamura spoke English, Parker took the lead. "We've learned that the Tomita samurai family records from Aizu may be stored here. Would it be possible to get a copy of them?"

"Of course. Strange that you should ask. I know exactly where they are. Is this for a personal reason?"

"No. We are doing some historical research for a book," Parker replied.

"Very good. I'll only be a moment."

"That's strange. Why does he know exactly where the records are?" Parker whispered to Terry. She shook her head and shrugged.

They watched Nakamura make his way past several aisles lined with metal shelf racks loaded with cardboard boxes from top to bottom. He ducked into the second-to-last aisle and, minutes later, reappeared with a documents box. He opened it and spread out fifteen photocopied pages on the counter.

"This is the Tomita genealogical table. It goes back to 1536. The Tomita family was quite illustrious. Sadly, their line was extinguished in 1868 when Tsuruga Castle fell to the Imperial Army."

He pointed to something on the last page. "These are the names of the last Tomita family members. Tomita Yoshi, the youngest brother, was a member of what was called the Byakkotai. He died on October 8, 1868. The two other brothers are listed, but their death dates are not recorded here. They just disappeared. Aizu's army was defeated by the Imperial Army, and . . ."

Parker interrupted Nakamura. "Did you just say that Tomita Yuki had *two other* brothers?"

"Yes. Besides Yuki's younger brother, he had an elder brother named Tomoyoshi. But as you can see here, his name was struck out. It was the usual practice when a person was disowned. I think..."

Parker interrupted again. "Mr. Nakamura, how can you be so sure the line ended in 1868? Maybe Tomoyoshi or Yuki had children."

"Perhaps they did, but there is no record in the kakocho, the book containing the death records kept at the Buddhist temple near where they lived. I already checked. I found Tomita Yoshi's name and date of death, but there are no death dates for Tomita Yuki or Tomita Tomoyoshi. I suppose that both were killed, but their bodies were not found. I think..."

"How about uncles, cousins, and aunts? Surely there are living descendants somewhere in Japan."

"I'm afraid not," Nakamura said huffily, having been interrupted a third time by Parker. He pointed to several other lines of handwritten Japanese text. "The brothers had one unmarried cousin, Matsudaira Nariaki, who was assassinated outside Edo in 1868. His father, Matsudaira Tokunari, died of old age earlier. So, in my opinion, the Tomita family line ended in 1868."

Parker knew from his experience at Greene & West that what looked like a barren family tree could still bear fruit. He was not ready to give up. "Perhaps Matsudaira Tokunari had a brother or a sister who carried on the line."

Tanaka nudged Parker not to press anymore, but it was too late. Nakamura gathered the papers in a huff and put them back into the document box.

Parker regretted his indiscretion. "Sir, please forgive me. I'm sorry for having interrupted you."

"I'll address what you just said, but that's it, no more," Nakamura said testily, "Matsudaira was an only son, and his son, Nariaki, died without issue. Once again, I believe no Tomita descendants are alive today. You have been barking up the wrong genealogical tree."

"Touché," Parker whispered to Tanaka. "We're done here. Let's go."

"One moment," Nakamura said. "Before you leave, you must fill out this form with your name, address, and the purpose of your visit. It is a government requirement."

Parker filled out the first box but stopped when he read the entry above his. "Jason, look. This morning, a Harvard University professor named Emory Keeting requested copies of the Tomita family records."

"Yes, he left about an hour ago," Nakamura said. "He's why I had all the information about the Tomita family at my fingertips."

Terry grabbed the register and examined the name list. "Hmm. In the last thirty days, Dr. Keeting and three other Americans, one German, and two Brits, came to research something called the *Byakkotai*."

"Mr. Nakamura mentioned that name before. What is the Byakkotai?" Parker asked.

"I don't know," Terry said. "Perhaps Mr. Nakamura would be kind enough to tell us."

Tanaka nodded toward the exit. "No, no. I'll explain things on the way to our next stop. We're running out of time. Let's go."

*What's that all about? Another one of Jason's secrets?* Parker grimaced at the thought.

Back at the Fukushima train station, Tanaka glanced at his watch. "Well, that was worthwhile."

"Jason, how can you say that?"

"Because we now know that Yuki had an elder brother. We may be able to find something about him in Aizu Wakamatsu."

# CHAPTER 3

PARKER WAS ON EDGE by the time they reached the train station in Aizu Wakamatsu. "Jason, are you going to tell me about that Byakkotai thing or not?"

"Sorry, Parker, I didn't want to rile Nakamura any more than he was."

"Yeah, I admit I was not very polite, but please, get on with it."

"Well, I'm fairly sure Yuki died during the last battle of Japan's civil war, as did his younger brother Yoshi. I hope we'll find something about his elder brother, but I'm unsure where to start."

"Jason, please get to the meat of the story," Parker said. "What about the Byakkotai thing Nakamura mentioned?"

Tanaka sighed. "Their story has haunted me since I was a child. The English term for the military unit is White Tigers. It was composed of about 300 teenage samurai. As we learned today, Yoshi was Yuki's younger brother."

"Teenage samurai?"

"Yes. Every Japanese school kid knows the story, but few foreigners know it. You need a little background first. In the old days, infants were deemed one year old at birth, so they became two on the first day of the Chinese New Year. According to the family tree we saw today, Yoshi was born one month before, so he became two years old on New Year's Day, when, by our way of reckoning, he was only two months old. Therefore, Yoshi was a fifteen-year-old squad member when the tragedy unfolded. On October 8, 1868, all but one member committed suicide when they thought Aizu had been defeated."

"Teenagers did that?"

"Sadly, yes. Ironically, Aizu did not surrender for two more weeks, but the boys did not know that. They were on a hill when they saw Tsuruga Castle engulfed in smoke and flames on the plains below. That is why they thought Aizu had fallen to the Imperial Army. They felt great shame in not being able to defend the castle and its surrounding area where their families lived."

Tanaka let the story sink in, expecting Parker and Terry would have questions. But for the remainder of the trip, they stared at the passing countryside in silence, lost in their thoughts about the tragedy.

金　金　金

THEY TOOK A TAXI directly to Mount Iimori, where the White Tiger tragedy had unfolded. Parker looked around for a mountain, but Iimori was more of a hill. There were few tourists, and Parker noticed that almost all the souvenir shops and restaurants leading to the site had closed.

"Visit the gravesites while I'm checking out the museum archives," Tanaka said.

Terry pointed to an escalator and laughed. "Only the Japanese would install one of these to climb a hill. Too bad it has stopped running for the day. It's got a rubber-matted walkway instead of metal steps."

They were out of breath when they reached the clearing on the side of the hill where the tragedy had occurred. They stopped and surveyed the plain below.

"There it is," Terry said, pointing at something in the distance. "You can barely see it, but that must be Tsuruga Castle. No wonder those teenagers thought it had fallen when they saw it engulfed in smoke and flames."

"Come on, let's see their gravesites," Parker said. He expected to find massive granite headstones. Instead, he found a line of simple slate markers with small incense urns in front of each one. Terry caught an incense vendor as he was about to leave. She bought three sticks and lighted them over his brazier.

They walked from left to right, Terry reading the name and age on each slate marker out loud. She stopped in front of the last one and pointed to it. "This is where Yoshi-San is buried," she said, handing Parker the smoking incense sticks. "Go ahead. This means a lot to you. He was your distant uncle."

Parker choked up, gazing at the marker. A gentle breeze sent leaves skittering over the paving stones. He bent down and planted the incense. He stood back, took a deep breath, clapped twice, and bowed. "Yoshi-San," he whispered, "I am your brother's descendant. Please guide me to Yuki-San." A shiver played about his neck, and before he dismissed the idea, he imagined that Yoshi was attempting to reach him from beyond.

Before they left, Terry pointed to a small plaque nearby and translated it. "No matter how many people wash these stones with tears, these names will never vanish from the world." She blotted her eyes. "I'm sorry, Parker. I'm a crybaby. It's such a sad story."

They found Tanaka in the museum, preparing to leave. "I couldn't find anything, and according to the curator, none of the other museums have what we are looking for. I guess my next step is Tosashimizu."

Parker was overwhelmed with so many Japanese words, especially the long ones. "Tosa-what?"

"Tosashimizu. John Manjiro's museum is located there. You remember reading Yuki's journal entry about him, right?"

"Yeah. Page six or seven."

"Close enough," Tanaka said. "Anyway, I'll leave tomorrow morning. The bullet train goes most of the way so it won't take too long."

"I have to say this again, Jason. It sounds like a stretch."

"Are you asking me to give up on this?"

Tanaka's blunt rejoinder made Parker feel like a spoiled kid being put in his place. "No, that's not it. It's just that you're doing all the work, and all I can do is follow you around like a lost puppy. I don't understand Japanese, and I'm nothing but a hindrance. You're right—it's important to check that Manjiro thing out, but all I can do is stand around and do nothing."

Terry grabbed Parker's arm. "Don't be so hard on yourself. We'll get to the bottom of this."

"I'm sorry. It's just that I'm so frustrated," Parker said with a hangdog look.

"Terry is right, Parker. Don't be so hard on yourself. You've been a great help," Tanaka said.

Terry patted his shoulder and wrapped her arm around Parker's elbow. "We're not going to give up. There's always a means to the end, and we will find it."

"Tomorrow, you two take some time off and go sightseeing or shopping. By the way, Terry, can I borrow your phone? I'm a dummy! I forgot to bring mine," Tanaka said.

Terry pulled it out and tried turning it on. "Sorry, Uncle Jason, it's dead. I'll have to recharge it tonight."

"Never mind," Parker said, handing his phone to Tanaka. "Take mine. It's all checked out and fully charged."

# CHAPTER 4

PARKER TURNED OUT THE lights just when the copy of the journal and the translation caught his eye. *It's like it's mocking me. Maybe I should go over it one more time. No, screw it. I need some sleep.* When he woke twelve hours later, the journal no longer mocked him; instead, it beckoned him.

While he dressed in front of the bathroom mirror, Parker walked himself through Yuki's story. "He arrived in Japan in late June of 1868. So, where did he go after he returned? Did he get killed in Aizu, like Nakamura said? Wait a minute…." He sat down and fanned through the translation until he found the entry he was looking for:

> *What would it be like to be free from the turmoil I have encountered? Perhaps I can find peace someday sitting on the veranda at Daiten-ji contemplating the Fourfold Truths of Buddha, away from all the cares of the world. I yearn someday to be at peace. But what would become of Mary?*

He tore open a packet of rice crackers and munched on them while he reread the passage. *Where the hell is Daiten Temple?* He grabbed his laptop and googled the name. *Daiten-ji is only an hour from here. I suppose it wouldn't hurt to go there.* He jotted down the address, finished dressing, and grabbed his briefcase. When he opened the door, he came face-to-face with Terry, whose knuckles were poised to rap his forehead.

"Well, sleepyhead, you're finally awake."

"Terry, what's up? Where's Jason?"

"Forgot already, huh? I got up early this morning to give him my cell phone and return yours. I charged it last night, but he'd already left. He's on his way to the Manjiro Museum, remember? But where are you going with that briefcase of yours?"

"Do you remember when Yuki mused about becoming a Buddhist monk?"

"Yes. He was homesick or something. So?"

"Stay with me, Terry. I think this might be important. Yuki referred to Daiten-ji in that entry. I checked out the temple, which is less than an hour from here."

"Parker, I know you want to solve this, but let me borrow one of your favorite phrases—it really is a stretch." She opened the door a bit wider and smiled. "Or are you just trying to avoid shopping with me today?"

"Heck no. We'll have plenty of time to do that when we get back."

"I suppose it won't hurt to go. When do you want to leave?"

"Fifteen minutes ago. Here's the name and address. Let's take a taxi."

"No. We'll go by train. It's faster."

# CHAPTER 5

A TSUNAMI OF COMMUTERS surged through the passageways and eddied about the ticket machines in Shinjuku Station. With 3.2 million passengers passing through daily, it is the world's busiest train station. Parker held his briefcase to his chest, fearing the human riptide might tear it from his hands.

"We're going to take the Odakyu Line. Stay close," Terry shouted as they climbed a staircase. "Let's go. We can grab the next limited express. It's leaving in two minutes."

They got to the train just as a buzzer sounded, warning that the doors were about to close. But something caught Parker's eye. He recognized a man dashing through the closing door of the train three cars ahead.

"Get in," Terry said, pulling Parker inside. "What were you looking at? The doors almost shut you out."

"There's a man…the guy we saw at that Shinto shrine two days ago. He had on a pair of aviator sunglasses and a baseball hat. He just boarded three cars ahead of us."

"Parker, don't be so paranoid."

"I'm not. He is the jerk I spotted standing next to the stone torii, pretending to examine it. Don't you remember?"

"Parker, I know you were traumatized when Blackwell and his

sidekick tried to kill you, but you may be overreacting." She took him by the arm, and they grabbed the last two open seats. "We'll see who it is when we get off."

Thoroughly chastened, Parker sat glumly as the train pulled out. Forty minutes later, they arrived at Ikuta Station. People flooded the platform when the doors opened, and Parker and Terry were swept along to the exit gate. Parker scanned the crowd, but he did not see the man. By the time they were outside the station, Parker had concluded he was wrong about what he had seen. Terry hailed a cab outside, and they climbed in.

"Take us to Daiten-ji," Terry said in Japanese.

The driver hesitated and called his office.

"That's odd. He needs directions," Terry whispered. "Daiten-ji must not be widely known here."

The driver hit the meter button, climbed a hill, and turned onto a dirt lane leading into a wooded area. A quarter of a mile later, he pulled up next to a granite column at the foot of a hill. Terry paid with her smartphone app, and she and Parker climbed the uneven path to a small entrance gate.

Many Buddhist temple gates are stately affairs with elegant sloping roofs. But Daiten-ji's gate was in obvious disrepair. Roof tiles were missing, and one of the supporting columns had severe wood rot.

"This place looks like it's on its last legs," Terry said. "I wonder if there's even a full-time priest here."

"Someone is here," Parker said. "The temple doors are open."

As they approached the entrance, Terry noticed a nearby cemetery shaded by a stand of ancient cedars.

"You're right. Someone is here," she said, pointing to a headstone. "Check out the incense sticks in the ceramic urn. They're smoking."

"Yeah, and someone is standing near the trees," Parker whispered, pointing to a man holding a broom. "He's staring at us."

"Ooo, I see him. He's wearing priestly robes. Use the term *Osho-Sama* to address him. It means something like Reverend."

The priest finished sweeping up a small pile of leaves and greeted them with a toothless smile and an arthritic bow.

They stopped several paces from him and returned his bow. "Osho-Sama, *ohayo gozaimasu*," Terry said.

The old priest smiled, squinting at them through his cloudy eyes.

"He's dirt poor. Look at his kimono. It's threadbare," Parker whispered.

"I hear you speaking English, young man. Visitors are a rarity, especially foreigners. *Ohayo gozaimasu*, good morning to you," the priest said.

"Sir, I mean Osho-Sama, you speak English?"

"I try. I studied your language from middle school all the way through the university. I won first prize in a national speech contest early after the Pacific War."

"Allow me to introduce ourselves," Terry said. "My name is Ando Teruyo. My American name is Terry, and this is my friend Parker West. We've come to see you."

"I'm sure you mean you've come to see the temple. Before the war, people visited and admired its architecture, but hardly anyone does nowadays. You must be looking for Ozen Temple. It's a few kilometers from here. I can give you directions."

"No, we came here to do some research and talk to you," Parker said.

"Ah, yes, research. The last person to come here for that purpose was a university professor. That was about fifteen years ago. Unfortunately, I have little money to care for Daiten-ji. It was built in 1558 during the Era of the Warring States, but no one cares about such things anymore. Young people have no interest, and the elderly cannot climb the hill."

"Have any famous visitors come here?" Terry asked.

"Famous? No. The temple served only poor farmers back when Ikuta was a small village. Once there was a school here where the priest taught the local children, but now the few visitors who come do so only to visit family graves." He paused and looked at his broom for a moment. "A merchant from the village once endowed the temple, and it supported a succession of priests and their families for over one hundred and fifty years. But now, it is just the opposite. The town of Ikuta is prosperous, and the temple is poor."

He pointed to the main building. "There is a donation box just to the right of the temple steps. Would you be kind enough to drop a few coins into it before leaving?"

Terry nodded. "Yes, of course, but …."

"Forgive me, but I have work to finish. I will hold a *hoji* ceremony the day after tomorrow. It is the third anniversary of someone's death. I will recite a sutra for the family, who will pay me for the service. Such donations and a small government stipend are my only sources of income. If you would like to visit inside, be my guest. The main hall is open, as you can see. There is an ancient effigy of Amida Buddha on the altar. It is about one meter high and beautiful to behold. It is finished with gilded lacquer. See for yourselves."

"Osho-Sama," Parker said, "I understand you are quite busy. We will certainly leave a generous donation, but we really did come to see you. We have some questions."

The priest held the palm of his hand behind his left ear, as if he had not heard clearly. "Questions? Me?"

"Yes. We want to know about someone who possibly visited Daiten-ji around a hundred-fifty years ago. His name was Tomita Yuki."

The priest's milky eyes suddenly darted from Parker to Terry as though he was unsure who had uttered the name. "Tomita Yuki, you say?"

"Yes."

The priest frowned. "I have never heard of such a person," he said with brusque finality.

"Perhaps there is a record of his visit, or maybe he was buried here," Parker persisted. "May we examine the kakocho if there is one?"

"No," the priest said, sweeping past Parker's feet. "I cannot spend any more time with you. I must get on with my work. Please be on your way. Good day." He turned his back, leaving Parker and Terry to look at each other in wonderment.

"He's a bit crotchety," Terry said. "We should just leave."

"Hold on," Parker said. "It's weird. Did you see his reaction when I mentioned Yuki's name?"

"He's just old. He probably doesn't realize how abrupt he sounded."

"No, his English is amazing, especially for a man his age. I think we're on to something."

"Oh, come on, Parker, don't be pushy."

Parker shook Terry's hand off his shoulder and called after the priest. "Osho-Sama, Tomita Yuki visited this temple quite often. He was an Aizu samurai."

The old man set his broom aside. He looked pale, and Parker thought he might be having a seizure for a moment.

"Osho-Sama," Terry said, "is something wrong?"

The priest glared at Parker through his cloudy eyes. "There are no more Tomita descendants," he said. "The family line ended with the death of Tomita Yuki and his two brothers."

"Bingo. I told you I was on to something," Parker whispered.

# CHAPTER 6

"OSHO-SAMA, FORGIVE MY impertinence," Parker said, "but you are mistaken. Tomita Yuki was not the last descendant of the Tomita family. I have proof."

The old priest hobbled closer to Parker. "Proof, you say?"

"Yes, I have a diary Tomita Yuki kept when he was in America. It's in here," he said, pointing to his briefcase. "In fact, I am a direct descendant of Yuki."

The priest cocked his head. "Diary? America?" He eyed Parker suspiciously before doing the unexpected. He stroked Parker's cheek with the back of his wrinkled hand. "Can it be?" You are not trying to trick me?"

"No, sir."

"Then come and show me the diary."

Parker gave Terry a surreptitious high five, and they followed him to the temple. They removed their shoes, entered, and bowed in front of the ornate altar. Over four hundred years of incense soot had darkened the gilded features of Amida, the Buddha of the Western Pure Land, the Buddha of Immeasurable Light. The priest bowed before the seated figure and lit three incense sticks, placing them in a bronze urn. Terry gave Parker a nudge, and they bowed as the old man struck a small bell. He intoned a prayer and then led them to a cramped room.

"*Dozo*, please sit down," he said. He retrieved a pair of steel-rimmed glasses that looked as if they came from the 1930s and carefully hooked them about his ears. "You are part Japanese?"

"Osho-Sama, have you heard of DNA?"

"Mr. West, I am ninety-five but still listen to the radio. I know what DNA is. Why do you ask?"

"Because the proof is in my DNA. We found a bloodstain on one of the pages in Yuki's diary." Parker opened his briefcase and pulled out a copy of the lab analysis. "We had it tested, and the DNA proves I am related to him. And here's something I wish to give you. It's a photocopy of his diary and an English translation."

Parker turned to the first page and slid it across the table. "Yuki was sent to America on a secret mission to purchase rifles. It is a long story, ending when he left America and presumably returned to Japan. We do not know what happened to him afterward. That is what I am trying to find out. A woman named Mary bore their love child, but I assume Yuki never saw the baby."

"Yes, I know about the rifles and the child," the priest said. "But give me a moment while I compare the writing."

He retrieved a folder from a bookshelf. He pulled out a piece of handmade paper and compared the writing with the handwriting in the copy of Yuki's journal.

"This is amazing," the priest said. "The handwriting matches. You must be Yuki's descendant."

"What is that document you've been comparing?" Terry asked.

"It's a farewell letter Yuki wrote to his elder brother. He was the priest here."

"Hold on. Yuki was here with his elder brother?"

"Yes, Tomita Tomoyoshi was the temple priest at the time. Yuki had a younger brother too. His name was Yoshi. Do you know the story of the White Tigers?"

"Yes, we do," said Parker. "We visited Yoshi's grave on Mount Iimori yesterday. But what's this about Yuki's elder brother?"

"As I mentioned, Tomita Tomoyoshi was the priest here in 1868, the year Yuki returned from America."

"But we assumed he was killed in Aizu along with Yuki."

"No. Tomoyoshi never went back to Aizu after becoming a monk. Parker-San, this diary brings both of us very happy news."

"I agree."

"You agree, but you don't understand yet?"

"Understand what?"

"You and I are related."

Parker and Terry stared at each other, not comprehending.

# CHAPTER 7

"OSHO-SAMA," PARKER SAID, "I'm not sure I understand. How is it that we are related?"

"It's a long story. Tomoyoshi became a young monk, and one evening, he came here begging for a bowl of rice and a place to sleep. His predecessor was on his deathbed, and he pleaded with Tomoyoshi to assume his priestly duties, to which he willingly agreed. The dying priest had a daughter who must have been a very kind and lovely girl because soon after her father's death, she married Tomoyoshi and gave birth to a girl named Saori."

"And?"

"And Saori was my grandmother. Don't you see? You are my distant nephew."

"I . . . I could never have imagined," Parker said.

Terry grasped his hand as he tried to make sense of what he had heard. Being related to the gentle old man sitting across from him filled Parker with a sense of tranquility, something he had never experienced before. The priest chuckled when he saw Parker struggling for words.

"There is even more, much more, my nephew."

"Please tell us," Terry said.

"Before I go on, let me finish reading Yuki's diary."

"We have all the time in the world and much to think about while you read," Parker said.

An hour later, the priest pulled off his glasses. "It's hard to believe, but it all comes together."

"Osho-Sama, do you know the date when Yuki left Daiten-ji for Aizu?"

"It was sometime in late September of 1868. In April that same year, he came to the temple with two commoners. An adult named Ichi and a boy named Ben. This is where the story gets a bit complicated. Yuki was supposed to meet his cousin in September and return to your country to get the rifles."

"His cousin Nariaki?"

"Yes. I just read his name in Yuki's diary. It is a sad story. A traitorous samurai by the name of Kuroi murdered him. He would have killed Yuki too, but Ichi drew the attackers away, giving Ben and Yuki time to escape on a fisherman's sailboat."

"What happened next?"

"Sadly, Ichi was killed, but Yuki and Ben somehow made it to Aizu. Weeks later, Ben returned to the temple. Tomoyoshi adopted him, and he eventually became a priest. Are you aware of the Japanese custom of adoption?"

"No, but what about Yuki?"

"Hold on, Parker, I think Osho-Sama is trying to make a point here. Let me explain," Terry said. "You see Japanese families without someone to carry on their name often adopt a male child who is given the family's surname. But this is where it gets interesting. Sometimes a daughter's prospective husband is even adopted to take on her family name."

"You're quite right, Terry-San. In this case, Ben became a Tomita and married Saori a few years later. He took over the priestly duties here when Tomoyoshi died. I am descended from their line. So, besides being related to Yuki, you, Parker, are distantly related to Ben by marriage."

"Incredible."

"That's an understatement," Terry said.

"Parker-San, there is even more to the story," the priest said. "I read in this diary that a commoner whose American nickname was Shorty was Yuki's assistant. You will be surprised to learn that he was Ben's father. The relationship is tangled, but Shorty is also your distant relative. It's because Ben married Saori. Shorty and Ben are your distant in-laws. I think that's what you would call them."

The old man got up and put his hand on Parker's shoulder. "I'll bring some tea while you think about all this."

When he was out of earshot, Parker turned to Terry. "I can hardly get my head around all this, but we must find out what happened to Yuki."

"I know he's been avoiding the subject, but just be patient. He'll tell us."

"You look like you're trying to hold back your tears. What's wrong, Terry?"

"Nothing's wrong. You've complained so much about not being able to find any clues here in Japan, but you've cracked the case. I can't wait to tell Uncle Jason."

The priest reappeared with a tray of teacups and a pitcher. "This is what you might call Japanese iced tea. It's made of roasted barley. Please enjoy."

Parker sipped the tea, thoroughly absorbed by the implications of what he had learned so far. "Osho-Sama," he said, "what more can you tell us about Yuki after he escaped on that fishing boat?"

The old priest sighed. "It is a sad, sad story, and I'm not sure I have the inner strength to tell you. Let me instead show you what Ben brought back. Lord Buddha has been waiting to give you some things. Things you've been seeking."

Parker looked wonderingly at Terry, but the old man got up from the table before he could respond to the priest's cryptic comment.

"Please follow me," he said.

# CHAPTER 8

THE OLD PRIEST BOWED before the altar and whispered a prayer. Parker and Terry stood behind him, gazing at the ancient figure of Buddha seated cross-legged upon a carved wooden cushion of lotus blossoms. The statue's placid countenance gave Parker an inexplicable sense of peace.

"The statue is heavy but very delicate," the old priest said in a hushed voice. "Please, Parker-San, carefully grasp it by its base and slide it to one side for me."

"Go ahead," Terry said. "I'll help you."

They slid the statue to the left and found a rectangular panel underneath.

"Remove it, and you will find a bag. It is very old, so be careful when you pick it up," the old priest said.

The panel slid free, and Parker extracted the bag. "It looks like an old rucksack."

"Bring it to my room," the priest said.

Seated at the table, he opened the rucksack, produced a small cloth sack, and gingerly undid the cord around its neck. "Parker-San, I have something for you." He produced a gold coin and placed it in Parker's open hand.

"Terry, look! It's a double eagle."

"Yes, a gold coin. It was part of Yuki's expense money. As poor as this temple was, my ancestors never dared exchange it for cash. It would have given the authorities cause to search the temple and discover Tomoyoshi-Sama's past identity."

"Why would that have been a problem?"

"Because for several years after Aizu fell, loyal shogunate samurai were sometimes hunted down and punished by the Imperial government. And if word had leaked out about Yuki's mission to America to buy rifles, Tomoyoshi could have been tortured to reveal what he knew. We've been suspicious of strangers ever since. My ancestors did spend the remaining expense money in the late 1800s, but not this gold coin."

Parker read the coin's small letters. "This was minted in San Francisco in 1860. Let me check what it's worth." He googled it on his phone and found one that had recently sold on an auction site. "Osho-Sama, it's worth about $2,600. I wish it were worth more, but there's no need to keep it hidden. I suggest selling it."

"Thank you, Parker. I can use the money. Oh, and here is something else."

The aged priest handed Terry a locket dangling on a leather cord.

She clicked it open, revealing a porcelain image of a young woman on the left and glass-covered hair strands on the right. "This must be Mary Butler, the woman who bore Yuki's love child, and this is a lock of her hair."

"There is one more thing," the priest said, "A most important item." He drew an antique tin canister out of the rucksack.

"Please, Parker-San, open it. I believe it holds a clue to what you seek."

# CHAPTER 9

PARKER TWISTED THE TOP off the canister and found a piece of paper inside. He carefully unfolded it. "It's a map," he said with uncharacteristic calm. Wide-eyed and slack-jawed, he looked to Terry as if he needed her affirmation.

"Parker, you did it. You found the treasure map." She reached over and hugged him. "I'm so proud of you."

"Let's see if it is really from the journal."

He placed the photocopy of the original diary on the table and fit the left side of the map alongside the gray vertical line on the left edge of the page from which the map had been cut. "It's a perfect match."

"Look at the X on the left-center of the sketch," Terry said. "It marks the spot."

"What do the characters next to it read?"

"*Kinoshita.* It means under the tree. That's where Yuki buried Shorty and the gold. Parker, you've done it!"

"Not so fast. Everything is here except an address. There's nothing even to suggest that it's in Rhode Island."

"At least it's a clue." Maybe we can find something about the small rivers in Rhode Island and go from there. River Oak, remember?"

"Fat chance." Parker said, "I thought we were close, but we are still a million miles away."

"Do not give up, Parker-San," the priest said. "I will pray that you persevere and someday discover the shogun's gold."

Having regretted his pessimism, he closed his eyes and considered his response. "Osho-Sama . . . uncle, I am certain that with your prayers, we will succeed. But please understand. The gold no longer matters. I am determined to bring Yuki's story to light. His love of Mary and his struggle against terrible odds. All of it. Terry's uncle has written several books on Japan, and I will ask him to write one about Yuki."

Parker paused a moment for effect and then continued. "And today, I've found a story about another treasure that must be told."

"What might that be?"

"You, my uncle. You and this temple are the greatest of treasures. When we find the gold, I will see that Daiten-ji and these grounds are fully restored."

The old priest seemed moved, although sadly so. "That is good of you, Parker-San. But my time is coming soon. I had hoped my son would succeed me, but he rebelled, preferring to pursue a life in the big city. That is why I never told him the secret. My death will mark the end of the Tomita family's history at Daiten-ji. No one will likely take my place, but he will not be a Tomita if someone does. But thankfully, you, my nephew, will carry on our American line."

Parker wanted to say to comfort him, but the priest's expression had already changed. He was smiling.

"By the way, a neighborhood lady visits me early each evening and provides me with a meal. I can ask her to prepare a few more things, and the three of us can dine here tonight."

"Osho-Sama, we cannot stay," Terry said. "But I promise to have a celebratory feast prepared when we return tomorrow with my uncle. May we borrow the map for one day?"

"Of course."

"Thank you, Osho-Sama. And I'll leave this with you," Parker said, pointing to the journal copy and its translation. "Besides the coin, they are the only things of worth I can give you for the time being."

Parker returned the rucksack and its contents to where they had been hidden. With Terry's help, he inserted the lacquered panel and slid the seated Buddha back to its original position. The old man stood fingering the wood beads of his *juzu*, and it was clear to Parker that his uncle, the priest, was very tired.

"Perhaps we should leave," Terry said.

"Before you do, I have something else to give you," the old priest said. From his folder, he produced a manila envelope. "There are two letters inside. Yuki recounts his last days, and Ben tells even more. Perhaps Terry's uncle will be able to translate everything. Please forgive me. I read them many years ago but cannot bear to do so again."

"Thank you, I understand. I will return them tomorrow."

"Nephew," the priest said, "this is the happiest day of my life."

"It is mine too."

"And mine too," Terry said.

"I have one more thing to show you," the priest said. "Years later, Ben returned to Aizu and recovered Yuki's remains. He interred them in the temple cemetery, and I think you noticed the headstone when you first came here. Come, let's look."

He led Parker and Terry outside, and they bowed and prayed in front of Yuki's grave marker. The old priest lit three incense sticks which Parker planted in the urn filled with gray ashes.

They said goodbye, and at the bottom of the hill, Yuki kissed Terry's hand. "Without your patience, I doubt this all would have come to light. What does all this mean to you?"

"History," Terry replied. "You discovered something historically important, and as you said, it's not about the gold anymore." Terry pulled him close and planted a kiss on his cheek.

"I agree," Parker said before planting one on her lips.

TERRY'S PHONE RANG AS they waited on the platform for the next train to Shinjuku. She pressed the speaker button and passed it to Parker.

"Jason? Where are you?"

"I've just arrived at the hotel. Let's have dinner in my room."

"Uncle Jason, Parker did it. He found the map," Terry said.

The ensuing pause caused Parker to think they'd lost the phone signal.

"The map?" Tanaka said. "Where?"

"At Daiten-ji, a small temple outside Tokyo. But don't get too excited. It tells us nothing we do not already know. The gold could be anywhere in New England, and...."

"Hold on, Parker. I have learned something important. I think we are very, very close. Get back soon. Bye for now."

Parker stared at the screen on Terry's phone.

"What is it?" she asked.

"Jason has a security contract on your phone, but I want it scanned anyway. Just in case Blackwell has somehow hacked it."

Terry shrugged. "Have it your way, Sir Paranoid," she said.

Parker called CyberSecure. "Can you scan this phone? I'm on a train in Japan."

"Relax, Mr. West. I see the number. We'll run a deep scan from here. But your phone is several miles away. Did you forget it, or was it stolen?"

"I loaned it to Jason Tanaka. I'm sure you know he's CyberSecure's client too."

"How about your laptop?"

"It's in my briefcase. I'll turn it on."

"Then, no problem. We have you covered. We get a new list of threats and hacks almost hourly. Some are very nasty."

Parker and Terry were getting off the train in Shinjuku when the CyberSecure agent called.

"Your computer and both cell phones are clean as whistles, Mr. West."

Parker gave Terry a thumbs up, and she flashed him an I-told-you-so smile.

# CHAPTER 10

WHILE PARKER WAS SLEEPING off his jet lag at the hotel, Blackwell had flown to Tosashimizu aboard a chartered jet. He beat Tanaka to the Manjiro Museum by three hours but failed to find anything. Discouraged, he reserved two seats on a charter flight back to LAX, one scheduled to depart that evening.

Fumio was waiting for him when he arrived back in Tokyo. "What you find, boss?"

"Nothing yet, but I know where to look. Did you keep them in your crosshairs while I was gone?"

"I'm sorry. West and Terry got away from me. I got as far as Ikuta, a station on the Odakyu Line."

Blackwell smiled and pulled out his cell phone. "No matter. I already know where they went."

金　金　金

THE OLD PRIEST WAS about to light an incense stick when Blackwell grabbed him by his neck and shoved him against the altar.

"An American was here. You gave him a map," he said in Japanese. He pressed the priest's windpipe to make his point.

"Please let me go. It's hard to breathe."

"What did you tell Parker West?"

"Please…"

Blackwell pressed harder. "Damn you, tell me."

The old man smiled and closed his eyes. "All will be well."

Blackwell's anger flared, and he slammed the priest's forehead against the altar. He dropped the body and checked for a pulse but found none.

"Damn," he said, "Fumio, start checking the other rooms. No, hold on."

"What do you find?"

"There's a track of incense ash and sooty fingerprints on the altar next to the statue. Help me move it." They shoved the statue aside and slid the panel open.

Blackwell pulled out the rucksack and unbuttoned the top flap. "I found something," he said. He grabbed Yuki's journal and the English translation but ignored the other contents.

"Where do we go from here?"

"It's time to act," Blackwell said, "Enough of this stalking bullshit."

On the way back to Shinjuku, he read the translation.

# CHAPTER 11

TANAKA HIT THE TV's mute button, and Parker and Terry pulled up chairs for dinner. After they finished, Tanaka returned Parker's smartphone. "So, tell me about the map."

Parker nudged Terry with his elbow. "Go on. You can tell the story better than I."

Terry took a sip of tea and coughed into her napkin as a prelude to recounting their story from when they got off the train in Ikuta to when the old priest said goodbye to them. When she finished, Parker produced the map from his briefcase, and Tanaka retrieved the original journal. He opened it and placed the map next to the page where Yuki had cut it out after burying Shorty.

"It's a perfect fit. I don't know what to say. I must have read the diary a dozen times, but it never dawned on me about Daiten-ji. Too bad the priest, your long-lost uncle, couldn't tell you what happened to Yuki."

"He knows what happened but could not bring himself to tell us. But I suspect the full story is here," Parker said, sliding the priest's folder across the dinner table.

Tanaka pulled out two pages from the first envelope and examined them. "It's a letter from Yuki to his brother. He wrote this on those blank pages he tore from the ledger. Look, there are brown streaks on them. Blood. That's a bad sign. I'm pretty much used to his handwriting, so let me try translating this on the fly. It's dated October 8, 1868. He likens Aizu samurai to falling leaves. It's his way of implying that something bad happened. I'm sure it's about the White Tigers."

"And a fellow named Kuroi too. Osho-Sama told us about him. He was a traitor who assassinated Yuki's cousin Nariaki and almost killed Yuki," Parker said.

"Sounds like danger stalked him from the very beginning, doesn't it? From what I've read so far, Yuki left nothing to his elder brother's imagination:

金　金　金

*Dear Brother,*

*The leaves of Tsuruga Castle have fallen, and a cold winter is in the offing. I pray that Ben has safely returned and has told you what happened after we left you. Kuroi murdered our cousin Nariaki and ambushed us by the Tama River the next day. Ichi sacrificed himself, allowing Ben and me to escape. After a harrowing journey, we arrived here in Aizu to the sound of cannon fire."*

"I wonder who Ichi and Ben were?" Tanaka said.

"Ichi befriended Yuki, and Ben was Shorty's son," Terry said. "Osho-Sama told us they are Parker's ancestral in-laws."

Tanaka shook his head in wonderment. "Amazing. Yuki's story gets more fascinating by the minute. Well, let me translate the rest:

*I was determined to fight alongside Yoshi, whom I believed had been assigned to Tsuruga Castle with his comrades. I dared not expose Ben to the danger, so I planned to take him to Uncle Matsudaira's country estate, where I assumed he would be safe.*

*We made our way over the hills to Mount Iimori, where I discovered a clearing littered with the bodies of Aizu soldiers.*

*Ben saw a farmer standing at the edge of the woods, aiding a survivor. His name is Iinuma Sadakichi. He sat leaning against a tree. The farmer used Iinuma's white headband to wrap his neck wound, and I helped lift him to his feet.*

*The young samurai steadied himself and pointed to Tsuruga Castle on the plain below. 'The castle has fallen. Aizu has lost,' he said. Then, he pointed to the bodies scattered about the clearing. 'I have failed in my duty to join them. I did not cut deeply enough.'*

*I was shocked when I realized his wound was self-inflicted. Iinuma told me he and the others had been assigned to a village on the other side of the hills, but they became lost and decided to return to defend the castle. When they saw it shrouded in flame and smoke, they realized Aizu had been defeated, and they took their own lives. Several soldiers, like Iinuma, chose to slash their necks. Many others attempted to commit seppuku, but some failed. To save them from further suffering, their companions beheaded them before taking their own lives.*

*When I surveyed the scene again, something struck me like a bullet in my chest. The fallen samurai were White Tigers. You cannot imagine my shock when I found Yoshi among the dead. I pulled his short sword from his abdomen and cradled him in my arms. Ben said later that my tears fell into our brother's open, unseeing eyes.*

*All the while, Ben sat next to me, reciting a prayer for the transmigration of Yoshi's soul. I considered burying him at Uncle Matsudaira's estate, but I knew he would have wished to remain with his comrades.*

*As I debated what to do, we heard enemy soldiers approaching, so we ran. One hour ago, we arrived at Uncle's estate only to discover that the beautiful gate and the mansion had been destroyed by cannon fire. The remains still smolder as I write.*

*It is getting dark, and I will finish this letter tomorrow. When I am rested, I plan to join the fight. Tsuruga Castle may have been destroyed, but that does not mean we've been defeated. I intend to send Ben back to you along with this letter."*

Tanaka paused to clear his throat. "My guess is that things did not get any better for Yuki the next day."

"'Yuki's tears fell into Yoshi's open eyes,'" Parker said. "How worse could things get?"

"We'll soon find out. Let me finish:

*It is October ninth by the Western calendar. Brother, my fate is sealed. This morning, I watched in dismay as a score of Aizu soldiers crossed the field in front of what is left of Uncle's estate. Armed with French rifles, they abruptly stopped and formed two lines. I was puzzled until I saw five enemy soldiers crowded around something not far away. Our soldiers fired and killed two of them, but the enemy answered with something called a Gatling gun. It spit out bullets from right to left, and our soldiers fell as though an invisible scythe had cut them down. I rushed to the edge of the field with my sword unsheathed, hoping to join our soldiers. But I was struck in the abdomen by a stray bullet. Ten Aizu soldiers lay dead, and the remaining ones ran to a stand of trees on the far side of the field with the enemy soldiers not far behind.*

*Unmindful of the danger, Ben helped me to my feet. I could barely walk, but we returned to Uncle's Garden. Ben wants to find a doctor, but I know my end is near, and I have refused.*

*I intend to send him back with all my belongings, including this letter and another I have already written to Mary, the woman I told you about. I asked Ben to find the French officer, a friend I have known for several years. He is currently stationed in Yokohama's foreign settlement, and Ben must find a way to deliver my letter to him before returning to Daiten-ji.*

*Tomoyoshi do not grieve. I am at peace. Ben is worthy of your benevolence, and I beg you to care for and raise him as you would a son.*

*Farewell, my brother.*"

TANAKA SIGHED. HE SLUMPED in his chair, removed his glasses, and dabbed his eyes. Terry wiped hers and grasped Parker's hand. He gave her a gentle kiss and wiped his eyes on his shirt sleeve.

Finally, Tanaka spoke. "The castle did not fall that day, but two weeks later, Aizu surrendered, and the civil war ended soon after...in Ezo."

"I wonder if Ben remained with Yuki until he died?"

"We'll find out soon enough," Tanaka said. He pulled the second letter from another envelope and scanned the first page. "This appears to be a letter Ben wrote. Very interesting."

"Why so?"

"He appears to have written this late in life. It's to Osho-Sama's father, dated October 8, 1908. That makes it the fortieth anniversary of Yuki's younger brother's death. Listen:

*To my son and his descendants,*

*I have kept a shameful secret hidden, and as my eternal journey draws near, I feel compelled to reveal my grievous sins, which I committed four decades ago. I have never stopped praying for Master Tomita, and ever since his death, I have striven to atone for breaking the most important of Lord Buddha's cardinal precepts.*

*I have fed and clothed the poor, patiently taught the village children, avoided sinful activities, and raised you to assume your role as the next priest to preside at this temple. But nothing I accomplished in the last forty years can atone for my deplorable behavior."*

"I wonder what's that all about?" Terry said when Tanaka paused to take a sip of water.

"We'll soon find out. Ben states that he will spare no details, and I believe it because of the length. His letter is divided into two parts. Let me summarize the first."

After reading the section, Tanaka recounted the story from the day Yuki and Ichi came to Ben's village until they disembarked from the *Takao Maru.*

"That's a ship they got on after escaping from the fellow Kuroi."

"From what you've told us so far, I'm guessing Ben was only fourteen or fifteen," Parker said.

"I would say so. Let me tell the rest of the story in Ben's own words. I'll try not to make any mistakes, but I'm not used to translating on the fly. The second part of the letter begins on October 8, 1868, when Yuki and Ben crossed the border into Aizu."

Tanaka readjusted his glasses and began to read.

"*On our way to Aizu, Master Tomita spoke about his mission to America and his love of Miss Mary, things he hesitated to tell me earlier. He said he intended to return to her after the Imperial Army was defeated, but nothing went as planned.*

*We found the body of his younger brother on Mount Iimori, and my master was severely wounded near the ruins of his uncle's country manor. I trust you have read his letter. It is the one I delivered to my adoptive father: your grandfather, Tomoyoshi-Sama.*

*The day after Master Tomita was wounded, he got up and limped over to a ginkgo tree with obvious pain. He took off his swords and sat formally on his calves and heels. There, he finished the letter to his elder brother. He described the horrific event on Mount Iimori and how he was wounded.*

*When he finished, he ordered me to return to Daiten-ji. On my way back, I was to deliver Miss Mary's letter, the one he had written aboard the Takao Maru. I was to give it to a French military officer in Yokohama. The other letter was addressed to his brother.*

*Master Tomita also gave me an American gold coin, Miss Mary's locket, and a big key. He instructed me to take them back too. I stuffed everything into my sleeve, intending to put them in Master Tomita's rucksack when I left.*

*Seeing how weak he had become, I begged him to allow me to find a doctor, but he would not hear of it.*

*I was puzzled when he removed the dagger his elder brother had given him, and, for a moment, he appeared to admire the blade. 'Go, now, and take my rucksack too,' he said.*

*I was powerless to do anything but obey, and I bade him*

*farewell. I was so distressed that I forgot to put the items from my sleeve into the rucksack.*

*'Sayonara,' he said in a gentle, untroubled voice.*

*I left him, but after I had walked a kilometer or so, I could not bear the thought of leaving my master to suffer and die alone. I returned intending to watch over him until his end. But shock seized my whole being when I witnessed him plunge the dagger into his bare abdomen. Blood drained onto his lap, but to my utter bewilderment, he sat placidly gazing at the trunk of the ginkgo tree. All was quiet. But a moment later, he took a deep breath and gave the dagger a forceful upward jerk. He slumped forward, and his shoulders heaved as his breathing became labored. His suffering tore at my heart.*

*He must have heard me whimper because he lifted his head and gave me a pained smile. I almost ran, but my compassion and respect would not have it. I drew close and, barely conscious of what I was doing, picked up the long sword and unsheathed it.*

*I was consumed by the horror of the moment, but duty overcame my urge to run. I held my breath, and with all the power I could muster, I closed my tear-filled eyes and ended my master's life. I killed him—the man I had loved and respected.*

*I was assailed by grief and weighted with guilt, and I fell to my knees and sobbed. Six months before, my mother had died, and Ichi-San sacrificed himself to save us only weeks before. And now my master was dead. I had ignored Lord Buddha's commandment not to kill.*

*After struggling to calm my muddled mind, I removed the letters, coin, key, and locket from my sleeve. I placed the heavy things atop the two letters so they wouldn't blow away, and with a shovel I found in the clutter of the gardener's shack, I dug a grave and buried my master's remains. It was noon when I finished, and I started to recite the alphabet poem:*

> *'Even as the scent still lingers,*
> *The flower's petals have scattered . . .'*

*But angry shouts interrupted me. I saw Kuroi and two of his men come running down the road. They were the ones responsible for killing Tomita-Sama's cousin, Ichi-Sama, and the fisherman. I grabbed the coin and locket and stuffed them into the rucksack. But when I grabbed the key, a gust of wind sent the envelopes sailing into the weeds. I dropped the key somewhere in the grass and chased after them. I snatched one, but the other skittered out of sight. Fearing for my life, I grabbed the rucksack and ran. My heart sank when I turned and saw Nibei, Kuroi's spy, standing by the grave, holding the envelope and the key.*

*I escaped through a collapsed section of a perimeter wall and blindly ran into a thicket of thorn bushes. A vine snagged my leg, and I slammed headfirst into a rotting tree stump.*

*On our way to Aizu, my master gave me his pistol and showed me how to use it. I pulled it out, cocked the hammer, and waited. Kuroi's bodyguard, a ronin, came dashing through the bushes. I blindly fired, and he fell. I had killed him. Kuroi cowered behind a tree, and I saw Nibei hand him the key and envelope. My heart sank.*

*'This is all I need,' Kuroi said when he read the American address on the letter.*

*'Do you know where the gold is?' Nibei asked.*

*'I do now, but we cannot leave until we capture Tomita.'*

*'He's there,' Nibei said, pointing to the fresh earth piled over my master's grave.*

*Those were his last words. Kuroi stabbed Nibei in his heart and killed him. That is when I got up and ran.*

*For some reason, Kuroi did not give chase, and a month later, I was back at Daiten-ji. I told Tomoyoshi-Sama that Master Tomita had died but did not reveal what I had done. Since then, I have been wrought with guilt.*

*Your mother and I have often told you that your grandfather was the first of the Tomita family's line of priests. He adopted and raised me as his son. I was a willing pupil and studied for the priesthood at a Buddhist school in Kamakura.*

*Four years later, I returned to Daiten-ji and married your grandmother. With Tomoyoshi-Sama's permission, I went to Aizu and recovered my master's remains. I then brought them back to Daiten-ji and re-interred them.*

*Now, it is nearing my time to join him on the journey we all must take. I have chosen to confess my sin of killing Master Tomita and the ronin. When I am gone, please pray for the peaceful transmigration of my soul.*

*Your father, Ben."*

# CHAPTER 12

PARKER AND TERRY HELD hands, lost in a moment of melancholy introspection. Choked up, Tanaka stared out the window at the crowds of fun-seekers below, attempting to calm himself.

"I always thought Yuki was killed defending Tsuruga Castle. How wrong I was," Tanaka stammered in a whisper.

"Now I know why Osho-Sama did not want to read the letters to us," Terry said. "The story is heartbreaking. It was as though the weight of the whole world had crushed Yuki. I cannot imagine how both he and Ben suffered. By the way, Parker and I saw Yuki's grave at Daiten-ji's cemetery. Osho-Sama places sticks of incense in front of it every day."

"Terry, dear, forgive me for interrupting, but we must get on with it."

"Jason, you're right," Parker said. "Please change our flight from tonight to tomorrow night. I'm sure you'll want to interview my uncle."

"For sure. Maybe he can give us another clue that we can use to find the gold." Tanaka held his index finger and thumbed an inch apart. "We are this close. We have what we need."

"How can you say that? The map indicates that the gold is buried under a large tree. We're not even close."

"Hold on. I haven't told you my story yet."

"We are all ears."

"Well, I found nothing at the Manjiro Museum, so on a hunch, I visited a museum in the nearby hometown of a famous samurai named Sakamoto Ryoma. He met, and sometimes corresponded, with John Manjiro. The museum curator showed me an original letter Manjiro had written to Ryoma in 1864. In passing, he mentioned Benjamin Butler and Captain Whitfield."

"Okay, so what are we missing?" Terry asked.

"The curator told me about a collection of Whitfield memorabilia, including his diary. It is in the Fairfield, Massachusetts, town library."

"Not another diary," Parker groaned, expecting his sarcasm would get a reaction. But something on the TV was distracting Tanaka.

Terry grabbed the remote and turned it off. "Uncle Jason, please focus."

"Terry, we need to hear this," Tanaka said. "Turn it back on."

Parker saw an older woman being interviewed by a reporter. "What is she saying?" he asked.

"She's being interviewed in front of Daiten-ji's gate. Parker," Terry cried out. "She just said she found your uncle's body. He's been murdered."

"Oh, God, no! Is she the woman who brings him dinner every night?"

"Yes. She says she saw a foreigner and a Japanese woman leaving the temple this afternoon, and another foreigner and a Japanese man leaving a couple of hours later. She took a meal to the temple when they were gone and found your uncle's body."

"What have I done?" Parker groaned. "I should have realized Blackwell was stalking us. I am why Osho-Osama is dead."

"Parker, it's not your fault," Tanaka said. "Listen up. We've got to act. The cops are probably already looking for you and Terry. Our flight leaves at 10 o'clock, but we'd better leave now. Let's get packing."

Parker got up to leave but stopped when he saw a set of grainy photos on the TV screen. "Damn," Parker said. "That's us standing on the platform at Ikuta Station. And look at the other photo. The short guy wearing the baseball cap and sunglasses must be Fumio, and the other is Blackwell. Why didn't I figure this out before? They've stalked us ever since I knocked on your door in Pasadena."

"How could they have known we were in Japan?" Terry wondered.

"I don't know, but we need to get our act together," Jason said. "It's probably only a matter of hours until the cops find out who and where we are."

Terry grabbed the remote and turned off the TV. "Both of you listen up. The police will be looking for a foreign man and a Japanese woman, so Uncle Jason, you and I will take the express train to the airport. Get your passports and give me the journal and the map. Parker, you go alone. Grab a taxi in front of the Gracery Hotel and take it to Narita."

"Wait a minute. Hotel what?"

"The Gracery. It's part of the Toho Cinema complex. Toho produces all the *Gojira* movies. You can see his giant likeness glaring down from the hotel's rooftop. It's one of Shinjuku's big tourist attractions. He gets angry every hour and growls loudly as he hisses out steam. Gojira is Japanese for Godzilla."

"Gojira is the way Japanese say Godzilla," she said.

"Oh."

"Go to the front to hail a taxi."

Tanaka handed the journal and map to Terry. "Parker, let me keep your phone. We're going to Fairfield, Massachusetts, and I need to make reservations before getting to LA."

He thrust a wad of Japanese banknotes into Parker's hands. "You'll need money for your taxi ride. Remember, it's the private terminal at Narita. Let's get out of here before it's too late."

They hastened outside, where an endless crowd of cosplayers wandered past the hotel. Parker was about to say one last goodbye when he saw Fumio and Blackwell shoving through the crowd fifty yards away.

"Get back inside and take the rear emergency exit. I'll lure them away," Parker shouted.

It started sprinkling as Parker dashed down the road. As he wove through the crowd, he saw Fumio closing the gap when he looked over his shoulder, but Kuroi was not with him.

He reached the back of the Toho Cinema complex and shouldered his way through the packed crowd to the front of the hotel. But there were no taxis, just a line of tourist buses.

He ducked inside the building and into an elevator. He pressed the hotel lobby button, but the elevator did not stop on the second floor. *Where the hell is it taking me?* He found out when the doors opened. The Gracery Hotel lobby is located on the eighth floor.

Panicked, Parker scanned the crowded foyer for a place to hide. He saw an exit sign. He rushed to the far corner where two glass doors slid open.

He ran outside and found himself on an observation terrace. Looking over his shoulder, he saw Fumio pushing his way through a line of guests in front of the registration counter.

Parker dashed to the far end of the terrace, but there was no exit. The glass doors opened, and Fumio strutted outside. Behind a fake rock wall, on Parker's right, was the gigantic figure of Godzilla, bathed in purple light, glaring down at the crowd of merrymakers on the street below. With no other way to escape, he climbed the rock wall and onto the scaly hide of Godzilla. He shinnied up its back and swung about to face Fumio.

"Come down and give me map," Fumio shouted.

"Screw you," Parker answered.

Godzilla's neck was over three feet wide and eight feet long. Its scaly hide, made of hard-cast resin, glistened in the rain, and the monster's fierce yellow eyes glowered at the crowd below. Parker straddled the monster's neck, his knees hard-pressed against the scales.

Fumio wasted no time. He climbed onto the prehistoric reptile and jostled his way forward. Parker pushed himself backward, not daring to look at the street below.

"You gonna slip off and die. Give me a map, and I'll go away," Fumio shouted.

One hundred feet separated Parker from the gathering crowd below. He held onto the beast's scaly hide and waited. "If you want the map so bad, come and get it."

"You gonna be sorry!" Fumio shimmied ahead until he was within arm's length of Parker. He pulled out his knife and slashed the air. "You make big trouble. Hand me map, or I kill you."

Parker was determined to decide the outcome. He pressed his legs against Godzilla's scales as tightly as possible and thrust his upper body forward, his forehead striking Fumio's left knee. Godzilla let out a roar, and Parker cringed, expecting to feel Fumio plunge the knife blade into his back. But he felt nothing. Godzilla let out another roar, and an ear-piercing hiss of vapor shot from his gaping mouth.

Parker pushed himself up, staring at the flailing man who had sent him to the Pasadena hospital. He saw his chance. Summoning his last ounce of energy, Parker grabbed Fumio's right knee and wrenched it. Fumio shrieked, dropped his knife, and slipped off, hitting his head on the safety wall before tumbling over the edge of the building. A moment later, Parker heard a startled howl from the crowd below.

He inched his way down and scrambled onto the roof. A crowd of shocked onlookers had gathered near the glass doors, and Parker barged through them. When he reached the ground floor, he jumped in a taxi that had just pulled up behind the last tour bus.

"Narita airport. The private air terminal, please," he said.

金 金 金

A FEW SECONDS AFTER Fumio and Parker disappeared into the bustling crowd on the road, Blackwell charged after Tanaka and Terry, who had disappeared into the hotel. He was jostled by a score of guests milling about the lobby. A night clerk stood in front of an emergency door, urging them to ignore the flashing red light and the loud clang of the alarm bell.

Blackwell pushed him out of the way and dashed outside. He craned his neck, expecting to spot Tanaka. But the bobbing heads of the rowdy crowd made it impossible to see more than a few feet in any direction. Kuroi guessed that Tanaka and his niece were on their way to Shinjuku Station, so he took the most logical route, but a wall of people slowed him every way he turned. Concluding it was futile to continue, Blackwell spun around, bumping into a cosplayer. The man was dressed in a gemstone-studded, high-collared jumpsuit and was sporting sunglasses and a wig with sideburns.

"Don't be steppin' on my blue suede shoes," the cosplayer said, pointing to his feet.

Blackwell was about to slug him when he heard the shrill sound of a whistle a few yards behind.

"Emergency, stand aside," a policeman shouted.

Positive the emergency had to do with Parker and Fumio, Blackwell shouldered his way to the Gracery. He was stunned to find Fumio's bleeding body on the pavement. Blackwell was able to save him from a gangland execution, but not from Parker West.

"Fumio," he wailed. But he heard two police officers pushing through the crowd, and he ran.

In front of Hotel Gracery, Blackwell caught a glimpse of Parker's taxi pulling out into the traffic. Another taxi pulled up, and he got in next to the driver.

"Sir, where do you wish to go?" he asked, but Blackwell did not respond. "Sir?" the driver asked again.

Kuroi shrugged. "Take me to the private terminal at Haneda Airport," he said in Japanese, "and make it fast."

Forty minutes later, he and five well-heeled passengers cleared security without incident. They boarded a Bombardier Global 8000 and prepared for the flight back to LAX. Minutes before take-off, Blackwell's phone vibrated. He put it to his ear and listened in on Tanaka.

# CHAPTER 13

AT NARITA INTERNATIONAL AIRPORT'S private terminal, Tanaka spent an hour on Parker's phone planning their next move. He chartered a jet from LAX to the closest airport to Captain Whitfield's hometown of Fairfield, Massachusetts. He made his second call to Crown City Security.

"Have six guards meet us at the private terminal at LAX. Rent one of those big SUVs and have it waiting for me at New Bedford Regional Airport. It's south of Boston. We'll be there around four o'clock in the afternoon to pick it up. Stock it with a couple of shovels, an ax, and a pick—whatever you think we need for digging. Throw in some hand tools too."

"What's all this for?"

"I plan to do some archeology on a plot of land I just bought."

"Cool. How about a low-frequency GPR?"

"What's that?"

"Ground-penetrating radar. It looks like a powered push mower. You run it over the ground, and it will find anomalies as deep as ten feet. The problem is, they run about twenty-five grand."

"Get one and have it ready."

Minutes later, Parker arrived at Narita, fearing the police were waiting to grab him. But a ticket agent hardly looked at him when she handed him a boarding pass. He cleared security, and an immigration officer stamped his passport without asking questions.

Terry and Jason were waiting at the departure gate. They led Parker to a private room and shared their escape stories.

"You had a lot of guts bumping into Blackwell with your blue suede shoes," Parker said after hearing his story.

"Sometimes, the obvious is the most difficult to recognize," Tanaka said.

"Terry, where were you all this time?"

"I was Raggedy Ann. Blackwell didn't bother to give me a second look." She gave Parker a peek at a red wig nestled in her purse. "But tell us, how did you get away?"

"I didn't. Fumio caught up with me on Godzilla's back."

Terry and Tanaka listened spellbound as Parker related his fight with Fumio.

"Oh, Parker, how very brave of you," Terry said.

"It had nothing to do with bravery and a lot to do with fear and luck. So, what's next, Jason?"

"I've made all the necessary arrangements. We leave for Fairhaven soon after arriving at LAX, but it will be Sunday when we arrive."

"So?"

"The library where Captain Whitfield's diary is located won't be open, so I reserved three rooms at the Delano Homestead. It's a great B&B named after one of President Franklin Roosevelt's ancestors who used to live there."

金　金　金

DURING THE TEN-HOUR flight to LA, Parker downloaded a Japanese-English dictionary onto his cell phone and entered two words: black and well.

"I'll be damned," he said when he read the definitions of the two kanji.

"What are you doing?" Terry asked.

"Nothing. I was checking out that B&B online. It looks nice."

It took Parker a couple more hours to put all the pieces together, and when he did, he realized Blackwell's motive was not all pure greed. But he decided to wait until they found the gold before telling Tanaka and Terry what he had discovered.

The Crown City Security guards met them after they cleared Customs and Immigration. They then cleared the security checkpoint at the private terminal, and another set of guards walked them to the Cessna waiting for them on the tarmac.

An hour earlier, another chartered jet had taken off from Hollywood Burbank Airport with only two passengers aboard. It, too, was bound for New Bedford.

A black Lincoln Navigator with keys inside was parked on the tarmac of New Bedford Regional. After checking out the tools and the GPR, they drove to Fairfield and registered at the B&B. Jet lag and the fear for their lives had taken their toll. They went to bed early, but Terry was late to the breakfast table the following day.

"I feel miserable," she said. I think I'm coming down with something. Let me know what you find this morning."

It was nine o'clock when Parker and Tanaka entered the Millicent Public Library. They washed their hands, and after the librarian made copies of their driver's licenses, she led them to a side room. She unlocked a bookcase door and presented Tanaka with Captain Whitfield's leather-bound journal.

Sitting at a small table, Parker opened the diary to 1840 and read the first entry. "It's way too early. Let's start with 1860."

They scanned page after page but found nothing. "Still too early," Tanaka said.

Parker shook his head. "No, let's hang in a while longer."

Moments later, he pointed to a paragraph in the middle of the next page. "Check this out, Jason."

Tanaka adjusted his glasses and read the entry aloud.

*"May 12, 1861: Benjamin Butler stopped by on his way to Boston. He's accepted an officer's commission with the 28th*

*Regiment of the Massachusetts Volunteers. Miss Mary is quite unhappy with the prospect of Ben going to war."*

Tanaka ran his fingers farther down the page and then the next. "That's all. There's no mention of where they lived."

"This morning, I checked out John Manjiro on the *Wikipedia* website. I learned he visited Whitfield in the fall of 1870. It sounds like he got off the hook with the new government because they sent him here with a diplomatic delegation. He reportedly took time off to visit Whitfield."

Parker found what he was looking for on page 151. "Jason, listen to this:

> *I am very much relieved. I had long feared that John had been killed, but he sent me a telegram from New York City two days ago. He survived the civil war in Japan and is now a member of the new government's delegation. He visited me yesterday and stayed overnight. It was a joyous reunion, and he told me about all the changes that had taken place in his country.*
>
> *John was saddened to hear of Ben Butler's and Mary's passing. Benjamin is buried in Boston, and maybe Mary is buried at their ancestral home outside Woonsocket. John was too pressed for time to visit their graves."*

"Give me a second," Tanaka said. He googled Woonsocket on his cell phone. "It has a population of around 41,000 and is in Providence County, Rhode Island. A farm near a relatively small city with a nearby cemetery beside a river shouldn't be too difficult to find. There's bound to be a historical society in Woonsocket. Somebody there should be able to give us what we need. Let's get Terry and go."

When she opened her door, Parker was shocked. Terry looked like hell.

"You guys go without me," she said in a phlegmy voice. "If you find the gold, call me, okay? I'll take a taxi out there and take pictures."

Parker gave her a lingering kiss on her cheek. "I'll call you as soon as we find it."

They got into the SUV, and Tanaka punched the address to the Woonsocket Historical Society into the GPS.

"We're on our way," Parker said, shifting into drive.

# JOHN MANJIRO (1827 – 1898)

# & WILLIAM H. WHITFIELD (1804-1888)

MANJIRO WAS 14 YEARS OLD when he and four others were stranded on a deserted island several hundred miles southeast of Japan. William H. Whitfield, the captain of the whaling ship *Howland*, rescued the starving party. He dropped the other members off in Hawaii, but "John Manjiro" returned to the US upon Whitfield's invitation. He and his wife cared for John and saw to his education in Fairhaven, Massachusetts. Manjiro learned English and studied navigation. During his ten years abroad, he spent more than six at sea. In 1850, he went to California and panned for gold. He made enough money to pay for his way back to Japan.

In 1853 and 1854, Commodore Mathew C. Perry visited Japan in what some have called an exercise in "gunboat diplomacy." The shogunate hastily summoned Manjiro to advise the government on how to deal with Perry. He was elevated to the rank of samurai and chose the name of his home village, Nakahama, as his surname.

Under duress, the shogunate eventually signed the Japan-US Treaty of Amity and Commerce. Japan was required to open two ports to American ships, ensure the safety of American castaway sailors, and allow the establishment of a US consulate.

In 1870, Nakahama Manjiro returned to the US on an official mission with the new Japanese government and visited Whitfield in Fairhaven. Manjiro's advice and insights helped Japan along its road to becoming a modern nation.

Learn more about Manjiro and Fairfield's famed Manjiro Festival at: *https://whitfield-manjiro.org.*

*Photos are in the public domain. Photo of John Manjiro courtesy of Fairhaven's Millicent Library. Photo of Captain Whitfield courtesy of Kyo Nakahama and Dr. Issei Imanaga, great-great-grandchildren of Manjiro.*

# CHAPTER 14

THEY FOUND WOONSOCKET HISTORICAL Society's brick building close to the Blackstone River. The librarian, a seventy-something woman with bluish-white hair, welcomed them.

"I'm Patience Stanbury. How may I help you?"

"We're looking for a farm owned by Benjamin Butler in the 1860s. A river runs through the property. Butler was a Civil War veteran," Parker said.

"Have you checked the title companies? They've digitized all the property records in Providence County."

"Yes, but we didn't come up with anything."

"If that is the case, it's quite likely Butler did not own property here, but I suppose the title companies could have messed up. We have plenty of rivers and creeks running through our farmland. Can you be more specific?"

"Well, it had a small cemetery on it."

"They are called pioneer cemeteries, and not all the graves are marked. You might try checking with the property registrar in Lincoln. It's on Route 126, south of here."

"It's worth a try," Tanaka said. "Come on, Parker. Let's go. Sorry to have bothered you, Miss Patience."

Parker opened the door and saw a large oak tree across the street. Something clicked.

"Miss Patience, a big tree was growing on the property we're looking for."

She laughed. "Oh, Mr. West, there are a lot of big trees around here, just like the one you're looking at, and . . ."

She paused and put her hand over her heart. "Oh, my, A big tree and a cemetery? Good gracious, perhaps it is where Nathanael Greene once camped."

"Who?"

"Do you mean to tell me you don't know about General Nathanael Greene? He was Washington's right-hand man during the Revolution. Greene is Rhode Island's most famous Revolutionary War hero."

"Sorry, I'm not much on American history. Why was a tree named after him?"

"It is said that Greene pitched his tent under a great oak tree near Mr. Wainwright's grist mill. It's still there, as far as I know—the tree. The Daughters of the American Revolution installed a plaque beside it. I clearly remember the ceremony."

Parker let go of the doorknob. "Whoa, a mill? The DAR?"

"Yes, a tributary of the Blackstone River powered a grist mill there long ago. In the early 1800s, several Woonsocket families lived along the river, and a local cemetery was established. Wealthier families built grandiose crypts and elaborate headstones for their dear beloveds. Then came the train. The tracks were too close, and the area lost its cachet. The homes were abandoned, moved, or burned down, and the cemetery surrounding the big oak fell into disuse. Mother took me there for the DAR ceremony I just mentioned. Except for some brick foundations, the mill was gone, and the cemetery was in ruins."

"How do we get there?"

"Look at this wall map. It's near the Black Hut Management Area. Take this road hugging the Blackstone River. You'll see a turnoff just before the river bends south. The twisted remains of an old railroad trestle are nearby. The cemetery is back in the woods somewhere."

"You have been a great help, Miss Patience."

"Good luck, young man," she said.

# CHAPTER 15

TWENTY MINUTES LATER, Parker pulled up next to the rusting remains of a railroad trestle, and Tanaka unfolded a photocopy of Yuki's map.

"See those two depressions running through that field?" he said. "They are wagon or tractor ruts. Could be decades old."

"You've got better eyes than I do, Jason. Let's go."

Parker negotiated the potholed ruts and stopped when he reached a break in the tree line to their left.

Tanaka examined the map again. "Yuki's scale is a bit off but, look," he said, pointing to an open area. "There's the river and the cemetery."

"Forget the cemetery, Jason. Check out the size of that oak tree."

Tanaka rubbed his eyes and squinted. "I can't believe it. Can it be?"

They picked their way between dozens of tilting headstones, broken pedestals, and fallen marble statues. When they reached the venerable oak, Tanaka gave Parker a congratulatory slap on his back.

"We've done it! But go check out the obvious first. Behind you," he said, nodding toward three stone mausoleums overgrown with ivy and crowded by fir trees. "They aren't anywhere close to this oak, but it's better to check them out first. Family names are usually carved over the entrances. If one of them reads 'Butler,' I just blew twenty-five grand on the GPR."

Parker took his time inspecting each one. "The good news is you didn't waste your money," he said when he returned to the tree. "I couldn't find the Butler name. Just Smith, Wainwright, and Underwood."

"Well, I guess it's time to crank up the GPR," Tanaka said.

They staked out a large circle around the tree, and Parker pushed the machine through the weeds while Tanaka walked beside it, monitoring the screen. An hour later, they were done checking every square foot.

"That was a waste of time. What now?" Parker said.

Tanaka unfolded the map and studied it again. "I guess we have to enlarge the area. As I said, the map's scale is a bit off."

"Underwood, Underwood," Parker muttered under his breath.

"Hey, did you hear me?" Tanaka said. "Let's get going."

"Jason, hold on a bit. Terry told me your shell company had something to do with your real name."

"Yes, but what's that got to do with anything?"

"Just hear me out. Terry drew two kanji for me and explained that Tanaka means 'field little.' She said you reversed the characters to form Middlefield, your company's name."

"That's true, but where are you going with this?"

"Well, Yuki said he buried the gold under the tree, right?"

"Yes, he implied as much."

"How do you write the word 'under' in Japanese?"

"All right, I'll play along." Tanaka scratched a character in the dirt with a stick. "It looks like the capital letter T with a finger pointing down."

"And the character for a tree?"

Tanaka bent down and scratched out another character.

木

"This is the tree trunk," he said, pointing to the vertical stroke. "Imagine it has four branches, two sticking straight out from either side and two drooping down. Come on, Parker, do you mind telling me what you're driving at?"

"Jason, just a couple more questions. What about the character for a tree? Does it have more than one meaning?"

"Most kanji do. The most common meaning for the tree character is wood. It can be pronounced '*moku*.'"

"Bingo! You just said the magic word."

"Moku?"

"No, wood. Combine the words wood and under, reverse them just like you did for your company name, and get the words under and wood. Understand now? The gold is there," Parker said, gesturing toward the largest of the three overgrown mausoleums. He ran to it and pointed at the name UNDERWOOD carved into the granite lintel over the bronze door. "Tomita stashed the gold in the Underwood family vault, or whatever this structure is called."

"By God, that explains everything," Tanaka said. He grabbed the toolbox and joined Parker at the entrance. "Yuki used a play on words in his diary, something he believed only he would understand."

Tanaka took a long, deep breath and managed a wan smile.

"Jason, are you okay? What's wrong?"

"It's just that when my wife died, life lost its purpose. I felt like a walking shadow, to borrowing a phrase from *Macbeth*. Then you came along. Parker, you gave me a new purpose in life. And by the way, I thought I was such a hotshot historian and linguist, yet you were the one who found the map and figured this all out."

"No, Jason, the three of us did it. But enough of that. Let's get to work."

Parker clipped off the ivy clinging to the door with a pair of shears and ran his hand over a large dent. "There are plenty of rocks

around here. I'll bet farm boys used this door for target practice."
He picked up a hammer from the toolbox and gently tapped the
lock's escutcheon. It grudgingly moved, exposing the keyhole.

"A lock pick wouldn't help even if we had one. We'll have to drill
out the hinge pins and pull the door off."

When Parker put the hammer in the toolbox, something hit the
granite steps with a clink. They looked down and saw a bronze key
next to Jason's left foot.

# CHAPTER 16

PARKER AND TANAKA SPUN around and found themselves staring into a 9mm pistol barrel.

"Well, if it isn't Charlie Chan and his number one son," Blackwell said.

"Who are you?" Tanaka demanded.

"Tanaka-San, I'm surprised. West hasn't told you about me?"

"Jason, he's Eddy Blackwell, the guy who has been stalking us."

Blackwell laughed. "Don't you think stalking is a bit pejorative? Just like the word hacking?"

"Huh?"

"You don't get it? Detective Smith delivered me your laptop and smartphone. I made a few changes, allowing me to hack Dr. Tanaka's computer via your phone. From there, I could link up with Miss Terry's smartphone. And Fumio tapped their landline. Hacking connotes brutality, but I spent many quiet hours devising and writing the code. It was a loving task. Just think of the money you wasted on CyberSecure."

"Jason, I'm sorry. I should have known," Parker said.

"Enough. Pick up the key and unlock the door," Blackwell snarled.

"Do it," Tanaka whispered.

The key was a perfect fit, and when Parker turned it, he felt the lock click. Tanaka grabbed the handle and shouldered the door open.

"Blackwell, how did you find the key?" he asked.

"Be patient. You'll learn soon enough," Blackwell said. He picked up the tool bag and motioned them inside.

The floor was set with large marble slabs. A white marble sarcophagus sat at the back of the vault, and two wooden coffins rested against the right-side wall.

"West, read the brass plaques on them," Blackwell said.

Parker brushed away decades of dust and read the first one. "It's Underwood's wife, Emma.

"Okay, check the other coffin," Blackwell said, pointing at it with his Glock.

Parker brushed the dust off the much larger plaque and read it. Little crosses served as periods:

> "Silas Underwood + Native of New Bedford, Massachusetts + Born January 10, 1820, + Died, January 25, 1855, + Owner and President of the North Scituate Woolen Company + Devoted husband to his wife Emma + Father of his beloved daughter Mary."

Parker swallowed hard when the truth finally hit him. "Beloved daughter Mary. So that's it. It's the reason none of us could locate River Oak. The title must have belonged to Mary Underwood, not Mary Butler. Benjamin Butler must have been Mary's uncle by marriage."

"Very clever, West. I have to agree," Blackwell said. He walked over to the marble sarcophagus and read the name carved on the lid. "Silas Underwood's coffin was inside at once, but somebody took it out and set it aside. I've got a hunch we'll find some gold inside. Open it."

Parker and Tanaka shoved the top just enough to get a grip underneath and leaned it against the back wall. Parker was the first to look inside. Time had shrunk the corpse's facial tissues, but it still bore unmistakable Asian features.

"His mouth is stretched as if he's smiling. It's Shorty," Parker gasped. "It's obvious Tomita removed Silas Underwood's coffin to make room for him." Looking closer, Parker saw something bound in an oilcloth atop Shorty's sunken chest.

"Take it out and unwrap it," Blackwell said.

Parker unrolled the cloth. "No gold. It's Yuki's long sword." He pulled hard on the hilt, revealing seven inches of a blade covered in congealed grease.

"Put it down and stand away."

Parker hesitated, his hands trembling as he stared at the blade.

"You've got three seconds. One, two…"

Parker knew he had no other choice. He put the sword aside and held up his hands.

Tanaka broke the ensuing silence. "Blackwell, listen up. There's no gold next to Shorty, and Silas's and his wife's coffins are sitting against the wall. They both couldn't fit inside the sarcophagus. It's a bit strange…."

Interrupting Tanaka, Parker tapped the marble floor with his shoe. "Look here. There are six slabs. Check out the names and dates carved on these two. Blackwell, you're standing on Emma Underwood's empty crypt. Mary Underwood's name and birthdate are carved on the one beside it. But there's no date of death because she's buried elsewhere."

Blackwell grinned. "You know, I think you've got something there. Get to work and pull up Emma's slab."

Parker grabbed a crowbar from the tool bag and pried the 4x8' marble lid up enough for him and Tanaka to get a grip. They hoisted and leaned it against the sarcophagus revealing five black-and-red-lacquered cases.

"Lift one of them out," Blackwell said.

Parker grunted. "Help me, Jason. It weighs a ton." They grappled with a case that slipped from Tanaka's hands and hit the floor. The brittle wood shattered, and hundreds of gold coins spilled out of the broken box. They stood speechless, looking at the treasure at their feet for a moment.

But Parker was not thinking about the gold. He wondered how he and Tanaka could get away before Blackwell killed them.

"The shogun's gold," Blackwell said in a hushed, almost reverential voice. He grabbed a handful of double eagles and let them slip through his fingers. "Pull up the rest of the slabs. Let's see how many cases there are."

Parker and Tanaka bent over to lift Mary Underwood's slab when a pickup truck stopped in front of the entrance.

"I wonder who that is," Blackwell said with a smirk.

Moments later, Lieutenant Smith shoved Terry through the door with his pistol. Handcuffed and crying, she collapsed next to Emma Underwood's coffin. Smith stood slack-jawed, looking at the coins littering the floor.

"Terry dear, it's all right," Tanaka said, reaching down to lift her.

Blackwell shoved the pistol in his gut. "Not so fast. Up with your hands, now!"

Terry tried getting up, but Smith pressed the barrel of his Glock against her forehead.

"Damn you! Put your gun away." Blackwell snarled. "You make me nervous."

"Eddy, cool it."

"I said put your damn gun away. You forget who's boss here."

Smith frowned and slid the gun into the side pocket of his jacket. "Suit yourself, but don't say I didn't warn you."

"Just shut up. I have a little story I want to tell all of you, and…."

"Is this all necessary?" Smith said. "West looks like he's ready to jump you with that sword. Let me take care of him, for God's sake."

Blackwell glowered at Smith. "For the last time, shut up and listen. This means a lot to me. It's time to set history straight, and I intend to do it."

# CHAPTER 17

B LACKWELL GLARED AT PARKER. "You fancy yourself a genius for solving the mystery of the shogun's gold, but that
diary is full of lies. Tomita Yuki was way over his head, and
when things went haywire, he left this gold and ran back to Japan.
In effect, he betrayed the shogun."

"Really?" Parker said, his voice laced with sarcasm. He considered his weapons: his hands, the crowbar on the floor, and the
sword leaning against the wall. None seemed promising.

Blackwell interrupted his thoughts. "Yes, a traitor, and he hid
when he returned to Japan. But the Bakufu sent a samurai named
Kuroi Taketo to capture him. He caught up with Tomita Yuki in
Aizu and executed him. That's how Kuroi came across the key and
a letter Tomita had planned to send to his American mistress."

Standing amidst the scattered gold on the marble floor, Tanaka
dared not rile Blackwell, but he felt compelled to counter him. "I
don't know where you heard that. The evidence does not support
your claim."

"Dr. Tanaka, shame on you. You don't get it, do you?"

"Get what?"

"Tell him, Parker, or don't you know either?" He pulled out the
bronze key and dangled it in Tanaka's face. "Tell him how I got this."

"Jason, Blackwell is the direct descendant of Kuroi Taketo. Remember Ben's letter? Kuroi got Yuki's key. It's been in the Blackwell family ever since."

"Parker, why did you keep this from me? I thought we were partners."

"I'm sorry. I figured it out on the plane yesterday. I translated Blackwell's name with a smartphone app. Kuro means black, and the third syllable, '*i*, connotes a water well. Hence the name Blackwell. But I wasn't sure about all this until just now."

"All right, enough of your crap," Blackwell said. "Now you know the truth—I am a descendant of a samurai."

"I am truly impressed," Tanaka said with unconvincing deference. "Allow me to speak further. "You are a man of intelligence, and you have everything you want."

"So, what's your point?"

"Just take the gold and leave us. No harm, no foul. You most certainly have an exit plan—perhaps to live like a Russian oligarch in some third-world country? There's no need for bloodshed. We'll help you load the gold and then lock us in with our bag of tools. It will take a couple of days before we can break out. By then, you'll be long gone."

"Very noble of you, Dr. Tanaka. I admire your concern for West and little Miss Sniffles here."

"I have had enough of this crap!" Smith shouted. "Let's get this shit over with," he said, slipping his hand back into his jacket pocket.

"I warned you," Blackwell shouted. He cupped his hand next to his mouth and whispered loud enough so they all could hear. "Dr. Tanaka, did you know Smith likes little boys?"

"You bastard," Smith yelled. He fired through his pocket, but the bullet missed, striking the granite wall inches above Blackwell's head. Blackwell shot back, hitting Smith an inch above his right eye. His body crumpled on the floor next to Terry.

Parker thought he saw his chance and grabbed and unsheathed Yuki's sword. But he was too late. The barrel of the 9mm Kimber stared him in the eye. "You're next," Blackwell said. "Sayonara, asshole."

A shot rang out, and metal clattered on the marble floor. Parker cautiously opened his eyes and saw Blackwell clutching his shoulder and reaching for his pistol.

Terry fired again. Blood and brain spattered the wall behind Blackwell as he crumpled atop a mass of double eagles. Parker and Tanaka stared at each other, their mouths agape. Blackwell and Smith were dead, and they were alive and safe.

Parker knelt and wrapped his arms around Terry. Softly weeping, she dropped Smith's Glock and buried her face in Parker's chest. Tanaka retrieved the handcuff key from Smith's jacket and freed her. They left the vault and sat under the shade of the Nathanael Greene oak. Tanaka made a call on Parker's phone while Terry huddled with Parker.

"Terry," he whispered, "it's all over, sweetheart. I love you."

An FBI helicopter landed in a clearing near the cemetery two hours later.

# CHAPTER 18

*Five years later—Downtown Los Angeles*

MIKE BURGOYNE, A *Pasadena Star-News* reporter, rode the elevator to the twentieth floor of the high-rise next to the Cortez Club. Next to suite 2013's door, the sign read Tanaka and West, LLC.

Burgoyne introduced himself, and the receptionist led him to a glass-enclosed room where Parker and Jason were leaning over a conference table inspecting several documents. Jason welcomed Burgoyne and shook his hand. "I must leave now, but Parker is ready to answer all your questions."

Parker gathered up the documents and motioned Burgoyne to have a seat. The reporter took out a notebook and commenced with his rehearsed interview. Parker obliged him by recounting Yuki's story.

"An incredible account," Burgoyne said when Parker finished, "but what happened to Vice-Admiral Enomoto and Captain Brunet?"

"The Republic of Ezo was short-lived, and only samurai were permitted to vote. A naval battle took place in late October of 1868, and the Imperial forces prevailed. Enomoto and Captain Brunet were arrested but were eventually released.

"Years later, Brunet became a high-ranking general in the French Army, and Enomoto was pardoned and became the ambassador to

Russia under the new regime. Incidentally, a Confederate warship captured by the Union, the *Stonewall,* was purchased by the Bakufu but taken over by the Imperial government and renamed the *Kotetsu.* It played a key role in the defeat of the Ezo Republic."

"Wow, what a story." Burgoyne finished his notes while Parker looked on. "Mr. West, what are those all about?" he asked, pointing to the two plexiglass cases on the wall.

"The one on the left contains two twenty-dollar gold pieces from the cache we discovered."

Burgoyne stood up and walked over to the other case. "And what about these medals?"

"The Japanese government awarded Jason, Terry, and me the Order of the Rising Sun, First Class. The one on the left is mine."

"So, what happened to the gold?"

"Lawyers for the Japanese government claimed that all Bakufu assets rightly belonged to the successor government."

"Did they prevail?"

"We came to an equitable settlement, and the case never went to court. They allowed us to choose four thousand of the best double eagles. We've loaned coins to various American museums, and the Japanese government lent more to museums and universities there. We auctioned the rest. The prices fell when the news hit that many rare coins had been discovered. Even so, our share amounted to thirteen million bucks. By the way, Jason is getting ready to publish his next book, *The Shogun's Gold: Uncovering a Historical Mystery.* Everything you need to know is in it. Maybe I can persuade him to give you an advance copy," Parker said with a wink.

"Thanks. I look forward to reading it, but what happened to Daiten Temple? You said it was falling apart."

"The grandson of my distant uncle was devastated by his grandfather's murder. He entered a monastery and became a priest. He and his family now reside at the temple. The publicity about the shogun's gold hit Japan like an earthquake, and everyone wanted a piece of the action. We donated money to repair the temple, and a big Japanese entertainment company built a museum on the site.

A major film company is in the process of making a movie. It will be released next year."

Burgoyne closed his notebook. "What an amazing story. Thank you for spending time with me. If I might ask, it appears you've gone into business with Dr. Tanaka."

"Yes. It's a logical outgrowth of our past occupations and backgrounds. We work with governments, museums, and, in some cases, private parties on research projects where some items, say things of historical importance, have gone missing."

"What are you working on now?"

"I'm not at liberty to say. Everything is necessarily held in confidence."

"I understand. But one other thing," Burgoyne said, pointing to the wall. "What about that photograph above the medals? You and Dr. Tanaka are standing next to the Emperor and Empress of Japan. Is that young woman in a red and gold kimono standing next to you, Terry Ando?"

Before Parker could answer, the glass door to the conference room opened. Terry and a child entered.

"Daddy!" the little boy cried out.

Parker gathered his four-year-old son into his arms and planted a kiss on his forehead. "

"Allow me to introduce Terry. We got married soon after we found the gold. And this is Ethan Yuki West, my son."

"Ethan West?"

"Yup," Parker said, "Ethan West have finally met. Pun intended."

Burgoyne and Terry burst out laughing.

# Acknowledgments

I am deeply indebted to the many who have contributed to this book, including the following:

**Ayako Tominaga Piper**: My wife and mentor without whose patience I would never have finished the book.

**Dr. Issei Imanaga**: A descendant of John Manjiro and a good friend. He provided me with many valuable insights into his awe-inspiring ancestor.

**Yoshi Saito**: Former executive at Nomura Real Estate. He accompanied me to Aizu Wakamatsu, where we visited several historical sites. He has given me much encouragement.

**Milton Meyer, PhD.**: Former professor of Asian history who first stirred my interest in Japan. He authored several books on Japan, Southeast Asia, and China. I am also indebted to my Thunderbird School of Global Management professors at Arizona State University and Waseda University's International Department.

**Phillip Arnold:** Author of two Christmas fantasies: *Big E and the Santa Man*, parts I & 2. Phil trudged through the very first drafts and gave me many helpful suggestions. Check him out on *Elvisblog.net*.

**MacDonald Stearns Jr., Ph.D.:** A linguistic scholar, author of *Crimean Gothic-Analysis and Etymology of the Corpus*. He set me straight after reading the first chapter of my first draft to him.

**Ed McGranahan**: Retired newspaper reporter and editor who spent hours editing one of my rough drafts.

**Robert Satterwhite**: Former managing editor of *the Asheville Citizen-Times*, published writer, and English professor. He spent hours editing and advising me about the *Shogun's Gold*.

**Paula** and **Rick Janczak:** Two avid readers and book club members gave me much-needed advice.

**Naohiro Ogawa, Ph.D.**: "Hiro" is a long-time friend who is a university professor and National Bureau of Economic Research member. He provided me with important information about the value of Japanese currency during the Bakumatsu.

**Jeff Dye:** A cyber-security expert who advised me on cyber-hacking.

**Chad Sailer:** Commercial pilot who advised me on private jets.

**Shibayama Yoshio:** President of the Shibaya firm. He is an antique sword dealer in Fukuoka, Japan, who provided much information about long swords.

Several friends have been kind enough to offer encouragement and suggestions. In alphabetic order, they are **Carey Fleming**, **John Kendrick**, **Daisuke Kimura**, **Ken Mizuno**, and **June** and **Tony Zimeri**.

# READING

*Most of the books noted below are available on Amazon*

**Romulus Hillsborough**: *Samurai Revolution*: A detailed account of the Tokugawa Shogunate's last years. An excellent read for those interested in the *Bakumatsu*, the period just before the shogunate's fall.

**Romulus Hillsborough**: *The Shogun's Last Samurai Corps:* A detailed military history of the *Shinsengumi* in the final years of the Edo Period.

**Nakahama Kyo**: *John Manjiro:* A description of Manjiro's life in English and Japanese written by a descendant of the famous castaway.

**Miyoshi Masao**: *AS WE SAW THEM*: A lengthy description of the first Japanese embassy to visit the US in 1860. A fascinating account.

**Dr. Milton W. Meyer**: *Japan-A Concise History*: An excellent introduction to Japanese history.

**Keiko Imai Packard:** *Old Tokyo*: An instructive read about what the city once looked like.

**Junya Nagakuni and Junji Kitani**: *Drifting Toward the Southeast-The Story of Five Japanese Castaways in Manjiro's own words.* Transcribed and illustrated by Kawada Shoryo.

**Charles Oscar Paullin**: *American Voyages to the Orient, 1690-1865:* This book includes an extensive report about Commodore Perry's arrival in Japan, which triggered the eventual downfall of the shogunate.

**Sato Masayoshi**: *The Shogun's Gold: A Novel of the Nineteenth Century Financial Intrigue:* Learn why The Treaty of Amity and Commerce, foisted on Japan, proved to be an economic disaster.

**Yamamoto Tsuneo**: *Hagakure:The Secret Wisdom of Japan:* Written three centuries ago, it summarizes "…the essence of the Japanese Samurai bushido.

**William Eugene Warner Ph.D.:** *Warships of the Late Tokugawa Conflicts: Japan (1853-1870)*: If you are a naval buff, you'll like this book.

www.ingramcontent.com/pod-product-compliance
Lightning Source LLC
Chambersburg PA
CBHW060156260626
47160CB00001B/297